for Judy —
And all those echoes resounding
over the years, ringing as true
as when we first heard the
sound --- All love D

APPOINTMENTS WITH THE DREAM FAIRY

A Memoir

by

David Evans

"The whole tale of my life is better to me than any poem."

ROBERT LOUIS STEVENSON

(Tusitala, The Teller of Tales)

First edition published in 2004 by TUSITALA
12 Ripplevale Grove, London N1 1HU
Tel: 0207 609 7005   Fax: 0207 607 4925

British Library Cataloguing in Publication Data –
A catalogue record of this book is available from the British Library.
Evans
Appointments With The Dream Fairy

ISBN 0 9533341 3 9

Printed in Great Britain by Antony Rowe Ltd, Eastbourne.
All type and graphic layouts created and produced by Melinda Sandell

Please call 0207 609 7005 for all sales queries.

Painting of The Cliffs at Birling Gap © Tristram Ellam-Bell
Author photograph at back of book © Sally Soames

BOOK I

TICKLED PINK

1947 – 1975

Writing this is a gratuitously selfish act and is done only for me. I probably will, but, at the moment, I regret not a word.

This book is dedicated to the memory of Pat and Mary Evans and is made with love for my families, both Evans and Quiney

My thanks are also due to John Tagholm for permission to use the 'white' extract from ELSEWHERE, his account of his walking journey across France, to Tristram Ellam-Bell for permission to reproduce his painting of CLIFFS AT BIRLING GAP on the back cover, to Sally Soames for permission to reproduce her photograph of me in later life and to Nigel Quiney, my own 'someone' who 'saved my life tonight, didn't you dear?'

INTRODUCTION

Islington, London.   November 1998

My friend Kris Ellam, assessing a group of men dining at an open-air restaurant in Ibiza, opined that they must be gay.

When I asked her why, she was quite succinct:

"They've all got extremely short hair, most have got moustaches, they're wearing leather waistcoats and those great big workmen's boots and they're singing a song from that musical ..."

We laughed but after the laughter, her observation remained with me. And as it turned out, she was absolutely right but it had set me thinking. They didn't have to be gay. Was there any common cause which had brought those individuals together to create such a recognisable shared identity? Is there such a thing as pinkness? Does the lavender consciousness exist? An equal but separate identity?

This conjecture begs a multitude of questions which I would not even attempt to begin to answer, only explore. Most of my early life I spent trying to conceal, disguise and hide this putative identity. Now, I too have short hair and a moustache, frequently wear a leather waistcoat, always wear great heavy boots and hum many a tune from the musical stage. What had happened to make me like I am and to get me this far?

1

Unfortunately I didn't take notes whilst I was growing up. The early chapters of my tale hereafter, therefore, must be taken with a pinch of salt for although I think I can remember, I really am not entirely sure that my life, as I unravel it, ever was. Having recently been unable to recall ten minutes after the event whether the burglar I saw shinning out of our bedroom window was wearing dark jacket and pale trousers or vice versa, I regard memory - anyone's - as inherently inaccurate unless two or three other versions of the same event substantially concur. Video cameras, tape recordings and photographs ... These I trust as factual although, Doubting Thomas that I am, it could be argued in the courtroom-of-life that, without context (and therefore meaningless), even photographs and magnetic tapes can be made to lie.

I can't help concluding that all truth, like most people, must therefore be a little bent. So why am I bothering to even try to recall anything at all about my time's span?

Purely selfishly, to remind myself that I have lived.

Merely curiously, to make sure I haven't wasted my time.

And variously, to add my own little bean to the larger hill. Though some might say that our whole hill is itself not worth too much, it will inevitably be examined by ensuing generations whose research and assessment will rely upon the information available. The more information there is, the greater the likelihood of the accuracy of the conclusions for my tale will be balanced by those told by others using different perspectives, opposing political attitudes, written from positions of opposite prejudices and points of view.

Finally, at some point in the future, we are all going to be the past and I want to play my part in the past as I once played my part in the future.

Chapter One

DAISY ROOTS

They told me I was born in the midst of the bleakest midwinter the world could remember in the shadow of the Malvern Hills, arguably one of the most distinctive ranges in England. But in Worcestershire, middle-England in what I later dubbed 'The Land That Time Forgot', my world on the Welsh side of the river crossing at Upton-upon-Severn was somewhat removed from the wider world of even bleaker mid-winters. But no one knew about that.

Theirs, mine, was a very, very small world.

Unarguably, it was February 1947 and through the thick snow piled high on the sides of Great Malvern's streets, my mother, then the twenty-five year old mother-to-be had been driven for my birth. This was my mother's, Mary's, first confinement. Full name Mary Nancy, nee Bray. Mary lay ensconced not at home where most babies were then born assisted by midwives and old wives, nor in the local Cottage Hospital but in Stokefield, a private nursing home in Malvern's gracious Graham Road.

The house was once a rather grand verandahed Victorian cream-painted stucco villa whose once unassailable social place had been elbowed in favour of trade. The gentle private house had been made over to mercantilist care principles, the National Health service being as mewling an infant as I was about to be and not to be relied on by 'nice' people who were quite used to paying for the doctor, thankyou very much.

And out I duly popped - a Pisces baby - on the 26th of that cold month of February. I don't think my birth was in the presence of my father, Pat. Full name Reginald Patrick. Fathers being around at such intimate moments was not at all the done thing. In fact, their having had anything at all to do with the birth of a baby was considered nothing less than a little mucky in the low church circles from which we Evanses sprang.

Sex ... Ugh!

I think I had all the requisite fingers and toes although the top of my more-than-usually malleable head had been apparently squeezed in the tunnel of birth into a frightening ridge. Fontanel indeed. What a wonderful word. My mother once joked that on first acquaintance, my appearance suggested that she had borne a devil. A joke? Yelling, covered in blood, squeezed through an opening ill-designed for the purpose, reluctant to leave the state of un-born, thus the do-or-die is cast for the rest of human life. Pain and suffering and worry and fear and much more before oblivion is regained at point of death. Maybe The Creator was in fact trying to put humans off reproducing rather than encouraging their multiplication.

But no one listens ... Especially to Creators.

My poor father's part in all this being born thing was severely limited to struggling through the deep-and-crisp-and-even with bags of coal on his back as it was cold in my mother's room and coal and its delivery was at a premium throughout the further-flung wider world across the river. So, there we lay, ma and I for a week or so before my father was allowed to bear us home which he did in our little grey Standard motor car.

Home was at 38 Blackmore Road, Malvern, a detached house in a leafy, well-gardened and highly respectable neighbourhood of a town upon which respectability had been forged like a chastity belt. Joyce King, the editor of The Malvern Gazette lived in our road. Mr. and Mrs. Sendall, the headmaster of

North Malvern Primary School lived there. Mrs. Girling lived next door. And the Reynolds further down, past the Nashes at 'Dunheved'. The Reverend and Mrs. Coley lived opposite us and next door to the Coleys there was still an open field over whose five-bar gate Thelma Hodges' horse hung its head and whinnied for sugar lumps and apples. The field is now a small Wimpey-ish estate.

In those days, there was much spare land in Blackmore Road, all available for building for most was owned by my grandad and little came under local government red tape then. My grandad on the other hand, as you will see, permeated everything and his shade looms blooming large over the battlements of my life, like Banquo's ghost.

Our house, number 38, was a brand new house which my father had built with (more-or-less) his own hands within the larger garden of a house my grandfather had built earlier and retained. This original house was called Craithie, after the church where the royal family worshipped when at Balmoral - my family were ardent royal familyists. Number 38 had had to be built within the restrictions of the post-war legislation governing private house construction limiting maximum square footage to one thousand and that to be achieved only with what materials were not being used by the newly installed Labour government in the building of the politically prescribed 'council houses'.

Pre-war building stock had to be used to fulfill much of this prescription. Little new had been designed, much less produced for the building industry since the cessation of hostilities. Little new? Not very much? In fact, nothing. Since my father's repatriation from the two *Kriegsgefangene Lager* - the first in Poland and the other near Ravensburg in Bavaria - where he had been incarcerated since being captured at Dunkirk right at the start of that iffy war, he had been learning and practicing the building trade. When he had volunteered for the army with his friend Geoff Woodyat in 1939, only just pre-empting conscription and therefore being eligible for a single stripe, my father, Lance Corporal Dad, had been training to be an architect at the Birmingham School of Art.

That future was not to be. Instead, prisoner of war camp.

Stalag 383. The university of life. Those German words now send shivers down my back though they meant little when I first heard them. In much later life I was to transcribe my father's memoir of that appalling time and only then did I realise that I was typing said memoir because pa had made a slight turn to the left whilst sheltering against his bren gun carrier on a road in Northern France whilst being strafed by a screaming Messerschmitt. The bullets meant for his heart instead zipped through the dust just past his right shoulder.

On such random reflexes hang whole lives and the future of generations.

Thankfully, I have never known war like my father and grandfather knew it. My world has probably paid for the exemption in many other invisible ways but the last fifty European years of peace have brought us a privilege which few other generations of humanity have enjoyed. That such a peace has been abused is only natural. I'm not a great believer in the propensity of human nature for doing much good. Now nationalist schism, inherent aggression - both male and female - terrorism, gang-fights, street-muggings and crime-related violence as well as one-on-one domestic battering are as endemic as they have always been but the difference is that now the fighters do it because they want to not because they've been told to by their rulers. Road rage isn't a disease that you catch. It arises quite naturally and only too lethally.

If my father's generation's sacrifice achieved anything it was that never again would a nation's manhood willingly, *en masse*, go off and risk their lives in order to rectify the mistakes of politicians. What was a healthy suspicion for politics and politicians has now turned - thanks to the Third Estate - into an indifference bordering on an apathy which probably threatens democracy itself but ... Weeell. *Plus ca change*, I suppose. But, back then in 1945 and back home in Blighty, one just got on with things, didn't one? Marriage and work had been set about with little thought of the youthful carefree years which my pa and the hundreds and thousands like him had been made to forego. They had been denied the chance to live, to sow their wild oats, to complete their childhood in the way they had been educated and brought up ...

6

The same story must have been played out in thousands and thousands of homes all over the world whence the heroes returned having undergone experiences which, far from being soundly constructive and character building, had in practice scarred them for life. And, of course, it was way before counselling. Way before popular psychology. The army pay my dad was awarded which had been so kindly saved for him by H.M.G came to some £450. He declined the two medals which were offered. I think he and his fellow veteran P.O.Ws likely told the army where it could put their medals. Does an army have a collective bottom?

Setting aside rank idealism for a moment but bearing in mind Mr. Beveridge had produced his report in 1942, at war's end three years later in 1945 it was thought that the country's war-weary pains could be assuaged and its discontent stemmed by throwing the ravenous the greatest popular sop in the history of power politics.

It was supposed to have had to do with Socialism. Ha! It was, in fact, the Welfare State. For this, natch, though they were not to know it then, the once-ravenous have been paying through the nose ever since. At some point in the mid-nineties, although it was acknowledged by the in vitro New Labour conceptualists that the spawning of their Socialist ancestors could no longer be afforded, the Welfare State is here to stay.

Notwithstanding ...

On with the tale of the little house that Pat built at Number 38.

De-mobbed Dad had added £350 of savings to his army pay and for £800 bought four cottages, the rent of which was my mother's for her own use. The cost of their own house was conveniently 'lost' in the company's books ... My family has always been a great fan of convenience.

The sentimental English middle class find names for everything and my parents had called their house Eastwell - at least it soared above Mon Repos or MarPat - and it was in the thousand-square-feet-maximum Eastwell that the three of us started family life. There was a bit of furniture - most bought for a song by grandad from a lady of the distressed gentlefolk variety who was selling up. There was a utility, uncut moquette, green three-piece suite and there was a cot. There was, judging by the wedding present list in my mother's Bride's Book, a lot of pyrex and an inexplicable surfeit of pillow-slips.

In those days, there were, of course, no central heating radiators, there was no fitted carpet, no refrigerator, no television although there was a radio (called a wireless then, for some only hazily-remembered reason). But it was more than many had and it was all bought and paid for. Hire purchase - credit, yeah? - was only just emerging as a form of payment but entirely frowned upon by 'nice' people who never borrowers or lenders were. That was for 'them', them being the poor. The never-never was one of the many available roads to hell as far as the provincial bourgeoisie was concerned.

Of the three of us who arrived at number 38 that March morning, I was the only one to come to the situation with no baggage or other agenda. At least, none but what I believe now to be genetic. But we weren't to know anything about that then, were we?

The other two, however, my ma and pa, had baggage aplenty. So a few words about the family ... bags and baggage and all.

My father has been able to trace back the history of our family to the end of the eighteenth century in Malvern and its environs. Malvern is a pretty town with something of Harrogate about it, something of Tunbridge Wells, a little of the seaside even, though the sea which covered the plain beneath it dried up millions of years ago. The town, overlooking the fertile Vale of Evesham and the Cotswold range beyond, nestles on the east-facing Worcestershire slopes of the Malvern Hills, riding the contours easily, its streets and houses like strings of little flags fluttering against the green of greenest England. At night, viewed from afar, the whole shebang looks like an ocean liner moored against the dark dock of eternity.

Malvern's population in my lifetime has always been some thirty plus thousand and the town had developed into a minor spa in the late eighteenth and nineteenth centuries, famous, as it still is, for its pure spring water. The fashionable came and went, with the successive seasons, for the water cure - a hydrotherapeutic torture - and the exercise needed to walk the steep slopes to the various wells and springs. Gradually, the cured or the merely gouty left behind a residue of spinsters, governesses, older relatives and certain of themselves in reduced circumstances, especially after the First World War. This pan-European disaster put the kibosh on much of the lifestyle of the idle rich at many a watering hole, reducing the ranks of the kept and creating a genteel but distressed poverty of which Malvern reeked for years after ... Like the residual smell of mothballs.

There were, naturally of course, always a sprinkling of the local quality. The Beauchamps at Madresfield Court, the Lechmeres at Severn End, old Mrs. Cartland (Barbara's mother) at Barnards Green, Radclyffe Hall at ... Radclyffe Hall !... You mean, her? She of the WELL OF LONELINESS? Oooh! Just the sort of population Jane Austen and Mrs. Gaskell would have adored. Oh, and the schools. Endless big and small public and preparatory private schools.

As far as I'm concerned, a boarding school is no better than an *oubliette*. Those aching dormitories. Those tear-stained back-stairs. Those vile communal bathrooms, the lack of privacy, the forbidden intimacies, the fear ... But there was still a British Empire then, whose furthest-flung reaches had to be staffed with military, civil service and legal personnel who would have to endure the rigours of absence, the privations of the lack of home comforts and so boarding school, I suppose, prepared them. All self-perpetuating, of course, because all those old boys and girls finding themselves in the godforsaken backs-of-Imperial-beyond had children of their own to educate who were packed off to England to endure the same loveless childhoods as their stiff-upper-lipped parents. A quite inhuman and grisly carousel.

There was Malvern College in its gothic authority fringed by patrician playing fields and Malvern Girls' College housed in the old Imperial Hotel by the Railway Station. There were the house masters and schoolmistresses and their attendant frustrations ... Their various wives, the letter-a-week lovers, the day-excursion tarts in London, their plaintive scattered loves whose names were never spoken. And what about those school beauties and the bullies, the warriors and the philosophers? Old boys like the movie star Brian Aherne. (Interesting autobiography, by the way). The painter Christopher Wood. Denholm Elliott. Gossip was engendered. Reputations were claimed. But the world of Malvern's schools was a world apart. Mixing with the town was not encouraged.

In the town, along with the many pubs which my family regarded as only one step removed from opium dens and the train to London, many churches had been built of all the denominations from chapel fire-and-brimstone to Quaker introspection. Religion was very popular in Victoria's England, like video arcades and wine bars now and each religious taste had to have its own temple. Outside the public houses of course, churches, chapels and meeting houses were the only social centres for both the poor and thrifty alike.

To cater for the wealthier laity, meeting rooms were established and concert halls were built - the biggest called The Winter Gardens - and a theatre was erected for the further cultural edification of the motley. George Bernard Shaw and local resident Edward Elgar provided the words and music to the annual show which was celebrated as the inter-war Malvern Festival. Sir Barry Jackson supplied the thespians and the chorus boys from his Birmingham Repertory Theatre company, several of whom turned out to be the summer chums of the likes of Errol Flynn and Stewart Granger, Wendy Hiller and Gwen Frangcon-Davies. My mother, helping with the interval teas and coffees as a teenage volunteer usherette at the Festival, gushingly remembers sitting on the stairs at the back of the gods next to the imposing - and obviously heart-fluttering - Donald Wolfit. But every name in this pantheon, I would say, became luminary despite rather than because of their repertory seasons on the *Cote Malverne*.

And gathered they rosebuds whilst they might ... All of this company are now pretty much unknown to most people under forty. More than half-a-century has past. And they're pretty much all dead.

Anyway, in Malvern's expansionist prime 1860-1914, there was plenty of work for the working-class Evanses to do in the building of the big houses in the grand parts of the town and plenty of work building smaller, rentable housing to accommodate the serving and labouring classes in our, less eminent, neighbourhood of Newtown. Malvern mushroomed.

However, against and amongst this company, no Evans did anything in any way illustrious or significant other than a fairly honest day's work for most of the nineteen hundreds; wives were recruited as marital needs dictated from the local countryside or, as in my grandmother's case, from as far afield as Burslem in The Potteries. Though they multiplied variously, my predecessors did not spawn anyone of note until my great great-grandfather John Evans, a bricklayer, established himself as a housebuilder in Newtown Road in 1870.

One of a very large family - I believe there were some ten siblings, five boys and five girls - from the tiny cottage in West Malvern where he was raised, John enjoyed a childhood with superb views across Herefordshire and further to his ancestral roots in Merioneth whilst enduring the privations endemic in living cheek by jowl with eleven other human beings in a two-up-two-down.

By the end of his life, John Evans had roped in most of his brothers in the associated trades, married his sisters to men helpful to him and left each of them a freehold house in which to live, a not inconsiderable achievement one hundred years ago. It was the start of a successful business which was to last until, with no apparent heir, my father sold the name and the premises in 1993.

My great-grandfather George Evans, married to Elizabeth from the four- mile distant village of Bromyard, didn't do much more than maintain the status quo. It seems he was far more interested in gardening for, although no mean builder himself, he was only too pleased to hand over the reins to my grandfather, Albert, his only child born in 1887. Elizabeth died when her son was only thirteen.

Albert Frederick Evans was a born businessman and it was thus the Evanses jumped the class divide and became middle. Phew! Bert, as he was always known, was a good scholar at Lyttleton Grammar School in the building at the corner of the shady churchyard of Malvern Priory where he learned the beautiful copperplate script he maintained all his life. But a career in a solicitors' office (hence the necessity of the copperplate) was not to be. Another bloody war. When Albert returned home in 1918 from the Battles of the Somme and Northern France, decorated and mentioned in dispatches ratified by the signature of Winston S. Churchill no less, he was conscripted yet again, this time into J. Evans and Son. The enterprise duly thrived.

This canny man began buying up property, often in lieu of debts of which the depression-stained nineteen-thirties Malvern had its fair share. By the end of his life in 1970 Albert had garnered over fifty properties which he had vested some years before in a discretionary Trust which bears his name and of which my mother and father and we children were made beneficiaries. Thankyou, grandad!

Although Albert was a simple Victorian man - he was an avid sports fan - he liked the finer, flashier things too ... I can remember his builders' van and lorry were converted Rolls Royces. That's showin' 'em, Bert! He himself drove a succession of fine cars, ending up with a swanky Mark VI Jaguar saloon. He had his suits and sports coats hand tailored from Bray's, one of the town's two department stores and in the rose-growing season, he sported a fresh bud in his lapel every day. Albert was made a Justice of the Peace and sat righteously and staunchly cheek-by-jowl on that stentorian bench with the Earl Beauchamp, the untainted one. Not the one who had suffered ostracism and even exile because of a congenital peccadillo ... But whoa, boy! People must have forgotten all that by now, surely?

Albert was also a member of Masonic lodge, sang lustily in church and local male voice choirs and was a local school governor, notably of my own and my father's alma mater, Hanley Castle Grammar School. No one has more exemplified the Protestant ethic and the spirit of capitalism than my grandad. Church - Holly Mount Congregational Church if you please - was the rock ... In its shadow Albert found respectability and validation and against all the odds, maintained a stern probity which held even in the face of family scandal.

Bert made damn sure it held.

He was both a holy terror and a bit of an unholy tyrant. My mother loathed him for I fear they were not unalike in qualities of intractability. My father played patient politician and mostly acquiesced and did as he was told. But I actively liked my grandad. I found him hugely glamorous and, like his God to whom I had been introduced at an early age, Albert was truly aweful (in the awesome sense) and therefore appropriately frightening.

However, I found that his apparent ignorance of that world just across the River Severn was blistering ... Boasting of my newly-made university friends from all over the world, as a braggart eighteen year old, I was advertising my admiration for some fellow from some African country.

"Black is he?" Grandad demanded earnestly offering me the customary Lyons Mint Choc from the famous hexagonal box taken, like a dish of wafers of communion host, from his bureau.

"Oh, yes," I said airily, demonstrating my sophistication.

"Tell me," he went on, "does the black come off on their collars?"

Dear Grandad. But after all, he'd only been out of the country once, to France, to kill other white people. The-Land-That-Time-Forgot was bounded by Kiplingesque borders where captains were still courageous and fuzzy-wuzzies were impertinent cannon fodder although basically good-hearted potential converts to the true cross in times of peace ... In my childhood, whole church days were given over for the raising of money for missionaries who were still civilising heathen Africa in nineteen sixty-three. Martin Luther Who? We had only three black people in Malvern and because everyone was so used to them, very few people realised that they were black. Oddly, my grandfather employed one of them as a painter and, I fancy, had never noticed.

In similar ignorance, I shook my collection box shaped like an African grass-roofed mud-hut with the best of them and thought I was being made a good person. Yes, me. The one who'd never even imagined that Jews existed outside the stories in the bible. I finally met one, a warlike lady-one at that, in the person of my sociology seminar partner Elbie Spivack. She upsticksed and hurried - too late as it turned out - to join in the 1965 war. Elbie was my - very humbling - first Jew.

But grandad Albert patently wasn't as silly as I thought. He was, after all, the first person to confront me ... At age seventeen or was it twenty? On one occasion when I visited him for the Lyons mint choc and the - fingers crossed - five pound note and I was banging on about a girl I was bearding the world with, he said quite matter-of-factly,

"But you don't really like girls, do you?"

Was it that obvious? I thought I'd been so clever. But, obviously, that I was a little gay boy was perfectly clear to him. How we boys do fool ourselves!

My paternal grandmother, Mary, whom we called nanny, died when I was thirteen. She was elegant, beautiful and kind. She bought her clothes at Warwick House which was the reigning department store in Malvern town and she loved me. I just knew she loved me. Warwick House sold gowns, not frocks, if you see what I mean?

Nanny made wonderful Scottish bannocks - pancakes - on a griddle pan and gave out sweets and chocolate bars from an old earthenware salt jar in her larder every Friday when we went to tea. Then, to each grandchild, a shiny half-crown from her suede snap-shut coin purse whose smell I can recall to this day. We found her, on Christmas morning in 1960 when we trooped in at half-past-ten with her presents, still lying in bed unable to get up, unable to speak.

She had had a stroke during the night. Albert hadn't even woken. Although nanny still had some facilities, stroke recoveries weren't usual then and she died two months later, a few days shy of my thirteenth birthday. She and grandad had come to stay with us for a few weeks but in-laws weren't my mother's style.

Nanny was transferred to Clanmere, yet another house in gracious Graham Road which had been converted into a nursing home. She had promised me a grown-up bike for my upcoming milestone birthday. On her bedside when she died was an envelope with the money for my bike. I loved her too and miss her even now.

Albert and Mary had had three children. In 1912, the twins, David and John, were born. In 1919, my father came along an embodiment of, and to celebrate, the peace that would last for ... well, 'til teatime. The twins were not identical. David, my namesake I presume, was obviously bright. They were both jolly good-looking in the photographs.

After Hanley Castle Grammar School, David gained a

place at Birmingham School of Art to read architecture. John was sent off to be articled at a quantity surveyors. Wily old grandad had dynastic ambitions ... What horizons could not be essayed by a capitalised builder with both an architect and a quantity surveyor in-house? But such dreams were dashed. David was killed in 1936 in a motor accident on the way back to Malvern at midnight from a student dance in Birmingham. On a dark country road. Light-less. He had borrowed grandad's car and so, in a twisted sort of way, the old man had contributed to his own broken dream.

Every early soul is mourned but none more than a child's. The family at Eastlands must have been devastated. My father was informed at school. David's friend and classmate went on to become a more than celebrated architect, Sir Frederick Gibberd. There were similarly high hopes for David, too. But whether he would have escaped into the wider world ... There's a thing.

John didn't escape. He married. Jenny Cresswell. Now you know where one of my *nom-de-plumes* comes from. The winds of war had wafted John away to the Middle East where he succumbed to a liver ailment. Jenny succumbed to a Canadian airman (overpaid, over-sexed and over here) and bore a child, Susan. Grandad, stony but straight-faced, apparently spread it incontrovertibly abroad in the town that John had come home secretly for a weekend. At least Grandad must have ended up believing his own fol-de-rol. No one else did for a minute. Like exactly how had John come back, Albert? On a camel?

John eventually did return from the war but he was a broken, sick man and after a spell away in Gloucestershire, he returned to Malvern and joined the family firm for as long as he was able. He masqueraded honourably as Susan's father, the Canadian putative poppa having long scarpered. But he didn't have long to wait before he too was excused life parade. He died in hospital with my father next to his bed in 1948. At least he'd met me. I wish I could have said, "Hello".

Two children lost. Grandad's plans for a dynasty were subsumed by the need for a mere succession and my dear old dad was really on the spot.

He'd met my ma briefly, before the war. Five years later,

as the town's only repatriated serving soldier on VE day, my dad was asked to take the salute at the victory parade on Belle Vue Terrace. Afterwards, Steve Bray, my maternal grandfather, introduced himself and asked him to come to tea with his daughter Mary, back in Malvern after a tour of duty on the bombing ranges at Shoeburyness but still on duty with the ATS at the newly developed and top-secret Royal Radar Establishment in St Andrews Road. Pat turned up for tea, they met and they went out together. They married in April 1946 at the Wyche Church on the Wells Road.

My maternal grandmother Annie had come from Yorkshire as a housemaid to a big house on Peachfield Road. She seemed to have come from no family to speak of. There was a sister, Dorothy, in Leeds, but my mother has never been one for opening closed and locked drawers. Yorkshire can't have been happy for Annie. She turned out to be the most restless, miserable, neurotic woman ... I know. I feel a lot of her in me. My grandpa Steve, equable and tolerant and patient and kind and adored by my mother, was a clerk at Malvern Boys College in the Bursar's office.

Steve and Annie Bray lived with my uncles Frank and Don at Welroyd in Peachfield Close, an unmetalled cul-de-sac adjoining Malvern Wells Common. It was their own house. Nice, middle class. Phew! But they weren't at all wealthy. The Evanses, however, were. Or were perceived to be. My ma had worked in the bank - Lloyds I think - before the war and so was at least a considerable prospect by Albert and Mary to enable the succession grandad sought.

I can't put my hand on my heart and say it was a match made in heaven. If it was, heaven had run out of love that afternoon. Good stock of duty, lots of perseverance and guilt ... But love? They'd been together fifty years in the year of their Lord, 1996. I had to think of something to say at the golden wedding celebrations and I found those few words the most elusive of my life. It's an achievement, sure, worthy of some sort of monument but ...

I did find some words and said them. Something about, "... the most difficult thing on earth, more difficult than being a mountaineer or a scientist or a sports hero is living with

16

another human being. That Pat and Mary have done so for fifty years is quite an achievement ..."

They liked it.

But, fifty years ago, after they'd unwrapped the parcel they'd been handed, they got what they got and so got on with what they'd got to ...

Set about by rationing, shortages and totteringly high expectations, on indeed we got with it in March 1947, we three people who'd known each other for such a riskily short time.

Chapter Two

CATERPILLAR

I was soon robbed of my starring role in the three-ring circus at Eastwell. In awful succession, I acquired my brother Richard - in 1950, I think - and then my sister Elizabeth in 1953, Coronation Year when we got our first telly. I loved the telly and the Grove Family more than anything but my brother and I maintained a mutual disinterest - still do - and I was then utterly indifferent to my sister except on the day when she suffered what were then called 'convulsions'. I can still remember that tiny little body, racked and perspiring and my parents' faces white and scared. My brother and I, tearfully, weeded the rosebed below her sickroom in the front garden of Eastwell and swore that if she died we'd weed the rosebed in her honoured memory until we too were dead.

Oh. There was another time. The awful day when we tried hanging said sister at the bottom of the garden from a pole stretched between the two pear trees next to the chicken run nearly resulted in juvenile manslaughter.

And people were shocked by the Jamie Bulger tragedy? That juvenile manslaughter doesn't happen more often is a miracle.

18

What Elizabeth's crime had been, I'm now not exactly sure, officer but she'd had her trial of course and she had, of this I'm surely sure, been quite fairly sentenced by the statutes of the day but ... Elizabeth gamely went along with our kangaroo court charade but finally cavilled at the execution stage.

Thank god she did. If she hadn't shouted out ...

And kids aren't influenced by the telly or books or ... Jehosophat!

But Liz survived; we boys were thoroughly and resoundingly walloped for our transgression and, anyway, we were soon to move house, rug-rats no longer. We said good-bye to the chicken run where the ten scratchy old brown hens laid the few eggs which my parents would still steep in isinglass in a galvanised pail to keep for winter when the hens stopped laying altogether. Outbreaks of myxomatosis had already curtailed the regular appearance of rabbit in our diet. About the same time, my grandfather gave up keeping the pigs and chickens he husbanded on a plot in The Knapp opposite his garage. The tangible realities of wartime life were at last slipping away over time's horizon. Things were looking up.

And we didn't move far. We merely skipped over the fence, next door, to Craithie which was reconverted from a two-flat rented house. Miss Law, large and old occupied the first floor and my Uncle Don and Auntie Jean had gone to live in St. Albans - my uncle worked for Schweppes – thus vacating the ground floor and basement.

So, the Evanses moved in, into the big house. Grandad's big house. I was ten. And deeply impressed. My father had just invested in a paint machine which mixed two colours and out came a flecked, speckled spittle. It was supposed to be used for painting public or institutional lavatories and thus was duly used experimentally in our downstairs cloakroom. Yes. We had a cloakroom. And in that cloakroom ...

But I hurry. More haste, less speed as the wise advise the child. At ten I wanted to be thirteen, at thirteen, sixteen, at sixteen eighteen and at eighteen anywhere in the world but Malvern.

What I wanted to be when I was three I really can't remember. I can't honestly recall my first memory. If I have one it was of Brian Harper, more a friend of my brother's, I fancy, at Applegarth nursery school in St. Peter's Road just around the corner, who died during one school holiday. No one actually said he died but somehow I knew. My father had extended the cramped Eastwell with a bedroom wing which had facility rooms beneath it including a second loo. I could pretend it was a cloakroom but it wasn't.

On the plastic seat of the loo, for what I remember as years, was a spot of indelible yellow gunk which I believed was the hardened urine which had dripped from the cock of the vanished four year old boy. I really didn't want Brian Harper to be dead but I was intrigued and often ran the tip of my finger over the hardened spot. It was my first experience of someone dying.

Odd. From that first death, people just keep on dying, it seems.

I remember nothing of the arrival of my brother to rob me of my solo, centre-stage spot - blot it out, blot it out! - but I remember being told when I was six by my unnaturally swollen-tummied mummy that I was shortly going to be provided with another brother or sister.

I was unimpressed.

I was operated on at three years of age for a congenital hernia caused at birth and due to a weakness in the stomach wall. I remember being in the hospital because Margaret Chisholm (nee Drysdale), my mother's friend and bridesmaid, was a nurse there and I had jelly. Ice cream too. I don't think either the surgery or being parted from my family was a particularly traumatic experience.

Other than falling out of my pram, the hernia was the incident of greatest mortal moment I suffered in childhood. The pram story on the other hand, being unscheduled, is quite awful. My father had volunteered to push me in my pram up the hill from where my grandparents lived in Somers Park Avenue. All went well until he reached our house when in the driveway, opposite, he saw his neighbour Dennis Baker. Dad parked the pram, brake on, so he thought and went to chat to Dennis.

But brake on pram not on. Pram rolls down slope. Baby David catapulted onto hard driveway when pram hits bump. Hits head. Men see. Eeek!

My mother's fury, needless to say, was apoplectic. Pa was banned from as much as touching me for weeks. The Baker house was not auspicious for our family. Ten years later, my three year old sister fell out of an upstairs bedroom window onto a concrete path. Ouch!

The Bakers and the Evanses were old Malvern families. Old Mrs. Baker lived in Scarborough House at the junction of Cowleigh and North Malvern Roads, a wonderful solid Victorian villa faced with what seemed to be dressed Malvern granite from the nearby quarry. In fact Malvern granite is too hard to be dressed. But I digress. Grandad had opened an electrical and plumbing accessories retail shop on North Malvern Road which was just across the road from the Bakers.

This shop, the last of Bert's ancillary, empire-building ventures was supposed to complement the builders' operation in Newtown Road. It didn't. I remember not only working in its rusty, metallic depths during deep mid-winter stock-taking counting a million light fitments and mountains of dusty, spider-ridden tap-washers but I remember the final closing-down sale.

J Evans and Son in Newtown Road was an entirely different operation. It was the 'mother-ship', as t'were. It was always run by my grandad and my dad in the company of Audrey Cook. Audrey, 'Olly' to some, had joined the firm to assist Miss Small on leaving school at fifteen. It was her first and has been her only job. Miss Small left eons ago but Audrey was there still, even under new management, over sixty years later. She collected rents, warded off unwanted sales reps, coped with the moanings and rantings of the payroll's malcontents ... At the height of the business, J Evans and Son employed some forty tradesmen and labourers and Audrey was having no nonsense with any of them! J Evans and Son finally closed its doors early in 1997 and Audrey, for the first time in her life at seventy-four years young, found herself with nothing to do.

The firm's offices were on the ground floor of 101 Newtown Road, the northerly of the double facade of the two granite-faced cottages built by my great-great grandfather John which he had tacked on to a previous building behind. The upper half of this barn-like edifice to the rear had been once the HQ of the Salvation Army before their new premises had been built across the road. When the Sally Army marched on, the space had been turned over to Tom Evans, my great-grandfather George's brother, as the carpenters' shop and that is how I remember it.

The huge room smelled of wood, both soft and hard and sawdust. There were always huge piles of curling wood shavings, wonderful for young children to roll in and excellent as cage floor material when the inevitable pet white mice and hamsters arrived. There were antique wooden tools hung on nails all over the white-washed walls, their redundant uses long forgotten; there were planes for making both skirting boards and architraving for doorframes, bowsaws and fretsaws for cutting barge board decorations. There was new stuff too, with an electrical smell of graphite and the whirring of the motors which drove huge metal planing machines and the vast whirling blade of the mechanical circular saw whipped into motion like a spiked, spinning top by the long drive belt, reminiscent of those of the binding and threshing machines from the steam engines of old.

It was, quite candidly, a magical place. I smelled it again only once after my father sold the business and that was in The Pit at The Barbican in London, light years and miles removed from Malvern, when Bill Bryden recreated Dennis Potter's SON OF MAN in 1995 and I went to see John Standing. Bill had set Dennis's play in a carpenters' shop in the writer's native Forest of Dean. I could empathise instantly. Dennis's wife had died two weeks before him in the hospice for which my mother always worked so tirelessly, St. Michael's on the Welsh side of Hereford.

Small world? No. Merely a cruel one. Dennis decided not to book himself into St Michael's for the train departing to eternity but instead to die in the wider world at St. Somewhere-Else.

Downstairs from the Evans's woodworks, the builders' yard was another child's dream-come-true. It was presided over by Arthur Pullen, the Yard Manager, who had been a fellow P.O.W camp inmate of my father's in Germany. I have a horrible memory of calling him Sergeant RolyPoly. From Arthur's little kiosk where he booked materials and tools and equipment in and out, he surveyed an empire of towers of stacked chimney pots, pyramids of pipes, baulks of pine roof timbers, arks of bricks, palaces of porcelain bathroom equipment bulging out of ancient stalls where the builders' dray horses had once been stabled, sheds and storehouses where the carts and wagons had stood. There was a paint store as bright and mysterious and alluringly challenging as abstract art itself, reeking of turpentine, littered with useless opened paint cans with that thick dried skim which was so satisfying to break to find the liquid paint beneath.

The door of the paintstore I always wanted to hang on my wall. It was a marvel of conceptual art on which had been spattered and sprayed a hundred years-worth of painters' experiments in brush cleaning and colour-matching. Adjoining this treasure house was the glass store with its cathedral stacks of sheets of every thickness and quality of glass along with the old stained panels and panes removed for 'later' from long-demolished or, worse in a way, modernised Victorian Malvern houses. The store was like Planet Krypton - a cold desert of shards of broken glass which crunched clinically and bum-crinklingly underfoot.

I was old enough to remember great-uncle Tom and his sisters, Aggie and Mary who still lived in Devon House, 99 Newtown Road, their half of the pair of cottages which John Evans had left their parents. These women, my relatives, are long gone but I have not forgotten them. I can still smell the old ladies' old-lady smell, feel their whiskered chins as they pecked our cheeks with welcoming kisses; I can see Aggie's black bombazine dress, shortened from an even longer one which probably belonged, who knows, to her own mother. Their ghosts need not be laid. They are quite content to do a little light haunting and they're there when I need to remember them.

I fancy that for these Evanses who were still conspicuously of the working class like George, our Milkman who was a sort of cousin and Ivy Thomas and the rest with whom we rarely had truck, it was easier to wriggle out of the dutiful respectability which afflicted grandad Bert. I never recall seeing Tom or Aggie or milkman George anywhere near a church. However, for Bert and his regimen, church-going at Holly Mount Congregational was *de rigeur*. Even Audrey Cook was press-ganged into attending which she did regular as clockwork with her friend Cynthia Sallis until the necessity died with my grandad.

Church was serious business. It was not to be shirked. It was after all a part of the family business, for God's sake. The 'topping out' ceremony for the spire of Holly Mount Church had been carried out witnessed by an Evans no less. Church was entirely socio-economic. All the Evanses I knew had absolutely no theological curiosity whatsoever. And not a single voiceable doubt.

For most of my church-going life, our minister was Conrad Bonifazi, a gentle and highly intelligent man steeped in the theological and whose thought-range was patently far loftier than the fundamentalist/neo-baptist mindsets of most of his flock.

Small towns in middle anywhere are infamous for the twitching of net curtains, the high street gossip, the whispering campaigns of the righteous. Malvern was a malicious microcosm of all this. My mother was prey to it, a willing victim. My father, somewhat less. All her life, what my mother thought of something or someone is as nought when held against what other people think. Small town morality is therefore always an ever-decreasing spiral of what other people think and everyone lives in fear of being 'fingered'. Church attendance effectively disguised a menu of behaviour which might otherwise be labelled censurable. As with all ever-decreasing circles, of course, one ends up faced with the hideous awfulness of one's own bottom.

Of course, I didn't suss all this in the beginning. It was fun at Sunday school with the hirsute, diminutive Miss Needham and the pompous, monotonous Mr. Underhill. It was fun on choir outings, on Sunday school picnics to daffodil glades and poppy-dotted cornfields. Later Margaret Clarke assumed Miss Needham's fallen mantle and led our childish voices in devotional song in that church backroom, her feet pumping away on the pedals of the panting harmonium which never quite kept up with her.

There was the youth club on Fridays nights chaperoned by one or two well-meaning parents whose embarrassed children vainly pretended all was hunky-dory. They were always the children whom fashion avoided. I have always been a major snob about stylishness for which I am now far too old to have to apologise. The main attraction of youth club, however, was when, having closed with a prayer, we would wing it on the walk home down the Worcester Road.

Though we were all bound to be in by ten o'clock at the latest, the mile walk home was dark and ... And, in those dim and distant days, there were girls. I really very much liked girls in my very young days and not just for theory. I very much enjoyed kissing Nicola Bonifazi, the daughter of our minister, in the bluebell woods at Eastnor in Spring 1955 gathering flowers for Mothers' Day. The Bonifazi family finally moved to California and I lost touch with my first inamorata.

I don't know what went wrong with me and girls or where or when or how ...

However, when I did start to notice that what church-people said they wouldn't do on Sunday, they seemed to embrace fervently for the other six days of the week, the practical cat was out of the spiritual bag as far as church was concerned. The commandments obviously could not only be fudged but were blatantly broken, even in my own home. Like the one about, 'Honour Thy Father and Thy Mother ...' My mother was essentially vitriolic about my grandfather and entirely unpleasant much of the time about her own mother and large swathes of the remainder of Malvern's population. And covetousness ... Well, that went by the board by Sunday lunchtime as we all knew that one of our esteemed and very married choirmen drove out with the wincing soprano from the front row pew and parked on Malvern Wells common after church on Sunday. Hypocrisy, as far as I could care, reigned and if it reigned I could, with impunity, render it willing fealty.

It seemed to a naive and impressionable youth that the real world had little place for such huge concepts as honesty and love and truth that we were supposed to abide by as taught by Christian Jesus and validated by the God of the Hebrews ... Who were one and the same and indivisible, by the way.

Hey? Hello!

That, and all the other patent contradictions of faith, of course made no sense whatsoever. I sat twice a day each Sunday for thirteen years staring at the holier-than-I-could-ever-be commandments emblazoned in gilded and illuminated lettering on Holly Mount Church nave's south wall before I could stand it no longer and began to rebel. Not only was there patently no cat of any ilk in the highly debatable bag but the escaped cat was shitting everywhere and someone had turned on the fan in my nasty little suspicious mind ...

But, once again, I accelerate.

Music and singing was always part of our lives. Both my parents, for example, played piano and I was sent at a very young age to Miss Holland's at the top of our road to be similarly instructed. Miss Holland was a white-haired old biddy who looked not unlike Sybil Thorndike but she was a knuckle-wacker. Maybe Sybil was too. Woe betide you if you made a mistake. Many's the time I walked back home, past the window where Joyce King's grey parrot sat in its terrible cage; whilst it preened its deeply pink tail feathers, I nursed my sore and pinker knuckles after Holland'd had at them with a ruler. I seethed, vowing hatred and loathing of the child-beating old bag and that, one day, I and the parrot would fly away.

I never got to grips with the piano. I regret it enormously. I gather Miss Holland was a Miss because her fiancé had been killed in the first war. Her father, the bandmaster of the Malvern Band, which played on the bandstand in Rosebank Gardens, was, sadly, never as enterprising as my grandpa Steve and no suitor was found.

In the end, Miss Holland died, as did Joyce King's parrot. It was very old and all its pink tail feathers had fallen out. I, on the other hand, knew I couldn't wait that long.

Both my father and grandfather sang in Malvern Male Voice Choir, conducted by Jack Hindmarsh the organist and head of music at Malvern Boys College. In church, they both sang in the choir, led by Holly Mount's organist Reg Marsh, succeeded by my friend Keith Wood's father, Freddie. My brother and I were early conscripts into the choir and as trebles, sat in the front choir pew next to a hugely bosomed and warblingly reedy soprano by the name of Jessie Knight who in turn sat next to our Sunday school leader, the blushing tiny-voiced Margaret Clarke. Jessie and her sister Maggie Grose often baby-sat us.

I still remember the words to all the hymns. It's where I first learned MORNING HAS BROKEN by Eleanor Farjeon, a hymn whose lyrics, I learned lately to my horror, that Cat Stevens, a.k.a. Yusef Islam, has now bucanneeringly appropriated as his own, apparently with the sanction of copyright law? If this is so, the world is, truly, barking mad and the tail is indeed wagging the once-beloved dog. And this from the man who was quite content to plagiarise a Hindi melody and adapt it so we could all go out and buy I LOVE MY DOG in 1966. But, thankful for small mercies, I'm glad he has at least left Eleanor her name. I wonder if she got royalties like him? She died quite recently, in the late 'sixties. Unfairly, churches don't participate in the activities of the marvellous Performing Rights Society!

For those of us who lived in the days when we sang hymns for free, it was the marching, quasi-Sally Army sort of singing that we Congregationalists favoured. I'm convinced that the dum-de-dum, evenly-rhymed and bumpity-metred lyrics spoilt me for more anarchic poetic forms in later life. And I've never aspired to any higher form of music than country-and-western which I regard as sufficiently grand-operatic for a boy from the Baptist backwoods. I'm also a slave to order and tidy beginnings-middles-and-ends forms. I have a knack for rhyme and metre which has never been used except in Vincent Carver's music room when that dear boy and I wrote two musical shows but that was when I was ancient in the faraway nineteen-eighties and nineties.

Enough already.

Malvern Junior Musicmakers claimed us early. Ray and Kay Mills who owned and ran Malvern Wells' Cottage In The Wood Hotel, were the momma and poppa of the thirty-or-so-strong choir which embraced both sexes of all ages between six and thirteen. We met on Saturday mornings at Ann Fisher's mother's huge late-Victorian house in Manby Road and sang in a large, high-ceilinged room with bare boards and a thumping upright piano. Ray Mills - who also for a time gave me piano lessons - usually played whilst Kay took the choir through its paces. Our choral performances were in old peoples' homes as well as on competitive concert stages where the choir won many prizes. Coach trips to the Llangollen Eisteddfodd, competitions at the musicfests in faraway places like the de Montfort Hall in Leicester ... Luverly trips.

27

But, the high notes were the shows ... Produced by the Mills and put on at The Winter Gardens (sadly not the plusher and more romantic and CV-enterable Festival Theatre, next door) I played Christopher Columbus in a show called THE SHADES OF NIGHT whilst my brother was in the junior production entitled THE BACHELOR MOUSE. In 1996, I stood at the base of Christopher Columbus' memorial column by the sea in Barcelona and looked up. I felt entirely no empathy whatsoever. But in Spain, I would have played a man whose name was not Columbus at all but Colon.

I simply adored my foretaste of showbusiness and although I would have to be satisfied with a three-night run, I wanted the show to play forever. I was intoxicated by the dressing rooms, deeply scarred by the greasepaint and infatuated with the costumes. Funny. I'd always liked what we called 'dressing up'. My worritting Yorkshire grandmother kept a box of old curtains and rags in the garden shed in her Peachfield Close house and I would quite cheerfully drape these around my person - shoulders or hips - and parade around the garden on summer days being whoever. I can't remember if I was a Tartar chieftain or a Tartar tart in my imagination but prance I did. Of course, now I think about it, to the watching grandparents and parents I must have presented an alarming sight.

So, on second thoughts, perhaps that's when it all started. Where 'it' went wrong.

You see, I never played football. And I hated cricket. I tackled a little tennis in teenage at the Manor Park Club but I really left all the macho sporting stuff to my brother whom they all adulated for he displayed an aptitude for virtuoso performance in team and manly games from an early age and both the Brays and the Evanses talked a lot about sport. It saved talking nitty-gritty one-to-one how-do-you-feel, what-do-you-think-about-art stuff. And why compete with one's brother? Stupid I wasn't. My sister was a wonderful tennis player, latterly appearing in Junior Wimbledon and teaching games and P.E for a living. But by then I had long left our sibling nest. It was to be twenty-five years before I knew and loved my sister as a person.

In my own teenage, I found it wiser to keep my own

counsel. I knew what real men were all about from the year dot-and-carry and have avoided them ever since. Especially men in suits and in sports jackets and flannels and men who ignore their armpits as airlessly as they suffocate their wives. No. Rather men knowing they're *acting* like men than men thinking they're really being men, please.

I suppose I must have started to develop the propensity for deceit from an early age. Now, I gather that most children do. Duplicitousness, invention, secrecy ... Lies? Yes. All that. And more. I always knew there were things I shouldn't tell, things I should keep to myself.

Thus I perceived my own to be eventually a seamless transition from innocence into sexuality. I thought I handled it all rather well. I never dreamed that my charade was being guessed. I am forever sussed!

If my brother was the warrior, I was the philosopher. Though we were never read to after infancy when THE STORY OF GINGER finally fell into saliva-stained tatters, I loved to read, unlike my parents who, when I finished my second brand-new seven-and-sixpenny Enid Blyton FAMOUS FIVE book in two days as a seven year old on holiday on Looe in Cornwall, reprimanded me severely for 'reading too quickly'. Not being readers, my parents had no idea about second-hand books and second-hand bookshops. Second-hand was tainted with 'can't afford' and that would never do.

Television and radio, regarded as probable evils, were both rationed and curfewed to be on the safe side. My childhood reading was haphazard - maybe that's how all childhood reading is - and ultimately cursory. The windows onto the world which it afforded me were glazed with frosted panes. The more I read, the more occluded was the light and, hence, my vision.

Throughout my education, 'though I was always expected to consistently do well, both my parents consistently failed to hold my hand and keep up with me. There was no back-up. I couldn't talk about what I read with them because they hadn't and would never read the same things. I think they were afraid of learning and certainly suspicious of the learned. They asked no questions and maintained this incurious remoteness assiduously. It wasn't 'done' to be too clever and yet how pleased my father was when his children were the victors in the general knowledge quiz at the local Rotarians' Christmas lunch thrown for their children. We Evans kids won in a public arena and were publicly applauded. In private, Pat and Mary simply didn't know what to do. Perhaps they couldn't agree? They floundered, lost.

It was in The Musicmakers where I met the friends who were to be my teenage. Ian and Judy Lockyer, Andrew Lett, Keith Wood, Diana Blake, Nina and Helen Mills ... Of course, I had others. Ann Bartlett was my great friend and neighbour in Blackmore Road and there were Robina Locke, Rosemary Steer ... These were friends from youth club who also came to the church and they came only and precisely because we all had so much fun. God wasn't a lot in it.

Before this socialising period, there was the pre-teen stage. Sometimes with my brother or maybe with Robert Jolly and Charles Wade or Peter Williams, my peers from houses just around the corner in smart St. Peter's Road and the latter from St. Anne's Road, we explored the farms and barns and fields and byways and hill slopes and woods. Preferably I would be on my own but it was difficult, for my other nature drew me to the company of my peers.

Those childhood days seem now to have been halcyon. There were no child rapists and mass-muggers in those days to speak of; no drugs other than nicotine being pushed on every street corner; no off-licences or supermarkets selling cans of beer to underage whomsoevers ... Beer came only in bottles and it wasn't 'done' to drink, eat or smoke whilst walking on the street. No one did.

We children were free as trespassers ever were and we roamed the Malvern Hills, the Malvern fields and the Malvern hedgerows of our town-limits environment, other people's orchards and gardens and potting sheds... My grandfather's land in Nursery Road where the fabled Rolls Royce lorries were garaged, adjoining the house where Jenny Evans (nee Cresswell) lived with my sort-of-cousin Susan was a mine of adventure, situated as it was opposite Scrappy Johnson's yard which o'erflowed onto the rocky, uneven road with strange bits of discarded and redundant machinery, the innards of old engines, chains, pulleys and ancient rusting boilers. Interesting and exciting and childishly collectible. For a week.

On Cowleigh Bank, two roads away, there was an abandoned brickworks and further up in West Malvern next to an old shooting range was hidden a playing field with swings and roundabouts where no one but us ever seemed to go. In the more immediate vicinity of Blackmore Road, there were a myriad vacant buildings ... Grandad's nursery-land, (it had once been a market garden) was ruled over by our gardener (and grandad's lorry-driver) Frank Howard who still produced vegetables there for his own use and some which he took as tribute to my nanny. The nursery was to have a heavy significance later, during the early years of my teenage. Something about doctors and nurses, don't y'know. We experimented with everything. Cigarettes were once spirited out of the house and down to the end of the garden where I had a 'den'. They were smoked and not liked. Then, cigarettes were made up instead from dried leaves rolled inside newspaper and smoked. We were sicker still.

Malvern, (our world) was our oyster and as long as we were back home in time for meals, who cared where we roamed? Of course we had errands to run. My mother would always give us her shopping lists. The grocer, the greengrocer, the butcher and the baker all had lists deposited each week and many of the resulting deliveries were made to the house. The Misses Bubb brought the greens and fruit, from John Evans came the sugar and tea, Mr Hewer brought the meat when it wasn't personally selected and collected by my father on Saturday morning; and the bread too, also duly arrived ... at the back door. As well as the milk. Nowadays, it would be an unheard-of way of life. All this was less than fifty years ago. Until the start of the internet age, it was only Harrods who seemed to deliver and at an enormous premium. But, now ...

"Hello, Sainsbury's? Do you deliver?"

Certainly, sir. As do Tesco, Waitrose ... How times change. And then change again.

Although I enjoyed my JUST WILLIAM existence with my friends, I always valued my own company. It was an early realisation, this contradictory pull between the man and his company. Being alone and being with.

31

Thus, I adored my schools ... Until I had to board in one. School was a sort of escape. I could be alone at school and yet still be with the people I liked. Free with my imagination and my private world and yet able to participate, competitively it must be said, amongst my peers. I could be me for I knew that I could make me shine. I was clever. Brainy. I learned basic showing off, really.

My first school, Applegarth was a huge alpine sort of house at the end of the unmetalled St. Peter's Road, in which some impecunious distressed gentry had started the inevitable private school. Wonderful grounds on the Cowleigh edges of Malvern, there were wooded bits and tennis courts and lawns where once had resounded the genteel but vicious knock of croquet mallets. This beautiful house has now been demolished and in its spacious grounds now stands an estate of modern, 'tasteful' designer homes. Happen in 1999, I re-visited the old house only the week before it was due to be eradicated from the risk of being further remembered.

It also appears that through this narrative seems to be emerging an indication that I was developing in surroundings way above our station and gaining a taste for big house life which, had I thought at all, would only have been available to me in my dreams.

Then I moved at six to Applegarth's senior school, St. Nicholas' in Cowleigh Road, again only up and around another corner, which was a similar institution to Applegarth, but bigger. There were proper classes, form monitors, rows of desks and teachers at blackboards.

An infant year or so later I was, at age seven, delivered into the thrall of Captain and Mrs. Lyster at their forty-pupil preparatory Hill School, a squarish, white-stucco country house built into the lee of the wooded slopes of the hills at the end of The Promenade, as the terraced part of the Worcester Road was known. My nanny Mary had first come to Malvern to work for her aunt, the manageress of the Rhodes China Shop on the eminently respectable Promenade. (There. One of my characters' names. Dear Norman Rhodes from A CAT IN THE TULIPS.)

The Hill School was at the top of a long drive, overhung by a green vaulted span created by the interlocked branches of beech trees, beneath which trickled a crystal-clear and ice-cold natural spring from the granite below. Hill House, once one of the homes of a part of the Foley family of Stoke Edith in Herefordshire, had handsome, walled kitchen gardens, stable blocks, garage blocks where we did woodwork with Sergeant Hirons, hidden tennis courts in wooded glades, lawns where in summer we played a sort of pre-rugger tackling game called Tripperbugs. Sometimes the older boys would trip you up and sort of roll on you. Funny feeling. Liked it.

Games were played on a site in Malvern Link some two miles away whence we walked three times a week when games were scheduled. We walked in a crocodile, smaller boys keeping up at the rear. Two miles there and two miles back. We were seven, eight and nine ... Barbaric, really. No wonder I had no appetite for the games when we arrived. Cricket was interminable, made bearable only by the thought of an almost ice-cold glass of water from the lady in the cottage at the end of the field who pumped the gushing water from her garden well. I've never tasted water as sweet.

The Hill School's site afforded woods too, on the steep slopes behind the house which stretched up to the treeline on the Malvern Hills behind. It was where we played at some point on most days, notably, memorably, Mondays after woodwork, or rifle shooting or something ... And it was in those woods where some of us, especially boys like Peter 'Pierre' Clarke and I, would be taken under the wing of those older boys and invited to accompany them ...

And then shown things.

Things that engendered experiences which I knew were not to be shared or, ever, confessed. I can't remember penetration being a part of the wonderment but I do recall a particularly violent frottage which left you, the underneath one, feeling pretty-well done in. And, in those days before tissues and handy-wipes, there was always a handful of leaves for the bigger boys to clean up and wipe themselves dry ...

Which is where, now I come to think of it I suppose, "it" all really started. I was eight. Maybe nine.

Mmmm. Quite shocking, really, I suppose.

Chapter Three

CHRYSALIS

The last two years - my own life's ninth and tenth - at the Hill School were most formative. The Gosden sisters, Daisy and Olive were memorable. I think there were other Gosden sisters too and they all lived in bucolic grace with goats and things in a cottage in the middle of neighbouring Castlemorton Common beneath Eastnor Heights. Daisy taught us how to sing. Another moustachioed lady, she stood squarely behind her trusty upright and pounded out DASHING AWAY WITH A SMOOTHING IRON, RAGGLE TAGGLE GYPSIES, MEN OF HARLECH and other classics and barked at us for laziness. I wasn't lazy. I loved to sing and still do.

Daisy's sister Olive taught me French. I adored French which I've always found incomparably useful: when in France, where I often am, one still has the need to speak it. French, typing and driving a car are, other than reading, the most useful things I've ever learned.

Mr. Gillot taught us History and, I think, Geography and was nice. Father Scutt, an ancient religieux from an ill-defined monastic house in West Malvern, arrived a couple of times a week on his futtering moped, his monkish skirts tucked up preventatively, to teach us Latin. Scutty on his Scooter. Pretty funky, really. Kind of, 'Brother Act'.

Miss Blackwood was divine and young and wore full and swaying dirndl skirts with cinched thick webbing belts and black flatties. What she taught I haven't the faintest recollection but she appealed to my appallingly undeveloped sense of style. And of course, our matron, Hilda who became Hilda Dudgeon and, remained a great friend to us all until her death in her homeland, Ireland in 2003.

The Captain, Mr. Lyster, had a rather chronic war wound, probably from the first war, I'd guess. He had no ear, basically and not a lot of the relevant bit of surrounding skull. His head was mostly and often wrapped around with bandages beneath which he'd tuck one of the arms of his tortoiseshell spectacles. Occasionally things would improve and he'd sport a pathetically un-lifelike prosthetic ear for a week or two before resorting once more to an existence under swaddling wraps. I'd say nicer things about him but he was cruel. Each day, before tea (doorsteps of bread and marge, a scraping of tinned mystery jam and a mug of Assam's finest floor sweepings) he would inspect our hands and nails. For those silly enough not to have scraped their fingers and hands raw with pumice stones to erase any speck of dirt, he would whack our palms with a board compass. Bastard. Children don't see dirt. Neither boys nor girls. It's a well-known fact now.

Lyster's wife, rather bemused and dreamy, seemed oblivious to his abuse of us as she moved through her kitchen, making those ghastly meals. But they were the days before abuse was thought of by persons who need to sell newspapers and make reputations. In my day, only poor people in slums (much-reported on) abused their children although Doctor Barnardo's took care of all that ... We were told so at church, believed so unquestioningly and collected money accordingly. We even went on Sunday school visits to actually see the poor little waifs and orphans at the local Doctor Barnardo's at Droitwich.

But never mind adults, children can be pretty abusive to each other and I can name a case in point. The Lysters' son Torrance was also a pupil at the Hill School and was no one's friend. A plain

35

and pulpy boy with thick lips. Talk about a fifth column. His life must have been hell.

Oh ... Cooking. Cooking was the next most important thing I learned but that all came later. I somehow knew that it was possible to cook properly. At least to cook better. Never was I going to be responsible for the kind of slop I was served in all my schools.

It fell to Mr. Ebden to take the prize as primo character in the Hill School's *dramatis personae*. He lived in a dirty room above the stable block and wore filthy clothes, sports coat and horrid corduroy trousers whose forever-unbuttoned fly always gaped like a raw black wound. He rarely shaved and smoked a vile pipe. He looked like Desperate Dan out of The Dandy. Or Bluto, as in the Popeye cartoons. We called Mr. Ebden 'The Ogre' and in return he taught us indecipherable maths. He was probably incredibly nice.

The Ogre's must have been the last generation before proper teachers. I have a sinking feeling that all these men were probably university graduates who had either done their national service or who were waiting to do so. Whatever. They were going nowhere and by the end of the 'fifties there were even fewer places for them to go because by that time most of the Hill Schools of Britain would have closed. Bloody good education, though. Thanks, chaps.

I was usually top of the class and have the prizes to prove it. THE BIBLE AS HISTORY by Theodora Wilson-Wilson. THE WEEKEND BOOK. Several Rudyard Kiplings and OLD SAINT PAUL'S. Little prodigy, wasn't I?

Undisturbed years, really. The only trauma was in my first year at the Hill school. In the upstairs classroom at the front of the building. Probably now someone's bedroom. My place was towards the back in a single form desk. Pine floorboards beneath my feet. I don't know why put I peed myself. I felt the pee running hot down my leg and watched it puddle on the floor. It began to seep away between the floorboards.

I think the experience was a trauma. At least, I remember it vividly as I do tooth extractions by Mr Minshull. I panicked when the foul-smelling black rubber mask was put over my face, flailed when the gas started to flow and on two occasions ripped the pockets off Mr Minshull's handsome white coverall.

I had my tonsils out at about eight in Worcester Royal Infirmary but this was definitely no trauma. I can't really remember it so it can't have been that bad.

On the other hand, at age ten, a tender ten in February 1957, I was taken to do the eleven-plus. For those younger than I, most will have been spared. The Eleven Plus examination ... It might as well have been the thirteenth labour of Hercules. It caused rifts, divisions, warped perspectives, removed aims and ambitions and destroyed confidence and initiative in both children and their families where one child passed and the other failed. Where one went to grammar school and the other to the secondary modern.

But then, there will always be the inevitable, odious comparisons ... I was brighter than my brother. He was better at games. I was older. He was younger. The rifts in families happen anyway, eleven-plus or no.

I'd already had a trial stab at a mock exam and I knew I had to pass this in order to qualify for the real exam to gain my place at Hanley Castle Grammar School, my father's and dead uncles' school in the village of Hanley Castle some five miles away on the road to Upton-upon-Severn. They'd passed whatever exam they'd taken. Hadn't they? Now I was on the same spot. I had to pass. No one told me that in my dad's and uncles' day, grandad paid for his boys to go. No one had to pass anything.

The eleven plus exam was held at the Pound Bank state primary school in Barnards Green. I was the only boy there from a private school taking the test. It was threatening territory, going public. I didn't like it. I felt entirely unspecial and very uninvited. The eleven plus exam was utterly confusing. A complete mystery. The maths and the composition I suppose I must have understood but I think I learned the way of tackling the intelligence test by rote. I could make neither head nor tail of the puzzle-solving questions. I think my IQ must be unmeasurably low.

But I suppose I must have passed the fucker (rather than being let in because my grandad was on the board of governors), for in September 1957, in my school cap and wearing my short grey flannel pants, with my satchel over my shoulder and my five bob for the week's dinner money in my pocket, I joined the other greenblazered lads (Black was for seniors only) at the bus-stop on Link Top and boarded the charabanc, one of the three permanently contracted from Hastelow's Coaches, destination Hanley Castle, for the first time.

The castle at Hanley Castle had long disappeared and so had the potters who had arrived down the adjoining River Severn in mediaeval times, from the Hanley in Staffordshire, who had named the place. The right sort of clay they had found in abundance close to the river bank and their completed wares were shipped out by Severn barge from a long-vanished wooden wharf at the bottom of Quay Lane, up-river to Worcester or downstream to Tewkesbury and thence to Gloucester.

The grammar school was an ancient foundation, initiated in the fifteenth century by some local big-wig - maybe her from the castle - who needed a permanent team of choristers to sing masses in the next-door church for the salvation of an eternal soul. The choir school was not a new idea. Many great British schools have been similarly founded. Private funding has always been a keystone of popular education. Contrary to middle class perception, education is not a majority priority in our fair land so if you wanna be taught, you betta pay and when you've paid, you'll be taught.

But whether you'll learn or not ... There's a rub.

After four hundred years of pay-now-learn-later, the school at Hanley Castle catered for the education of some two hundred and twenty boys, forty of whom lived on the premises as boarders. In conforming to the demands of the local education authority from which, since the end of the war, all funding came, the school still struggled to maintain some of its independent traditions and was in fact run as a minor public school. It was therefore somewhat pretentious.

Somewhat?

The dormitory section, the prefects' and housemaster's room were in the oldest buildings, black-and-white half-timbered mediaeval in origin which bordered the churchyard where there was still a gateway directly into the school grounds for the choristers' easy access. The remainder of the school building was red-brick, constructed in stages over the past hundred years, the front section of the school having been built by my ubiquitous grandad, no less. All this in an unspoiled English hamlet of incredible beauty and remoteness called Church End, shaded by a magnificent cedar of Lebanon. It was a cul-de-sac. No one passed through. You could only leave. Or drop down dead-drunk in the quarry-tiled snug of George Roberts' ancient Three Kings Inn.

So, on disembarking from the charabanc on my first day in September 1957, other than the school's facade, I will never forget the school milk in third-of-a-pint bottles in crates outside in the playground which was vast and tarmac grey. In winter, the milk froze and pushed off the red foil caps and the blue tits had a feast. In summer, the blue tits gorged more easily and the milk was often rancid - Gone off by eleven o'clock, dumped in the sun just next to the canteen kitchen's dustbins. It made it all the easier for provision of statutory school milk to be stopped, one of the achievements of the then unknown but rising junior Tory Minister Thatcher.

Margaret Thatcher, Milk Snatcher ran the refrain.

At Hanley Castle Grammar School, there wasn't a hint of Hill School lawn or the softening effect of o'erhanging boughs. My 'Country Life' childhood was about to be nuked by a blast of Dotheboys Hall.

We had to be outside in the playground during breaks and on the playing fields at lunchtimes, boiling hot or freezing cold. Dickensian, do I hear? Even legitimate sick notes barely excused the vulnerable. Opting out, taking stands, student strikes ... No way. The sixties were yet to happen. There were the rules and you obeyed. Or you didn't and suffered the consequences. A lot did. I learned early on that choosing not to obey, mindful of the consequences, is also a legitimate option and, to some, an entirely rational and necessary choice. Later on it's called breaking the law. Early exercise in dealing with my school's rules helped me come to terms with the fact that as a little queer person, I had only partial freedom relative to the het boys and often acted utterly illegally until 1967 and, even thenceforward, am still only partly legal despite paying the same taxes as my straight peers.

However, back then, my aberrant future was harmlessly nascent and there, dispensing playground comfort, was the red Co-Op van - or Mrs. Preece's smaller travelling shop dispatched from her Malvern Wells HQ - which parked at morning break under the horse chestnut tree in the playground to tease out the coppers and tanners from torn and fluff-stuffed pocket linings. Those who had this spare cash bought Wagon Wheels and Chelsea buns, chocolate bars, Refreshers, sherbet dabs and doughnuts.

The Haves and the Have-Nots were soon respectively penned by the sheepdog of envy. I could never work out why I, with the wealthy grandad my mum was always reminding me about, never had money but kids whose dads still worked with their hands and lived in rented accommodation sometimes on council estates could afford any number of KitKats and, worse ... cigarettes. Of course, the mothers of these boys often committed the unpardonable sin ... they went out to work.

Voiding one's bowels at school was to be avoided at any cost. Especially by me. To pee was not much better. The school bogs, the condemnable vile bogs, the bogs from hell with their foul-smelling urinals and shit-stained privies, were at the rear of the playground. People smoked there. Smoking was an expelling offence. There was no practical 'behind' to our particular bike sheds which bordered the front of the playground and so what traditionally went on behind the bike sheds went on at lunchtime on the Glebe playing field instead, around the pavilion or on the school's allotments (referred to as The Plots) where Martin Rice, who had been at school with my Uncles David and John, tried to teach us digging and vegetable lore and reaped the rewards of our labours by taking all the produce we had helped grow for himself. Fair? Justice? All grist to a rebel's mill, this. I can't wait for the 'sixties.

Oh. The toolshed on the gardening plot, by the by, amply lived up to time-honoured toolshed myth. Wonderful things are often to be discovered hanging in toolsheds.

But back to those bogs for a moment. In the school ones, I felt vulnerable and mucky, I looked not to right nor left and I was nauseated by the smell. In the other, non-educational bogs in both the town and on family holiday locations of whose hidden agenda I was already aware and where I learned far more about myself than in any classroom, I found the smell of piss and Izal not only inoffensive but positively aphrodisiac.

To fuel our schoolday bodies, most of us partook of

school dinners - two courses, two sittings, all puddings with runny custard and very few second helpings - which were eaten in the dining room. It was a Nissen hut, really. Converted. So much in England then was make-do-and-mend. The school meals - all-in for a shilling a day - were nutritionally adequate but entirely unimaginative. The headmaster always presided over first sitting when grace was said. One boy from each end of each of the six long tables was appointed daily to serve his peers and the presiding prefect. Prefects and sixth-formers sat on the headmaster's table and were expected to converse with him on matters of the day or local, topical interest. We were encouraged to voice our opinions, say our pieces. It was an invaluable introduction to the dinner party thing ... I don't know what I would have done without the basic training and I fear for those now who are denied it and rely on sandwiches.

Mrs. Butterworth was in charge of the staff of three or four, all local country women. Mrs. Tainton, apple-cheeked Mrs. Tainton from Hanley Swan who was specifically the after-hours school cleaner also worked in the canteen as relief, when needed, for the extra money. I liked her. I thought her motherly but what did I know?

The classrooms were in school buildings which, in all seriousness, would now have been long-condemned. The desks and furniture were much abrased and deeply scored with the names of generations of previous inmates. The coke-fired central heating was patchy, at best, tended valiantly by our caretaker Phil Gibbs from the cottages on the road to the Rhydd. Church End resident Joe Little tended the school's grounds and playing fields on a tractor so old it might have come from an original Ukrainian collective. Joe Little looked after things on the headmaster's private patch too where Mrs Headmaster had more time to oversee Joe's planting technique. Perks bain't only in the Archers, my beauties ...

By the 1990's standards, classes were huge. Though a grammar school, there were regularly thirty-eight and more in my class until GCE weeded a lot out. Contrary to a lot of perceived current wisdom, the class size made no difference. And, we had the best teachers, men of intellect, erudition, creativity and passion ... Even our headmaster, Ernie Nichols whom we nick-named 'The

Bock' for some long-obscured reason. Other than manners, protocol and conversation, he taught me French, later, some Spanish and German and introduced us to the joys of French and Spanish culture by playing us Edith Piaf records and de Falla concertos on the school's single gramophone.

There was no equipment to speak of - the science laboratories were primeval - and we learned from only the tattiest old battered textbooks but we had Alan Gilchrist for English, Harry Cross for Economics, David (Hugh) Ottaway for History and Musical Appreciation, Peter Powley for French, John Clapham for German, Sol Gurney and Billy Burchell for Maths, Dick 'Binnie' Hale for Geography, John Byl for Physics and Chemistry and then Harold Dudgeon ... Fantastic men. And, of course, dear old Daisy Gosden pounded the ivories once a week just in case one of us ever thought we might forget the words to DASHING AWAY WITH A SMOOTHING IRON, which, we were assured, were going to be much-needed in our later life. And she was right. Many's the time I've *T'was-on-a Monday-morning-oh*'d away long stretches of tedious motorway.

Alan Gilchrist had fought in the Spanish Civil War and was a novelist. He later left teaching and went to work for Corgi books. I wish I could talk to him now. I could do with his wisdom and balance. But he's dead. One of his sons, Patrick, used to run the Teatr Clwyd in Mold in North Wales. And then there was Harry Cross, a diminutive man with a dangerous line in tobacco pipes, who was also a writer. His novel NO LANGUAGE BUT A CRY was a formative perspective for me. Both the work itself and its doing. He's dead as well but he was giant alive.

David Ottaway knew more about music but taught history just as passionately. He was a well-known broadcaster - on the BeeBeeCee no less - on matters musical and died far, far too young. And all the others, even the ones I didn't get on with like John Harrison, succeeded by Chris Smith, (PE, Games and Art), Martin Rice (Biology), Harold Dudgeon (senior physics and chemistry). Wonderful.

And friends? Of course friends.

My first was Chris Hewitt. What was wrong with Chris, we were never really told but he was no more than three feet tall ever, lived in a wheelchair and had a normal-sized head on an impossibly malformed body, long spindly arms which worked and dangling useless twisted legs which didn't. He was my first introduction to bravery. Games captains? Mountaineers? Heroes of shot and shell? Perhaps. To some. But Chris Hewitt was my own brave icon. He had a wicked sense of humour and was most naughty. We got into terrible trouble for giggling. In the days before ramps and special needs, I and Robert Horne carted him around the school in his wheelchair, both up and down stairs and in and out of inaccessible buildings, often, where necessary, in our arms like a sack of spuds. After going up to Birmingham University, he went to America and became a poet. He was at a mid-Western university and I saw him, once, about fifteen years ago or so. We didn't keep up. There was no need. We had our time. He now lives in San Francisco, at least he did in 2000, according to his eighty-something year old mother, Joan. But life made us catch up. We reconnected in 2003 and in 2004 he sent me a book of his latest poems, one of which I read over my father's grave.

But, other than Chris, I now have no friends from school.

I think we all had our time, as did it.

The school is now a standard co-educational comprehensive. To revive the past in terms of reunions and Old Boys Associations seems irrelevant ...

I used to be able to remember our form register. Let's try now.

"Angel, Ashby, Arrowsmith, Bishop, Coxshall, Evans, Hall, Hewitt, Horne, Griffiths, Knapper, Nixon, Noad, Peace, Phillips, (Ron) Simcock, Shuttleworth, Shepherd, Underwood, Vaughton ..."

Yeek. Only half.

And Ron Simcock died, too.

Other names come, admittedly, later ... Tony Ditchfield. Phil Nield. John Tallis. Michael Fender who had appalling asthma and who too was so brave. Brian Bates, from Smethwick, a very small person and as such proverbially aggressive and arrogant and so, so sad. The Whelan twins, Gordon and Brian. I thought Brian rather unstable and very frightening. And Philpotts. I think his name was Roger. He had fabulous copper-red hair and he was a

43

fabled shagger of girls from the secondary modern schools in the town and he lived in some disrepute in West Malvern. Chris Berning, who lived in North Malvern Road and who was willing to experiment in the holidays with his wonderful thing. Well, once. Chris Wagstaff who lived at a farm in Hanley Swan and who was the last pick-up in the morning before the schoolbus hit Hanley Castle. His mother Connie did the make-up for our school plays and was a leading light in Malvern's own AmDrams. Oh, Keith Wood, of course. And Phil Hughes. They're gradually coming back. This paragraph has been written over three days. So far.

'Jock' Anderson. There's another. There were the Deeks boys, Arthur and Johnny - from America for a year - too. Dishy wasn't in it. Gorgeous!

(Fifth day of remembering) - Mietek Wankowski who lived in Frederick Road, had Poles for parents and was a wonderful runner. Peter Pinson from Worcester Road.

I lived with these names for eight years. Eight years when somehow, somewhere, sometime I fell irretrievably in love with the male. *Le Male* in Jean Paul Gaultier-speak. Essence of male. Not real male, you understand; fantasy male. Fantasy fuelled by the passing reality of bodies, by mental images of shapes, by memories of musculatures, by the look in the eyes, by wondering what whiskers feel like, by hair, by un-held hands and faraway fingers, by the scent of someone left floating on the air in their passing wake, by the lure of forbidden closeness, the urge to touch skin, to communicate, to bond ...

Some of the boys to whom these remembered names belonged I liked. Some I loathed and there was one I loved and lost. But it's better, isn't it to have loved and lost than never to have loved at all? Gore Vidal loved the dead Jimmie Trimble for sixty years before ... But later. I too have loved the dead ones. They're so much easier. Can you guess which one I loved out of the school register so far? Maybe I won't tell you. Maybe I can't.

There were bigger boys, of course, in higher forms. Richard Bryant, Harry Whalley ... Older boys let me see yet more wonderful things at Hanley Castle. Same bit of anatomy but each bit totally different, each with different needs, each with different uses. The wonderful things never stopped coming but we never talked about it, of course. Couldn't.

Games were a nightmare. We played them twice a week, at least and underwent enforced PE in the barren gymnasium once a week. It was undiluted rugby and hockey in the winter and spring terms and cricket in the summer when I was forever hiding in the long grass. Athletics during the summer term broke the pattern. House points. You were supposed to go for the 'standards', the lowest achievement considerable. These were then credited as points to your house total - Lane House, Hall House or Rhydd House - in a pathetic competition.

"Forgot my games kit, sir!"

"Then you'll do standards tomorrow, Evans."

Shit.

What did it all prove? What the fuck did it ever prove? Someone or something is best or better and someone who isn't as good loses. An 'X' foot throw in the javelin. Cor. A 'Y' foot distance in the high, long or triple jumps. Wow! An 'A' second run in the hundred yards sprint, a 'B' second two-twenty or four-forty, eight-eighty etc etc. Yeh, yeah.

I got no standards whatsoever until I discovered that I had great, strong legs and could run, jump and go with the best of them. If I'd wanted to, that is. But by then I was sixteen. It was too late. I hated it and them and I wasn't over fond of me and didn't want to ...

I ended my time at Hanley Castle severely dysfunctionally socialised. Winners and losers. The former were lionised, the latter ignored. All very well except judgments came in somewhere along that continuum and that's dangerous. Like winning was good, losing was bad ... That's really dangerous stuff.

Punishments other than the brain-dulling occupation of writing lines, 'I must not run in the corridors ...' - earned or not - often took the form of a gang of us being put to labour rolling the aforesaid sports pitches with a huge - repeat huge - iron roller some eight feet wide and three feet in diameter which was the undercarriage to a wooden platform with shafts at the front in which the shire horse stood. Except there was no shaggy-footed shire horse, merely a gang of boys on punishment detail. We had to push this confounded roller up the pitch and back again, up and back, turning it at either goal's end, struggling with it, slipping in the mud, dirtying knees, trousers and hands when we fell and all under the eagle-eye of the duty prefect. In cold, wet and whipping winds. Some things I will never forget. Mindless.

For our ongoing pleasure there was a swimming pool at the back of the school on Quay Lane. It was unfiltered and its water was changed once only, at the end of the summer term. Green, soupy water. Squiggly aquatic life forms vied with us thrashing school kids ... No wonder I hated swimming although I have to admit that I loved the changing afterwards, upstairs at pool's end in a rotting wooden loft. I can still recall the smell of our clothes hanging up on the rusting hooks, the black lace-up shoes, with socks tucked in, kicked beneath the benches. Wonderful things were often on display if one was patient and well-positioned. By this time, 'it' had not only started, 'it' was well-down the line.

Morning assemblies singing piano-accompanied school hymns (me pressed in a throng with bigger boys - bliss!), monthly marks accompanied by 'A's and 'C's (I was usually in the top three - arrogant little bastard), school plays on a rickety temporary stage in the gymnasium (they never asked me), Founders Day ("my grandad's a governor, you know and what sort of car do your parents have?")

A gentle pull-bell whose rope dangled from the ceiling of Big School was used for years to signal lessons' ends until a polluting electric one was installed in a neighbouring corridor. Prefects on duty had to ring it. Farewell romance. The old bell rope was right out of Tom Brown's Schooldays.

Then, at four-thirty ... General exodus - desperate flight - and into the charabancs, one for Barnards Green one for Malvern Link and our own back to Link Top. Twenty minutes to go watched over by bus prefects Don Stevens and the sumptuously sexy Greville Rose. Later Phil Kilford (swoon) from the pub at the bottom of Queens Road and later still, by the skin of his teeth and after a lot of tears and heartache, me. But I'd had to undergo four horrendous years of boarding at the damn school before I was permitted to get out from under, return to being a day pupil and ultimately, wow, to be made a bus prefect ...

School days were ultimately thoroughly wrecked by my

46

one persistent physical impairment. I had the most dreadful stammer. I still do. Some days it's worse than others. I sort of cured it a little at university by joining the drama society when I realised that, acting the role of another person, I wasn't me and therefore never stammered once onstage. As a child, one invents ways of getting round stammers. Kids know the syllables or the word formations where they're going to trip and they compensate by thinking ahead and circumventing the speech hurdle via alternative ways of saying the same thing. Choosing different words meaning the same thing. It's another form of dissimulation. Cheating, really. Dissembling. Lying? Of course.

However, as a child and as an early teenager, I could never raise my hand in class for fear that I wouldn't get the words out. I was teased for it too, which of course made the stammer worse. Children are very cruel. Nowadays, my speech-challenged state would more likely have been picked up by whole teams of experts at the earliest evidence and help - at least, sympathy - would have been at hand. Was it that by acknowledging my problem, it would become real? Did ignoring my speech impediment mean that it was more likely to go away? Or even that, for them - parents and teachers - it didn't really exist?

I'm presently over fifty years old. My old *betes noirs* were Bs and Ps but I notice that I now find it almost impossible not to stumble over any word beginning with 're'. And I tried to say "hysterectomy" today. I nearly convulsed my neck muscles and swallowed my tongue. A friend calls the operation which the word describes an "ex-directory". I think it's a more accurate name for both the operation and, betimes, its implications and what's more it's gone into my lexicon 'cos it's a damn sight easier to say than hysterectomy.

My schooldays. Aaahh.
The best days of my life?
In my dreams.

Chapter Four

SEASONING

Whilst I was still a child, before I became a rebel, I had other lives. I realise that I have had so many lives and have been so many different people that I can hardly believe that one individual could have impersonated so many. What, now, do these other Davids share in common with the David who taps on these qwerty keys?

I feel I am the amanuensis to strangers who are long dead and yet the intervening years seem to be a passage of time marked only by the moment it takes me to blink my eyes. Where did they all go? And which one emerged at the end of the chrysalis stage? Or are they all still there, wound round each other, separate but indivisible like the woven strands of some ethereal rope?

Whilst not at school ...

My brother and I would steal money from my mother and buy sweets at a shop on Cowleigh Road on our daily morning walk to The Hill School. We also shop-lifted. Just sweets. But entirely criminally. With malice aforethought, your honour.

We obviously did not connect our actions with our parents' and grandparents' involvement with the police and the bench. We just did it. What we did we knew, I suppose, was wrong but knowing it was wrong was no impediment. Right and wrong had absolutely no meaning. Thankfully, we were caught, one day, stealing from Mr. Ryder's shop at the top of Somers Park Avenue. That Gordon Ryder informed my grandfather, with whom my brother and I were staying at the time, instead of the police was sufficient. Justice was swift and terrible and I never stole nor shoplifted again.

I don't know. Ten-year-olds. Remember Jamie Bulger.

However, ten-year-olds are at least aware of one helluva lot more than they're credited with. Take sex. The mysteries of the orgasm had been unlocked for me from the age of eight beneath many bushy trysting places in the wooded afternoon undergrowth in the playlands of the Hill School. I think it must have been those woods which wedded me to outdoor activities like huntin' 'n' shootin' 'n' cruisin' in the open-air locations I would later colonise such as Putney Towpath, Wimbledon Common and, finally, Hampstead Heath. However, then, at ten, after the huntin' it was always other older boys' shootin' that I watched and wondered at and I could not understand why I couldn't perform in the same way.

At eight and at nine and ten I wondered this and will never forget that my first encounter in a public lavatory was with a man from the Salvation Army in one of those young years. I can hardly believe that the place itself is now probably a listed building and is being converted into a private residence!

As you can gather, we were told nothing by anyone about either sex or what these opposite sexes did with their dangly bits and what could or couldn't, should or shouldn't be done to whom by whom and when. A lot of trial and error, therefore, resulted. Those results were then riddled together with the stuff we had cobbled together from other boys' tales and half-truths and misperceptions and the, frankly, fantastic.

Puberty was like being handed a biology set with no instructions. My brother and I were, however, left a booklet, mysteriously, one day. It appeared on our beds and explained what we already knew about sex and across the top of the cover had been printed in large letters: NOT TO BE TAKEN OUT OF THE HOUSE.

Such was the danger inherent in the written word perceived by the unknown supplier of that booklet for neither it nor the information it contained was ever discussed. That the written word could be memorised, turned into knowledge which could and had to be taken out of the house in our heads seemed to have escaped the writer of that *caveat.*

Experimentation with that knowledge took many forms. One of which was on one hot summer morning spent playing in grandad's nursery land in Nursery Road. Me, my brother Richard, my putative cousin Susan and my friend Ann Bartlett played the Show-Me-Yours-And-I'll-Show-You-Mine game. Susan must just have gotten into puberty. Her breasts were beginning to cone and I think she had pubes. Ann, I can't remember but neither my brother or I had anything even approaching a flowering follicle anywhere below the belt. But, at least we saw and were shown and examined.

We had seen a lady's one before, I think my infant sister's and so it wasn't a shock. It was a quite clinical experience, memorable, obviously but entirely unexciting and more anatomical than anything. I was neither attracted, nor repelled. I felt - as the girl in Michael Bennett's A CHORUS LINE sang - nothing.

I heard recently, in fact on the twenty-seventh of April 1996, on the occasion of my parents golden wedding, that the said Susan had died a couple of years previously, of cancer. She had married and divorced and, childless, had returned to live with her mother, Jenny who many years previously had married a Mr. Gray and who had in turn moved, quite sensibly, far away from Malvern to Dorset; or Devon ... Or anywhere.

On hearing the news of Susan's death, I have to admit, I felt ... nothing. Somewhere, across the world in Canada or wherever, the father of this Susan may have still been alive. What did he feel? Did he know? Probably not. Easy come, easy go ... *Ca c'est la guerre,* after all. In Boublil and Shonberg's MISS SAIGON, such children are known as *The Dust Of Life.* Strange, isn't it. I wept buckets when Kim dies in the show. Make-believe, you know. It's often more real than real-life.

However, in the downstairs cloakroom in our new house Craithie, at twelve boiling years of age, I finally did feel something real and at a stroke, (sorry), broke my duck. It was a spit-'n'-a-spot to be sure but it was fascinating, endlessly pleasurable and, thank heavens, still affords the fundament of consistent joy thirty-five years later. Masturbation is a wonderful therapy and an inexpensive alternative to violence and aggression and, for those who care to follow, can lead through that secret door into the imagination and thence to the world of fantasy without which this whole life thing would be an unendurably bad joke which no-one with even half a brain could sit through.

Fantasy should be an enforced study in the national curriculum to at least 'A' level standard.

My friend Kris Ellam has pointed out to me that in that previous paragraph lies the essential difference. Between Us and Them, boys and girls. Whereas I welcomed my spit-'n'-a-spot, she regarded her first period as a harbinger of constant apprehension and fear. For her, missing one of those bleeding monthlies signalled the shame that dare not speak its name ...

Now, maybe not all girls had Kris's experience but we men know absolutely nothing of this fear. Our easily worked-up spits-'n'-spots are quickly wiped-up and they don't hold a candle to women's experience and perceptions of sexuality. Moreover, the nature of our orgasm precludes us males from needing to know anything substantially more about our own sexuality. For us, there is no P.O.T. No pre-orgasm-tension. Whereas P.M.T? Science hasn't even scratched the surface.

Willy-nilly, that day in the cloakroom gave me my sexuality.

Though I didn't know it, it was the greatest gift I could have been given. That day in the cloakroom defined my whole life. There was something in my life, at last, of which I was in sole charge, that only I, at the time, could control and effect. I sort of knew then that my life was going to somehow be my own after all. That it was just a matter of time.

But the confusion continued. I had tons of girlfriends. Judy Lockyer, Robina Locke ... The 'Who's Going Out With Who' question was permanently on our lips. Going out never lasted too long and only very occasionally got serious. By serious I mean fucking, of course. Judy and Robina were succeeded by Sandra Hartley (highly disapproved of by my parents, especially my mother who nearly had a conniption when she discovered the girl lived on a council estate) and then Maggie Knight and finally Gill Phillips, who was the last. Nice farmer's daughter from t'other side of Worcester who went to the Alice Ottley School with my friends Ann, Nicola, Rose n' Robina. I gave up the me-and-girls charade after ending my flirting with Gill Phillips and I apologise unreservedly to those whom I ignorantly upset. Gill Phillips I feel badly about. I should have told her.

Told her what?

Simple.

That this teenage Don Juan was in fact pursuing not only a double but a multiple life. As soon as there was movement in the gonads, this translated into standard junior queer behaviour. First stop, the public lavatories. With all that writing on the walls. All those scribbled hopes and scrawled dreams and smeared invitations to a bliss beyond paradise. But did they ever show up, these men to whom I wrote biro replies on walls dripping with condensation? Especially, poignantly, did they ever show up whilst I was on family holidays in Tenby, Pwllheli, Looe and Saundersfoot where there were only two weeks for the supplicants to reply and turn up and me with no guarantee of my being able to get away every night to check?

Then those occasional meetings whilst walking on the Malvern Hills. Occasionally, I'd luck out and get a date. There was a junior assistant manager at the Abbey Hotel. His room was on the ground floor. Easy to vault out into the flower bed. Oh, the frantic, fumbling ... the frantic, fumbled fucking. No! I wish. The ineptitude of our coupling reflected a tragic combined ignorance. God, I wish I'd known then what I know now.

To cloud the issue completely, there was also the lusting and the longing and the equal pleasure derived from kissing girls and exploring their wobbly bits. Breasts were really something else for me. Anything below the waist left me not only a cold but a trenchant coward.

But then I was a lionheart at dancing. I loved to dance. And was good, too. Records and music had assumed a huge part in life. Our first Dansette, a mono-turntable with a tinny speaker arrived one Christmas and The Avons' rendition of   SEVEN

LITTLE GIRLS SITTING IN THE BACK SEAT was duly bought, much to my shame in hindsight. Thereafter, Soeur Cliff, Adam Faith, all the contemporary British raves and hearthrobs were in our eclectic collection. Oh, how I lusted after tight-trousered Cliffy in our pop-book annual albums. Little did I know ...

Mother sometimes bought our records or we were given record tokens, otherwise they were furnished either as birthday and Christmas presents. We really didn't have pocket money enough to buy regularly and our taste was circumscribed by that of our parents and what we were allowed to watch on teevee. We listened to Radio Luxemburg, sure but we rarely went to the cinema. I remember my parents refusing to allow me to go and see JAILHOUSE ROCK in Pwllheli where we were on holiday. Like with the books business, my parents were intent on not keeping up with their children. Being a good choir singer, my father always banged on about how 'they' couldn't sing, not proper singing, you understand. Well, that just made me think he was silly.

When we did buy records in Malvern, there was the coffee bar on Barnards Green, with the record shop in front where we went everyday when we were a bit older and on holiday. As well as being able to listen to records in the private sound-booths, there was a juke box and the whole shebang was run by a very groovy lady whose name I've forgotten but who liked us. Rowena, perhaps? We were 'nice' teenagers in angora and mohair sweaters which sprouted bodyless polo-neck inserts, black suede Chelsea boots and green-stiched black jeans all of which added a swinging image to Rowena's enterprise. Ah! Frothy coffee and the beginning of Detroit sounds. Potently addictive.

Of course, in reality, we knew from shit and yet we felt so, so grown up. Our touchstones were iconic teevee programmes like Six-Five special, Juke Box Jury, Jack Good's Oh Boy and later, in the middle sixties, Ready Steady Go! was the apogee; oracular. I was in love, successively, with Helen Shapiro and then Dusty Springfield. I liked the Beach Boys and the Beatles and remember feeling a certain pride that the emphasis was definitely moving away from America as the fount of all things groovy. English pop music and movies had always seemed a bit second-best, a bit of a country cousin. The dawning of the 'sixties reshaped that perspective forever.

But our parochially-bounded lives in The-Land-That-Time-Forgot revolved for a long time around another band of whom the wider world never heard.

The (Malvern) Sundowners were the creation of me, Ian Lockyer, Andrew Lett and Keith Wood and a succession of locally culled different drummer boys. Dickie Bond was one I remembered. I couldn't sing for toffee and dropped out after the first rehearsal but the band enjoyed a couple of years of playing gigs around the county, doing radio broadcasts and we followed them with huge enthusiasm wherever we could. They played other people's songs and weren't original in the slightest but we thought they were the greatest when they played at the Malvern Winter Gardens. When I returned to the Winter Gardens it was ten years later as the management representative of a rock group appearing there, "For ready money", as Joyce Carey might have said. Money I had to collect. It was the Kevin Ayers' band. Andy Summers played lead guitar for them. The Police? Who the fuck'd ever call a band The Police?

And don't think backing dancers are a Madonna invention. 'Jock' Anderson, my classmate, was the best twister in The-Land-That-Time-Forgot and often gave exhibition routines onstage with The Sundowners. He was small and Scots and lithe and wiry and had a face like a shiny apple under a thatch of golden curls. He danced to Chubby Checker songs like a dervish rubbed out of a Portobello-bazaar lamp.

Ian Lockyer later became a professional guitarist. It gave him his passport to leave Malvern for he had none other except a rather fragile single 'O' level. Someone told me he worked on the cruise boats in the bands. The awful thing was, a lot of Malvern people thought it odd that anyone should want to leave at all. I shudder to think what would have been my fate without the benefit of my education. Ian Lockyer went back to live in Malvern. He wasn't gone long and stayed away, I suppose, just long enough to see the world. His son made it, though. Became an actor with the Royal Shakespeare Company, I hear. Or perhaps it was his step-son.

Generally, in the currency of youth culture, the Teddy

Boys, born in the age of the Spiv, died away. The Mods and Rockers came and new tribal allegiances were chosen. I became a mod and ran with the Anna Smith crowd and started to learn to dress and get attitude and be cool. Girls were at an advantage, I decided, in the groovy stakes for girls, it seemed, were taken shopping by their mothers and bought stuff. Boys either went without or had to save up and go on their own. Fathers and sons never shopped and certainly never for clothes! I remember many a dandy *manqué* having to survive youth club in a nicely home-knitted long sleeved jumper and grey flannel keks.

Now, of course, I would have chosen to be a rocker but ... fickle, fickle callow youth. I'm running ahead of myself again. Before we got to this high point in the sartorial and stylistic rite of passage at fifteen, there were the two early teenage years.

Life had improved for us all. The nation acquired another television channel. Then another. The Evanses acquired a refrigerator and ate frozen peas for the first time. There was a tiny freezing compartment in our primitive Electrolux and my mother of course tried to make ice cream. I think she made it once. It was an indicator. People were finding it easier, more convenient and altogether better to buy what other people made. Home-made was on the slide. Store-bought was the new thing and shopping caught on like a rickfire as consumer demand, un-naturally arrested by wartime privations, out-stripped supply. It is almost unbelieveable that in those days when one ordered a car one had to wait for it to be made and delivered. There was often a six-week waiting list for a perfectly ordinary marque.

My mother learned to drive taught mainly by my father. It was almost as explosive a combination as when he subsequently taught me. In the Easter holiday, almost to celebrate this new-found independence, I remember mother driving she and I to Brighton where we stayed with our friends Jack and Meta Hindmarsh at Brighton College. It was a memorable first visit to that most excellently raffish and naughty of places. Brighton lends itself to first times. Maybe virginity should be statutorily surrendered in Brighton.

It was a memorable trip for me for no other sordid reason but that I saw the movie of West Side Story. But I saw it in a huge cinema on a huge screen. This was modern America brought indelibly romantically to life. Those Sharks and Jets behaved like I felt. That distant land across the water was getting closer. And in the tradition of catching up with America, we acquired our first 'second' car. It was a tiny bathtub Austin. Sweet. Would there be no end to this unaccustomed luxury?

Which? Magazine started. Another indicator. We subscribed to it assiduously. There were now mass consumer items available on the market in sufficient abundance to warrant comparison. The people now earned to spend instead of to save. The British class system was being eroded by an even more pernicious and divisive phenomenon which our island capitalism - forced into being less insular by the year - had spawned from an American pedigree. The Rich and The Poor. There was no longer any shred of dignity or nobility left in poverty. The growth of advertising with the spread of television made people without want to be people with. It made malcontents of the hitherto governable great British unwashed.

I have observed that in the main, things American don't sit comfortably or easily on things British. On the other hand ...

However, it was because of America that mine was also the era of the teenager. I became a teenager and on a severely blighted budget we did the only thing teenagers could do way back then.

We had parties.

The party was the be-all to end-all. Parents were pleaded with to let kids have parties and for them - the parents - not to be there. Beseeched. Souls were sold for parties. "Take mine ... Take mine!"

It has to be admitted that most devil-parents forewent the bargains on offer but there were a few acquiescent suckers in whose absence Postman's Knock and Spin-the-Bottle would be played when a lot of kissing in darkened hallways would go on. Do you know, some bastards refused to kiss the ugly girls? Me? I never said no. I just wanted to be popular.

After the dancing and the cheese-and-pineapple on sticks and the dainty cocktail-frankfurters-from-a-tin, our parents would come and collect us at ten o'clock. Eleven at the latest.

Really liberal parents would allow their sons to ride their bicycles home. Girls were always collected.

My school holidays would be spent either at the Musicmakers' choir practices or at friends' houses or chasing parties or on World Friends Exchange holidays. At thirteen, as pictured on the cover of this book, I crossed the heaving North sea and went to Sweden. I remember intimate islands and birch trees and the taste of dill and Jussi Bjorling records and the Tivoli fairground and a Stockholm underground *pissoir*. At fourteen, preparatory to the GCE French oral exam, I was dispatched to Menton in the South of France. Of this I remember nothing except a girl called Barbara Craig from Edinburgh and two very zany sisters called Carmichael. I was incredibly impressed that the latter lived in Chelsea.

When I was fifteen, I went with a Malvern World Friends party to Austria. I went with Ian Lockyer and stayed with a boy called Hans and his mother in a rural area on the outskirts of Vienna. I was there ostensibly to brush-up my 'O' level oral German. Hans was small and muscly and sun-tanned and we went for a weekend walking in some alpen-like mountains outside Vienna and stayed in a shelter in a male dormitory with large communal beds. We were the only three guests. When Ian was asleep, Hans tried to jump me.

To my eternal regret, when he offered to show me a wonderful thing, I declined. No oral there. How did he know not to jump Ian Lockyer? Hey ho. Instead of heiling Hans, there was a girl called Sylvia Diesner who had the most wonderful breasts. I felt them at every opportunity but the thought of going any further frightened me. I actively didn't want to. The thought of having-to filled me with dread. I can still feel the feeling. It's the one I get when I think I should go out and get a real job.

Later, at the German oral exam, I was told that I spoke well but with an execrable accent, Wiener being the very poor relation of Hoch Deutsch.

Otherwise, holidays were spent hanging around in coffee bars. One particular summer, my mother had to go into hospital in London for a while. St George's, lately converted into The Lanesborough Hotel on Hyde Park Corner. It was induction by fire into cooking for a family. My father must have undertaken some but I remember learning the basics of cooking then. Peeled potatoes take twenty minutes to boil, pastry is twice flour to fat. That kind of thing. None of us ever went up to London to see our mother. No one knew why she went ... It was never mentioned again.

As teenage progressed, the nearby city of Worcester beckoned. At the cathedral-end of The Shambles, The Flamingo was the 'in' coffee bar. It boasted a wall-hung juke box system and a state-of-the-art selector mechanism. And all this excitement in the afternoons and, as far as I was aware, drug-free. None of us even smoked cigarettes.

And then, of course, there was the swimming pool.

In its very beautiful Priory Park, spread out around the glorious Victorian Gothic pile of the Council House, Malvern boasted a plain but very practical open-air swimming pool which was altered and juggled with over the years. Now what was original is all but hidden beneath a glass and red-metal building of supra-teck invention housing a thing called The Splash, a motorised version of the Severn Bore in which shrieking children develop synchronised aquatic hooliganism under supervision.

In my day, we hung out on the concrete surfaces around the pool on very thin, old towels. It was a very confusing time. I loved lying about with 'the gang', the girls in their various stages of bosomly development; the Davison Twins, Lesley and Susan were of especial fascination because they were older and the big boys I knew liked them. The Twins liked me too. These associations did wonders for my self-esteem and laid the foundations of a rather horrid habit of knowing who best to hang out with for social advancement purposes ... Social profiteering, I call it and it really is a horrid habit.

But, simultaneously, way back when, there were those stolen earthy moments entirely free of any hidden socio-political agendum which were of infinitely greater sexual excitement and basic meaning than the aforementioned networking. Moments when the torn and haphazardly hung canvas curtains drawn across the front of the men's changing cubicles parted to reveal ... Yes! Wonderful things!

Sometimes the wonderful things were being revealed on purpose. I don't know how long it took me to work out that such exhibitionism could indeed be carefully conceived and stage-managed but when I did finally work it out, the gesture was reciprocated and several mind-blowing, heavily-breathed encounters provided the fuel for later fantasy self-entertainment sessions at the end of that pier formed by my right hand.

Of course, away from the cubicles, no acknowledgment was necessary between conspirators ... And none was offered. We just quickly returned, admittedly a little flushed, to 'kicking the gang around' as the French father of my friend Jackie Jesse used to term teenage social life.

Of course, this hectic social schedule had to be paid for. As I've said, pocket money wasn't a strong point of sixties teenage life. A lot of kids had to work for what they got from their parents and a lot had to work earning money from other employers. Apart from annual stock-taking work at our builder's yard, I variously washed-up at the Abbey Hotel or picked fruit during the summers either at Fruitlands next door to my granny Annie or at Beard's Farms in the Leigh Sinton area some three miles away.

My favourite holiday and weekend employment, however was working for Charlie Green at the cafe at the top of the Worcestershire Beacon, the rustic wooden refreshment-site which had been open on and off during the Easter-October season for a century. It has now burned down and will not, I guess, be replaced. Not only I but Ann and Mary Mooney, Sue Gibbons and many others bulked-out pocket money by working there. To get there was a long climb to the summit of the thirteen hundred foot high hill which had to be walked until I gained a special dispensation to ride my Lambretta motor scooter up the wide trackways which Lady Howard de Walden had built a century earlier to accommodate the carriages of the quality.

The cafe was franchised by the Malvern Hills Conservators to Mr. Ballard from Colwall who, because he grew and sold them, we all thought invented Michaelmas Daisies. Mr. Ballard, in turn, employed Charlie Green from Ledbury to manage and run the cafe. Charlie was my first gay man - not to have, you understand, but to know.

And we never once talked about 'it'. And of course he's bloody dead now too, isn't he ...

Charlie was a scrubbed, shiny, hairless chubby gourd of a man. He was kind, funny and during the off-season he modelled at local art schools for the life class. He was a fair and decent role model and we all liked him a lot. No. We loved Charlie Green. Thankyou, Charlie.

The best times at the Beacon Cafe were when I was entrusted to open and run the place on my own. It was where I learned to prepare, cook, to serve and to store food. Charlie taught me. It was where I learned that coffee didn't only come in powdered instant form, where there was such a thing as salad-dressing made from oil and vinegar instead of industrially-spawned salad cream splatted-out on lettuce, tomato and cucumber from a waisted Heinz 57 bottle. I just adore Heinz salad cream!

I met a lot of people on the top of that hill. Walkers would materialise from the swirling depths of the worst mists and rain and be amazed that there was a hot plate of bacon eggs and toast to be had with a decent cup of tea. Staring into those mists and rain clouds, I also exercised my fertile imagination. Images would dance in front of my eyes. Images of the past, of the future. Superimposed. Then trans-substantiating ... Blood into wine, bodies into bread ...

Being alone up there by the toposcope, a person could see thirteen counties. Perched on the summit of my particular world on the edge of an incomparable panoramic view, I memorised the tapestry of folding greens and gentle earthen hues which was elegaically English. An all-but mystical brand was seared onto my soul. If ever you have listened to Edward Elgar in the rain, with the windows open, you will understand. If you've ever seen Ken Russell's marvellous evocation of that Worcestershire man's creative environment, you will indulge me.

It is up there on that bald hill that I want most of my ashes to be laid for I want to return there. Being up there, on top of the highest Malvern Hill, me, self-cast as a latter-day Piers Ploughman contemplating the coming hellos and goodbyes of my life ... Entirely without the aid of magic mushrooms or prescience ... Just being so close to the great blue yonder made jumping off and flying away, borne on unidentified flying hopes and thus having a future seem entirely possible.

Chapter Five

DEATHS 'N' ENTRANCES

My life between the ages of ten and thirteen saw three deaths and one ominous entrance. The first of these deaths was my grandpa's. Steve Bray's.

I had been sent to stay with my granny, Annie whilst Steve went into hospital for a hernia operation. He was due to be in Malvern Hospital about two weeks, they'd said. It was summer. When I stayed with them, my nan and I would walk every day on the Wells Common, waiting for Grandpa Steve to appear at the top end, silhouetted against the trees. We followed the little track his feet had made on his daily journey through The Furse to his work at Malvern Boys' College.

When he was in hospital, it was too early for conkers. Ordinarily, Grandpa would help us knock them down from the horse-chestnuts bordering Peachfield Road and then conspire with us in their baking and piercing with the obligatory meat skewer and the stringing and thence, the tournaments ...

Steve Bray was fifty-nine. He never came out of Malvern Hospital. The operation went fine but he died a short time later after a blood-clot had formed in an artery. Embolism.

Then, you lay in bed and didn't get up 'til you were better. Now they get people up and walk them round within twenty-four hours of coming round from the anaesthetic.

Dead.

My mother was deeply distressed. She loved her father deeply. My grandmother never recovered. Without her Steve, Annie withdrew into a distant and protracted *adieu*. She took no interest in the world and merely watched it going by as she sat in her window and waited ...

The worst thing for me was that I felt she blamed his death on the fact that I had brought some peacock feathers into her house whilst playing with Richard and Eric Dee next door on the Fruitlands fruit farm which their father managed in Peachfield Close. Peacock feathers indoors are supposed to be the most terrible bad luck. Like May Blossom.

For a long while, I felt that I'd killed my grandpa. It also made me incredibly superstitious. I am still superstitious. These country matters are threaded through all my reactions. I always bid good-morning to magpies. Still.

Next to go was my Auntie Mavis, married to my mother's brother Frank. She was okay one minute, then got a fever which worsened to the point at which she was taken by ambulance to hospital in Worcester where her condition deteriorated rapidly. Polio myelitis. The End. There was a lot of it about, then.

As she flashed into glory, Mavis left behind her husband and her three tiny children, Andrew, Susan and Margaret. My mother helped, my grandmother sort of helped but was pretty useless. Mary Spring helped too and even though Frank married again and had other children - one of whom also died as a result of cot-death - I shall never forget the night when we were taken back from my granny Annie's where we had been staying whilst my mother and father attended upon Frank and the dying Mavis ...

I remember seeing my bereft Uncle Frank silhouetted at the door of my cousins' house in Lower Wyche Road and feeling for the first time the momentousness of death. The gaping awesomeness of it. Understanding and yet not understanding what life was all about.

The third passing was my other grandmother, Mary and

we've done that.

I was thirteen.

One day I too will die.

And yet I was only thirteen when I made my forced exit from childhood and entered the brutal world of growing-up. I was thirteen when my pupil status at Hanley Castle was changed from a day basis to day and night. Twenty-four hour attendance. In short, I was made to board and thus I was thirteen when I realised that I was a distinct person, on my own, helpless and that it was only I who could or wanted to save me ...

I realised my parents and I were not on the same side. I knew what team I was playing for but had no idea for whom they were batting. To say that I kicked and struggled and fought and loathed the idea would be an understatement. I abhorred the prospect and the reality fell not short of but amply exceeded my forebodings. My father recently, discussing some financial matter or the other, said,

"You see, it takes an awfully long time to trust your children."

Awful as that statement may sound and as much as I wanted to reply, "Ditto, dad,", I have to admit that I must accept his observation in our case for it takes, indeed, also takes an awfully long time for a child to trust his parents after an experience such as mine.

After that longago teenage experience, I'm still waiting for the trust thing. I wish both sides could have started out trusting. Starting out MIStrusting isn't a kind or auspicious way for either.

And what was the reason for my being sent to board at a school not five miles away from my own quite serviceable front door?

Ostensibly it was because my father, in his day, had also been a boarder. I didn't believe it then and even if I had for a moment taken the rationale on board, I thought it ridiculous and unfounded. Didn't they realise they were talking to a boy who knew more Latin at ten than they'd ever been taught? Who had prizes for his brains? Who'd been telling more lies for longer than he could remember and could smell a flawed alibi from the other side of Offa's Dyke?

I later learned that the real reason was my brother. Richard had failed to pass the eleven-plus and also, later, the thirteen-plus which was the latecomer's second-chance exam. The school however, would be prepared to take him on the understanding that we both became boarders. Huh! Sacrificed on the altar of my younger brother for whom I'd never cared greatly in the first place!

Trunks were packed, tuck-boxes were bought and our names painted on solemnly by my father who, you'd've thought, had a bloody degree in sign-writing the painstaking pleasure the job seemed to give him. Yet more Cash's woven name-tapes sprouted from the inside-tops of knee-length grey woollen stockings and inside the waistbands of the three pairs vests, three pairs pants etc on the outfitter's list which was obtainable from the oft-aforementioned Messrs Bray on The Promenade and fulfilled by my erstwhile mama to the last hanky.

Ugh.

The day I was to be incarcerated, we went, for some goddam obfuscating reason on a family picnic to a Severn riverbank site at Callow End near Worcester where in a moment either of warped melancholy or seething brooding, I picked a handful of wild grasses for my mother. She kept the damn grass for twenty years and only threw it out when they finally moved house for the last time. It can hardly have reminded her of a perfect day. Or, horrors, could it? Each time I came home, I wanted to burn that grass.

And so to school.

When I transcribed my father's memoir of his life, there were some sixty pages covering seventy years. Over forty of the closely-typed pages were about the five year period when he too was incarcerated, equally against his will, in Kriegsgefangene Lager far, far from the hills of home. At least I could see the Malvern Hills from my particular prison. But for me, seeing them made it so much worse. So close yet so far away. That left just twenty pages for the whole of the rest of his life. Including his children. Including me.

I too could, I suppose, write the majority of this memoir on the four years I remained prisoner in the boarding house of

Hanley Castle Grammar School but I won't. I don't want to give them the satisfaction.

I'll merely cut to the chase and get to the juicy bits.

How fathers who have been to boarding schools can forget so much of what goes on there to the extent that they willingly send their own sons to undergo the same experiences, I do not know. That their son will be buggered is pretty likely. I won't lay odds. That their son will do a bit of buggering is equally likely. Better odds. That their children will bully or be bullied, will suffer unfair punishment or inflict same on weaker boys, will enter into a power warp where seniority is all and obedience the only course, where competition is taken to mindless extremes, where home is not where the heart is but where the parents are, where the institutionalising is begun so early that when the adult is failed by an institution, he or she has no recourse to individual resources ... This is a series of ponderables which for many luckless children begets a case which is not only arguable but winnable.

I was not physically big or strong and certainly not emotionally sound and I found the whole experience of being sent away from home confusing. It taught me paramount virtues such as that to survive, you'd better be 'nice' to the big boys and not say 'no', never volunteer for anything, always look to be very busy, always sit at the back and - most important - never to let other boys in the dormitory know that you're wanking. To this day I remain the quietest wanker and am jarred to the quick by Theo Fennell telling me that at proper boarding schools like Eton there were no dormitories. At Eton, ergo, you could make as much noise as is required.

Some boys I didn't mind doing it with. Others, I didn't take to doing it with at all. I had no friends. Only a lover. I had a crush so hard on this nameless boy that you could have made *marc* out of my tears. Games captain, tall ... Just the way I like 'em. Was it love? Felt bloody like it to a fourteen year old. And of course, it's only when love strikes with the mutual wanking and the ragging in the showers that a boy turns queer, isn't it? If love was part of it, all men'd be queer, I reckon.

The only way I could get close to my worshipped one was to help him with his homework, mainly French 'cos, I must admit, he wasn't the brightest. But against all his better instincts, I actually, finally got him to be friends with me. I eventually got him to let me come with him on the obligatory walks we had to take on a Sunday afternoon after obligatory church when we'd listen to Jules and Sand on the BBC Light Programme's Round The Horne and not know what the fuck they were talking about.

I more easily got him to come home to tea back in Malvern when my parents realised they could, with impunity, drive down to collect us and have us back at Hanley Castle in time for another tea at five-thirty.

Michael Carson's character Benson called his 'My Dearest Him' and when mine was made a prefect and I wasn't, I'd make excuses to John Clapham, our housemaster, that I could help my particular dearest him if I was allowed to stay up and 'study'. We'd sit, alone, in the warm fug of the boarders' prefects' room, washed and changed for bed and gradually, I'd work it so that his dressing-gown and then his pyjamas would be parted to reveal the wonderful thing which I would then excite, manually, I think for I can't remember fellatio figuring on the sexual menu then. I was a manipulative little sod and very clever with wonderful things.

The only trouble about dearest him's wonderful thing was that it was a very tiddly wonderful thing and I already knew that it was the big wonderful things I could do most with. I believe I was the same with sticklebacks and tadpoles. Not cruel, mind. I merely threw the tiddlers, as Steve Bray, my grandpa, called them, back into the sanctuary of the slow stream.

There was often a long time to wait between the appearances of the wonderful thing. Taking up that time were prep, listening to John Tallis's record player throbbing to Buddy Holly and Elvis and more of that Detroit sound in classrooms empty of their daytime babble and life. Oh, and talking about 'The Charts'. It was very important which record was number one and what was on the way up or down. Pop music became very, very significant in our lives, on a par with sports and spoken of by boys with the same macho fervour. The soul patrol was being recruited.

Movie stars and all their manufactured, middle-brow, mediocre respectability moved over and the icons of the new music moved in, far more in tune with the perceptions of teenage rebels without a cause.

Teenagers had become an overnight sensation. They became famous for not liking to be told what to do by their elders, their betters and in particular their parents. This implied, sullenly-borne parental yoke did not presage mere disobedience. Unruly teenage unrest was spoken of in the same tone used in our history text books to refer to revolting peasants in Tsarist fiefs and rebellious settlers in King George's Thirteen Colonies.

Schism and breakaway and deconstruction were in the air in my nineteen-sixties and indeed by 1968, the youth of France had taken once again to the barricades, a significant American youth uprising had fundamentally questioned the patriotism of the Viet Nam war and in England, student campus murmurings erupted. There were riots in Grosvenor Square and every weekend a different demo to go to if that was your bag. Man. The Campaign for Nuclear Disarmament politicised a generation.

The first pitched battle in my own one-man guerilla war of teenage rebellion was fought over religion. As in all civil wars, this first battle was on home territory. I was fourteen. Ish. Other battles came later.

Increasingly, I was unable to suspend my disbelief as all audiences must indeed do in order to stay with the plot. As far as church plot was concerned, I was failing dismally to see the point in these Sunday observances into which my parents forced me. Arguments during Sunday lunch about god and religion became dangerously more aggressive until one day, I just blew ... Affronted for the last time and fuming with powerlessness I quit the table and slammed out of the house, so hard that the panes of glass in our partly glazed inner front door cracked and smashed.

Off I ran down the road; the taste of freedom was a high I shall never forget and I felt exultant and yet scared. My father ran after me and then chased me down the road in the car yelling at me to get in and return home. I ignored him and ran all the harder and as soon as I could, I broke through a fence into some waste ground on the slope at the side of Queens' Road and hid, crouching beneath a green bramble scrub canopy until I could no more hear and feel his presence on the street below. I don't think I was crying. I do think I was exhilarated beyond my wildest dreams. And, heaven for fend, it was all more empowering than any orgasm I'd ever had.

I made my covert way to my friends Ian and Judy Lockyer in Somers Park Avenue although, of course, I had to confess to their parents, Betty and Roy that I had run away from home. I wasn't to know that Betty telephoned my mother to let them know I was alright and later in the afternoon, she engineered for my father to come and collect me.

I can safely say that from that moment on, relations with my parents were never mended. Not properly. Not even to this day, when both of them are dead. I felt their withdrawal of love and support and understanding not, alas, for the last time but for yet another time to make me question their loyalty.

Quite simply, I had shown myself no longer controllable and I became the enemy. Dramatic? Perhaps. But not at all inaccurate. I felt it. Therefore, it was true. And also, looking back, maybe I was just a teency bit wilful. But my dad didn't go to church anymore. Only my mother went now ... Occasionally. It's a time I regret to the bottom of the pit of my soul for it robbed me of the chance to believe, of availing myself of the facility of faith. I look back, now, and realise that I had confused two very different phenomena: man and God. I had turned against man because, for a moment, I had lost sight of the face of God. Afterwards, pride kept me away and now ... I take huge, tearful comfort in the occasions when I still, but only very infrequently, once again glimpse the face of God. It has happened, most significantly, in India. Twice. Once in the face of a *saddhu*, a holy man at a temple in Gujrat and the other in the depths of the shrine to Shiva in the temple at Madurai. Oh, thankyou, God ... Just for letting me know you are still there.

Politically, my family were of course Tories of the truest blue. Politically, I was a passionate socialist, revoltingly red. We were diametrically opposed. Perhaps I reacted to their total lack of idealism which, had it ever existed, had been consumed by a blanket pragmatism which rendered dreaming useless. I pounced on any issue that provoked confrontation. The scandalous dealings of a tenement landlord called Rachman had hit the headlines and I immediately tarred my father and grandfather with the same brush. Rather hurtful than wilful, I fancy.

I worked for the local Labour Party in at least one

general election. I even asked my mother to drop me off at the local Labour headquarters on her way to help with the local Tory's campaign on election day. She refused point-blank in case anyone saw her. There was more than a little of Hyacinth Bucket in my ma. And a lot of the trust-fund Tolpuddler in me. I remained wedded to the Labour Party well into my twenties until I realised that socialism was only politics and as such as pragmatic as any of my family's one-nation Toryism.

Riven along faultlines made even less stable after many clashes of personality, by 1963 the unit formed by the three people who had returned to number 38 Blackmore Road in March 1947 was certainly a unit no longer and were fated never to be one again.

Looking back, it was as though on both sides of the generational divide, we were all were being trained for rebellion. On Saturday mornings at boarding school we were made to sweep the yard and the playground with bass brooms and to collect all the litter from around the school grounds, litter dropped not by us but by day boys who knew that it would be us who had to pick up whatever they dropped. Kinda mean.

Sundays engendered yet more church, not the Congregationalist variety but at St Mary's, the good old Church of England. Sitting in the beautiful old country church made me think not of God but of the men and women and children whose hard lives formed the continuity of ancestry which had brought about the village and its church. Religion seemed to have made of me an entirely secular little sausage, e'en though stuffed through and through with more than a hint of mysticism.

Saturday and Sunday afternoons the rules dictated that we were forced out of doors on endless walks across grassy green pastures or muddy fields of turnips, loitering on bridges by frozen streams with transistor radios flattening our ears, waiting for a sign, impatient for the signal which heralded revolt. But all we heard was Alan Freeman on Pick Of The Pops at four-fifteen. I later knew him as Fluff ... Small world, eh?

All this torture went on and on and on like some seemingly eternal treadmill until I finally persuaded my parents that I had to leave the boarding school. I had suffered an appendectomy right in the middle of my 'A' levels at the end of my second year in the sixth form... Needless to say, I failed the exams.

I convinced my parents that I would work better at home for my second shot at the aborted 'A' levels. Once again, it was a set of exams I had to pass but, unlike the eleven-plus, I wanted at last to pass on my own terms.

I had to pass. No. More than merely pass.

I knew that good results were my only passport.

The spectre of university had raised its head and it loomed out of a blank and bleak horizon just slowly enough to climb aboard, as one would a dirigible, the vessel which would enable me to at last take off from my hilltop fastness and really get to grips with the bright lights and colour and panoply of the world which I knew lay tantalisingly just beyond the borders of The-Land-That-Time-Forgot.

Chapter Six

LOVE SCARS

Despite dearest him, I was heavily into going out on weekends and did so with a variety of 'the gang' and to a variety of places including Jazz Club at some venue close to Foregate Street in Worcester where we perfected the Art School Stomp and, less boisterously, Folk Club on a Sunday night at The Nag's Head's function room just below Oxford Place on Link Top.

"... all around the bloomin' heather, Will ye go, laddie, go?"

Will he, fuck! Of course he will. Given the chance.

But, love hurts (breath) Love scars ... as the Brill writers writ large. Love wounds (breath) and mars ...

Boy, it sure did.

In my new and hard-won freedom as a day-boy, it was tough leaving behind my dearest him at four-thirty every afternoon when I caught the charabanc back home but all I can say is that absence made the heart grow fonder. However, to cap all my best-laid plans for his successful 'A' levels, his mother died from a protracted bout of cancer which had materialised in her jaw before metastasising throughout her body after part of her jawbone was removed.

I hope I was some solace to my dearest him. I thought he bore his loss with exquisite bravery. Two days after her death, he came to our sixth form dance in the early days of January at some god-forsaken village hall near Cradley in the depths of the Worcestershire countryside. It wasn't a prom and I felt like no homecoming-queen. I was just incredibly sad for him. What a horrid, horrid night.

I had learned to drive, at seventeen, as soon as I could and I used to drive down to school in our second car (by now a Triumph Herald) to collect 'him' as usual and bring 'him' home for tea on Sunday.

But living at home had returned me to my life - my real life - and I had plans. As far as dearest him was concerned, my plan was still, despite the mourning, to make sure he and I got good 'A' levels after which we would go off on a camping holiday to Scotland.

Thereafter ...

Strange. Onward plans didn't encompass being close to dearest him at all. Didn't even encompass dearest him. Scotland was obviously set to be the watershed. At long last, the dirigible had stopped at my *stoep* and it had stopped for me. I had all but climbed aboard. I was really, really going away. At last.

I had gained a conditional acceptance at the brand new University of Kent. I was going to read sociology. It was all the rage. Quite the thing. As were the new universities. The school wanted me to stay on and try for the Oxbridge entrance exams but it would have meant a fourth September in the sixth form and I was just too impatient.

I knew bugger all about sociology and zilch about universities of any description. I was to be the first in my family to go up to one. Green and sappy, I would have picked any course as long as it was at a college far, far away from Malvern.

I first interviewed at some college in Newcastle. Bit grim, that, I thought. And a bit too far away.

But then, Kent. Crossed London to get there. On my own. Liked that. It was either that time when the London thing began or ... Perhaps the previous year when David Ottaway had taken a party of us on a school trip to take in a play at The Royal Court and then dinner at, heavens, a Chinese Restaurant! Sounds odd now, but Chinese food then was as rare as moonrocks.

In Canterbury, I stayed overnight at the Chaucer Hotel by the imposing Westgate and was interviewed in Beverly Farm house by Professors Hagenbuch and Stirling the following morning. I liked the blowy emptiness of the hilltop campus overlooking the magnificent cathedral; I took to my heart the juggernaut earth-moving machinery and the banked mounds of bright earth. It was all as virgin as I was. But as wise ...?

I don't know about wise or foolish but I do know that it was after going to that interview and crossing London again on the way back to Malvern, that I realised that as well as sexuality, I had somehow been presented with another of life's great gifts. The opportunity of London. I realised that London was possible. London, where no one knew either me or my family.

London, via Scotland, that is.

'A' levels over with and the last Founders Day and prize giving, dearest him and I drove up to the Lake District in convoy with my parents where we spent our first chaperoned night in a cottage which the parents had rented for their holiday. Thence we continued our car journey into the southern highland fastnesses where we pitched our tent for our first night alone.

I have no idea what I was expecting and have no recollection of what happened on any of the ensuing days of the holiday except that it was all designed by my pea-brain to be some sort of bizarre honeymoon to what was in fact a doomed marriage. As things turned out, I rather fancy the whole thing self-determined and became a frightful *auto-da-fe*. Both for dearest him and me.

What I do, painfully, remember is the utter bungled failure of the love-making which I had conceived and planned and schemed to be the acme, the zenith, the pinnacle of what I had always fancied was our shared passion.

Wrong.

Dearest him, it transpired, had absolutely no desire to want to fuck. No way. Any way. Not then. Never. His distaste was obvious and as it dawned that no consummation of my shenanigans was likely, I felt dirty and humiliated and ashamed. Unmitigated disaster. I've never been in a tent smaller than a marquee to this day.

What would have happened had I received the fucking I was expecting, I don't know. Together-forever didn't seem to figure. Passionate letters scorching across the counties on clicketty-clack overnight mail trains was never a real option. What on earth had I been thinking?

I was far too young to know about the difference between sex and love. Did I assume, like many of us at that age, that it is the same, that there was no difference? I know I did. It would have been impossible to even begin to appreciate what I now know about love, which is that there are indeed many different kinds of it, none better or worse than any of the others.

And to add insanity to ignorance, I also now know that there are many different kinds of sex. Try pinning the right tail on that bastard combination. I still am. It's like catching an unwilling iguana. The tail falls off in your hand.

But as a catharsis, 'the Scottish play' - for the tragedy shall never more be referred to - was purgative and thus I left Malvern for Canterbury in October 1965, as cleansed a pilgrim as had ever made the return journey telling Chaucer's vanished tale, that of *Ye soryye Studennte yf Moel-y-Varn wyt ys scarres.*

Well, I at least packed an unfettered heart along with my vests, three pairs and my pants, three pairs. There were no obligations on the list. Oh. Except to Gill Phillips, of course. Sorry, Gill. I know, I've said it before but I'm saying it again.

As we drove - my mother, father and I - along the A40, through the Mitford-steeped Cotswold villages, through Oxford, past High Wycombe, by Beaconsfield, me for only the second time on that London road, I remember saying rather reflectively that I was leaving home.

At least, they say they always maintained they remember me saying it.

True or no, leaving home was exactly what I was doing. I'd got my scars but they were healing. And I knew that somewhere ahead, stored for me like destiny in aspic, was a huge bottle of Doctor Fewtcher's Famous London Linament.

Chapter Seven

CATS IN THE WASTELAND

Of course, in 1965 the Old Possum had yet to write his famous musical. Nevertheless, someone had decided it would be okay to take T.S's relatively unalloyed name and use it to dub the first college of the new University of Kent in the county town of the garden of England.

Thus, Eliot College.

Five hundred cool, undergraduate cats went up on that Monday, the eleventh of October 1965 and took their places - some in collegiate rooms, some as lodgers in Canterbury, Whitstable, Herne Bay, Harbledown, Bridge - for the start of the first term in yet another one of the twentieth century's educationist experiments.

Physically, Eliot College was the work of the architect Lord Holford and was only just built. Surrounded by freshly turned earth and, everywhere, the evidence of the building site which effectively was the status of the campus, Eliot College was a cruciform concrete structure, clad in pebble-dashed concrete panels. It comprised a central empty square of contemporary cloisters - entirely redundant as no one ever needed to go through them - surrounded by four square blocks of mixed usage - teaching, administrative, studying, recreational, domestic and, ultimately, residential.

The macro-concept of the University had been Oxbridge in theory. Therefore, the college-unit was deemed to be the microcosmic nub of the logistical part of the Oxbridge principle. Hence, Masters, Bursars and the Porters whose lodge, the only entrance to the college, was reached by a long, raised brick-metalled causeway. I think there was a flag somewhere too.

Was this Camelot? No, not-a-lot, but it was on this causeway that many of those first-day photographs were taken which hit the national press and which made us all, I imagine, feel rather special. None of us said as much, of course. Uncool. However. It was a sort of celebrity. Our own. Ergo, my own.

I had never before felt myself at such a finely drawn boundary between past and future. I felt weirdly detached - pivoting as opposed to pivotal - as I said good-bye to my parents who drove away, convinced, I'm sure, that they had merely dumped me at a different sort of boarding school and that everything would be alright in the end. I still wonder what they thought was to become of me, for I had absolutely no idea whatsoever.

We were all of us new boys and girls. Tradition didn't exist. There were no antecedents of any description. Not even ghosts. This grove of academe was a transplant, dumped and then spread over these innocent downland acres. We were living on what had been, until a year ago, Kentish farmland upon which we had been turned out from a randomly collected jamjar of provenance to fall where we would and grow like so many seeds. Fred Whitemore, Chris Cherry, Louis James, Frank Parkin and all the other docs and dons were just as green about the gills as were we undergraduates.

I know I felt very much on show. Despite my mod jacket and mod trousers and mod haircut, I felt very vulnerable. Like the bumpkin in me was showing. Like my accent was too fruity. Like my roots were too dark.

It was a very levelling experience. To find out that many of those who were to teach us were only four or five years older than us was quite re-orienting. The respect with which we were treated by all the academic staff turned angry adolescence fast on its head. Though later I was to discover it patently wasn't, I was also awed by the social and geographical mix of the intake. Maggie Nairn from Newcastle-on-Tyne, Susan Sowery from Kensington, Penny Milnes from Sheffield, Donald MacDonald from Scotland, Pru Norton (now Cherry). However, beneath the egalitarian facade, the roots of the institution were planted very firmly in the home counties.

Lovely. Suited me down to the ground. My intuition was confirmed. London was going to be the hub. But first things first.

First night, we queued up to go for dinner in the dining hall. Modernistic chandeliers over-hung the wide square parquet space. Bare, unadorned brick walls on two of which hung a cantilevered balcony as access to the other wings of the building. Were we served or was it self-service that first night? I fancy we were served, silver-service from stainless-steel, and probably suitably addressed from Professor Whitehouse's High Table, the Master of the College's sanctuary on its raised dais beneath a huge plate glass window in which was framed Canterbury Cathedral in the centre of the town spread out below.

Almost from that first night I met those who were to be my immediate friends. Donald, Felicity Ward, Julia Naish, Gillie Willis (now Denton) Richard (Willing-) Denton ... Very soon there were others. Sally Fenby (now Tagholm), John Tagholm, John Pidgeon, Susan (Bubbles) Sowery, Sarah Auburn, Sue Lermon, Alison White, Julian Ruddock, Steve Godfree, Sebastian Graham-Jones, Lisa Vine, Jenny Stern ... Most of them London people.

Also, to be in an environment where women were your colleagues was an unbelievably liberating experience for me, hailing as I did from a single-sex school. Girls and I may not have been cast for the horizontal in life, but vertically, I loved them, always have and still do. And to be with people who actually went to the Ready Steady Go! studios in Kingsway was amazing to me. People who knew Eel Pie Island and The Marquee like I knew the Malvern Winter Gardens ... I was gobsmacked.

I felt euphoric as we shuffled, en bloc, from the bar in the junior common room towards the double doors, patiently waiting to be admitted to our first dinner.

I had been allocated one of the college rooms for the first year. They were called study-bedrooms. Rather Kinseyish, I thought, that hyphenation of studying and bedrooming. However, although the college was co-sexual - deeply shocking to many in those antediluvian nineteen-sixties - the corridors were not for co-habitants of any sexual combination. The contraceptive pill had that year become widely available and our girls swallowed them like kiddies with smarties, all prescribed by dear Doctor Miles. To satisfy the baying of the moral lobby, boarding school-type rules had to be applied in this new Eden. Like, definitely no girls after midnight. Curfews and time limits governed all night-time intercourse.

There were so many 'Thou must nots ...' and all over-seen and enforced by the prowling more-than-my-jobs-worths college porters who immediately became identified as the fascist enemy. Shades of Porterhouse. We were not free to come and go. We were indeed in an only slightly modified boarding school. Exeats - how very public school - had to be applied for to cover weekend breaks and nights spent away.

My room, like all the others, faced out and was simply if ascetically furnished. There were rules about the walls, about what could be put on them but they were quickly swept aside. Each corridor had eight rooms and in the middle of these there was a bathroom and a kitchenette about which there were, of course, rules. It was very salubrious. Very proper. Each corridor had a cleaner; ours was a very jolly deaf-mute who darted and bobbed about her work, chattering incomprehensibly like a sparrow on speed.

We were encouraged to join societies. All very well except we were also expected to start the societies. We were the founder members. I felt like a pioneer, a colonist in a wilderness world until I realised that I had never joined anything in my life. I was used to life coming to me, not vice versa. I fancy I joined the Labour Society along with John Hine and Reg Race - who later became an MP - because I remember canvassing on some grim damp night in Erith in North Kent for no other reason than ... I forget. There was a Folk Club too at which Roger 'Earl' Okin performed as well as the junior commom room which sported its share of wannabee Bob Dylans, including Richard Denton who was possessed of a superb blues voice and played a pretty mean guitar for a boy who'd been to Shrewsbury.

I also became a ligger ... The word hadn't been coined then but for those who don't know, it's a music business moniker for someone who hangs around, waiting ... For a chance. To be invited in. To be asked on board. Until the dust settled, our society of peers was molten and viscose as it found its levels and stratified. The In people, the Movers and Shakers ... Who were they to be? Where did I belong amongst all these elements?

It never really shook down like that at all. People certainly watched each other, assessing, wondering, some cautious, some too hasty. It was fascinating watching people pal-up and grow up. We metamorphosed before our eyes from being schoolchildren into students. The means were various, one of the more embarrassing being the playing of Pooh sticks.

On the first weekend we spent in Canterbury, at the end of our first week, some bright spark had the idea of generally convening us on Sunday after lunch on the bridge over the river which ran in front of the great West Gate of the city and, like in the Winnie-the-Pooh stories, to emulate the adventures of same (plus his friends) and throw sticks into the current on one side and then run across to see whose stick emerged first on the other. The townsfolk who watched us must have thought us indeed quite mad. And as a piece of elitist showing-off, this would surely take some capping? The bright spark, m'now thinks, was the incredibly socialist and egalitarian John Hine.

During that first year, I was also interested in INCANT, the student newspaper founded by Tim Duvivier who died much, much too young in 1996. The current rag (c.1996) is now inexplicably called KRED. I have a copy. Kind of in-your-face.

There is not only a generation between the two names ... INCANT was much given to student politicking and campus causes and was rather more earnest than worthy. Tabloid it wasn't. Forming the Students' Union was a pressing activity. My friend Donald MacDonald stood for the first presidency but the election was won by John Harwood, who is now something really important like the Chief Executive Office for Oxfordshire County Council. Fuck me! The kind of man for whom the grey suit was invented. And, of course, the recent recipient of an honorary degree. He'll probably be a Sir by sixty.

And then of course, there was the Entertainments Committee. It was the responsibility of this august body - with a fairly zonking budget - to provide entertainment for the students. This meant bands. Dancing. THE WHO, THE ZOMBIES, MANFRED MANN, THE KINKS ... Unbelievable. These bands actually came to your door. You could hire dreams! You could rent fantasies! Although I didn't put myself up for election for a while, it was working on this committee and, later too, being part of the drama society which set the seal on my post-graduate life. I gravitated effortlessly to like. I suppose I should have heeded my 'O' level physics electro-magnetic theory - Opposite poles attract: Like poles repel ...

But unlike those who spent most of their first terms shagging their brains out in their study-bedrooms, I didn't spend much time in mine at all. Though the rules said nothing about boys after midnight, there didn't seem immediately to be any boys I wanted to have *in flagrante dilecto* in my room at any hour of the day. None at least upon whom I might have worked my wicked magic and after the ... The Scottish episode, I wasn't much into persuasion. Rogue immediacy was to be my romantic milieu for the foreseeable future. In fact I wasn't much interested in sex at all for a week or two. The people I was meeting were entirely more fascinating.

For a week or two.

I regret perhaps appearing gross but it became perfectly obvious to me within a very short time that the most pressing matters about life in university in the mid-nineteen-sixties fell under the umbrella of hedonism and specifically, in no particular order were, for the majority, sex, drugs, music, clothes and then ... Doing as little work as possible. In any order. As many sexual liaisons seemed to be being made between students and academic staff as between students themselves.

And then, of course, there were the students with already established relationships - Jill Peacock brought down Michael Barker as often as she could, Sally Fenby was going out with Murray Head, no less, a pop star yet, whom I was to meet ten years later in very different circumstances. Gillie Willis was going out with Richard Binns ... yes. Well. That didn't last long. And I of course ... This shabby little bastard was still keeping up with aforementioned Gill Phillips although after her visit to coincide with the Christmas dance, the liaison was well and truly over. I have a horrible feeling we spent a sexless night together in a single bed. Oh, the horror and the shame and the non-event for her.

I really am consumed with guilt. It's one of the most shameful episodes of my life, second only to not looking after two horses I had stupidly purchased in the depths of a cruel winter in 1978. Both events are only recordable because of my utter, unjustifiable ignorance. I was fumbling with little or no knowledge and, with dear Gill, a great deal of fear. I really wasn't ready to come out. 'Coming-out' as a precept of homosexual life just wasn't one in common currency then.

In those liberating nineteen-sixties, amongst my peers, no one muttered a word about queers except Richard Denton who bragged endlessly that during his sabbatical *vie bohemienne* in Paris, he'd virtually lived with an American queer called Jack. I suppose we must have been reverently impressed at the time in a *gauloise 'n' gitane* sort of way although later I wondered ...

The week or two of being insularly fascinated passed fairly quickly and then I discovered the town of Canterbury and what it had to offer. The cruising for sex which takes up and has taken up so much male homosexual time over the years finds atavistic roots, I am convinced, in the instinct men have for hunting.

Now, here's a theory.

The gatherers in those long ago societies would seem to me to have been the women. Gathering can be a very comradely, group kind of thing. Like shopping. I hate shopping. Hunting, I maintain, would have more often than not been solitary, the members of the hunting party still having entirely separate, individualised functions. But then shopping can be a lot like hunting, come to think of it.

Cruising, for we queer people, took (takes) the form of walking or loitering or riding or driving in 'productive' areas like heaths, commons, woodlands, beaches, sand dunes, road lay-bys, motorway rest areas, public parks, graveyards etc. 'Loitering' (as the law would have it), sitting in one's car listening to the radio or merely smoking endless cigarettes whilst waiting to see who might go into a certain public convenience or wander into a particular patch of dappled shade has wasted the best part of many a good man's life.

We wait, we stalk, we pounce ...

The kill is as good as the feast. That we can still do it seems to be the propellant motivation and each conquest becomes immediately the stepping stone to the next. End becomes means, endlessly. A serial loop.

As far as Canterbury was concerned in 1965 when one could still drive down the high street, apart from several 'cottages' - the Izal and piss variety and none too productive - there was the pub. Every provincial centre in Great Britain sported at least one pub - boy! Was I learning fast - and Canterbury's was the aptly named Queens Head which being the closest to the stage door was also the Marlowe Theatre's pub. Deeply GOOD COMPANIONS.

There I met my wider world. Not in the Junior Common Room of the University, nor on the student demos when we paraded down to the Administrative Headquarters at Beverly Farm but in the public bar of The Queens Head. Peter Moore and Andrew Thompson from Christchurch teacher-training college introduced me to a society of queer peers which included actors, farmers, locals and ... yes! Prelates! Princes (or Princesses) of the church, yea. Andrew Thompson reminds me that The Long Bar in the Johnson's Queens Head was the meeting and mixing place for both queer and straight alike. It was the real world, more real than my campus society which was so, so liberal but yet so unbelievably rarefied. No one had identified themselves as a university queer to encourage me to want to do the same. I was content to mix with the teacher training college students who seemed much more prepared to stand up and be counted and when they were, they were thoroughly embraced by their straight peers, men like Malcolm Bell, big, rugger-playing and thoroughly tolerant.

It was all quite head-turning, especially one's successes like when dearest me was invited to spend an evening and have breakfast at the ecclesiastical knocking academy known as Lambeth Palace. Golly, I thought as I pondered all the Archbishops who'd been burned at the stake or sent to the Tower for less carnal transgressions, is this wise? I can now remember absolutely nothing of the occasion except that it happened and the following morning, the little postern door in the huge Tudor red-brick main gatehouse closed behind me and there I was in the cold light of morning, buggered (probably) but not bowed, alone on the Embankment, only just across the Thames, albeit two bridges seaward, from Charing Cross.

Whether Queen Eleanor's spirit still adjudicated in the ether above Charing Cross is purely my whimsy but there was some good fairy looking after me - or do I mean some good-looking fairy after me? - whenever I arrived there to catch the train back to Canterbury West. Some days, when I really got lucky, I just never caught the train.

In the gentlemen's conveniences on that station, I met a whole cast of characters who were the stout parties to my fey ingenu in the farce which was my socialisation as a functional homosexual. My apologies, but I have forgotten all of my encounter group except two and I wish I hadn't forgotten for all were as instrumental in my education as any formal teacher or tutor and I would love to accord them credit.

The first I remember was a man called Rob who lived in Grove Road in St John's Wood and who was something in advertising - very romantic and glamorous in those days. He was tall and thin and fucked like a stoat and was wonderful to me and taught me that penetration was not only possible but a truly Heineken experience. And all done to lit candles. Well. What was a boy to do? Run screaming out into the night?? Puhleeze.

The second was Michael Handford, a teacher. The experience with him was more on-going and yet entirely unsatisfactory for expectations crept in. I still see Michael around ... At theatres. In the street occasionally. He doesn't recognise me. In those days there was a pub called, I believe, The Green Man, at the top of the hill leading from Greenwich up onto Blackheath. Now it is demolished and there are flats on the site. Then, there was an established music hall in the upstairs theatre-ised first storey and it was where Michael took me after he'd met me at said Charing Cross for it was at weekends when I would go up to London to meet him. We'd catch a suburban train to Blackheath and then walk across the heath to the Music Hall in which Michael was very involved, I think betimes as Chairman. It was theatre, after all and of a sort I'd never experienced and it was a further expansion of 'the real life'

Michael's friends were very nice to me and didn't look

at me like I had two heads or my bumpkin was showing. I felt almost normal although very, very young. In being so concerned about my bumpkin, my naiveté and youth trailed behind me like a torn hem. After the varieties, we would go back to his flat in a huge Victorian villa overlooking Blackheath and try and shag. It was always so cold there - he said, suddenly used to centrally-heated student monkishness - and I was just not good with him. Quite shaming in the light of later acquired expertise. I'm so sorry, Michael. Put it down, I beg you, to callow youth. And if anyone out there wants to seduce a tender nineteen year old, do it with a bit of finesse, a heater and a lot more lube.

And thus back by British Rail to Canterbury and thence by bus up the Whitstable Road and back to campus. Back to tutorials in sociology, seminars in economics, lectures on economic history and ... dread, horror, shiver ...exercises in statistics.

The first year, our part one, was a mixed curse. Sorry. Mixed course. Very early on in my first year, I realised I had made a truly terrible choice in the matter of what to study. I came quickly to loathing sociology and sociologists who seemed whether from textbook or lecture lectern to be spouting merely what was perceived common-sense for us all. I saw no practicable application of the discipline especially after we were firmly told that sociology had absolutely nothing to do with social work.

Despite every graduate sociologist worth their two-two having since been absorbed into a *corps de social service* expanded purely to accommodate otherwise unwanted social science graduates brandishing their irrelevant certificates, I can only trust that the pioneer Canterbury sociologists sincerely believed their own bullshit. That they themselves were bullshitters to a man and woman, I now have no doubt.

Why didn't I change course? I think I resisted because I had made so much of wanting to study sociology to my parents at home who, quite rationally, had wondered what I could do with a degree in such an 'ollogy'. I was kind of hoist by my own impractical petard, really and I doggedly decided I would not be beaten.

But my stubborness meant that I fell out of love with academe incredibly quickly and I contrived for the next two and a half years to do as little work as possible although sufficient to maintain maximum credit from minimum profile. I still have nightmares about ignored revision and incompleted tutorial and seminar papers and wake up thinking I am about to go totally unprepared into my finals. I believe actors have dreams where they forget their lines ... Well, snap.

University did a great deal for me but it was my attendance which was the dynamic; the course and the work and the ethos left me colder than a witch's tit.

London beckoned more and more insistently although it was to the queer bits that I was drawn most. The pursuit of love was not facilitated by the presence of friends from Canterbury. I usually went up by myself although I did on occasion go to London with girlfriends such as Jenny Stern. Jenny lived with her mother and father in Highgate, opposite the school playing fields and other than Highgate I was introduced to neighbourhoods like Kensington High Street and Kings Road Chelsea in order to hunt for clothes.

Biba in Abingdon Road I thought a magical place, redolent with myth and the mystery of glamour. Kind of legendary. Same with Mary Quant in her shop BIZARRE next to The Markham in Kings Road. Ossie Clark's shop too. The cutting edge. Carnaby Street was an obvious attraction although I have to say I found the John Stephen empire and the other boutiques on the main drag somewhat down-market. Thrilling to go into Foale and Tuffin, however, tucked away in a side street. Sally Fenby looked wonderful in Marion and Sally's (now-Dennis) clothes.

Sadly, in all my three student years, I never went to any of the clubs and coffee bars that other chroniclers such as Peter Burton in PARALLEL LIVES have described. I knew they existed but to me they were places where you went as a social event, in and with company. Not as a man alone.

My experience of gay (not a word in much common parlance then) London was limited to the obvious West End, Soho (but not the back streets) and the vicinity of Charing Cross as my compass naturally pointed back to Canterbury. But London did the trick, alright.

The alternative hunting grounds such as Earls Court, Hampstead and Notting Hill Gate ... These areas were unknown to me during my university years. They proved all the better for the waiting.

Thus, on any visit to London, I usually ended up in The Salisbury in St Martin's Lane. Very close to Charing Cross, you see. The plush, brass and gilt theatre pub has been used for so many film productions that I now can't place the reality of it way back then but I can confirm it was a wonderful place for cruising and furnished many an encounter.

How did I cruise in those days? Did I stand simpering with a half of bitter and wait to get picked up or did I flagrantly flash in the gents loo down in the basement? I rather fancy it was the former for the brazenness which later characterised my approach strategies hadn't yet hardened in me and I was rather shy. Forward but shy, eager but retiring if such an infuriating contradiction can be imagined. And of course, there was always the constraint of the last train. There really wasn't much I could do, pro-actively. If it was a question of, "Yours or Mine?", I had no place to go.

I suppose I have to take a moment to examine this cruising urge. It's something so natural in gay men of my acquaintance, the phenomenon seems to have been taken very much for granted. Just what was it that I was looking for? Love? Whatever that might have meant then, other than 'pairing off', I don't know. 'Finding someone special', 'settling down' ... Yes. Perhaps. But in mock-monogamy? Like the straights do? I very much doubt it as reason *numero uno*. That sort of comes with the territory of age and apathy. Truth to tell, we really only cruised for sex. Simple sexual gratification.

Without doubt, what socialising we had been bequeathed was to materialise in codified form in 1967 when certain (read unspecified) homosexual acts between consenting adults (for gay males read over age of 21) in private (read unspecified) were decriminalised. Homosexuality itself was never legalised. It was beckoned out, encouraged to show itself, falsely lured like so many of its individual adherents mistakenly thinking that it was safe to come out of the shadows and into the sun ...

Wrong. Light too bright.

Two people, and only two, enjoying certain sexual activities in private was, after all, no more than what straight people were allowed to do. That's certainly what we young queers thought and, therefore, perceived that we could, and probably should, do. A generation of gay males was bred where pairing up and settling down was held to be a fair norm and an applaudable aspiration. I'm sure it is. But like with marriage, there are no guarantees and togetherness is no fail-safe. Co-habitation with romantic/sexual love as a foundation is as inherently an unstable a confection as nitroglycerin nougatine for, without being legitimate, two queers coupling-up and settling-down are doing so with the added drawback of having no legal protection whatsoever. And, as we know to our painful and humiliating consequence, the law is the only freedom for civilised man.

If we were obliquely being told that we were supposed to live like straights, we were being expected to do so in 1967 entirely unprotected by the law. As I grow older and wearier, I find it increasingly peculiar that as a civilization, our culture in the west - ownership, property, law, wealth, civil rights - is based on such a volatile arrangement as the marriage of a man and a woman for love. Why should we self-respecting gays, given an opportunity to choose, want to play through the same charade to fall into the same traps?

All this got to be very confusing for me. Still is, forty years later. We were too young and freshly out and it was all too early for us to realise that there was to develop something called 'a gay perspective', that it doesn't have to ape any straight one. It seems we will never stop learning how to be properly queer. Leastways, I know I won't.

Even then, underlying the Homes and Gardens and the Habitat catalogue motives for making sexual contact, there is, I contend, an underlying male need to survey, to assess, to pick out, to approach, to contact, to mutually pleasure, finally to come and then, to ... To what?

Mostly, it would seem, to say, "Thanks" and, "Goodbye", if you get good-mannered trade. If not, it's just a grunt and a murmured, "Well, see ya," and off.

I also contend that for most straight men, this urge - laid out in precisely that order - is identical. Male sexuality has always seemed to be indivisible. It doesn't really matter what a man does with his dick or where he puts it to do it. That's merely a matter of mechanical preference. I feel more in common with the sexuality of straight male friends than I ever do with women's. Given Gay Man A and Straight Man B are each entirely comfortable with their sexual preference, their sexuality is one and the same. I intend no chauvinism nor mean no exclusion. I just think ...

Sex and love, I was discovering, don't always come and go together. Only very infrequently do they come together and, even then, I think the co-incidence is as much to do with current circumstantial pressures and needs as it is to do with an innate desire in either party to 'couple up' in the way of forever, 'til death do us part. That part just sort of happens. Much more luck than judgement.

So the first year in Canterbury passed and although I must have been changing, to me it was imperceptible. I still felt much too young. And arrogant? God, I must have been awful. The work got no better. Studying in the temporary library was an enforced doldrums every two weeks or so in order to turn in the required essay or seminar paper. Did I care about extended families in Bethnal Green or the customs and culture of the Trobriand Islanders? Really.

I became, for reasons unfathomable, rather too caught up with the superficial and developed a vanity. I wanted to be a male model for a time and even went as far as having some silly test photographs done for an exorbitant amount of money in London. Total con, of course. I don't know how I got the message about 'forget it', but I did. I think I was rather relieved to realise that I was endowed with quite ordinary looks and that the best score quotient I could ever make of the merits of my physiognomy would be a mere 'interesting'.

One more-than-interesting social observation which I could safely make about other people as the first year drew to its close was the natural division of the student body into those involved with the Arts and Humanities and those reading Science subjects. It seemed that never the twain would meet. Looking back, I suppose the roots of the schism are traceable to the curriculum adopted in schools for both 'O' and 'A' level GCE exams.

There came a point in one's entirely flexible and amorphous education when the fourteen year old had had to choose between the arts and the sciences and, once the choice had been made, there was generally no going back. Such are the arbitrary divisions which have no natural place in the world of curious, inquisitive evolving teenage minds. Surely, if it was mandatory to study religious matters at school, the existence, or not, of any god is surely as discussible by enquiring teenagers as the basic philosophy of mathematics and physical science even if one cannot do the sums in either lesson?

I wonder if this same academic schism existed at faculty level? Would the urbane, essentially Oxbridge Brian Keith-Lucas, professor of politics, with his fabulously tasteful Georgian house in the cathedral part of town have felt at home for a whole evening with a flock of science students in his drawing room instead of us airy little artistic types? Maybe it's down to types. The more deconstructivist Professor Stirling, to whose home we were also invited, might have proved the contrary. Whatever. These visits to our tutors' homes all conspired to aid and abet the greatest lesson that some people ever learn - How to juggle a plate, a fork, a glass and a napkin and at the same time, eat, talk, listen and politely put across your point whether it be the talents of your college's domestic bursar (in our case, Barbara Harris) or the existence of God (name and sex unknown).

And on the God front, as first year students, we still thrashed he, she or it about quite a lot in late night discussion ... God and socialism and moral rights and wrongs. The Bomb. Viet Nam. We were, when we chose to be, an earnest bunch and there were great questions to be asked to which answers were obviously desperately needed.

I can't tell you how many sleepless nights I spent worrying about the dropping of the hydrogen bomb. It is something that patently now would not raise a hackle on hamster. In those days, the day of armageddon was uncomfortably nigh.

That no real answers ever came to our intellectual quandaries, however, gave us no particular disquiet. Several of us even foolishly dabbled in scratchings of the ouija board in the quest to penetrate the deeper, non-rational mysteries. Those who venture into unknown territory, without maps and without an accredited guide can be safely said to be dabbling in foolishness. It was not to stop even when the medium glass nearly flew off the table when we enquired as to whether or not there was a god. But more of that foolishness later.

Being car-less and mostly bike-less, we used to walk quite a lot around and about the campus and explored all the new buildings taking shape. Rutherford College, the university's second, had to be ready by October 1966 which deadline looked decidedly dicey. We found that there was an old railway tunnel which lay beneath our greenhill and we used to walk through it in the dripping, dank darkness, torchless, of course and found that rather exciting. There was a huge depression, perhaps a crater caused by an exploding jettisoned German bomb, where we often sat and vowed one day to do something wonderful in. A great many plans were laid whilst musing on the subject of the site of that greenfield amphitheatre.

Much of our wanderings, especially in that first summer term, were because of the Film Society which I had also joined. Richard Denton was the society's first film-maker and he set out to make a film of John Donne's poem "Come live with me and be my love and we shall all the pleasures prove ..." Richard's first and very short film rather lacked the bite and precision of his later celebrated documentary works like PUBLIC SCHOOL, COMPREHENSIVE and COMRADES and was rather bogged down in Bergmanesque imagery and sex. I remember quite a lot of effort going into both pre-production and subsequent filming of an obligatory pair of naked Bristols. Said boobs were ultimately owned by Julie Box, both a member of the faculty and also married to one of our sociology lecturers. A very heavily made-up girl, I remember. She took little persuasion. Great fun was also had planning to audition people. Bit laddish, I suppose but pretty harmless.

And all grist to the mill. Hand-ground, of course.

And there came too soon the end of of the first year. I moved out of my college room. The next twelve Kentish months were to be spent in digs. Location as yet unspecified. I prayed fervently I wouldn't be billeted in windy Herne Bay or gusty Whitstable. Wheresoe'er, Donald Macdonald and I had elected to room together and, not being allowed cars, I was determined to acquire that most necessary of a mod's accessories. A motor scooter.

So I bid farewell to all my groovy new chums for the duration of 'the long vac' and drove with my father, the car packed full of a year's worth of accumulated stuff, back to Malvern. My father, who had never been abroad since his repatriation, had acquiesced to my mother's apparent urge to travel and had agreed to a continental summer holiday.

It was the last family holiday we were to take and it was to be taken, due to my mother's fear of flying, by coach.

Chapter Eight

WE'RE ALL GOING ON A
SUMMER HOLIDAY

By coach!!

Horrors! What were these parents of mine thinking?

And to Yugoslavia!

My new-found milieu migrated to Provence, to the Dordogne and to Tuscany. Or to long-held family cottages or second homes in the countryside and by the coasts of Great Britain. And they got there either by aeroplane or by ferry and car; even by train. They did not, however, go by coach, anywhere and they certainly did not go to Yugoslavia!

I had turned into the nastiest little snob ever. Not a happy event. The purgatorial prospect of the holiday was at first only mildly offset by the palliative provided by my securing a vacation job at the local theatre for the first revival since the war of the fabled Malvern Festival.

Mine was not an acting job; it wasn't even ASM'ing. It was selling programmes and ice-creams and working in the coffee bar. It was to prove a galvanising experience. But at the outset it was a job. No job. No money. No money. No motor scooter.

The festival's policy was to put bums on seats with a revamped diet of Elgar and Shaw with a few modern items to spice up the plot. The music side of the project I had nothing to do with. That part of my education was thwarted when I was no longer exposed to the passions of David Ottaway. Of classical music I was and still am woefully ignorant.

The theatre part of the Festival was being organised by Bill Boht, a huge, shambling and charismatic man who had had charge of one of the Birmingham entertainment complexes. He was more like a landlord of a vast city pub or a manager of a boxing arena than a theatre man. Bill dominated the proceedings, ably and surprisingly compliantly abetted by his wife Jean. A dark-haired young actress of the sweetest and most caring disposition, Jean Boht was the mother to the repertory company which had been assembled as well as to all us little odds and sods whom the theatre anywhere attracts. It was all a bit Dodie Smith, I suppose with a touch of Broome Stages but I straightaway felt right at home. Many years later, as Ma in Carla Lane's BREAD, Jean Boht developed her art and craft to institutional proportions. She was and is magnificent. I don't think Bill lived to see her triumph and I know not what happened to their marriage but he would have been proud of her career achievement.

For the first time in my life, I was seeing stars. And my head duly spun. Glamour, howsoe'er it is perceived, is definitely contagious. I became living proof. There, in the flesh, was Betty Marsden who had delivered those mystifyingly camp lines in ROUND THE HORNE which had baffled me for years on my Sunday afternoon boarding school walks. Betty was one of the repertory company's leading ladies along with Helen Christie. The camp was a tad less mystifying now but still as deliciously secret as what lay between an 'omey's bonar lallies!'

I remember Betty starred in a French play called THE LAUNDRY which concealed the terrible secret of her having a grossly malformed son whom she loved but could never admit to the world and over which I broke down and wept at every performance. Did I identify or what!

Then there was something suitably historical ... I think it was to do with Mary Queen of Scots when it was Ms. Christie's turn to shine. With Rio Fanning and Donald Someone, all being courtiers or swashbucklers. The ASM (Assistant Stage Manager, darling) was Virginia Denham, Maurice's daughter. We became friendly, nay close and it was my first of many, many friendships which I realised needn't be continued or worked at or perpetuated beyond a certain mark in time. One can become terribly close to someone because you just have to, given the requirements of prevailing circumstances and then ... Wheeee! Away it floats, safe in its little bubble of time. Like all the best holiday romances, repertory friendships should be bidden adieu at the end of the season, only to be waved at occasionally from passing trains at Crewe on wet and wandery Sunday afternoons.

Well, all this is sounding very cosy and Priestley except a special addendum to the repertory season popped up and upset the applecart ... which was one Shaw play not being revived, by the by. This interloper took the form of a touring booking. It might as well have been The Alien from Outer Space.

Top rank West End-bound productions have always toured out of town and PUBLIC AND CONFIDENTIAL by Ben Levy was no exception. Starring Levy's wife Constance Cummings, the play which was about political scandal or something was produced by someone called Michael Codron. Such a frisson of appehension rippled through the backstage corridors on the occasion of the first performance when Michael himself arrived from London - or was it Uranus? - to check out the state of his production. I expected to see Captain Hook or Ebeneezer Balfour or at least Beelzebub materialising in our quiet little backwater. Instead, a very handsome, dark-haired man arrived, looking every inch a distinguished leading player. We acknowledged each other in the crush during both intervals but didn't speak and then he was gone, back to London. Everyone breathed a sigh of relief. All had been approved, god had returned to his heaven and it was to be seven years before I would at last be properly introduced to Mr. Codron.

In the meantime, I found myself spending more and more time with Colin Dudley, the company manager of PUBLIC and CONFIDENTIAL. I was nineteen and he can't have been more than thirty. We were drawn to each other in lust. I sensed nothing of love and cared less. The lust was quite exciting enough and I was entirely intrigued by the insider's knowledge of the theatre which I was gaining through our acquaintance. He would climb the Malvern Hills with mates from the cast or the stage crew and visit me at my day-job at the cafe at the top of the Worcestershire Beacon. (Motor scooter fast approaching, please, dear Lord.) When the show came down at night, we would have a drink in the pub or even go back to my parents' house and have coffee and sandwiches. It was all quite proper ... and he was only in town with the play for an all too short week. But there was a plan. After Yugoslavia. Somehow, I was going to have to hold myself until after Yugoslavia.

Yugoslavia started with a train trip to London and a night in an Ebury Street Hotel. The following morning we boarded said coach at Victoria, somewhere and thence to the continent of Europe. I have no memory of the outward journey - blot it out, blot it out! - until we arrived at Opatija, on the Adriatic sea, a resort whose previous significance the fifty years since the start of the first world war had obliterated. Safe for the existence of a rather grand hotel in which our package holiday had been billeted, Opatija was a forgotten cairngorm in the tiara of the Balkans. And there I was, afraid of the prospect of gusty Whitstable. I should have been so lucky.

The coach trip was very long. I think we went through Switzerland and therefore some tunnel or the other but I have really forgotten. The only fellow coach passengers I can remember were a sweet couple very much in their later middle years of whom the husband was a London bus-driver. Talk about a busman's holiday. I think they were Irish. Anyway, at work, he was to be found on the eighty-eight route and his name was Tom.

When we'd been through Venice - not the tourist Venice - and through Fiume/Trieste and we arrived at Opatija, it was wonderfully, roastingly hot and I discovered heavy sun-bathing for the first time. About getting seriously brown. There was little else, during the day, to do. I'm amazed I haven't yet developed skin cancer for no one in those days knew about high-factor lotions. Suffer the little red ones ...

The hotel's food was simple and interesting and of a Mediterranean character. A welcome change from home-cooking. I can recall that carpetless, 'yesterday' smell, mixed with a whiff of dill to this day. It was in Opatija, I'm sure, that I also developed a taste for long, lazy days in tall, cool rooms where graciously proportioned double-doors still sport intricate bolts and locks and where the air of intrigue and breathless, flushed, suppressed passion floats like a perfume on a hot night. It was a time for ghosts and daydreams.

I don't know what my brother and sister and my parents did, but after dinner, of course, David went for his little walk. Into the public gardens bordering the *promenade* at the sea's edge. There was no proper beach, as I recall, merely rock ledges about which the warm, crystal-clear tideline lapped lazily. The breeze off this dream-sea at night was refreshing but barely penetrated the velvet darkness contained by the thick canopy of foliage beneath which the pathways of the gardens meandered from seat to seat. Of course, wonderful things grew in that garden. They knocked ice creams into a cocked (sorry) hat.

But we went nowhere and worse - apart from the bus-driver and his wife - met no one. That in a way was the worst. I think one could go to the Great Wall of China and yet without company to share the experience with or people to highlight the event, it would be just another wall. A big wall.

The return journey from Yugoslavia in that infernal coach across four countries was memorable only in that on one very long leg between comfort stops, my mother was taken so short that her need for a lavatory was painful to witness, so painful that I took it upon myself to insist in no quiet way to the coach-driver and our bespectacled lady courier that the coach stop immediately. It did. Ma went and everyone was rather quiet after my so un-English an outburst. I loathe coaches. Not to say I'd never go on one again. That I will have to at some point is fairly obvious but, will I like them? Never.

Once back in London and the obligatory night over with in the anonymous Ebury Street hotel, I was on my own again. My parents having met aforesaid Mr. Dudley back in Malvern had found him to be charming; so, it had been arranged with them that I would stay on in London to spend a few days with Colin in his - at last - Chelsea flat. I suppose I could pretend that I felt like Christopher Isherwood arriving in a strange and puissant city but I really felt like Sally Bowles. Or, rather, Elsie. Wilkommen, bienvenue, welcome ...

I left my parents at Victoria and, still unfamiliar with the buses, took the circle line on the underground to Sloane Square and walked the length of the Kings Road, brown as a berry and more than ready to be picked and eaten. Colin lived on one floor of a mansion block where the road kinks just about where Vivienne Westwood was. Is.

And there I suddenly was, from half-a-world away, knocking at this theatrical person's front door.

"You are expecting me?"

Perhaps.

"Bet you thought I wouldn't show up?"

Not a high priority worry, obviously.

Within about three minutes, it seemed, we were in bed and it was around that point that I began to think quite seriously about the business of choice. *Vis-a-vis* sex. I think up until Colin Dudley, I had gone with anyone who'd have had me. Anyone who'd looked at me, smiled at me, talked to me and asked me home'd had me for the price of my eager unquestioning inexperience.

After Colin, I started to get the drift. I realised that I had likes, therefore preferences, types of people I preferred ... Queers weren't just all the same. There were some that did one thing, liked one thing and some who were the opposite. And not the same things all the time. One could swap about, depending on the moment, on the mood. The your-turn-on-top-dear option had not been on my menu. There was choice in this great game of sex. I could say 'No' just like the other guy could say 'No'. Sounds simplistic, I know, but to me it was a revelation.

Not that I regret anything that had gone before. Far from it. Without the lessons, nothing would have been learned. And why did it all suddenly click into place? Easy. Colin Dudley's flatmate. Such a dish I had never seen. His name was Brian. I can't remember his last name but he was the manager of Leon Maybank's Calabash Club, a gay coffee bar in a little pedestrian walk-through off Fulham Road, five minutes walk away. The coffee bar too was a revelation. Here were queers not merely mixing with other straight people, but perfectly happy with themselves in their own society and having a jolly nice, often intelligent time.

And there was, of course, Brian.

I have no memory of how long I stayed with Colin and

Brian although I do remember that nothing came of my 'pash' on Brian, prematurely grey-haired and with an aura of quiet, sexy *savoir-faire* ... With all my new-found knowledge about choice, it didn't for a moment occur to me that a) he might not have fancied me or b) that we would have made the driest bread sandwich. A question of Martha and Martha as Arthur the American often has it.

So back to Malvern once again on that Paddington train. I came to likening the journey to Malvern as my own Via Dolorosa, the stops we made being my particular Twelve Stations. Hilly Malvern was obviously no Calvary but it represented the end of my road.

But at least it was back to buying the treasured motor scooter which I immediately contrived to drive full tilt at the garage door. A week in the motor scooter garage corrected the damage and then, time to return to Canterbury. News had come through of our billet. As luck would have it, Donald and I had landed the closest digs to the campus ever established, with Mr. and Mrs. Lowry in the house at the bottom of the hill, below Rutherford College. The house was a bungalow and Donald and I were to share a room at the front of the house with, as Donald pointed out, easy access through the window. I fancy that there were still rules about keeping late hours.

I think my father and I drove my stuff down to Canterbury and then returned to Malvern before I made the great solo trek on my motor scooter through every kind of weather condition to Canterbury. Never had I made a solo journey which was so long ... I have since known longer.

Eliot College was never the same for me again. Where you sleep most nights each week is where you live, as far as I am concerned and life had irrevocably opened out. However, I wish I had opened out more. I can remember feeling much more in charge, that I had somehow grown as a person since arriving on campus twelve months before but I still went through the same old social charades, rather half-heartedly I have to admit.

Donald began 'going out' with the very beautiful Sarah Auburn. Her elfish, exquisite face was like porcelain and she had indeed done some photographic modelling before university, notably for Vogue. Instant extra glamour 'cred'. She also had a friend - went everywhere together - called Sue Lermon, now married to Steve

Godfree and ... I look back now and I don't understand me. But then, I wasn't me. The me I am now. Sorry, Sue ... No great damage done, I'm sure, but I am sorry.

And then of course there were the new arrivals. We had a second year intake of undergraduates. Rutherford College had not only been completed, it had been filled. There was now a university history, albeit only a year old but there were traditions, dammit! We were introduced to Caroline Hebbron whose premature death in Australia was such a tragedy, Micky Sheringham and Michael Jacques. Mandy Pierce-Higgins materialised too and was the first in my small world theory of life which goes something like, "The further you travel from your own front door the more likely you are to bump into your neighbour."

Mandy's father, then Canon John Pierce-Higgins of Southwark Cathedral, had been the Vicar of Hanley Castle for several years although his time had been just before I went to the boarding school. I never heard him preach and I never really heard him wax significant on his personal particularity which was to do with the existence of spirits, of possession, of haunting and, therefore, exorcism, which interest had marginalised him in the Anglican church. I had to be content knowing that I believed him. I hope he knew.

So many years and miles away from Worcestershire, I meet his daughter, thence John himself and his wife and their other children Ben, Lucinda and the amiable Daniel at their beautiful Georgian house in Lambeth Road and also at their cottage-house at Froxfield Green, near Petersfield. I loved this mad, intelligent, artistic, vagabond and truly eccentric family and I wanted one just like it for myself. Of course, they saw it all rather differently but then ... The grass always is greener.

Sarah Harman, ex-deb-of-the-year swept in with her mane of Fergie-red hair. And, of course, David Meyer. David. Dear, dear David.

Having been so intimately connected with 'the profession' if only for a month in the summer holiday, it might not be surprising that in this, my second undergraduate year, I gravitated like the Newtonian apple to the Drama Society, despite the still-stuttering stammer which only served to prove that gravity can be delayed by *les forces majeures.*

I remember being auditioned by Anthony Miller and Sebastian Graham-Jones in a lecture room for the part of Ezekiel Edgeworth in Ben Johnson's BARTHOLOMEW FAIR which the society was to present at The Marlowe Theatre no less, at the end of the Winter semester in 1966. I've just seen Tony on TV doing an 'ad' for Imodium. Those pills that block up your bowels when you have diahorrea. Ten out of ten for perseverance, Tony, I thought. But then he is also the very successful writer of television's CITIZEN SMITH and THE BRITTAS EMPIRE.

Why my life took so long to be dramatised, I don't know. I'd already been charmed and intrigued by the idea of 'the theatre' whilst playing Christopher Columbus as a thirteen year old in THE SHADES OF NIGHT but now I really fell deeply in love ... On second thoughts, infatuation is a better word that springs to mind. Let's keep love for later. The Drama Society also provided my next important stepping stone for I learned that as someone other than myself, I could indeed fly ... deep into Never-Never Land with as many fairies as I cared to count. I thought I knew how to pretend very well. I seemed to be getting away with my current impersonation rather well. A few more layers on the top wouldn't hurt.

Oh. And I got the part.

I also got my Part One examination pass. Somehow. That was the greater surprise. I had thence elected initially to read sociology but I immediately diluted this agony by asking to read for a joint degree, adding economic history to my curse. Sorry, course! I must get this right. Although the course change certainly relieved some of the symptoms and spread the burden, the dull, uninteresting load still had to be carried.

But there were some of us who didn't pass and those people vanished from campus. One of these was Richard Hoyle, tall, thin, fine-featured, he wore polo-neck sweaters all the time. Nice burgundy and bottle green ones. He was always gaunt but obviously became more gaunt. He rarely smiled; he could have been called morose. He failed part one exams and left the university although he still kept up with fellow students.

He killed himself.

He was seeing Sarah Auburn at the time. I believe she found his body on a camping trip they had undertaken with her sister and boyfriend. It must have been shattering for her. For us, it was numbing. For me it was the first reminder that if you really wanted to, you really could be in control. Whether Richard was helped by the hard drugs on which he had started, who was to know? It was profoundly sobering.

There were several users in college. An aura of secrecy and impregnability developed around them. I smiled, I cheerfully always said hello but I was awkward. I felt uncomfortable, knowing that I would never know what they knew, would never feel, see or hear what they had experienced. I felt excluded. And frightened.

But back to reality ...

BARTHOLOMEW FAIR was my equivalent of being bloodied. I became passionate about acting and even tried a little writing, for sketches and comic pantomimes performed in the Eliot College Junior Common Room. PETER PAN especially got a dreadful pasting one Christmas with all the obvious innuendoes and attendant poovery.

Oh yes, Tink ... I believed alright. But, did they?

Other productions followed. NF Simpson's THE HOLE was given at the New Universities Festival at Keele. We were nearly killed on the way back to Canterbury. The driver was being fed neat alcohol as we drove.

By the beginning of summer 1967, I really thought I knew it all. At some point, I know I was on the Entertainments Committee and I found the pace and the pressure of the commercial side of showbusiness telling. It takes several rounds with the demons before anyone realises what their weaknesses are. My first bout was up against being faced with some huge financial loss because of unsold tickets or whatever - a responsibility which I naively seemed to shoulder alone - and ended up with me weeping uncontrollably in Mandy Pierce-Higgins' room in Rutherford College. I got over it, of course but I had felt the feeling and when it came again, I knew what 'losing it' was all about.

Some time at Easter had been spent on the Helford River in Cornwall staying in Donald Macdonald's parents' cottage there. The Macdonalds were sailors but we did no sailing. It was a magical few days, however, in a truly enchanted setting. We had had a couple of family holidays in Looe, further down the coast. Cornwall has always been wild and free. I like it. Why oh why do we have this need to tie ourselves down?

But we do.

And, as I've mentioned, David Meyer had indeed arrived ...

To say he was a beautiful youth would not have done him justice. He was not only blonde and physically beautiful but he also had a completely open and trusting nature. It appeared that life hadn't grafitti-ed David Meyer's wall at all. It was like he was handing you the spray-can himself.

It really is the people. Not the places ... I can recall much of what I thought about David Meyer but little of the event of my life in 1967. I remember writing a great deal of bad poetry. It wasn't even poetry. But I wrote of love, that aching, melancholic, idealised kind of love which I thought I was in and which I also then thought was poetry's essence. Lying in the long grass in the summer field below Eliot College with Vicky Wingate and her friend Patti Howe and David too and coming up with pages and pages of crossed-out and re-written heartspew, at least I thought I was happy ... So I'm also heartglad because I know I fell in love for the first time. Not just schoolboy infatuation like with 'dearest him'.

But although I got the love bit right, I flunked the sex test. And that, of course, screwed-up the love bit. Turned out to be another cruel twist of fate and I know I hurt David a great deal and, again, for that I am truly sorry. He didn't even know he was queer. I knew I was, but despite the bravura performance I hadn't a clue as to how to do it. How to be one.

While David and I lasted, we must have seemed a golden couple. I felt invincible for the first time in my life. We were both cast in ALL'S WELL THAT ENDS WELL performed in the Eliot College cloisters directed by Mike Hattaway. I played Parolles, a clownish jester to my lady Lisa Vine's Countess. Type-casting, do I hear you groundlings call? I notice from the programme that David played Bertram, a loving courtier. He was, indeed, incredibly loving.

And we went away in the summer holiday of 1967, hitch-hiking no less through France. We were en route for Sebastian

Graham-Jones' grand-parents at their *Villa Pace* in Sestri Levante although when we got there ... Let's just say there was no Eighteen-to-Thirty rep to meet us. I remember arriving in Lyons and sleeping under a bush in a public park which turned out to be Lyons' biggest outdoor cruising area which of course I was unerringly attracted to like a magnetic screwdriver to a screw.

It didn't take a genius to know that the trip was not going well. I also knew that at the time, I was suffering the first of many sexually transmitted diseases I was to contract in my life. Except that I didn't know it was a sexually transmitted disease. That was the bit where I could have used a little genius.

This particular visitation was an outbreak of anal warts, virally-transmitted, I now understand and which went as mysteriously as it arrived but only after a few months of unbearable discomfort, bleeding and inner panic. All this, blithe prat that I was, I did not impart to David or anyone and underwent in ignorance and terrified silence as though it was something dirty. Which, I suppose it was but nothing to do with shame or guilt ... But I didn't know.

Somewhere in all this, I was taken home to meet the Meyer momma and poppa at their stockbroker home in Harpenden, Hertfordshire where, as every Eliza knows, hurricanes hardly ever happen. David was also a twin. An identical twin. I met Antony, his brother but to say we got on like a house on fire wouldn't be right at all. Antony was at a Cambridge College, an entirely alternative universe. He himself was quite correctly suspicious of this flamboyant, intellectually fluffy chap with whom his womb-mate confronted him.

I didn't go down in the Meyer household at all well. I felt it. I knew it. I might as well have been that unheard-of hurricane or, at least, the harbinger with news of bad weather to come. What David had told his parents about me or him or us, I don't know but the ignominy of the visit is scalded into my sensitivity. I imagine Mrs. Meyer got used to the idea of homosexuality since then for David tells me that in recent years she has been acting as guide to visitors at Charleston Farmhouse and we all know what J Maynard K and Lytton S and naughty Dunkie Grant got up to in those creaky old beds.

Another year over and still deeper in life's debt, it had

been decided that Richard Willing-Denton, Gillie Willis and I would share a flat together and we found the tiniest, doll's house of a place on the first floor at number 72 Whitstable Road, again, a mere stone's throw from the university.

This was, at last, real-grown-up stuff. But amongst such best laid plans, then, oh why did David and I have no intention to move in together? We could have done. There was no one to tell us no.

No one even knew.

Much.

Chapter Nine

A TIME FOR EVERY PURPOSE UNDER EVANS ...

This is the coming-out chapter and what followed ...

Although I am a very secret person, I have a betimes auto-destructive need to be open and honest. Utterly contradictory I know, but then I am discovering that I am a very contradictory - and hence, contrary - character. I've always loved being on my own more than anything and yet I cannot bear to be without people. Someone. If there is a definition of a Pisces personality, rather than the usual depiction of the two fish swimming in opposite directions, it should be of single person with two opposite personalities born from entirely different and separate needs and yet having to co-exist in the same body. It was time to test my friends with my secret life.

Some purpose.

I had decided that no sooner than we had moved in to our new flat, which we did during the summer vacation so much did we all not want to be at home, I was going to tell Richard and Gillie that I was gay. Queer. Homosexual.

I bided a little time and steeled myself. I called them into my room announcing that I had something to tell them. Poor darlings. They tell me that at first they thought that I was going to say that I no longer wanted to share with them, they being a well-established 'item' and that three's a crowd an' all that ...

Instead they heard all about 'it' and ... Well, of course, in the best British tradition of *sang froid*, they declared that they had already guessed and who cared. Was 'it' David Meyer? Yes, I said, 'it' was David Meyer. I should have known then that for most straight people, any understanding of 'secret lives' is centred upon a person, not upon that multiple and concurrent and baffling phenomenon that being queer embraces. But, hey? Was I complaining? I hadn't been ostracised. I still had two of the sweetest friends a person could have, my life was open and above-board and I felt ten storeys tall. For at least that afternoon.

Coming out is an awkward expression. It's associated with freedom and joy and liberation and yet there is another very significant side to the story.

Once out, you can't go back in.

Coming out is also casting off, letting go the security of the past. It might have been an illusory security but there was safety in secrecy. There was a strange comfort in the subterfuge we developed; secrecy can be cosy.

But now it was grown-up stuff. David of course duly came to stay. It was all a bit like sleeping with someone in your parents' house. I imagine Gillie, now divorced from Richard, coming to that point with their son Oliver. Sorry, Ollie. And Richard? He has a whole other family, his twins to deal with.

But David Meyer and I were not to be. 'It' all came to a grinding halt and if I felt indulgently wretched, he must have justifiably loathed me.

But we each get our come-uppance.

How quickly can the dumper become the dumpee. There is a justice, if you look and wait for it. Lately, I've noticed that for every love affair you spurn and walk away from, the next one walks away from you. I don't know when my next one was but it was certainly snowing when Richard and Gillie drove me in their little standard car to the airport at Lydd in Kent to catch the plane to Paris.

Well, this finally was the whole enchilada. It seemed that a chance meeting in - ugh! blot it out! blot it out! - the Piccadilly

Circus underground station men's public lavatory had made an international gigolo of me.

Except I wasn't. Patently, that accolade still eluded me for I had paid my own fare that winter's day. I was off to see one Claude Licard, a Parisian boutiquier who had zithered m'heartstrings, dammit and rogered me rotten in a hotel near Regent Street one dismally wet Winter's afternoon.

Now, on a snowier one, I was up-up-and-away in some kite-paper and waxed string contraption to Beauvais in northern France from where a coach - ugh, coach! - took the flight to *destination Paris*. I must sound like some Mame Dennis clone and I really don't know why I'm telling this story except it made me feel fucking wonderful at the time and was my introduction to *le chic Paris*. I mean chic, not glamorous, not vampy, not loud, not raucous ... Claude indeed had a boutique which purveyed the finest in jersey *couture*, the *tricot* stuff as opposed to the island. Here, *le tout Paris* came to don the knit-like-heavy-silk garments which were the epitome of elegance. The shop was somewhere either on or just off the *Rue St Honore* - gasp! - and right next door to *Les Jardins des Tuileries* where *le tout Paris*, it appeared, also came to get laid. Most afternoons.

"You were expecting me?"

Sort of.

"Bet you never thought I'd get here?"

Cared little. Mattered less. I had, after all, been at this sort of door before. And for the weekend, I indeed loved 'it'. The tiny flat. The silly kitchen where gastronomic delights such as would have befitted Elizabeth David or Paul Bocuse were brought forth from the sort of cooker that refugees have in newsfilms. The French, deservedly, quite shame the world when simplicity and essence is *de rigeur*. Most of the rest of the world succeeds only in complicating what is best left entirely alone. A leek is a leek is a leek. Fuck around with a leek and you're merely left with the flavour of fuck. A tomato salad is only a tomato salad when the tomatoes are just ... Mmmm. *Parfait!* And peeled and pipped, for heavens' sake! Otherwise you have red slush with seeds in it. I had a wonderful time and was really pleased I'd paid my own fare. However, I knew I'd never see Claude again as the plane bumped down in that Kentish field and I was home. The end of my first return flight. My first aeroplane ride.

I had been somewhere else, learned something more but I realised that however far I might travel, there would be one thing that I could never change. My soul. That is unalterable, sadly, some might say. England was and is my home. I had and have an irredeemably English soul. Not Scottish. Not Welsh. English.

Maybe I should add middle-class to this apprehension. Perceptions of Englishness like mine depend on at least three factors - good health, an appreciation of history and access to at least some money. In the third year at university, I had a friend called Steve. I can't remember his surname. He was a mod, a real one, not a pretend one like we little wimps were. Steve was a proper, working-class, metropolitan mod, hardened and honed and very determined. He lived in Grays, in Essex. I got to know him very well and visited his home with him on a couple of occasions.

It was through Steve I got to know about the other Englishness, the one that wasn't village greens and Worcestershire and bucolic, caring, integrated one-nation-ness. It was not about next year, or the distant future or the far-flung past of ancestry but about tomorrow. Or, at furthest, the end of the week. It was about not anticipating, not catering and, ergo, not saving money for rainy days. Quite bluntly, there was no spare money for saving and every day was as rainy as its neighbour.

These circumstances breed a different Englishness. Perforce not gently, not particularly nicely, in fact quite barely, where the community chest means not a communal safety net but a tart who puts out for a milk stout underneath a dark railway arch in an England where the next town is foreign, where the other football club is the enemy, where dogs eat dogs and where every dog's day has already been had. The England where the idea of the Welfare State had taken root and flowered not like delicate honeysuckle but like rampant Russian vine, turning ecologically-sound hedgerows into burgeoning landscapes of Japanese knotweed. This alternative England which largely ignored the breathtakingly huge range of education on offer stuck with the old when faced with the economic revolution and was therefore sunk with the arrival of the new technology.

Young men and women who twenty years before would

have been craft and trade apprentices laughed at us silly middle-class youth for wasting so much time in an education which didn't necessarily end up in a well-paid job. Vulgar consumerism was on the rampage and intellectualism and cautious middle-class values tottered.

It had been a long time since the Evanses had been working class and it was a shock to understand that Disraeli's Two Nations was not only alive and well but had mutated. Instead of the rich dog wagging its poor tail, the poor tail was beginning to wag the rich dog.

I didn't start revising for my finals until the Easter vacation 1968. I had just been twenty-one and my parents had given me a car. A Triumph Herald. Saloon. Powder Blue. CUY 962B. Best steering lock available. Still elegant, even thirty-five years later. It had been the family's 'second' car. They replaced it and hence, it came to me on my twenty-first birthday. We had a party at home where my university friends - including Connie Rung from Chicago, Mandy Pierce-Higgins, Richard and Gillie - could mix with my family and relatives to show how remarkably well I'd done.

Later, we had a dinner party in the formal private dining room in Eliot College. I think my mum came. Not sure about my dad. They gave me a watch, nice Swiss stainless-steel self-winder which I still have despite many repairs and new straps.

The car was the best, though. I had abandoned the scooter months before under a row of conifers in the Lowrys' front garden after it had broken down. I have a phobia about having things mended. Once they break or whimsically cease to function, I abandon them. Not a nice trait of character I admit, especially if it's a person who fails to function.

But, hey? If you believed that the biter, at some point hence, unfailingly became the bitten, I figured what the hell? Well ... Perhaps not, although I wish I had believed that, then. How I wish I had. My dad said something to me on my twenty-first birthday which sank in and hit home. I don't know if he intended his words to be taken as sonorously as sensitive little me interpreted them but he said,

"Well, you're on your own now ..."

I thought it an odd thing to say. I kind of believed him.

109

I've always felt on my own. Since.

Anyway ... The car was the prize of prizes and was the ultimate accessory on campus where, I believe, third year students only had very recently been allowed to keep cars. Kids with cars in 1968. Bit too Californian for comfort. The sensible British university authorities obviously thought it was a confinable conceit.

But the birthday celebrations had been in February. In April, panic set in. The more I knew I had to work, the less was the work I could do. I realised just how little attention I'd given to the course work and of what little interest it had been to me. It must have been that I had instinctively known what little use the result would mean for my future. And there were drama productions to divert me. An exemplary production of A MIDSUMMER NIGHT'S DREAM, directed with inventiveness and a deftness of touch by Sebastian Graham-Jones. He was wonderful with actors. Finally we got to use the big hole in the ground for which we'd had so many plans. Ultimately, it was always a natural amphitheatre. It was as naturalistic as foolish mortals could have it. Norton Knatchbull (Second Year) who was advertised as being something to do with Lord Mountbatten even brought his cousin Princess Anne to have a look. No one stared, natch. Well, not so baldly as to gawp. Just ... Just act natural. What? Like how? Like forget it and just stare!

Richard Denton's Puck, my Oberon, Sarah Harman's Titania, Gillie Denton as Hermia, Lisa Vine as Helena, David Meyer - obviously - as the young romantic Lysander - or the other one - and Geoff Wilkinson as Bottom. Geoff is now Tom (he of THE FULL MONTY) and as famous as fuck on three sides of the Atlantic. He was always a wonderful thesp and a damn good bloke. Jolly serious, though.

I think Penny Cherns directed us in something too - Ionesco's THE BALD PRIMA DONNA. Yes. I played Mr Smith. Ummm. Forgettable, I'd say.

But back to finals. And finals ... Fer, fer, fer finals. The Final Examinations.

Alison White - later Ruddock, (now back solo) - got locked in the lavatory in her flat just a little further up Whitstable road. She arrived on her moped burning rubber at the Examination Hall, wailing and sobbing but just in time. Most of us would have

110

loved the excuse ...

"Door jammed, sir." "Forgot my kit, sir!"

Oh, yeah. Get real.

Anyway, final it was. It was positively the last time in my tender or tough years that I would sit one in a row, row upon row, of examination candidates waiting for the hammer to fall. Loathsome exercise. Worth it, possibly, if what we were going for held any sort of candle to a chance in life. We knew already we'd been conned. Too many of us, luvvie. Too many graduates chasing too few jobs and what your three years' worth got you wasn't worth the bit of paper if was written on. An eminent Victorian Quiney family ancestor is oft quoted as saying:

"You get nothing for nothing and very little for sixpence."

We'd started applying for jobs, of course. The real world beckoned. But it was patently obvious that we were not being courted *en masse*. For some damnable reason, the world wasn't knocking on our door. Not that any of my immediate circle really knew what it was they wanted to do in life. Except, Anthony Miller, of course. He wanted to act. Richard could have done. So could Sebastian. So could I, I think. We talked about going for RADA auditions. We didn't.

I fancy most of us had had enough of learning. We wanted to do something. But what? And with whom? And where? Still so many unanswered questions, so many uncertain alternatives on the signpost. What had gone wrong? Why? What had it all been for? It was not unlike how later I learned my father and many thousands of his peers had felt at the end of the war.

Forever, the unanswered question. Why?

Had the university experience and the countless hours of 'O' and 'A' and Degree study, the angst, the panic and the worry all been the fault of ruthlessly self-seeking, face-saving politicians, academic place-seekers and insidiously Janus-faced, self-serving civil servants?

Of course it had.

So? Get a life, guy.

I did. In fact, I'd already started.

Chapter Ten

HELLO, THIS IS LONDON
CALLING ...

Did you know the awful Lord Haw-Haw, the bearer of the Third Reich's fanciful world news in English during the second world war had come from Malvern? You didn't?

Odd. It'd been drummed into me from an early age as part of that necessary suspicion of things foreign.

Lord Haw-Haw. So many people listened to him in those desperate war days when hope, like a banana, was unobtainable. Why is it that regarding any yellow journalism, so many decry it, yet so many read it. Take me. In 1968, I believed any broadcast that emanated from any source in London whatsoever. I was hooked. I even reeled myself in.

The job application thing ground on. I didn't get the first job I wanted, nor the second and after the third, I stopped counting. The university careers advisory service was worse than useless. I think it vaguely pointed us in uncertain directions but it was all a case of answering advertisements, really. We knew we had to find our own way. Any successful outcome was going to be down to luck; judgment didn't even enter into it.

I worked at St Augustine's Theological College on some overseas student English course with Ruth Bundey that summer. I'd started to write better poetry and we put on a pretty good poetry evening with the help of some other lights in the Poetry Society. Through either that aegis or another, the poet W.H. Auden had come to visit Eliot College for a day. He sat, tall and imposing and wrinkly, like a huge Char-Pei dog, in one of those tiny and uncomfortable armchairs in the Junior Common Room and folk flocked round.

I flocked round and, d'you know, I had no real idea around whom I was flocking? I had no academic background in literature, no knowledge of the official poetry line and, ergo, I didn't even realise he was gay! I felt, as the very marginalised SEX PISTOLS were later to sing, pretty vacant. All I did was write stuff that I called poetry. I didn't know about writing *per se*. It was a lesson too late to be acted on. In order to be a writer, one had, then, to be literary. I wasn't. Either. Then.

But the seeds I had unconsciously garnered were beginning to germinate. In reminiscence, I realise that writing had kindled a niggling uncertainty within me. Not a vulnerability, not a neurotic, angst-ridden fear. Nothing definite at all except ... I felt my life snag on something sharp, like a lamb leaving wool behind as it scrambles through a thorny hedge. I was a long time acknowledging the nature of the itch this snag was to provoke. Yes. Maybe it was there that the other great 'it' in my life began.

Whilst waiting for interviews to come through and also for finals results, the London thing was hotting up for me after meeting Pierre (Tito) Arenas. I met him on the St Martin's Lane corner of Trafalgar Square one evening on my way back to Charing Cross and ended up back in his tiny single bed in his little shared room in Hans Crescent in Knightsbridge. He worked in the hairdressing department at Harrods and was Spanish, despite the 'Pierre' bit. But he looked incredibly aristocratic and wore clothes beautifully and smelled of delicious French colognes and was pretty good in the sack. But the shared room and all ... His room-mate was called Paco and was very sweet but ... I wasn't as much shy as ... It was just tacky, methinks.

Our liaison endured over the summer, even to the extent of his coming down for an end-of-our-world party which Jennifer and Michael Graham-Jones gave, both at their house in nearby Rodmersham and in the village hall just across the green. Me and Pierre. Proper couple just like the others, all cummerbunded up in tux 'n' such. He was so incredibly glamorous and worldly and ... Look! Look at me, I'm Sandra Dee ...

But it also made me feel incredibly embarrassed and it must have made the others feel ... What? Incredibly tolerant? I don't know. Most of them, yes. Probably. At least, homosexuality was now on both the national agendum as well as Rodmersham's village green. I felt like a spearhead. Like it or lump it, Lord Wolfenden had achieved something and removed the immediate cause for a lavender clarion call to arms.

Homosexuality at last had a face. I wonder if Jack Wolfenden ever thought it looked a lot like his own son, the fated Jeremy. However, it was my own face which looked back at me every day from the mirror and about others' faces, I selfishly cared little. Then. Dear God, political will is a fire that is often a helluva time in the stoking. It took a holocaust to establish the state of Israel. All Aids has done is marginalise we faggots-with-faces even more. Angry? You betcha. It's so damn slow. There are still so many faceless ones.

Finally, the examination results. Me?

A two-two.

Surprised? You bet. And, together with the degree, an interview with The British Council at 65 Davies Street London West One and thereafter the offer of a job, starting September in their Study Tours Department. Salary? A whopping nine hundred and eighty pounds a year.

Not even twenty pounds a week.

I had four hundred-and-something pounds in a Post Office account which my parents had started for me and into which had gone every penny and pound which had ever come our way from relatives and god-parents like my Aunt Barbara. Our earned money had always been our own to do with as we wished but everything else was duly saved. Spending was not smiled upon by grandad or my father unless it was they who decided upon the spending. Ours was called saving for a rainy day. My rainy day had arrived but it was accompanied by a rainbow.

I decided in parental consultation that the money should be blown at one spending on the major extravagance of a London flat. (Very sharp intake of breath ...) The only thing my family had ever had to do with London property was grandad's dabbling in a lucrative investment in building private houses in Kidbroke. But his was a quick in and out. A killing. Permanent involvement with anything to do with London might be interpreted as something approaching the satanic.

Number 80A Ashley Gardens, on the third floor of a red-brick mansion block next to Westminster Cathedral somehow came to my attention. And it was in SW1. Priggy little snob that I now undoubtedly was, the postcode was one of the main attractions. I had met an old farming poove in some 'cottage' in Canterbury one night who had told me that as long as you talked right, smelled right and dressed right, you'd be alright.

Now, that's as maybe but without his help I was already deeply into the delusion that where you lived, what car you drove had some totemic effect on what became of you. I was patently still so insecure and so untrusting in my own abilities that I clutched at these straw-strong, superficial and entirely insubstantial considerations as a kind of validation. Splash on the Eau Sauvage and try not to roll your country ar's too much was how I perceived the prescribed order of the day.

The four hundred pound premium was what was used to be called key money but we shall call it politely the price paid for the lease on the flat which, together with the mainly orange carpets and curtains - Orange? Yes. This was the 'sixties - were being bought from Diana Macleod, the daughter of Tory politician Ian Macleod. The next-door neighbour was one of the elderly and poorer Vesteys. In the entrance hall, there was a porter. Shades of ... Crikey!

To make such a sickeningly sweet spoonful even easier to swallow, Richard and Sebastian had agreed to move in with me and pay third shares of the rent. I think we paid something in the order of twenty pounds a month each. Fiver a week. Not a ransom. The lease was for a little less than five years. But they couldn't throw us out ... I'd be a sitting tenant. It seemed to make sense. I don't think my pa would have let me if it hadn't.

But maybe he knew he wouldn't have been able to stop

me and didn't want to risk the confrontation ... Maybe, too, they had realised that it was better to have me safely away from Malvern rather than as a potentially scandalous embarrassment on their doorstep?

Richard and I moved in first, Sebastian slightly later because he was away in Italy. The neighbourhood was wonderfully special. A new Sainsbury supermarket in Victoria Street, the Army and Navy Stores just round the corner, the Byzantine edifice of Westminster Cathedral in the next street, Buckingham Palace so close, St James's Park next to that and, just across the Park, Piccadilly and the West End. Parking was hell but we somehow paid the tickets.

I knew I was lucky. But this lucky? Wow!

The degree congregation ceremony at Eliot College on a fine summer's day brought back memories of all the Founders' Days I'd ever known. Parents and flowery hats and suits and gowns and mortar boards. Then standing in the long line snaking up to the Master's dais where we bowed, shook hands with with the still beautiful Princess Marina, our Chancellor, and rejoined our families. But no piece of paper. Hadn't been printed. Sent on by post later. I still have mine. Somewhere.

We spent a lot of the summer in London. We brought up furniture both from Canterbury and also from our homes, Richard's at Middlewich Manor in Cheshire, Sebastian from his parents' town house in neighbouring Lower Belgrave Street and me from auctions and family hand-me-downs in Malvern. I bought first a huge Victorian bed in a Malvern auction which my father helped me convert to take a conventional mattress. It dominated my bedroom and was destined to be well, if unconventionally, used. The three bedroomed flat with its spacious bathroom and kitchen looked pretty sprauncey by the end of that summer.

Of course, Victoria Station immediately displaced Charing Cross in my affections because of its inordinately busier gents loo and its cosmopolitan - nay, international - potential. Victoria's and Pimlico's was for the most part an essentially migrant and impermanent population. Mass air travel was not that far established then and most non-British arrived in London at Victoria Railway Station or at BOAC - as British Airways was then known -

at its superb Art Deco terminal in Buckingham Palace Road. Victoria coach station catered for ... well, coaches.

The Biograph cinema in Wilton Place I discovered at a very early stage. The Biograph had started life as a news theatre but when I chanced upon it was celebrated as catering to a rather sleazy audience mainly of men. The seats slammed up and squeaked down with what must have been infuriating frequency for the serious moviegoers although of those there were few. Mainly, the three-and-sixpenny tickets were bought by old homeless dossers getting in out of the weather and old local tossers in for a wank between meals. Most of the clientele were homosexual men on the make.

One sat down either next to someone or in a vacant and un-neighboured seat. Legs touched. That was the signal. If the pressure was returned, then thighs were explored before the fly was fumblingly unzipped beneath the decorous mac-on-the-lap disguise. Alternatively, if one was sat next to by an unfanciable prospect, one merely got up and moved to another seat. This audience choreography was therefore entirely random and accompanied by the staccato percussion from the ever-slamming folding seats. Squeak, bang, squeak, bang, squeak bang bang ... Get the picture?

For three-and-sixpence, this wasn't robbery. This was living art.

The gentlemen's lavatory was thus throbbing with activity. Being able to be certain that who you were picking up was what you wanted, my bedroom was only a convenient few minutes walk away. Many's the afternoon I've spent ten-and-six (50-odd pee to you age-istly unchallenged people) on three shots at the Biograph on a wet Sunday. And I did see a huge number of movies. I saw FUNNY GIRL thirteen times!

" ... but guess who's gonna be dessert? " she sang. Thirteen times.

" Me, Barbra. Me! Here. In the twenty fourth row. I wanna be dessert!" Thirteen times.

I didn't use the car much during that first year in London; life started to open out pretty damn quickly. And totally unexpectedly.

I met Patrick Connolly somewhere or the other. He was something in the rag trade. Berners Street rings a bell. He was Irish.

Kinda invented it. Suave. Wore clothes beautifully and although he looked a million bucks with Jermyn Street shirts and jewelled stock pins through the Windsor knot of his tie, once again, like Pierre the hairdresser whom I unceremoniously dumped, he hadn't a bean to his name. He later emigrated to America where he had a successful living. But, before all that, Patrick introduced me to a place that fundamentally changed my life for there I met ... Aaah!

The Rockingham Club in Soho was downstairs in Archer Street behind the Queens' Theatre. It was run by Toby Rowe (sp) and was the queer answer to a Mayfair gentlemen's club. In fact, I would bet a pound to an old poofter that many of said clubs shared a large percentage of their membership with Toby Rowe's establishment. Low lighting, comfortable armchairs and some two seater sofas, newspapers, a quiet bar rather removed from the central salon and, in the main, polite hushed tones. It was also, in its way, a commodities and futures exchange where the materials invested in and sold on and the tips given and taken were of the rawest kind.

The Rockingham was basically a meat market.

It was where gentlemen of breeding, tone and quality willing to do business went to rent, if necessary, and always to trade. What could be fairer than a bit of dick for a bit of dinner?

Done deal. And yet done, as Kenny Everett a.k.a Cupid Stunt would have said, in the best possible taste. There was certainly nothing to intrude upon the mercantile atmosphere. No piped music in The Rockingham ... *Pas chic, cheri* ... The whole ambience was seethingly discreet.

The queer 'forties and 'fifties in Britain had been, like everything else in the culture, a warmed-up leftover of the pre-war practices of gentlemen going with anything but their own. Class was everything. Read James Gardiner's A CLASS APART. It's all you need to know. There were very few openly queer couples, very few obviously queer people. Read Morgan Forster's MAURICE too. And read Quentin Crisp's NAKED CIVIL SERVANT for most of the out queers not in the theatre or on the halls were out on their own save for an odd mate or two on the deeply dangerous 'dilly.

The Rockingham catered for and vaguely embraced all this but ... We were now, don't forget, at the arse-end of the sixties - sorry, bumpkin showing - and people were changing. People like

Patrick were useful to Toby Rowe's Rockingham. They found the fresh meat and brought it in to sit on the barstools. Did they sell too? Were the people like Patrick mere brokers? Middlemen? I've often wondered. Whatever, progress away from the grandee/navvie sort of coupling had been made and the evidence was around to be seen.

It was in the Rockingham that I was introduced to Andre Moussoulos. I'm not quite sure where my queer life would have led me had I not taken up with this fascinating man. And gotten myself into a dangerous situation which I was to encounter several times in my life before I was experienced enough to be able to smell it coming and walk the other way; except for once, much later ...

Dyed yellow, this dangerous thing looks vaguely like a field of oilseed rape, or a Brazilian poisonous frog or an angry wasp. They all say - go away! Less analagously, I'm talking about where people are still involved with other people and where those other people aren't involved with you and yet you still wanna be nice to everybody. Yeek! And I was still only twenty-one.

Half-French and half-Greek, Andre was incredibly intelligent, a graduate of the London School of Economics, already a fearsome entrepreneur, a landlord in the days when converting old houses into flats decently with a degree of chutzpah and style was still a rare achievement. He was also the business partner and, supposedly, ex-lover of one Gerald McCann. Gerald and Andre still shared their connubial house in Battersea though they did not share a bed. This latter involvement was, I fancy, both Andre's bitter pill and his own spoonful of sugar. Although no longer lovers, their lives were one and the same. Though neither knew it, there was little real room for respective 'significant others'. And they are still friends to this day.

Gerald was and is - *grace a dieu* - a fashion designer. In 1968, his name was up there with the Quants and the Muirs and he'd made that name in the suits and coats area of the fashion arena. His showroom was in Lexington Street in Soho and the clothes he produced there were both elegant and progressive, beautifully cut from entirely design-compatible fabrics. Jerseys, camels, tweeds ... Blazers and pants like ... Like Donna Karan. Ish. But what do I know?

Gerald had already had great success in America and

yearned to move to New York. Andre had no such desire. His family in France and Greece exercised as important a call on his time as did Gerald and the various ex-fashion business interests in London which he ran from his office in Regent Street. Andre's empire would not have benefitted from moving anywhere.

In those days, I knew I knew nothing, or little, and was quite content to sit and listen in order to learn. Andre, being some years older than I, had some fascinating friends. He loved to entertain - dinner, drinks. The drinks-party circuit was well-established then in what Armistead Maupin was later to call 'A'-gay circles and it was into that milieu that I was introduced. Bernard Sarron, a wonderful theatre designer, the Royal Ballet star Alexander Grant, television producer Derek Grainger and the interior designer Kenneth Partridge, television designer Keith Sproule. Men who were artistic and successful and who appeared to my twenty-one year old perception as suitable role models. Edward, Lord Montagu, Ben Colman, the mustard heir. The party circuit fairly sparkled with the rich and famous. Some other couples, too. Eric Howes and Michael Geery. Eric had become the chief designer and managing director of a London fashion house called Dorville. He was small and sparkling with incredibly bright bird-like eyes. His partner Michael was younger. Urbane and very laid back, he was also funny and kind. The pair constituted a great role model for me.

Andre had recently bought a flat on the top floor of a building in Chichester Terrace in Brighton, overlooking Duke's Mound by Lewes Crescent and I enjoyed the extra dimension of being introduced to the Brighton I had obviously never met when I went there years earlier with my mother. The Brighton society was, if anything, even more interesting that the London circuit because it was always off-duty when I met it.

Though never off-guard.

Godfrey Parker, Sir David Webster who ran the Royal Opera House and his friend Jimmy Cleveland-Bell, film producer Michael Topping and Norman Wallace Metcalfe who lately has been fund-raiser at the Sussex Beacon Aids Hospice. There were animated Sunday drinks parties where the new 'trade' was exhibited and, betimes, poached. Show business luminaries were much in evidence, some floated about, most flitted - Douglas Byng, The Oliviers who then had a house in Royal Crescent, Dora Bryan and Flora Robson. I found my head spinning as I started seeing stars once again. Later, of course, Toby Rowe (sp) himself moved his Rockingham operation to Brighton as did Christopher Hunter in his latter years, opening and closing at least two restaurants with Cherry Brown. And now Christopher too has been gathered. And Cherry.

Andre enjoyed going to the theatre and we saw a lot at The Royal Court in Chelsea as well as in the more mainstream West End. 1968 saw the opening of HAIR! at The Shaftesbury. It was tinglingly thrilling to see it, to be it and of course, afterwards, to dream it ... Albeit for that brief, incandescent first night, HAIR! had brought flower power to London and I, for one, embraced it. In fact, I don't think I've been quite the same since although I have several times washed the hand that touched. The talented company cast in HAIR! was later to figure largely in my life although when I took the HAIR! principles on board, I was not prescient. In that original London cast were Annabel Leventon, Oliver Tobias, Paul Nicholas, Peter Straker, Tim Curry, Kookie Eaton ...

Andre adored cinema too and introduced me to the National Film Theatre and then ... Uh oh. Andre got a nasty something, down there ... His doctor was John Gallwey to whom he went privately at John's consulting rooms in Ovington Square. I was also duly taken for an examination where it was found that I was, entirely unbeknownst, carrying round a nasty case of secondary syphilis.

When John told me, I became hysterical. Fear. Confusion. Ignorance. All these malign dervishes trampled my little boy's lavender-blue heaven to tatters and I honestly thought my world had fallen apart. Like, where had I got it from? Who had infected me? Who had I infected? My mind raced. I could have re-written La Ronde there and then, blindfold. Blind! Oh, God, no!

Both John Gallwey and Andre gave me a severe shut-up-and-grow-up talking-to after John had jabbed the first of a dozen or so very painful injections of penicillin into my bum. Duly cowed, I learned a very important lesson. Sex came with an invisible price tag. Sometimes there was nothing to pay. Occasionally there might be hell to pay. You never knew. I had been previously blithely unacquainted with sexually transmitted disease. My anal warts experience had been unconnected with anything medical.

From this first occasion, my association with STD deepened, as did my knowledge. I began to hear more about 'Clap Clinics', as STD hospital departments were called. I also acquired the impression that it was better not to have such history kept as public record in National Health or general practice files. There were tracing agents in those days. People who followed up sexual contacts whose names you had given who might also have been in need of treatment. There were many queer people who lived at home, those who were bi-sexual or even the straight guys who were married and only did it occasionally ... None of these would ever have wanted a tracing agent either call on or write to them at home. Queers were still reluctant to write the names of other queers in their address books for fear of association by ... Who? 'Them'?

The syphilis thing scared the hell out of me. Andre had very sweetly and generously paid for my private treatment. I will always be in his debt. There were, relatively, quite a few doctors to whom one could have gone to be assured of such discretion. Patrick Woodcock in Pimlico. Rex Warren and Gordon Atkinson in Shepherd Market. But one had to know about such options and all of the foregoing charged. A lot.

I felt heart-sorry for those who couldn't afford the luxury of anonymity. Fear of being recorded as a homosexual because of a sexually transmitted disease could also, easily, have meant that infection went untreated. So many of the diseases went into asymptomatic mode. People often thought that whatever they'd got had just gone away ... like my anal warts.

Queers were still very suspicious and very careful. Laws may have been passed, but we still lived in times when being fingered as 'queer' also made one a blackmailable possibility. Teachers still went in fear. Civil servants and diplomats too. And that now meant me because when I joined the British Council and arrived for my first day's work at the Study Tours Department in Bloomsbury Square, I had already signed the Official Secrets Act. Maybe I lied on the questionnaire but I honestly can't remember anyone ever asking me whether or not I was queer. Maybe the foreign office rules would have been different, stricter but with hindsight, it seems that security risks vis a vis blackmail were all but invited.

Having survived the fortunes of both peace and war, the British Council in 1968 felt pretty tired to me. The Council sort of exported British Culture by promoting the English language wherever in the world there was a diplomatic or political need and a suitable invitation. A sort of cultural embassy, represented by characters very similar to those in The Fortunes Of War, it dispatched tours of plays deep into the Middle and Far east, put out dance productions in South America, mounted book tours and art exhibitions. Anywhere where English wasn't the first language. Although the Council had been spoken of highly by those who knew I was about it join it, when compared to the Foreign Office, the British Council was about as sexy as a Reliant Robin alongside a Rolls Royce.

Its study tours department, exiled in Bloomsbury as opposed to being embraced by Mayfair, was the poor relation to any other department in the organisation. It arranged for groups of overseas professionals (teachers, lecturers, vets, architects etc) to come to this country and be chaperoned about on a pre-arranged tour which the department had set up.

Does this sound sexy?

God! As a first proper job, I just knew from day one that this one was gonna turn out to be a dog.

I worked with two women, one youngish and nice called Ruby and the other middle-aged, curmudgeonly and about as ugly as anyone has ever been and called Jean. Pompous, nervous, self-righteous, opinionated and ... well, weird. She sat at a desk around which she had pinned a full-length skirt of brown paper. She said it was to keep off draughts. I thought it could have been to hide behind. Whatever, she must have worked up a fair old fug under the brown paper for the air around her desk was always fetid and rank.

The director of the department, a very benign man called Burroughs, I think, worked in an office on the first floor as did a gentle and delightful elderly Scottish queen in the accounts department who very quickly worked out my number. But my proclivities were hardly ex-directory. I wasn't exactly sheltering under a bushel.

I can safely say that the only good thing about working

in that handsome building - now one of the offices of the international accountancy practice Coopers and Lybrand - for the nine months I was there was the British Museum around the corner where I went most lunchtimes and cruised.

Yes. I know. I hear you. I was supposedly stepping out with Andre Moussoulos, wasn't I?

But I tell you, no. I really didn't. I honestly never saw any moral conflict. I was never in any dilemma about this marginal cruising. I confess to being immune to any Scruton-esque 'moral shock'.

Although I shamelessly chased - and was chased by - guys around the corridors and galleries of the museum, I would not have *slept* with anyone else. I would not have gone to anyone else's bed.

However, as my first year in London unravelled, it was obvious that I would never be moving in with Andre. I only ever overnighted in Battersea and I can't remember that he ever spent a night at Ashley Gardens. Looking back on what I thought was a major romance, I realise that we only ever dated.

However, the relationship lasted for the best part of a year and the year was full and varied. We went to all those clubs which existed in London at the time. The sleazy ones in Leicester Square, names like the A and B spring to mind. The dancey ones such as Henrietta's in Henrietta Street in Covent Garden and of course, El Sombrero in High Street Kensington. Yours or Mine as it had been dubbed.

Being boys and dancing together was still an arrestable offence and although one could shug and frug and twist and locomotion as much as one liked decently apart, dancing pressed together, smooching slowly round the tiny dance floors, constituted the indecent and was often accompanied by an angry admonition from a man with a torch (flashlight) who would patrol the dancers.

Fears of police raids were still quite founded. At Yours or Mine, the licence for selling drinks was so archaic that we were provided with supper tickets on our way in, entitling clubbers to a paper plate on which there was a limp lettuce leaf, a teaspoon-sized dollop of Russian salad and a rolled up slice of store-bought ham. This constituted a meal, therefore a supper and only on the grounds of the availability and provision of a supper was a licence to sell drinks granted by the local magistrates to the club's proprietors.

In America, they were having Stonewall for heavens' sake!

Andre was also a fair old cook. He loved good food and introduced me to many restaurants - Christopher Hunter's La Popote in Walton Street and Inigo Jones in Covent Garden - as well as favourite eating places such as the Swiss Centre in Leicester Square, the Boulevard in Wigmore Street and of course The Chelsea Kitchen, one of the cheap 'n' cheerful Stockpot restaurants. Other than the Italian invasion which had seen trattoria blossom like *funghi* all over the town, over in Islington, there were men like Robert Carrier who was doing great things to Camden Passage, fuelling the revolution in the British food arena where gays were playing a vanguard role.

I must have still seen friends still at University. I have a book dated Christmas 1968 from David Meyer in which he thanks me 'for everything ...' So, maybe I hadn't been the shit I've always thought myself to be? David added his own haiku to his message:

"A hell of a lot/can happen/in two years."

It was through David Meyer that I met the other David who was to play a major part in my life. One evening, I had gone to the station to meet David Meyer off a train coming from Cambridge where he had been to visit his brother Anthony who had been assistant director on a Cambridge stage production of Jonathan Miller's. The costumes had been designed by Hugh Durrant who had been at the same Cambridge College as Tony Meyer. Walking down the platform with the Meyer Twins was David Minns who had been working for that play company as Hugh Durrant's assistant. Younger than us and from Lymington in Hampshire, David was jolly and funny and witty and had, so I perceived, a very glamorous job. I think he was about to clatter off to work on the Cecil Beaton picture, ON A CLEAR DAY with Barbra Streisand and then to start a stint with Noel Howard at Berman's.

Glamorous? You betcha.

Through David Minns' friend Murray Clarke, we went to see every queer-boy's favourite, Dusty, La Springfield, perform in a very pink frock beneath a very big blonde hair-do at the Palladium at which the support act was a very willowy young David Bowie who was enjoying his renegade SPACE ODDITY hit. David Minns was living in Murray Clark's appartment off Wimpole Street in those days and although we saw each other, our lives didn't really meld for at least another twelve months. David Bowie was still living in Bromley and in the early 'seventies was a friend of one of my later flatmates and an occasional visitor. Despite his admiration of the work of Lindsay Kemp, Bowie's life didn't really meld until 1972.

I remember introducing Andre to David Meyer. To say Andre was struck would be an understatement. I think it was from that moment that I got the message that I wasn't after all going to be the next Mrs. Moussoulos. I actually had no idea whether or not Andre was seeing other boys and I wouldn't have cared but there came a time when Andre, probably very astutely, eased himself away from being the focus of my life and I did begin to expand otherwise solely social evenings and go to bed with other people.

I was to introduce David Meyer to another of my friends a few years later who was also completely bowled over and remained so until his untimely death. The friend was Colin Higgins; after Colin, I stopped introducing David Meyer to anyone. A boy can stand only so much competition and limelight isn't necessarily big enough for any more than one person at a time.

But talking about limelight ... In those dying days of the 'sixties, the Kings Road in Chelsea was incandescent. Its attraction was magnetic. Every life form in the known universe could be found there from the ancient Bohemian artists, teachers and writers, fashion gurus like Ossie Clark, to crystally honorable ladies with second homes in Wiltshire, from crusty queens like Quentin Crisp to groovy little Lulu raucously rushin' about for frocks for the telly.

And of course, the general public.

There were Joe and Jean Public who came to gawp and tut but mainly it was Kevin and Sandra Public who'd never had it so good and who came with their pockets stuffed full of cash from their readily exchangeable unskilled jobs to spend, spend, spend in the proliferating boutiques. I saw the Kings Road explode twice in ten years. The second time was when the punk thing hit. The phenomenon is hypnotic. You can't stay away. The energy was tangible, transferable and the chances of meeting the sex-gods of your wildest imaginings many times more likely during both these eruptions.

Walking down Oscar Wilde's Tite Street in Chelsea, I met film-maker Malcolm Leigh. He might not have been an obvious sex-god but he was a fascinating man, erudite and creative and was married, with a child and we became friends. We saw each other when his extremely understanding wife was away in France and he and his life provided a sane perspective against which backdrop I started to evaluate my own future. Especially one of being a perpetual ephebe playing younger totty to Andre's older and wiser mentor role. I'd sat and listened for a year and I was beginning to think that I had learned sufficient of what I needed and wanted in order to be queer on my own account. Malcolm agreed. Independence manoeuvres were begun.

Independence was in the air. Perhaps it's contagious. The Russians drove into the ideologically unsound Czechoslovakia one day, causing an international outcry and causing me contiguously enormous problems. The following morning, the Study Tours Department of the British Council were expecting a party of Russian teachers to arrive at Heathrow. I was given strict instructions emanating from 'the highest level' that on no account was I to raise the subject of the invasion in discussion.

Although I can't speak for Czechoslovakia whose independence had been equally stifled, I can unequivocally state that my sense of hypocrisy was stung. I rather bridled and from then on, my fragile commitment to the British Council snapped and it wasn't easy keeping the jagged edge from breaking through the skin-deep veneer of polite lip-service I managed to maintain. The Empire's sun finally sank below its own yard arm.

Glug, glug, glug.

It must have been one evening in early summer when Richard, Sebastian and I arrived back at the Ashley Gardens flat from work at the same time. For once there were no girlfriends around, no lovers, no dates to be gone on and we started to talk. We realised we hadn't really talked for ages. We'd each been working off reference points almost a year old. We were coming from the past, not going to the future.

It had been clear for some while that none of us was particularly enthralled with what we were doing. I was totally disenchanted with life in a suit, Richard hated his advertising job at Young and Rubicam and Sebastian was a disillusioned English tutor at a crammer in Tottenham Court Road. We decided to give up our jobs there and then. Both of these young men were extremely talented, perhaps too talented. None of us knew what we were going to do but we had experienced enough to know for sure what it was we didn't want to do. When I resigned from the Council, our director expressed his regret and said that I was exactly the kind of person that the British Council needed.

"I know," I said.

I got a temporary job at BUNAC, the British Universities North America Club in Tottenham Court Road and worked for a woman boss for the first time. Judy Milligan. BUNAC organised work programmes for British students going to North America for the summer vacation and who had to work over there in order to finance the trip. There was a reciprocal programme too and although I had been employed ostensibly to assist Judy with the organisation and implementation of orientation courses for incoming American students, our main work was processing the visa applications which necessarily accompanied the ticket-holders on our outward-bound flights.

Nightmare.

Students waiting up and down the stairs for days on end whilst we sorted through mounds and mounds of documents and passports. Such frayed tempers and in such heat. But although it only ever was a temporary job and despite there being a hint that permanent employment might be a possibility, I terminated my stay there because Andre, dear, dear Andre, had offered to help out with a spell in Europe, in the South of France.

It seemed that every summer he went to St Tropez and, knowing how much I wanted to upsticks, he arranged for me to go and stay with friends of his, Andre Cluzel and his friend Franco, who lived close to *Tahiti plage* in a villa in the middle of a *provencal* field. The plan was that he would then come down and stay and together we would go off and explore the *Cote d'Azur.*

I had a car to sell ... Ouch! Further arrangements were made with the flatmates and once again, we planned to convene at the Tomlinson *Villa Pace* in Sestri Levante in a month's time. Richard and Gillie were camping in ... yes! Yugoslavia! Sebastian was ... I've forgotten.

Suddenly we were all on the move again.

128

Chapter Eleven

LES VACANCIERS

When I set off that summer having, I thought, successfully navigated my first year in London, it was with great joy and an air-sprung step for I fancied that for the first time I was on my own. Alone. Having given up my job at BUNAC and having arranged for someone to stay in my room at Ashley Gardens to cover the rent, I had a very important agendum. I was going to write my novel ... The itch now had to be scratched. The preceding twelve months had not been without their creative moments. Richard Denton and I wrote a musical based on the story of THE PRINCE AND THE PAUPER, set in Henry VIII's London. I think our motives had a Bart-ian whiff about them, OLIVER having laid Lionel's golden egg. Nothing whatsoever came of The Evans-Denton show. I can sing the songs to this day although the book I wrote is missing.

I learned a very important lesson writing THE PRINCE AND THE PAUPER. I taught myself to type. Not Pitmans, mind, but type I could. I also learned something even more important. Suffering needn't be endlessly endured. Being able to typewrite was all very well but such a pain when you had to make corrections and editions. This I could do nothing about until the arrival of the word processor when instant editing became a second-nature facility. Photocopying then was not such a widely available option and you still had to fiddle with toners and ink powder. There were no KwikPrints on every street corner. It was easily understandable why people without secretaries (Ha!) wrote in long hand and didn't type a word until all the rubbings-out and re-writes had been done. You had to be seriously in funds to have a script properly typed and presented. SCRIPTS Ltd. in Bond Street and all the other typing services were big business.

Richard and I wrote other songs too, one about an Eskimo called Emily - Hello? - which we sent to Rolf Harris. We would have been pleased to have had an acknowledgment with the rejection. We received, almost by return, a three page closely argued treatise about why EMILY THE ESKIMO, as written, wasn't right ... Intrinsically, fundamentally not right. I saw recently on early morning television that said Rolf Harris had recorded, had issued and was performing a version which he and a scratch country-and-western band had concocted of my friend Freddie Mercury's glorious BOHEMIAN RHAPSODY. If you read this, Rolfie my little scaramouche, a treatise-length critique, written in Beelzebub's blood, is on a website near you. Source it and weep!

I remember feeling rather writerly as once again I arrived in Paris en route, not via my hitch-hiker's thumb but on the train, south to Le Midi. Being on my own, the first time I had been so in a very long while, I began to notice that there were in fact two people travelling on my one single ticket. There were, clearly, two quite separate David Evanses and it's been like that ever since. There was the me who was doing the living, the travelling, the sight-seeing, the endless cruising and then there was the me who did the writing. I wrote every day. I. We ... And I, the one doing the writing, watched the other one doing the living. No wonder this first novel turned out to be the tortured tale of two young gay boys who set off from London separately but at the same time only to meet up later for a frolic in the South of France. One boy, John, was basically a tart with heart, out for pleasure and a good time before he got old ... The other, Tim, was in search of love, the real thing, his heart's desire and soul's true complement ... I called their tale THE HOLIDAY MAKERS. *Les Vacanciers*. I never did anything with it and

130

consigned it to the back of a drawer. I've just unearthed it.

In it, I now see that I made all the classic mistakes. It was supposed to be a gay thriller. It was a gay thriller. Reading it twenty-seven years later, I have to admit that although the style on a scale of ropey rates a ten and it is (to me) embarassingly autobiographical, it is nevertheless (to me) invaluably evocative. The writing experience taught me that there were indeed two separate and yet entirely complimentary me's and that for my life to progress, both, somehow had to be assuaged. One could never be out of step with the other. The one who lived couldn't, for example, do a job that the one who wrote disapproved of. The one who wrote couldn't write a tale which wasn't sustainable by the experiences of the one who lived.

I learned about being a writer on that holiday. About how the writer had to live. And I realised I would not be ready to be a writer for some years.

There are lots of people in the world who have ideas. Good ideas. But these people and their ideas aren't necessarily creative. Being creative means that not only do people have to have their ideas but that they have to also have executed them. They have to have completed the vision, held it up for wider examination and inspection and, therefore, criticism and, perhaps, ridicule. These people, according to the lights of others, may have been considered to have succeeded or failed but whatever, they are nonetheless creative people for they have completed the creating process. No one can deny or take away that experience. The really creative people are the ones who add the ninety-nine percent perspiration to the oft-trumpeted one percent inspiration.

In the face of both criticism and ridicule, I finished my book. I wish I could say that those who criticised and ridiculed have managed to do the same. Instead, they became publishers, editors, television producers and alcoholics. The reason I couldn't start being a writer then was that I couldn't work from a platform of insecurity. I knew I had to be certain of my funding. My middle-class, Congregationalist, bumpkin roots were showing again, I'm afraid.

I loved being in St Tropez. To say that it was a dream come true was no overstatement. I had no money and it mattered not a jot. I wasn't into drinking and doing drugs - little around in those days but weed and acid - and I was brown enough, young enough and thin enough that just being alive was sufficiently vital. Life still came to me. It was that time when the only thing a boy had to chase was a bus.

Everyone paraded in their glad-ragged finery around the harbour and the town every night. It was my first experience of that very Mediterranean phenomenon, the *paseo*. The harbour was crammed with every kind of expensive sailing and motor yacht, moored by their sterns. Their occupants would dine on their aft decks, showing off magnificently and shamelessly, apparently unaware of the passing, prying tourists for whom their performance was rigged.

Hot nights, beautiful men and women dressed in white, in espadrilles, tanned and with every type of silver and gold bracelet and bangle clattering and clanking, the chains of the 4S slaves. Sun, sea, sand and sex.

There was of course an enormous amount of sex available of every conceivable permutation - listen to Harvey Fierstein's lyrics for CAGE AUX FOLLES - and there were men and women ready to take your order and fulfill your every whim. Alternatively, the same pimps could recruit you to be part of the necessary human hardware to ensure that other people's fantasies were fulfilled. I don't remember having much sex except a few nights down on the jetty - the seaward side where the siren Mediterranean night lured the men who weren't fussy onto the very rocks where they found me kneeling.

I was, after all, waiting for Andre (remember him?) and the Andre business was unresolved. And I really was working. I even wrote on the damn beach, scribbling and scrawling to my heart's content all day long. Jesus! How much more pretentious am I going to get in this chapter?

Not much more because Andre arrived lacquered and luscious in a white convertible sports car and yet it seems that we left St Tropez as quickly as he arrived. He made some excuse, I forget ... He drove me to Nice, or maybe Cannes, where he found me a hotel room and basically left me. I think he paid a couple of nights at the hotel. Then he was gone. I knew we wouldn't see each other again. We didn't 'finish'. There was no big scene and I can't remember any argument. I can't remember being particularly impossible, either. When I got back to England, I called a few times but ... Nothing. And so it ended with a whimper. We'd had all the bang.

But I hadn't had all my holiday entitlement yet. Nice was nice but nicer was Villefranche-sur-Mer where I got myself a very much cheaper room and went everyday to the Cocteau chapel and the mediaeval arcaded harbourside and ate *bouillabaisse* with tranches of coarse dunking bread and drank wine and felt just marvellous. Everybody deserves a time like I had in summer 1969 in their lives. I'm so grateful for mine.

And I wrote. And on and on I wrote. I learned that writing a novel was a concentrated and extremely protracted business.

Pottering along the *Cote d'Azur* both hitch-hiking and by train, I eventually left France and arrived at Sestri Levante once again where I met up with Richard Denton (now virtually Willing-less) and Gillie Willis and we stayed for a week or so in the Tomlinson's appartment near the main *Villa Pace*.

I have to record regret about not knowing Mr and Mrs Tomlinson better. They had a solid if progressive educationist principle for their establishment having opened and run Beltane School in Melksham near Bath. My friend John Jesse was a pupil there between 1945 and 1948 but was so unhappy he ran away, the only pupil ever so to do. Andrew was nicknamed 'Tommy', rather predictably and John only remembers him as a remote figurehead. I presumed that Joan and Andrew also wanted to impart English in their British Council-ish, Fabian-ish sort of way because they always had paying guests from all over the place staying in their Bloomsbury-by-the-sea to live and eat and learn English. Or maybe it was we who were supposed to be learning Italian? Whatever, they were untiringly charming and unfailingly tolerant, Andrew being big and shambling, one of those men who look like God in a renaissance painting. Joan was smaller, slight, with a wonderful head of up-swept white hair. In many ways still quite girlish. Kind and loving and giving, the world will not see their like again. They came from a vanished age and there was no where for them to safely go but eternity.

Whilst In Sestri Levante, we lazybones swam and

sunbathed in the cool Mediterranean and ate lunch and dinner *al fresco* on the Villa's terrace beneath a trellised ceiling of cool green vines. In the evenings I had a short but delightful dalliance with a furniture and interiors designer from Milan. Talk about Italian stallions; when Italian men shag well, they can be positively Ferrari-like.

And of course I wrote. And wrote.

But it came time to go. Time to go home as we used to sing at the end of Andy Pandy. Denton, Evans and Willis drove back up through Europe in Richard's little VW Beetle, a journey about which I can remember nothing except that we camped *en route*. In fields. In tents. Ugh.

And home we came, returning to ... To? We had of course, we dimly remembered, done a Timothy Leary. Tuned-in, turned-on (metaphorically speaking) and dropped out.

Having put ourselves well-and-truly outside the pale of polite society, we somehow had to survive there.

Chapter Twelve

WILLOW, WEEP FOR ME ...

The absence of Andre Moussoulos in my life was palpably apparent as I settled down to assess the bleak prospect which was the autumn of 1969. As to what Richard and Sebastian did, my memory once again falters but I must have still had some money from the sale of the car left because I had enough to go to clubs. It was in a club, Yours or Mine to be precise, that I met Peter Blum, visiting from Geneva where this handsome, tall, blonde Swiss *boutiquier* had opened his men's clothes emporium.

I am by now convinced I am a complete accidentalist. I have never planned any course of action or behaviour in my life. I have merely tripped over incidents. Maybe that's what is called the 'The Gay Perspective' which I am beginning to hear about and in which I instinctively invest total credibility. It's all about life born from knowing one has no dependents. Something about randy and random? Adrian is an actor acquaintance of mine and when I saw him last and asked him what he'd been doing, he replied:

"I've been being a professional homosexual ..."

Pithy.

He didn't mean selling himself. He merely meant getting

135

up in the morning, walking down the street and taking up the sexual opportunities as they presented themselves and, while it suited him, following where they led.

Hey ho.

Anyway. Opportunity - and we're not only talking promiscuity here - consistently presented itself in my path and, instead of ignoring it or going around it, I've always blithely embraced it. I certainly embraced Peter Blum. Many a time and oft and after he set off back to Geneva, I followed in a shamefully short time. After all, as my friend Sarah Standing was later to wisely opine, there was nothing in London to walk away from.

Think about it.

It was one of those magical times, three weeks whose magic was marred not a jot either by the mercifully quick mutual realisation that Peter and I were not for each other or my instant departure. I remember having taken a job at some cock-a-mamy Teach-'em-'n'-Fleece-'em English school where I felt very impermanent. But for those three weeks it was interesting playing couples in Peter's tiny flat. It was actually my first crack at living with someone - trust me to attempt it in three languages - and in the abscence of any other advice or role model, I just did what I'd seen my ma do for my pa. It seemed right and it was, of course, totally wrong because domesticity in the wrong hands is a real passion-killer. I also thought Switzerland was a mite too ... clean?

Clattered back to Calais once again on the *chemin de fer* and once again beheld those white Kentish cliffs, like the teeth in the smile of England. Back to Ashley Gardens and ...

And good old Sebastian, probably via his mother Jennifer, had found one of those employment agencies of which several had sprung up in the late 'sixties which catered for the whims of the newly rich and famous. The particular one with whom Sebastian had signed up was called Organisation Unlimited, run by Willow Morrel from a tiny office in Sydney Street. Both Sebastian and Richard had already had cleaning work. Richard? Cleaning?

So off I, too, went to see Willow.

You see, I just knew that I couldn't return to the fold. I knew I could never again wave my meaningless degree certificate at a Personnel Officer and fill in application forms and then don the grey suit and go through the interviews and swear alleigance and pretend I had goals and hobbies and ambition for, in truth, I had none of what the straight, business or civil world needed. I would have been a frightful let-down not only to me but to them. I couldn't put them or me through it.

So off I went to see Willow.

I somehow knew that, self-cast out, I would always be alright and that I could go it alone, not part of a team, not having to dissemble and lie and hide. I wasn't interested in the world of work, its ethics or practices. I wasn't interested in being a cog, in playing the team-role. I wanted to be that little gay boy I'd been on the beach in St Tropez that summer for ever. For ever and ever, amen.

And finally I was seeing Willow.

Willow Morrel was one of the best things to happen to me. She was so instrumentally important in my life that I'm once again ashamed to say that if she jumped, today, out of a passing van and bit me on the ass, I wouldn't know who the hell she was. I think I only met her half-a-dozen times.

Anyway, I gave my particulars. Yes, I could drive. No, I didn't object to cleaning. No, I didn't mind babysitting, or washing up after parties, or being a waiter. Mind? Why should I mind? It was just like all the vacation work I'd always done. That doing it could also earn you proper money, more than I'd been getting from the British Council, I'd never even thought ...

Not bad. Not bad at all.

I went back to Ashley Gardens and waited. I didn't have to wait long. The following morning, or maybe it was that afternoon, the telephone rang and it was Willow.

"Would you go to 37 Monckton Court in Kensington tomorrow morning?"

"Sure. What is it?"

"Cleaning."

"Oh, okay. Yes."

It seemed that the wildly successful film director Silvio Narizzano and his wildly extravagant boyfriend Win Wells needed their penthouse cleaning.

Why Win, struggling to escape his past as Arkansas' most famous drag act, couldn't do his own cleaning will become all-too-clear all-too-soon.

Chapter Thirteen

SIN AND WILL

Monckton Court is a horrid 'sixties apartment building of some five stories built on the corner of Holland Road and High Street Kensington in what must have been the garden of some larger and probably more gracious mansion for this was Norman Shaw land. This was where Michael Winner lived in The Tower House. This was where Lord Leighton lived and whither *le tout beau monde* flocked at the end of the last century to sniff the heady and daring smell of barely-dry paint on fashionable canvases.

The march of the twentieth century replaced static images with moving ones. Hence the movie directors with money to burn. Silvio Narizzano, Canadian born, was enjoying great current success. He and his wife Bea (trice) who was a literary agent were very much at the heart of the 'sixties well-spring of 'new' talent. Having cut his teeth in award-winning television, notably for Granada, his GEORGY GIRL with Lynn Redgrave did for size sixteen girls what Walt Disney had done for dwarves.

Then Silvio and Bea split up. Silvio's homosexuality was too up-front for him to wish to continue in a marriage he didn't want. But, if the path of true love's a little bumpy, the path of true guilt runs a damn sight crueller ... Silvio never let go of Bea. He was always in contact with her, he was continually buying her presents. Faced with this, she thought he was simply weathering an aberration and she waited.

However, Silvio had met a young man called Tony and together they went off to America to make BLUE, a western. During the making of the picture, Tony was killed. Car accident. As a picture, BLUE fared no better than Tony although soon after, in a bath-house in New York City, the distraught and grieving Silvio schtupped one Win Wells, a rather pudgy, pasty, plain drag artist from Arkansas who was visiting in the city for a while from his current headquarters in New Hope Pennsylvania, the home of one of America's better-know summer stock theatres, the Bucks County Playhouse.

I don't think Win had been doing so great either 'til Sil materialised that afternoon through the steamy veils of vapour. Like Win was no Danny La Rue, right? Boy, but it didn't take Win long to realise his ship'd come in with a manifest rich beyond a drag queen's wildest dreams ... Talk about Quinquereme of Niniveh with its cargo of ivory, apes and peacocks ... Win was schemingly ambitious. Sil was his ticket. There are many multi-talented people in the world. It must be very galling for them to know that without that lucky break, their talents will spill merely as pearls before swine. Win was a wonderful artist, an acid wit, an entertaining (putatively) drag-queen and obviously a really good-fun-fella.

On his own.

But put an air-ticket and someone else's cheque book in his hand and he turned into a volatile and potentially vicious monster to which Ayeesha and Catherine the Great had donated ova and into whom Genghis Khan and Bluebeard had poured seed.

The newly homosexualised Silvio made a poor gay. In his former life, as a mere queer, he may have been unrivalled but what Silvio found in Win was what he hadn't had with Bea. A wife not only with balls but, more importantly, one with a dick. And Win, the personification of the rapacious pre-gay lib queen, who also hailed from a once-married, we-wuz-jus'-po'-white-trash pedigree, slipped into the role of the second Mrs. Narizzano like Zsa Zsa Gabor into legend.

Oh, and look! I'm talking about gay people, probably because in re-reading my unpublished 1968 novel, I noticed I was calling us gay. So, from hereon-in it's gay, right? Around 1968, thanks to the burgeoning American press and the political rumblings unleashed since the passing of the civil rights legislation, the word gay had slipped into common parlance on both sides of the pond. Its arrival, in hindsight, was convenient, for the word itself serves as a watershed. If I offend, I apologise, but it has to be said that some homosexuals remained stubbornly queer whilst others took to being gay like ducks to water. The gays were out 'n' proud. The queers were not at all convinced ...

Win Wells in Kensington was all a bit too Beverly Hillbillies to be true. It was like Dolly Parton at Ascot. I think they'd just had a party the night before and Mister Wells came to greet me at the door on the morning I first arrived wearing a kaftan, a cigarette dangling from his lips, his long, thin hair dischevelled and looking all the world like Shelley Winters slobbing out on testosterone. He called me 'Honey', asked me in and I just adored him.

There was a secretary working in one of the downstairs rooms of the duplex penthouse. I think her name was Annie and she is very important in this *histoire*. I started to clear up and wash-up and chatter and it seemed that Win and I were getting on just famously. He came on all avuncular and magnolias with tales that even Scarlett O'Hara couldn't have made up and I'd simply never met anyone like him in my life. I did my work and left but was asked to come again and then, at the end of the second day, asked whether I'd like a permanent position in the household.

Well, that was it. I was cast as 'the maid' and the whole thing turned more into CAGE AUX FOLLES than ever the movie, the stage show or the movie of the stage show or the movie of the movie ever was.

I'd by this time met Silvio, a most attractive, mustachioed man who obviously liked having his balls crushed in the vice that was Win Wells. All Win had to do to get his way was to whinge and he whinged superbly. He whinged his way into a full-length mink coat, into as many clothes as he could wear and in return he cooked and cleaned and husbanded his husband. The act was okay for a while but even I found it rather too cloying to be convincing.

Silvio was in pre-production for shooting Joe Orton's LOOT at Shepperton produced by Arthur Lewis. Joe Orton and Kenneth Halliwell, the only two openly gay icons this country had yet furnished, had died in the infamous Islington bloodbath Kenneth Halliwell perpetrated some eighteen months earlier. Sadly, I never met them. Well, not knowingly.

On the fourth day of my employment, Annie validated her importance by leaving. The 'I-can't-take-any-more' variety of leaving. I don't think anyone had ever left Silvio before. He was very taken aback, even offended but through his pain, he managed to show a little presence of mind sufficient anyway to ask me if I could type.

Could I type? Could I bloody type!!!

Absolutely, I lied.

And that's how I got my foot in the door. Annie's departure marked my very own 'right place at the right time'. Although I wasn't working on the production itself, working for Silvio involved going down to the film studios most days either driving Win - who, being a drag queen, had never learned to drive - to lunch with 'the boss' or gophering for the boss on several menial details.

Loot's American producer Arthur Lewis and his wife Evie, seemed ill-matched to Joe Orton's black comedy and, although paying lip-service to the 'out' Silvio and the even outer Win, I don't feel they really approved. Fay, the nurse, was played by Lee Remick only recently involved with her lifetime partner Kip Gowans; the Inspector was played by Richard Attenborough and the boys were variously Hywel Bennett and Roy Holder. I think Milo O'Shea figured somewhere too in all the casting *brouhaha*.

I found the whole thing thrilling. I stayed late most nights, helping Win with supper and dinner parties - he was a pretty wonderful cook if fried chicken and black-eyed peas are your particular favourites - and quite seamlessly insinuated myself into the fabric of the lives of my employers.

And then one afternoon, the telephone rang. It was a hospital. They were calling for Mr. Narizzano. Was I Mr. Narizzano?

No but I'm his secretary. Could I take a message?

Yes, they'd be grateful. Would you tell him that Mrs.

Narizzano died a few moments ago?

Mrs. Narizzano? Who? There wasn't one. Did they mean Win?

"Did you say dead?"

Yes, they'd said dead. Silence.

Hello? Hello?

"Oh ... Yes. I'll ... er, tell him ... Thankyou."

Of course, at that point, I never even knew that there was a Mrs. Narizzano let alone one who had been invisibly dying from kidney failure.

I didn't know what to do. I'd never taken a message like that in my life. Suddenly there was a dark past to contend with, like in that play THE LAUNDRY where Betty Marsden was shielding a deformed child. Like in 'O' level English Literature in JANE EYRE with Grace Poole and the west wing and stuff. Shades of REBECCA. Life was alarmingly beginning to imitate art and it was uncomfortable.

Imparting the message to Sil and Win, of course, embroiled me deeper into the foundations of that pair of lives. Bereavement makes temporary intimates out of total strangers, like friendships in repertory companies or on movie shoots and in the course of the next few days, I learned more of Sin and Will than anyone else on earth. But literary and theatrical London gathered and paid their respects. I met Silvio's agent, Barry Krost who, together with another ex-partner Liz Evett, had once had a business with Bea. I first met Lila Burkeman too. And talked to Rose Tobias Shaw. Death is a great little networker and I was on the hub-end of a stream of calls. Win, of course, grieved superbly, like Ava Gardner. No. Maybe Genevieve Paige. Friends came to call. The jazz singer Marian Montgomery, her husband, that musical man-for-all-seasons Laurie Holloway, Cathy MacGowan then living with Hywel Bennett, Lynn Redgrave and John Clark, Carol Channing and her husband Charles ...

And there was still a film to make. Joe's old TOOL still had to be taken in hand. Bea was therefore duly dispatched and life was gotten on with, basically. Ultimately, at Monckton Court, her obsequies were made to seem nothing more than a glitsch. There seemed to be no substantial grief. Hey? What did I know from grief? I wasn't there

142

to judge. I was there to heed, 'n' secretary an' clean and gopher 'n' stuff ... And no, thankyou, Barry Krost. Thanks, but no thanks. I like my job. I really can't consider coming to work for you in your glitzy high-profile theatrical agents' offices in Mayfair. I have my loyalties. Sil and Win need me, I couldn't possibly abandon them ...

And then Silvio broke his ankle. Maybe he tripped over an invisible thunderbolt? It was about the same time that he and Arthur Lewis were having to decide on the music for the movie. Ummm. Music to LOOT? The news of Sil's broken ankle was certainly music to the ears of my flatmate Richard Denton whose waxings about queers and pooves lessened noticeably when this movie-maker-wannabee was faced with the prospect of a) a paying job on a film set acting as wheelchair-pusher to Silvio and b) making a pitch for writing the music for the movie.

Was I the tooth-fairy, slave of the dream fairy, or was I not?

There was at least one other candidate for the music job but Richard submitted and waited and waited and of course ultimately got the gig. It was around this time too that he and Sebastian had a flirtation with Tony Stratton-Smith's Charisma records and were given contracts presumably as nineteen sixty-nine's answer to Peter and Gordon. At university they had played together in concert as THE NEW TWO. Nice public school boys. They even put down tracks for an album.

But whereas broken promises remain livid, broken bones mend. Silvio no longer needed a wheelchair, shooting was over and there was the delicate question of the impending arrival of 1970 and what do we all do now?

Sometime previously, Silvio had purchased an ancient house in the hilltop village of Mojacar some eighty kilometres north of Almeria in Spain. The village was about half-a-mile from the coast and both Win and Sil loved it. Work was being done on the place whilst LOOT was being filmed and it came time to go over and check on progress. In fact, it became time to think about moving there for some length of time for Silvio had no other work on the horizon other than the editing of LOOT and I fancy that living with Win in London was getting expensive.

I was asked if I would like to go to Spain with my movie

queens and to work in the house as secretary/factotum for Win, who was going to work on two screenplays and to keep the man company during Silvio's enforced absences in editing rooms back in England. Of course I said yes. I had made this odd couple my life.

What my poor old parents must have made of all this as they peered out between the palisades still surrounding the Land-That-Time-Forgot, I hate to think. They must have thought they'd really wasted their money and I can't blame them if indeed that is just what they thought. I was probably so scared of their reaction, I never even told them the truth.

Win's friend Howie Uible from New Hope, Pennsylvania was due to come over to London and wanted to travel through Europe and so it was arranged that I was to drive said Howie and a vanful of furniture and household effects from London to Spain. The van in question was the orange mini-van featured in LOOT which Silvio bought inexpensively from the production which, when used for the trans-continental *demenagements*, was to be left in Spain as the household workhorse. Packed to the gunwales with stuff Win couldn't possibly live without, we set off on the first of two similar journeys I was to make from London to the South of Spain. It was set that Win and Sil were to join us in about a week.

Howie Uible was a bespectacled, bearded very intelligent man whose restaurant at 8 Mechanic Street had done very well. Howie's trip was in advance of his wife Linda's by some three or four weeks to enable the couple to have a sensible winter break. Howie was good company on a winter's drive through France, beneath the Pyrenees and across the dull, grey expanse of Northern Spain. The trip took at least two days and on the third, as soon as Murcia was behind us, the sun came out.

By the time we reached the one-street fishing village of Garrucha, it was positively tropical and thus it was in the fading afternoon light on the third day that we drove up the steep, winding hill which led away from the immediate coastline to the hilltop fastness that was the ancient village of Mojacar, traditional centuries-old centre for witchcraft in this ancient Spanish region of Andalucia. Halfway up the hill, we passed a laundry house, a roofed structure familiar and unchanged in the Mediterranean since Greek and Roman times. Water was diverted from a spring or well and flowed through this wash-house where the women pounded the soapy clothes against bare rock, rinsing them in the purest cold water. This was another land-that-time-forgot but it was an entirely different one from the one in which I'd grown up.

Win had already been busy colonising his future. Another friend from Bucks County, Salvatore "Sammy" Fiorello had already transplanted himself to Mojacar and had opened a bar, courtesy I imagine, of a loan from Win via Sil. Other friends were supposedly on the way. Win had talked a great deal about one Theresa Sweet, a supposedly wealthy widow with whom he had lived for several years at her dog-breeding farm just outside New Hope. She was supposed to be selling up and moving out.

As far as I was concerned, arriving in Mojacar was about the most romantic thing that had ever happened to me. Nothing to do with love but with equally significant visceral, atavistic emotional reactions like adventure, like travel, like discovery ...

One of the typical *pueblas blancas andaluz,* Mojacar was still essentially mediaeval. Sure, in the square there was an hotel and a very big new hotel was being built just down the hill. But all this was in a very remote corner of pre-tourist Spain at the time I arrived. There was a disco, a couple of shops and a bank and a post office down a backstreet. But these were the meanest of facilities. Ten paces behind the main square were narrow, steep mud and rubble streets with whitewashed two-roomed, single-storey peasant houses which hadn't changed in a thousand years. Behind the town, several tracks led into the hillsides where terraced farming was still practiced with no greater mechanical aid than a mattock, a hoe and a skeletal mule.

For those to whom this simplicity had appeal, Mojacar was already proving a magnet. It was peppered with ex-Pats who were always in the square at eve of day at tables in front of the cafe, sun-downing the *Larios* and looking out over the *vega* beneath them through a haze of *Ducados* smoke. And it was all so bloody cheap. Gin was had for a song, fags for a ditty and simple, dirt-still-on vegetables for a crotchet from women who came down from the hills and sat in the square with pannier baskets of produce spilling out like rivers of Cornucopia.

There were the Napiers, proper gentry. There was an ex-

145

academic from America suffering tertiary syphilis. There was the proverbial rich young American drop-out, Tito de Lama, in a fabulous Fellini-like whitewashed paradise on the very top of the town with Mellie, his driftingly ethereal Welsh girlfriend. There was Sammy Fiorello. A short crust of assorted dessicated dykes. Several very nice people all of whom probably drank. Paco the Mayor who was also everyone's builder. David Lean had a house along the coast. It was all very *recherché* as well as being the supreme *cliché*.

But I just loved it. For those first few days, I just loved it.

Silvio's house was called *Mono Alto* which meant The High Knot, knot referring to the bun-style which was how many older Spanish women wore their hair. It was at the back of the village and was a mish-mash of several houses - both middle-class and peasant - which Sil had bought one-by-one and was in the process of knocking together. The plan was wonderful. There was a huge drawing room replete with ante-bellum porch swing, a cavernous (literally) master bedroom in which the bathtub was an excavated pool cut from the living rock. There were guest rooms and studies and a balcony and a verandah and always, more plans ... Always room for expansion.

It wasn't a folly, it was a *folie*. It was a bottomless pit with an appetite that no finite amount or money could ever assuage. I was to spend six months there and it was a clearing house of perspective, morality and ambition which brought me huge happiness, the most painful sorrow and every other emotion in between. But the only thing I remember about the house itself is that I first heard the Paul Simon and Art Garfunkel BRIDGE OVER TROUBLED WATER album in *Mono Alto's* cathedral-like drawing room. Hearing it, almost in wonder, I knew I had heard the future of music and that I knew, somehow, I was to be part of it.

I returned to England in late January, a solo journey which I found in retrospect terrifying. I had to collect the second vanful of vanities and to accompany me on the return journey, Paul Hillyer decided to make what he thinks was his very first exit from England. We drove via Paris and Madrid and finally Murcia on this second great trek - God, do I know how the West was won in covered wagons filled with whole households? For Paul, it was the trip of a

146

lifetime. For me it was yet another leaving of England, ostensibly forever for I had no return ticket.

How many times can you leave something forever?

Chapter Fourteen

INDALO

There are very few people in my life who have been thoroughly nasty to me and for that paucity, I am grateful. Conversely, it is my most fervent hope that I have never been really nasty to anyone but the people I have loved most for that is the way of love sometimes. So when I use the word hate, I do so with a great deal of forethought and precision.

I don't know when I started to hate Win Wells but hate him I surely did. Not one whit less than I later came to hate Silvio. I think I had good reason. By the end of the summer, I was more than prepared to acknowledge the evil that hovered over that tight little town. The totem which everyone seemed to wear about their necks worked no magic for me. *Indalo* was its name and it was the stick-man representation of the giant who, in mythology, stood with one foot on one mountain and the other on the neighbouring hill and who generated Mojacar beneath his all-powerful magical loins as a rainbow formed above his head between the tips of his outstretched arms.

Indalo was a powerful symbol. But it wasn't special, far from unique. I later found it in other Medierranean places. Ibiza even. *Indalo's* magic, like old elastic, had obviously lost a lot of its former snap.

In the Will and Sin economy, money was obviously getting tight and Win didn't like it one bit. He only seemed really happy when he had his hand on a cheque book or credit card. Silvio was more philosophical but then he didn't spend as much although he was nonetheless cavalier to the extreme. Especially with people's lives. I'm thinking of Quina Ferreira, Bea Narizzano's Portuguese maid who had been previously living in Bea's flat in Coleherne Court in Earls Court. Economic retrenchment meant that Win and Sil were having to move out of Monckton Court and the plan was to re-occupy the flat where Sil had once lived with his wife. Such are the demands of privation. It surely must have stuck like so much humble pie in Win's craw.

But what to do with the resident maid? *Problemo.* Solution? Silvio offered to bring her to Spain. Therefore, Quina, a Portuguese peasant whom the English language had barely scratched despite several years residence in London, arrived in a barren, dusty village full of Spanish peasants with whom she had absolutely nothing in common, especially linguistically. She'd managed to avoid learning English and so she certainly wasn't about to learn Spanish. She spoke Portuguese, after all. It was quite enough.

Mojacar was a long way from the Brompton Road and I'm not sure the journey was one which Quina ought to have been encouraged to make. She and I did not get on well. She looked upon me as a servant, just as she looked upon herself. I'm afraid I've never looked on anyone as a servant in my life. She was treated not unlike Californians treat their Mexican maids, patronisingly, mostly ignored and at worst, like a pet.

I started to learn a little Spanish, vocabulary and *argot* rather than grammar. I had to in order to communicate with the builder and the shopkeepers. All very well.

After a month, Paul Hillyer left to return to England I was by myself. Despite the wonderful walks we took in the hills behind *Mono Alto* where wild spring flowers carpeted the mountainsides, the visits to Almeria once a week for shopping and the amusing comings and goings each night in the square, I knew I was lonely and heartsick.

Silvio came and went. When he was around, there was a vibration in the house. When he was away, Win slobbed. He always wrote a little, every day, dictating most of the work impromptu. Occasionally, he would emerge in the morning from his bower-bedroom with legal pads covered with scrawl and notes and hand them to me to type up. He was writing a screenplay called THE SKY IS FALLING and he was also writing an autobiographical work as well as a novel. Because of who Silvio was, Win had managed to get a literary agent. Ergo, in addition to all his other selves, none of whom he ever discarded, Win was now Win the Writer.

By the end of the second month in Spain, I was taking it upon myself to rewrite huge chunks of his work and correct others to hike the pieces to some level of credence. Win never noticed I'd changed things or if he did, he never let on. I respected the English language too much. Even the American English language.

Mojacar was proving a very small place. Ex-patriate society was mean and small-minded and bitchy and as a sort of cross between Agnes Gooch and Man Friday, I had no natural place. Win was very frustrated too. Sexually. We both were. Any sighting of a new man in town and he'd be dressed and perfumed and sashaying off to the square like Mae West going bowling. At night, when they were speaking to each other, Win would spend hours in Sammy's bar.

I only had two sexual contacts in Mojacar the whole time I was there, one with a delightful Madrileno called Paco who was a poet. It should have been a time of enormous celebration. Instead my months in Mojacar were practically celibate. Win was forever looking for hitch-hikers. He'd often order a drive around in the orange mini-van during the afternoon to cruise the local road junctions. I don't think he ever trawled anything but it was like driving the spider to the flies.

Then Sil would return and it would be all kissy-kissy and lovey-dovey and indeed Win'd often throw jealous tantrums when he thought Silvio's eye or interest was wandering in other directions. The hypocrisy and the deceit were truly mesmerising.

A couple of American dykes arrived to buy a house and they were diverting. Then came Theresa Sweet. With bags and boxes and cases. She'd come for good. She followed her Win. For a while she stayed at *Mono Alto* until, predictably, they all fell out and Sil ordered her out of the house. She found her own flat and then, with the money she received from her son 'Doc', money left over after the sale of her property settled her mountainous debts in Bucks County, she bought a house in Mojacar and then a second in a mountain village some few kilometres from Mojacar where all was utter peace.

Theresa was in her mid-fifties when I knew her. She smoked, drank and swore and could make clothes like those from any Parisian *atelier*. It transpired that she had, of course, made all Win's drag costumes and she was soon using her sewing machine to make money for herself by making clothes which sold in the two or three Mojacar boutiques. She was one of the most fascinating women I have ever met.

She was also my saviour because there came a time when I became so unhappy that I couldn't stand living in *Mono Alto* any longer. I hadn't been paid since I'd arrived in the town. *Manana* wasn't in it. Unlike tomorrow, pay-day never came. But always there were the promises of better things to come, of the opportunities which Silvio was exploring, of the films that were going to be made in Almeria where indeed a lot of movies were shooting.

It was all eyewash. Neither had the decency to tell me that they were virtually broke. My anger and frustration exploded one night and I left *Mono Alto*. I couldn't get far, though. I had no money. I stayed at Theresa's and by the following afternoon, Win had apologised and asked me to come back to work. I said I would but only on the condition I didn't live there.

Some two or three days after that I was walking up through the town when across a street intersection infront of me passed an apparition ... A sun-tanned vision of such male pulchritude, it took my breath away. Whoever it was wore denim cut-offs and a short, zipper jacket made out of the American flag. I ran ahead, up the hill, but the boy was nowhere to be seen. I tried all the neighbouring streets but I appeared to have lost him.

Later that afternoon, I was sitting in the square having a *fundador* with my American friend Mary Bruschini from New York and telling her all about my vision which I was by then prepared to admit could have been a fiction. Mary was a wild and wonderful girl; the daughter of a Long Island orthodontist, she was 'travelling'. She was tall and had long, wild, black Italian hair which was always in a frizz and had a mouth as big and a smile as wide as Carly Simon's. However, in those days she rarely removed her make-up and so most of the time looked like Alice Cooper after a bad night. The black garbed and shawled *Mojaceras* would shout *'bruja'* after her. 'Witch!'

Suddenly, into the square came the very boy I'd seen earlier. He stood for a moment, saw Mary and I and came over. Whether he asked if he could join us or whether Mary made her usual direct move, I know not but into my life at that moment arrived Michael Hannah.

I don't need to describe him although his photographs do him scant justice. I fell instantly and deeply in what I can only call love and knew that I didn't stand a hope in hell in any sexual outcome. Mary Brushini was going to be the lucky horizontal one that night.

But my feelings confused me. I knew Mick, as I always called him, to be perfectly straight and I'd never fallen for a straight boy after 'dearest him' taught me what a straight boy was. But there it was, that feeling of adoration, of need ... Yes. Need for intimacy. Not sexual desire. Not remotely. Desire, now I analyse, never came into it. Only need. A desperate, visceral need for my intimate feelings to be acknowledged by him. It was the purest love I've ever felt and I can say no more because our story has a ways to run yet.

Mick had arrived in town as part of the crew of a Dutch yacht which had moored overnight in the harbour of neighbouring Garrucha. Hans, the captain, had plans to sail across the southern Atlantic to go and search for emeralds in Bolivia. In the course of our evening together, mainly spent *a deux* as Mary had to go off to her waitressing/dancing job in the discotheque, Mick and I swapped our life stories. We were the same age.

My story is my story. Mick's will always be better.

Illegitimate and abandoned after his birth in Hammersmith hospital, he'd been brought up in a Doctor Barnardo's home until his early teenage and thence, after a series of unhappy fosterings, ended up with Margaret, a dear woman in Twickenham; Margaret who adored him. He was indeed lovable and highly intelligent but his schooling was fucked and so he left as soon as he could and worked, odd-jobbing here and there, putting up tents and marquees, getting by.

Then, one day in Richmond, he'd met a girl called Lynn Annette Ripley, who the world then knew far better as Twinkle. Twinkle was a pop star. One of the rash of sixteen-year-olds who had major number one hits all over the world and whose careers were over by eighteen. Twinkle's self-composed hits had been TERRY, the death-dirge legend of a motorbike boy who gets himself killed and, second, GOLDEN LIGHTS, the story of a boy who becomes a pop star whose fame takes him away from his faithful love-lorn girlfriend.

Discounting what money she'd earned from music, Twinkle was the favoured daughter of Sidney Ripley, a Greater London Councillor and a wealthy man. Twinkle had a lot of money. But more of Twinkle later. She deserves it.

Twinkle and Mick got together and when, after the passion was spent, she thought she was losing him, she started buying him. It was the worst trap. He moved out and went to live with another girl whom he'd met called Judy. Twinkle went crazy, threatened both Mick and Judy with death and worse and yet herself ended up in Bowden House, a hospital for the mentally ill after attempting suicide. It was the final wedge. The split was complete. Whether Mick was supposed to feel guilty or not, I know not. What he did feel was terrible. Twinkle had made it impossible for him to stay even within her catchment area.

So Mick had left England and was now sitting on a Spanish wall with me at mid-night, outside *Mono Alto;* we sat swinging our legs and scuffing the dirt with our shoes. I felt entirely complemented. I felt as though I'd met my missing twin.

Silence.

Very dimly, far away, there was the bassline thud coming through the disco's speakers but mainly there was that limitless velvet silence around and above us as we sat beneath the cloudless canopy of the many-starred midsummer night sky. I knew that shortly he'd be making his way over to meet Mary, after work. That didn't matter. That had nothing to with anything except lust.

"I wish you'd stay," I said. "Here."

"I know," he said. "But I have to go. Early tomorrow morning. It's arranged."

He stood up, stretched out his arms and I might swear that the dark of the arc of the night above us turned into a rainbow.

The *Indalo*?

Chapter Fifteen

THE REIGN IN SPAIN

A couple of days after Mick had walked out of my life, Silvio and Win offered me an airticket back to London to attend to several details in England on the condition I returned to Mojacar. Condition? I had no alternative. I had to return. They still owed me money, dammit!

Back in London, I checked in at Ashley Gardens for an update. Nothing really had changed except the place was like a tip. Richard Denton was and, so I understand, still is the most untidy man and I was pretty upset to find what had been such a lovely flat looking like a doss-house. Strange, like phlogiston, the substance of our life together had flown and the place resounded with echoes. At that moment, London held nothing for me and I was left with little option but to return to Spain. I can remember nothing about that two week trip back to London except that I had papers to deliver to Barry Krost, Silvio's agent, whose acquaintance I rekindled and that I made the journey on an Iberia Caravelle jet, my first jet flight. You got into Caravelles through a rear staircase. I thought it novel.

Back in Almeria, I think it was Theresa who met me at the airport in her little Citroen Deux Chevaux. No, not a lot of news except that "that guy" was back in town.

"What guy?"

"You know, the one you and Mary met. Mike? Is that his name?"

"D'you mean Mick?"

"Yeah. That's him. Came back a coupla days ago looking for you. We told him you were in London."

"Is he still here?"

"Don't know, honey. Sorry."

I was in an absolute dither for the remainder of the eighty-or-so kilometres back to Mojacar. We parked and unpacked and as it was about time for drinks, we went to the square. There, at a table with Win and Silvio, surrounded by all the usual cast of sundowners, was Micky Hannah.

No, he hadn't gone to look for emeralds in South America.

As destiny was to work its way through our lives, I only wish emerald-hunting was just what he had done.

Win and Sil were effusively welcoming. I hope I was gracious. Mick was pleased to see me but equally pleased at having attention danced upon him by a famous movie director and a fawning southern beau-belle who was coming on to him like a menopausal Tallulah Bankhead. I joined in, as much as I could, rather weakly, feeling very much the plain country cousin, knowing it was politic to defer to Win whose libido was patently in overdrive. Silvio, a tad more discreet, was content merely to beam and drool.

Was I jealous? Damn right I was jealous.

This is not a pretty story.

Mick, of course was invited to move in to *Mono Alto* for as long as he wanted. I forget if he did but over the course of the next few days, he became the cat amongst the pigeons of Mojacar's society. Other than the women who ogled him shamelessly, the major complication was Jay Steffey, an American interior decorator who was staying with Tito de Lama and Mellie in their eyrie. He too spied the handsome Mick and set his cap accordingly. Although Mick knew what was happening, he had no idea of the *imbroglio* he was unwittingly causing. Mick wasn't going to bed with anyone he didn't choose. He wasn't even gonna let anyone touch him. He wouldn't

156

have been nasty, he would have merely declined, politely to start with and with increasing firmness depending on the degree of pressure put upon him until a simple "Fuck off!" accompanied by his exit spoiled another potentially beautiful friendship.

Jay Steffey wasn't too much of a problem. He would soon be leaving. And Jay was so obvious, he was endearing. Worse were Sil and Win who were already planning production schedules and rewriting scripts to accommodate their new find. Mick was well and truly falling for their pitch. I had no option but to explain that this fabled movie of theirs had no funding, no producer and would never be made. The only thing Sil and Win planned to make, I bluntly explained to Mick, was him.

And, knowing this, I also realised that my goose was cooked either way. Certainly when Mick moved on, they would have even less use for me and my chances of being paid would be gone forever. I told Mick that I had made up my mind that I was going back to London and that he would do well to come with me. I promised that I would help him become a photographic model - which he could have done easily with no help from me - and eventually an actor, which we acknowledged would be more difficult.

He agreed. We said our secret good-byes to Theresa, to Mary, to the dykes and to Peter Ermacora, a fabulously exciting American I had met for a torrid three days which yet again had opened up huge windows of sexual prospect in my life. The verbal thing. We arranged to meet in London. And did. And in New York. A whole lotta verbal.

Finally, with invaluable help from Jay Steffey who was also leaving for Paris, Micky and I got a ride very early one morning into Almeria. We only went back to Mojacar once. In the summer of 1972.

One should never go back to where one has been unhappy.

Anyway, first part of the escape plan over. I think it was the first time I'd abjured accidentalism and made a proper decision in my life.

I went into the travel agency on the main drag in Almeria where I was known through booking so many tickets for Silvio and

Win. As soon as I walked in, the agent produced from Silvio's file the return part of an un-used first class ticket London-Almeria-London. He wasn't to know I'd just quit my job and I sure wasn't about to tell him.

"I have been meaning to ask you, *senor*, what I should do with this?"

"Do?" I murmured weakly. "Oh, that's simple ... I can use this for myself and *Senor* Narrizano's friend to return to London." Mick was by this time at my side looking every inch a glamorous movie star. "I was going to pay with real money," I joked, "Spanish money, but now I don't have to!"

"Very good, *senor*," the travel agent replied, laughing, joining in the joke and in five minutes Mick and I were in possession of our tickets to London, routed via Paris where we decided we would stop-over and take up Jay Steffey's invitation to stay with him and his friend Ray Kassar at the Hotel Meurice.

Landing in Paris, the plane bumped and rocked alarmingly as it touched down. I thought we'd had it. Mick, on his first aeroplane flight ever, thought nothing of it. My palms sweated and I blanched visibly. All he said was,

"You alright, Dave?"

"Umm," I managed. "Fine," I then was able to say. "Bit bumpy, though."

At Orly, we were temporarily stranded. We had no money and I rang Jay at the Meurice. At his behest, "Just take a cab. I'll pay it this end," we were off and for the next couple of days we had a fab time being tarts in the oldest game on earth. I got chased around the many-tall-doored, many-tall-roomed suite in that gracious hotel and so did Mick. Like him I started off saying no, no, no! It was pure Feydeau.

But fine no's butter no parsnips.

I knew Mick'd never give in, so it was yours truly who found himself on his back several times thinking of England and lunch and taxis and then dinner on the Left Bank and swearing to myself that somehow, Micky Hannah would one day return the favour.

What am I saying? It was no hardship, your worship, no hardship, your lordship at all! I felt like Jane Russell looking after

Marilyn in GENTLEMEN PREFER BLONDES.

But Jay and Ray were going back to America and time came when the tune came to an end and the piper had nothing left to play. We said our *au revoir* which turned out to be *adieu* and taxi-ed out to Orly and got on the 'plane back to London.

It was August. 1970. Back to reality.

Why does reality always have such a hollow ring to it? And why, oh why does it always have to be gone back to? People escape into fantasy. Why can we not live life the other way around? Escape into reality, come back to fantasy?

Chapter Sixteen

WHAT MAKES BARRY RUN?

Mick went back and lived with Judy for a while. Indeed, she was at Heathrow to meet him. She was a good person. Kind. A little ray of realism. I took the bus back to Victoria.

Re-ensconced in a room at 80A Ashley Gardens, I took stock. I say 'a' room because I had sub-let my room to Mark Dotteridge. Mark too was a model and, for professional purposes, used to drop the Dotter bit to become the more hard-edged Mark Ridge. I'd met Mark through Ian, a mutual friend and he was looking for a flat-share to accommodate both his real work - he was writing some sort of history of art - and his fairly hectic and far-from-exclusive social life and relationships. His regular girlfriend, Felicity Downer, another model, lived a few streets away in Pimlico and was a frequent and very welcome visitor.

Sebastian Graham-Jones must have moved out to live with the actress Pam Farebrother who was to become, briefly, his first wife. I therefore re-possessed his room and flounced about the town for quite a while in some of the most outrageous clothes I have ever worn, *gratis* Theresa Sweet. Pirate shirts with huge billowing sleeves years before Viv 'n' Malc 'n' Adam Ant, floor-length waistcoats and trousers with so much flare I forgot what my feet looked like ... It was the nineteen-seventies, after all. Just.

But needs must and the devil was driving hard. I had to get a job. My ceevee was so full of holes you could riddle slack through it but somewhere in the growing pile beneath the seive, lay a key. The past always holds the key to the future although it's not always straightforwardly under the mat. You have to scrabble.

I kind of knew where my key was although I was reluctant to use it. I was afraid that Sin and Will could - sorry - queer my pitch. But, in the end, I did pluck up the necessary courage and I telephoned Barry Krost to ask whether or not the job he had offered me a year ago was still open?

Was this another decision? It didn't feel like one. Just another logical accident, perhaps?

Anyway, off I went to Claridge House, Davies Street, to BKM (Personal Management) Ltd. It was an interview, at least and, ironically, just across the road from the headquarters of the British Council, where I had had my very first job interview barely two years previously.

Barry Krost ... He was the first truly gay man I had ever met. He was one of the new out 'n' proud variety. Not a queen, not a queer, not a pansy, not limp and camp and fey ... Just gay, shamelessly, openly and extremely publicly. From the moment he woke up in the morning to the second his head touched the pillow at night, Barry was unmistakably not merely homosexual but gay, gay, gay!

Barry Krost ... He was also a short, tubby, ebullient, irrepressible Jewish ex-hairdresser in his early thirties who had infinite charm and plausibility. Barry was a sort of *wunderkind*, I suppose and a closer relation to Bud Schulberg's Sammy Glick in his novel WHAT MAKES SAMMY RUN? than could ever be co-incidental. Genetic, schmenetic ... The great London impresario Harold Fielding was once heard sagely to remark about Barry and, presumably for the edification of all those in earshot,

"Barry Krost? You wanna watch that boy!"

Barry Krost ... He'd been a child star, in Hollywood yet but his thespian career had proved a non-transferable asset as child

161

grew to man. Presumably his lustrous and plentiful hair had been a good advertisement for his subsequent trade as hairdresser although it was as artistes' agent that he had finally found his niche. In that role, he could still perform, still toss that magnificent mane which topped his leonine head and indulge his manipulative and persuasive skills all at once. He found that, simultaneously, the actor in him could be applauded, the ego in him assuaged and his rapacious need for money rewarded. He had infinite amounts of what now would be called street-cred. His parents, Pearl and Charlie, had run some kind of pub in Victoria or Vauxhall where Barry and his brothers Roy and Jackie grew up and where the bouncer was reputed to have been one Maurice Micklewright. Not many people knew that the burly bouncer would grow up to be Michael Caine. Of the three brothers, only Barry and Jackie remained in England. Roy had gone to Canada and had involved himself in film production.

Barry Krost ... As far as I was concerned - me, Miss Zilch-for-brains - Barry's gayness was his only qualification as a potential employer for I knew nothing of what I was getting into. I was instinctively drawn to him. Instinct must have been the only reason for we had nothing else in common whatsoever. Not that I didn't like him, I adored him and that - God knows - had always been my undoing.

My fingers should have been burn-proof surely, but love him, I did. We might not often like the people we love; we might even go so far as hating them on occasion, but we never stop loving them.

Barry's immediate offer of a job certainly was a relief. It also instantly converted me to the idea of the existence of a gay mafia for it seemed it was because of some gay *schema* that I was luckily being employed once again. I realise that for many people, the concept of such a *cos-y nostra*, an almost Masonic order based loosely on sexual preference, must be an anathema but I have found that it is only too real, both as a concept and an institution and in September 1970 it offered a deal that I could not only not refuse but for which I was actively desperate.

In truth, Barry showed himself to be more than a little bit of a Godfather for in offering to employ me, he risked incurring the wrath of Sil and Win and perhaps losing them as clients. But then perhaps Barry knew that Mr Narizzano's career would never really pick up again? And perhaps the thought of Win The Writer/Performer/Producer on his agency's books was just more than even a nice Jewish boy could stand?

The brotherhood worked and it didn't merely depend on the exchange of sexual favours. If you didn't let it down, nor would it, you ... Contrary to many perceptions, there are not hordes of gays running showbusiness. Certainly there are probably a few more than there are in chemical engineering but not, I hazard, that many more. Showbiz ones are just a bit more vocal, a teensy bit more obvious and perhaps not quite as married as those in chemical engineering.

Barry lived with his longtime lover, the actor Tony Beckley, in a flat on the third and fourth floors of 27 Curzon Street, a building which housed not only Rahvis Couture - a sort of expiring, wheezing House of Elliott - but also a gentlemen's tailor/outfitter, whilst in the basement the Curzon Street Hand Laundry steamed through Mayfair's dirty linen.

I wasn't to have too much to do with Tony Beckley for some time as for the first few months of my employment, I was solely involved with the operation at Davies Street and he was away filming. It might even have been the now-classic movie Barry's client Peter Collinson directed called THE ITALIAN JOB. I saw a zippy little red Mini today and its model name was indeed "The Italian Job". It's a sort of immortality, I suppose. Peter Collinson died years ago.

Barry was still involved in a financial arrangement with William, (Sir William that is), Piggot-Brown, owner of SHARKS tailors and begetter of that famous South Moulton Street emporium, BROWNS. When I started work for Barry, he was beginning to extricate himself from this arrangement with the wealthy, knight-about-town William and enter into a similar one with Michael Medwin and Albert Finney's Memorial Enterprises. Medwin who had started his career as a kind of wide-boy ingenue actor - notable for his television appearances in THE ARMY GAME - was an aspiring film producer and, I imagined, an astute businessman. Finney didn't seem to have much to do with the nuts and bolts. The prospective arrangement seemed to be mutually beneficial and Barry was like a little boy with an excessively sweet tooth to whom an infatuated benefactor had bequeathed a chain of sweet shops.

I rather think that in company where gays were a majority, Barry's behaviour and *modus operandi* would have self-marginalised in five minutes flat, leaving Barry relegated to the theatrical end of the bar. In those days, Barry's act depended upon most of the other players onstage being straight.

The Michael Medwins, the Finneys, the lawyers like Oscar Beuselinck from the Soho Square-based Wright and Webb and Michael Simkins of the Grosvenor Square Simkins Partnership were obviously not put off the flamboyant Barry at all nor by Barry's in-your-face behaviour. In those days, it was still these rabidly heterosexual men, often mutely homophobic behind their usurers' smiles, who were irredeemably in control of the asylum. But Barry's tireless flaunting of his gayness and his particular, home-made denomination of Jewishness was patently not only deemed acceptable but also considered passing charming. Its very destabilising effect also proved shockingly potent in his business dealings and had been so for years. Hasn't done much to change the establishment, though. Despite feminism and all the other emancipation and social enfranchisement of the past thirty years, those old, plain straights are still running the game.

After Barry offered me a job, he then told me what the job was to be. The money was minute. Barely more then twenty quid a week. I realized that I wasn't immediately going to rise to be a member of the board after signing myself up to Barry's hastily glossed-over codicils presented in characteristically throwaway small print.

ITEM: I had to acquire a car which I would buy but for whose use the agency would compensate me on a per mile basis. (This later would come to mean cheap taxi.)

ITEM: I had to be prepared to run a few errands in the course of a working day. (This was before I'd become familiar with the American word 'gopher', a small scampering rodent which runs itself ragged trying to stay alive.)

ITEM: I would be expected to do a little 'valet' work. (This immediately turned into doing all Barry's ironing and taking care of his personal laundry.)

The making of the odd cups of tea and coffee was

jokingly referred to as an aside and - ha, ha, titter, titter - it surely wasn't as bad as working for Silvio Narizzano, was it? At first I laughed too. No, it wasn't as bad as working for Silvio. At least I would be paid. But no foreboding dissuaded me. It wasn't one of those make-your-mind-up crossroads decisions like leaving Mojacar. There was no question but I would choose Barry's road ... But, a bed of roses, I knew it was not to be. I think it's because of the ensuing years of qualifying for the unbestowed title of male-secretary-of-the-year that I still empathise so much with the lot of women at work. The very mention of the words overtime and staying late still provoke echoing reactions in my soul, nightmare associations with sweatshop exploitation.

Item, the last: Leave off the big shirts with floppy sleeves. (No one upstaged Barry Krost.)

Though I wasn't to know it then, over the next few years, I was bound to learn something not only of the law but also accountancy and business administration. And office management. And contracts ... Reading legal documents became a favourite pastime. Barry was obsessed about the whereabouts of the contracts he had with his higher-rolling clients and was forever sending me hotfoot to check that the contracts were still in the filing cabinet. I learned to develop filing to a fine art to avoid the tantrum which would ensue if a contract had to be declared temporarily mis-laid.

Only later did I begin to wonder why, if such contracts were so valuable, why the originals weren't kept in a bank vault leaving only a photocopy available for mis-filing? Or perhaps he trusted no one? Not even the estimable crew at Harbottle and Lewis who were later to leave and emerge as the legal titans of the 'eighties and 'nineties. Men like Robert Lee, Charles Levison and of course the one-time jazz musician who gratefully accepted Queen's shilling, Jim Beach.

Despite this on-the-hoof apprenticeship, the knowledge one gleaned, by definition, lacked any real depth or quality. The trouble about falling into things - accidentalism - and then being thoroughly consumed by a way of life which is basically addictive was that should anything go wrong and you found yourself high and dry, there's very little else you're fit for. Careers in showbiz aren't ones which garland you with transferrable qualifications. "You

165

worked as what?" would be most employers' horrified reaction to being told that the applicant being interviewed for the job on offer had spent five years as a rock 'n' roll roadie or the bass player in a now-defunct band.

So why did I leap so haplessly into this arena with so little armament?

Blessed, blissful, blithe ignorance.

And, truly, the whole prospect was under-pinned with stomach-churning excitement. I can't fully or with any justification explain the vibrant atmosphere, the highly-charged energy levels which crackled through the Barry Krost Management offices in Davies Street that long-ago summer when I started work ... Not only was my life amongst film, theatre and television stars going to continue, the horizons of my life were about to be widened further for I was going to get to meet another of my heroes. Not only was I about to meet the much-trumpeted Twinkle but, as I left to go home after my interview, Barry handed me a copy of an album called MONA BONE JAKON.

It seemed that Barry had just signed up the re-nascent mid-sixties pop phenomenon who went by the name of Cat Stevens.

Boy! Had I landed in the big-time, or what?

Chapter Seventeen

LOVE AND HATE

Amidst the pervading euphoria I felt, LOOT was scheduled to open in London at the Prince Charles cinema off Leicester Square. Surely, I should have been feeling elated at the prospect of the first public showing of the first 'big' project with which I had been involved?

The British tend to stage non-charity premieres and industry first nights rather badly and LOOT's opening was especially under-stated. Theresa Sweet had arrived from Spain for the occasion and was staying with me in Ashley Gardens.

But I, of course, had not been invited to the LOOT do.

I say, "of course ...", although I really can't see why I should have felt bad about Silvio having never paid me. Sure, he could have been somewhat pissed off that I had used his forgotten air-ticket to get home but I don't think he ever knew about that. It was Theresa who, adorably supportive, insisted that I be her date for the occasion and so it was as her guest that I went to the premiere of the first film in which I had ever been involved. I think I had misgivings about going but Theresa sharply dismissed them.

We duly got ourselves up and swanned off only to be

assailed in the cinema's foyer by a ranting Silvio and Win swearing that they would cancel the performance if I as much as entered the building.

I suppose I should have been flattered at this outbreak of my own importance but instead I was humiliated, cut to the quick, in fact and I have a quick which the lightest scratch would cause to haemorrage. Theresa was outraged and we both never got to see the movie that night. We even paid to see it a few days later.

That opening night was the last time my path crossed those of Will's and Sin's. Win's since died and I did see Silvio at the ballet once, but he didn't recognise me ... I, on the other hand, shall never be able to forget Silvio Narizzano.

After Theresa's departure, in the Ashley Gardens flat, there were radical cast changes going on. Paul Hillyer, a protégé of Jennifer Graham-Jones and my companion on the Road to Mojacar had moved in. Paul was Mancunian, utterly charming and completely roguish. He had ambitions to be a dancer, which he later amply fulfilled, working notably with Danny la Rue on many British tours and summer seasons. Later, Paul became a choreographer and then both model and dancer combined when it became fashionable to have music and choreography in fashion shows and he toured extensively in Britain and Europe. Paul was also a jack-of-all-trades, cleaner and painter 'n' decorator bar-none. Immensely capable, hugely motivated and incredibly applied. I liked him and his kind heart tremendously.

Paul's successful love life seemed charmed. Joyce Ingalls, the American model I seem to remember him introducing as a sometime resident of the flat. I've followed Joyce's career down the years. At the time I knew her first she was involved with Tom Jones. Lately, I read she was knocking off Sir T. Hopkins and responsible for the almost-break-up of his marriage with the lovely Lady Jenny. Joyce certainly hung in there but Jenny won in the end. Later, Paul's girl was the lovely Melanie from *Le Bistingo* in Kings Road. Later still, Paul struck up with Marti Webb and after that Alison, currently married to Alan Price. Paul always did very well with girls.

Well? Perhaps more to the point, did they?

Paul wasn't, then, the settling-down sort. I wonder if

168

men regularly fantasise about a one-night-stand sex life or do they really get off on the prospect of the couple-of-months' long affairs? I have a fancy that Paul was one of nature's rarely honest men.

David Minns also moved in to Ashley Gardens. He found himself homeless after his lodgings with pioneer lighting designer Murray Clarke in Arthur Pinero's old house in Devonshire Street became, shall we say, unavailable. David'd also left Bermans and was, as the profession has it, resting ...

So, it was an eclectic mix, the company which faced the onset of 1971 at the back end of December. We weren't assembled for any reason other than chance which is never, ultimately, a good enough reason. Other than David and I, the meld was purely temporary. Richard soon moved out to live at Vale Court in Maida Vale with Geoff (Tom) Wilkinson (of later FULL MONTY fame), Terry Pilchik, Tony Miller and Richard de Friend, later one of our alma mater's pro-vice-chancellors.

Sadly, the original Ashley Gardens *coterie* of Kent alumni was never to re-assemble. Our youth had indeed become stale. Or was it that gay and straight perspectives didn't (and don't) utimately converge?

Until another room in the Ashley gardens flat became available when Mark Dotteridge moved out to finally live with Felicity (Flickie), his extraordinarily forgiving and patient girlfriend, David shared my room for quite some time, purely platonically and our relationship flourished. Being tremendously good mates, our *hors-de-travail* social life might have been a bit make-do-and-mend due to the shortage of money but we were never short of places to go or invitations and by the beginning of 1971, the pattern of my life for the next five years was set.

Friends, yes. Long-term live-in lovers ... No!

Being thus footloose, I was free to invest my fancy in my job and my job became my life.

At work I was received extremely kindly. Barry's assistant was Sara (Sar-Rar) Randall and the other agent was Gordon Black. Gordon was tall and elegant and later, sensibly, left to become an interior decorator. Fenella Fielding, on being first introduced to the office when she became Barry's client, was overheard rather cruelly to refer to Gordon as 'the suit in the corner', but that, coming from a woman who rarely washed her wigs and wore her lower false eyelashes stuck on her cheekbones an inch below her eyes was, I thought, a bit rich.

It was undoubtedly Sara and Barry who were the engine and dynamo of the outfit. Barry was forever at lunches and always out at theatres, screenings or dinners in the evening. Apart from covering for him, Sara was developing her own talents despite Barry's being really horrid and obstructive to her a lot of the time. Sara was in the process of being divorced and had a young child, Natasha, to bring up. And on what Barry paid us, her task was doubly difficult and her eventual success, therefore, doubly estimable.

Barry was a bully and if he could find a weakness in someone which he could then use to make himself appear superior, he would. Barry had to feel good to function one hundred percent Krostian and if he had to do so on someone else's back, he would and did. Achilles' heels were his speciality.

His misogyny was not only theatrical. Although he was charm and adorability to his female clients who, initially at least, loved him, he was a shitty employer, wringing the last ounce of energy and loyalty from people who really were not in a position to fight back. Of course, they - we - could always have quit but human beings generally aren't quitters. Barry knew that.

I will always be grateful to Sara. Her sufferings were my blackboard for I learned from her how to cope and how to perform many of the same functions when she later escaped - sorry, I mean left - to start her own hugely successful theatrical agency, Saraband Associates.

Other than the agents, Sally Moore was with us and did the company's books whilst William Piggott-Brown's half-sister Sarah Radclyffe also worked in an administrative capacity. Sarah didn't stay long. She sensibly had better things to do, notably working with Tim Bevan at Working Title to produce such movies as MY BEAUTIFUL LAUNDERETTE, A WORLD APART and WHITE MISCHIEF as well as Derek Jarman's THE TEMPEST and other of this dead hero's work. I think that's testimony enough. William's sometime girlfrind Vanessa often worked the old-fashioned plug-in switchboard and she deftly made those red and black plugs rattle in and out of the holes as skillfully as a gunner would feed bullets into a machine-gun. And the switchboard was truly a battle-zone. The client list throbbed like shellfire on the Somme.

The list itself read something like this ...

Jill Bennett - Actress. Married to playwright John Osborne. Some people found her grand. She was always superb to me, from the moment I first met her to the last time I saw her in the Crush Bar at Covent Garden a few weeks before her untimely suicide. Fabulously elegant, she wasn't the prettiest woman but one of the most fascinating and alluring people I have ever met.

Fenella Fielding - Aforementioned. Was all set to be a big star after appearing in the musical VALMOUTH. Had a sub-Joan Greenwood extra-fruity speaking voice and had appeared in a few British movies, notably as an outraged woman in a train compartment in a CARRY ON film.

Jane Asher - Famous then for once having been Paul MacCartney's girlfriend and for having appeared gingerly in THE MASQUE OF THE RED DEATH with Vincent Price.

Maureen Lipman - Just a girl from Hell, really. Sorry, Hull. Great promise. Good appearance in Nell Dunn's UP THE JUNCTION. Had a very Jewish thing and a very Jewish mother even in those days. Not pretty then. Bit of a problem. Now a very Jewish mother in her own right and married for long, long time to the wonderful Jack Rosenthal.

Ann Lynn - Lovely girl, especially after she had her nose done. Really an up-and-comer but she went a bit weird and woolly and moved to the country and was a bit new age before new age hit, if you see what I mean. Forever on the 'phone. Forever being fobbed off and far too sweet and scared to tell Barry to fuck off.

Suzanna Leigh - Frightfully energetic and blonde, a very sweet girl who was once in a movie with Elvis Presley with whom she remained very friendly. She was very professional at being a starlet for a bit in Hollywood. She deserved better than she got. But then what she got was maybe what she wanted?

Sheila Steafel - Very funny lady, from South Africa who later did good on the telly.

Sara Kestelman - Now close to damehood, I imagine. In those days, she lived with the actor Norman Rodway. She was very freckly and sort of ugly-beautiful. Very poised and a magnificent, under-rated and under-used actress.

Faith Brook - Lovely. Sort of Coral Browne character.

Patience Collier - Frightfully grand with a very good Kensington address if rather tottery on her pins. A stalwart at the Royal Shakespeare and very clever at promising young actors the world in exchange for a bit of rumpy pumpy.

Sheila Reid - Always a favourite. Highly intelligent with a special gift for the Nordic writers, I thought. Very kind.

Sheila Allen - Nice woman, married to David Jones at the good old Royal Shakespeare. Went to live in New York for a while and sort of never really got back on the wheel.

Edina Ronay - Edna Ronny as Sally Moore called her. Now much better-employed by herself doing fab knits and clothes.

And the gentlemen ... Loosely speaking.

Mike Pratt - Big and sub James Coburn-y and later did good in Randall and Hopkirk (Deceased) before he too became untimely deceased. Re-runs now on UK Gold. Hope his royalties go to someone nice.

Victor Henry - An angry Northernish, plain young man. When asked by Laurence Olivier after a very heavy audition at The Old Vic why exactly he felt he should be joining the National Theatre, Victor thundered from the stage:

"'Cos I'm a fuckin' star!"

He didn't join the National Theatre. He died too good and far, far too young.

John Thaw - Sort of a man's man. I found him a bit unapproachable. Polite to us minions but never matey.

Michael Cashman - Michael and I are the same age. I really liked him. He was a breath of fresh air in the office and would stop by just to come and see us rather than using us to inveigle his way into the offices to barrack the agents and feather his career. I'm very proud to have known him in the light of the huge achievements he has made by always and only ever being Michael Cashman. Michael has always been gay. Other actors, it will be recalled, spent years trying very hard not to be gay before they realised there was much more mileage in coming out. Puhleeze. Whilst working with Elizabeth Taylor in Z AND CO, they all had their marks and one day

Elizabeth didn't find hers. Reprimanded by a cameraman, Michael remembers her turning and snapping: "What's the matter? No fucking focus?"

Norman Rodway - Very nice man. Bit blustery and a wonderful company member at the good old Royal Shakespeare.

Keith Buckley - Useful client. Married to a casting director, Mary Selway. A very useful client. They de-married and he went off to not make it in California.

Doug Fisher - Good-looking young lead. Has appeared in a lot of telly since.

Dennis Waterman - Like Barry, like Michael Cashman, Dennis had been a child actor. I think he must have been an attractive child. As a grown-up, however, he seemed not to possess one iota of sex appeal. He made the odd movie in the late sixties and seventies but gained a reputation in our offices for being excessively ambitious and pushy. He was forever arriving with a guitar and auditioning himself so that someone would make him a pop star. He had to wait a long time before he finally got a hit off the back of one of his television series. It was a jolly good job that being laddishly cockney came into fashion for I found the pre-famous and the post-famous versions of Dennis Waterman thoroughly charmless.

I think we also looked after Nigel Hawthorne too. I remember him as being incredibly shy and particularly uncharismatic and not in any way queer. And certainly not gay. Rather earnest in fact. Dare I say dull?

In the non-thesp category, the agency handled the work of ...

Peter Collinson - Aforementioned director. Pretty much a rough diamond. Lot of flash and white Rolls Royce. One of his drivers, Dick, was a dear old poove of the old school from the West London margins who was forever regaling us with stories of his successes with suburban 'chicken'. Chicken, for those reaching for their childlines really did mean any young males, between the ages of sixteen and eighteen who could be enticed out of their trousers. Collinson's own life, chivvied and cherished by his secretary Caroline, was pretty much like a picnic-size bag of M and M's. Meetings and mattresses.

Mike Hodges - Now esteemed movie maker. Then, he

still had to hit the big time. GET CARTER came out and it was far from a hit. It took years for its cult status to accumulate. He was very earnest, very focused. Little banter and not a lot of humour, really.

Silvio Narrizano - We know.

Robert Kidd - *Wunderkind* Scottish theatre director, very much part of the Royal Court Crowd - Bill Gaskill, Bill Bryden, Lindsay Anderson - who died far, far too early. Very ambitious and very motivated.

David Bailey - The legendary fashion photographer of the sixties was desperate for a career at twenty four frames per second. Had to wait a long time. Fascinating character. Committed, great insight. So glad he was straight and girls had to deal with him. Very complicated person. But great to us. A fund of funny stories. He lived at the time with Penelope Tree, a little bit more of whom later. Bailey was magnificent. He once arrived at the offices swaying and staggering and obviously completely drunk. It was so out of character we were all amazed and, in truth, rather shocked.

"What the hell's wrong, Bailey?" I asked.

"Oh ...'Ello, Daisy," he replied,smiling, bleary-eyed and completely charming, "I jus' bin takin' some shots of winos .. Y'know ... Drunks. So," he sniffed, "I thought I better know what it was to feel like 'em." He paused. "So I drank a bottle of neat vodka ..."

That, ladies and gentlemen, is a pro.

And then there were the writers ...

Charles Laurence - Old friend of Barry and Tony Beckley. Had been an actor but was now writing. Couple of good tellies in the early days and then his career took off with MY FAT FRIEND with Kenneth Williams and Jennie Linden and later SNAP! (originally entitled CLAP!) with Maggie Smith.

John Osborne - The original angry person. LOOK BACK IN ANGER was seminal, breaking the mould of the polite, nineteen-thirties Binkie Beaumont school of theatre-going. In 1956, when set against the gentle Noel Coward and the veiled Terry Rattigan, John Osborne came on like Sid Vicious. It was like high school bends to the street!

Not surprising, this tall, rather fey figure was a very strange man indeed. Languid, almost drippy. Foppy. Whined and bitched his way through life which seemed to pivot on an axis of the Kings Road which ran from his house in Chelsea Square to The Royal Court. Barry always said he said that: "... my head tells me I'm gay but my crutch tells me otherwise."

That's as maybe. There are some who maintain that the crutch deceived itself and the head wasn't that great either.

John Osborne's theatre work carried on at the Royal Court but although Barry secured several lucrative movie deals including an early CARRINGTON project, Osborne's celebrity didn't embrace the other media as was the destiny of other Royal Court writers like Christopher Hampton. His refusal to fly in aeroplanes didn't help. It put America and Hollywood just too far away even though the Atlantic Queens bore him hither and thither across the single language separating the two cultures.

It was on board the QE2 I last saw him in 1984, with his third wife Helen Dawson. His deal was obviously to give a lecture for their freebie passage. He duly gave it.

He was either drunk or drugged. Most of the very small audience in the ship's cinema got up and left. My last vision of him was outside the New York Cunard Pierhead on the Hudson totally bemused as to how to progress. There were no taxis. I felt sorry for him in one way and yet I thought ... Dear John. Get a life.

He became cussed and curmudgeonly and cruelly vitriolic towards the end of his life and was beastly about people including Jill Bennett in an autobiographical tome which saw him out. His last play, not a success, was hours and hours long and he steadfastly refused to cut it, losing, in the process several fine actors who rightly couldn't see the piece playing as it had been written. They were right. It was cut and John died. He had become, in his turn, a very traditional writer. But, for all that, he was indubitably a very, very important figure in British life.

Every couple of weeks, a client information sheet was composed by the agents, the news of what so-and-so was doing and when they would next be available for work. This was sent to all the working casting directors and active producers in television, films and radio. The information was typed onto a kind of skin which became a floppy printing cylinder when placed onto the roller of a contraption called a Roneomaster duplicator. This predecessor of the photocopier used real - very messy - ink and one turned a crank handle which activated a sheet feed and out from the arse-end of the machine came the reproduction. This exercise and the subsequent collation and stapling and the typing of envelopes took forever. Whether anyone ever got work from the exercise, I frankly doubt but many agencies stuck to the format. I actually think that actors get their own work, never directly but always because of work and contacts they've made in the past.

For all our clients, success was obviously the motivating factor as indeed it was for the agents. When one lives by that rule of thumb, it frightened me how quickly one loses the compassion and the very ability to care, to listen and to want to advise and help, all of which qualities are some of the most important tools in an agent's toolbox. How innuring are those wingeing, currently unsuccessful actors who ring their agents five times a day, insisting on speaking in person and only to their agent. These poor desperate - but to you irritating and infuriating - souls, tortured and driven nearly to madness by the fear that they will never work again.

They were treated like pests. Sighs groaned out when the switchboard operator announced that so-and-so was on the line ... Eyes went to heaven and whomsoever's assistant or secretary girded their loins to take the call in place of the agent to invent some damned lie or excuse fuller of holes than a colander to fob off the non-working client. These poor, wretched thesps sometimes spent periods of months being fobbed off before either reluctantly taking the hint and finding another agent or miraculously landing a job. This latter, of course, meant that they were instantly re-classified as successful and therefore put through immediately when they telephoned about the tiniest and most insignificant detail of the job they were doing. All actors, it has to be said, love complaining about their agents for doing so validates their being unemployed.

Being polite at the same time as, in fact, being incredibly rude to someone is a talent which few have and which even fewer can develop. I could teach courses in how to get rid of people. Read these lines below. I've used them all in my time:
"Hello, darling. Sorry ... Barry's at lunch."
* * * * * * *
"He's not answering his 'phone, darling. Can he call you

176

back?"

       * * * * * * *

       "Where are you, darling? In a call box ... Oh. Then he can't call you back later, can he?"

       * * * * * * *

       "Barry's in a meeting. Sorry!"

       * * * * * * *

       "He's tied up at the moment."

       * * * * * * *

       "He's left for the airport, darling."

       * * * * * * *

       "He's in The States ... Sorry. Back next week."

       * * * * * * *

       "You just missed him, sweetie."

       * * * * * * *

       "Oh, he is naughty. Didn't he call you?"

       * * * * * * *

       "But I gave him your number, darling."

       * * * * * * *

       "Cheer up, pet. I'm sure something will happen for you soon."

       * * * * * * *

       "You've taken how many mogodon, darling?"

       * * * * * * *

       "The cheque wasn't signed? Oh ... the accounts department's just too much, isn't it?"

       * * * * * * *

       "I'm here all on my own, sweetie, would you believe? Sorry."

       * * * * * * *

       "Sorry, darling. Can't give you his home number. You wouldn't like me to give out yours, would you?"

       * * * * * * *

       "You might just catch him at The White Elephant ..."

       And out on the end of the thinnest limb of our client list was of course 'that pop singer'.

       Cat Stevens.

Cat Stevens' given name, Steven Demetre Giorgiou, furnished him with the name everyone called him. Steve. Despite his second name-change to Yusef Islam, I shall call him by the name his parents and family and what friends he might have once had used. Steve. Tony Beckley always referred to him as Pussy. But Tony liked cats.

Barry was also, patently, a cat lover. He seemed besotted with his new signing and spent a great deal of time with this totally unproven commodity. The first renaissance album which Island Records issued entitled MONA BONE JAKON (Titter, titter. D'you get the allusion? If you don't, you too, maybe, need a life) was not an immediate soaraway success although the single taken from it, LADY D'ARBANVILLE, charted.

Despite the lack of immediate success, by the end of 1970, it was noticeable that Steve was taking up a disproportionate amount of Barry's time. Discontent rumbled like the thunder of distant guns through the telephonist's headphones.

Why? People wondered.

Why? People gossiped.

People drew their own conclusions. They always do.

So, it was, thus comported, that BKM (Personal Management) Ltd, licensed to act as employment agents by Westminster Council in accordance with the strictest bye-laws, squared up to the vicissitudes of the showbiz market place at the end of 1970.

The deal with Memorial had obviously freed some money for Barry and plans were made for he and Tony to move from Curzon Street. By using the Mayfair flat for business premises, although there was never proper planning permission, Barry could charge his company rent. A lot of rent. This could then be used to make mortgage repayments on a house. Tony and Barry found a house at 20 Walham Grove just off Fulham Broadway. SW6. Not a bad address. Lord and Lady Rendlesham had a house opposite. Clare Rendlesham was just starting to open up the boutique promise of the Yves St Laurent pret-a-porter range in London. It was all very up and coming.

Pussy wasn't far behind and soon had bought the house opposite at number 44. Who says you can't mix business with pleasure? Everyone looked just dandy in their bits of St Laurent. When they remembered to wear them.

By the end of 1970, Barry's business had therefore moved out of Claridge House in Davies Street and over one hectic weekend removed to 27 Curzon Street. On Monday morning, it was business as usual, conducted, as usual, on the traditional wing and a prayer.

I hasten to add that the fobbing off treatment never happened to the Cat Stevenses of the client list. Steve's calls were always put through instantly.

But, change, as Steve wrote, was surely coming. From another side of time.

Chapter Eighteen

RACING CERTAINTIES

Both backwards and forwards, time was, time is and time will come ... Faster, admittedly in the car I bought which was a Austin Mini Cooper, twin carburettors, finished in British rally colours; green body, white roof. It went like a rocket. Its exhaust sounded like one long, angry fart. I adored it. Where I got the money, I have not the faintest idea. Probably from my long-suffering parents. Or, rather ... Hire purchase. Buying on credit was the only way nineteen-seventies Britain was able to be part of the twentieth century. Cheque guarantee cards were just coming on stream and in four years, credit cards would become readily and generally available. Consumer appetites were hotting up in readiness for the onset of the Milksnatcher Factor.

Very soon after I bought my zippy Mini, one of those cheap taxi moments arrived due to Peter Collinson. Interviewing actresses for a film, one of the last that afternoon was a sweetly-smiling but absolutely zonked Marianne Faithfull. I was rostered to drive her back to some godforsaken village in Buckinghamshire. I suppose they thought they couldn't just tip her out onto the pavement in Curzon Street. Poor benighted soul. She spoke nary a word the whole way down the M40 and thence onto the byways of Bucks except to murmur worryingly unconvincing directions. It was an interminable journey. It rained incessantly and Ms Faithfull's hand, rather her finger nails, gently scratched the glass of the passenger window as though she was trying to touch and gather the raindrops outside before they ran down the pane and disappeared forever, just as tears go by ...

The next time I saw her was in a lavatory at a party in a New York appartment in the 'eighties. On that occasion, she was talking a little more than she needed. She's now an icon, I gather.

But I digress.

Stars aren't like people. That they are people is self-evident but that they conform to the predictable, assessable and forecastable mores shared by the rest of us is simply outside the remit of being a star.

The musicbiz as a distinct part of showbiz was still only fledging in 1970. The knocks were just as hard, though. Being unfitted to do any other job applies to artistes as much as to their minders. Financial necessity often dictates that not only has the ex-pop star have to get another life but also they have to earn some kind of living. It is therefore no surprise to read that some once-glittering creature has been re-discovered by a prurient newspaper hack working on a production line gutting herrings. It's all grist to the run-of-the-mill.

For most of the fallen - let's be kind and call then former - stars, the only real alternative is to peddle the fame for as long as the tarnish can be kept at bay whilst actively pursuing the inevitably disastrous come-back. Very few actually want to get out for good. There isn't a Stars Anonymous, dedicated to helping an individual to become ordinary again and staying ordinary. Taking one day at a time on the road back to anonymity ...

I mention this only because it came to pass that Barry, and therefore we who worked for him, made a career out of the Come-Back Kids.

It also came to pass that I happened on my own Come-Back Kid in the shape and form of the infamous Twinkle. It was inevitable that we should meet.

Micky Hannah's stay with Judy had been scuppered by

the erstwhile Twinkle who had obsessively sought Mick out and relentlessly worked on him to move back into her Hampton High Street flat. An 'E' Type Jaguar was produced, clothes were bought, sumptuous meals were cooked ... Micky basically surrendered. Not because he loved her, but because he didn't.

Twink actually was one of those who should have had the availability of a Stars Anonymous. She really didn't want to carry on or go back to being a star. In her disabled state, she saw Mick as her passport. She wanted to be married. To cook meals. To have babies and care for the cats and dogs which, willy nilly, became her whole life that she envisaged him taking care and control of.

She did make it through in the end. But not with Micky Hannah.

Although Twinkle made a fair stab at pretending to trying to like me, I fancy she always loathed me. I was a convenient villain when she could not bring herself to blame either herself or Mick. Her ambivalent attitudes swung, flailing, from putting it about that she had bought a gun and was going to kill me to sending me hugely expensive presents from Bond Street booteries. Confused? Hardly. More like scared to death! Twinkle's instability terrified me.

Although Mick, in turn, didn't end up loving her, he was always Twinkle's very loyal friend, believed fiercely in her talent and actively never wanting her to give up. Ultimately, it was only because of him that she went back to work.

Via me. The enabler ... Who would do anything Mick asked me.

Twinkle had been managed by Philip and Dorothy Solomon for her briefly topical career on Decca Records. That she had never been accorded the accolade of being a songwriter is not surprising. That no one had thought of her making an album was perhaps commercially short-sighted but not, in those days, sanctionable. Women were very poorly treated in that respect - even major stars like Dusty Springfield, Twink's contemporary - in the male-dominated music business and, in fairness, Twinkle herself didn't see her talent as anything particular. Nothing special. It hadn't even been work to her. Just something she knocked off ...

That's work, Twink. To most of us.

Professionally, (sorry, dear), Twinkle suffered badly

from having no natural performing talent according to the tenets of the age. Now, she'd've been perfect. Then ... Well, kinder to call it showing off, perhaps, but not performing. Even speaking in public trounced her. What she said sounded too little-girl, vacant and unconvincing. Drunk, she was great. Sober, she was stiffer than a wing collar.

She lived behind the mask of Twinkle but, like a lot of the 'sixties stars, hadn't yet worked out who she was underneath. Ultimately, it was easier to be Twinkle the Star. She lived in a tiny world, mostly inside her head, buoyed up by all the other enablers, her mother and father - by then divorced - her sister Dawn who had been a pop music journalist and significant in the start of her celebrity and those people whom she saw as enormously important such as her cleaning lady, a teenaged fan from down the road and round the corner, the people who kept the pub opposite in which she would drink herself to distraction, treating everyone within hailing distance to drinks. And of course she thought everyone loved her and was duly devastated when she discovered that Mick didn't.

Her brother Beverly sensibly kept them all at arm's length as did her father Sidney's partner Pida. Both knew that the music money had been replaced by money from Sidney and that one day, Twink's bubble would burst. However, it was not to be until 1972 that Twinkle was persuaded by Mick to seriously try for a come-back. The intervening two years were not peaceful ones. Twinkle spent most of them plotting dire consequences for Mick's subsequent girlfriends, one of whom was probably the only girl who ever told him, "Sorry, no." Everyone has their come-uppance, even the beautiful people.

Just for the exercise, may I invite you to set the readily comparable situation of Cat Stevens, Twinkle's contemporary against her own case. Both artists wrote their own songs. Both had had established managements behind them. Both had been on the Decca label, Steve the first to be released on Deram. Both had known hospital life, Twinkle after a suicide attempt and Steve after having contracted tuberculosis after abusing his body with late-nights and alcohol.

But surely, wasn't it Twink who'd had the number one hit? Steve hadn't.

Steve, however, was a man.

And a very attractive man at that, leaner and moodier than ever after his tussle with the TB virus. Early photographs of him in the mid-sixties show a youth not only aware of his sexuality but unmistakably keen to flaunt every inch of it. In his renaissance mode, although he professed humility and an aversion to being photographed, he nevertheless, when photographed, presented himself extremely professionally. He dressed apparently insouciantly. He wore velvet suits, tight pants, boots and his hair, although tousled and curly was never dirty. He dressed, in the tailoring sense, very obviously and on the left and was either completely at ease with the sexual vibes he exuded or entirely unaware. Personally, I harboured no secret desires about him. I never fantasised about him and never reacted to his sexual vibe. But he wasn't really my type, then, and we were the same age. I was also cognisant of his special relationship with Barry which immediately quarantined him. I have never made it a practice to invade other people's special friendships. I suppose I regarded Steve as my equal, a sort of brother of whom I was fiercely proud. He really was special.

Steve had broken with Mike Hurst, his original manager, producer and enabler using the legal advice and resources of Oscar Beuselinck, co-incidentally the father of Paul Nicholas who was probably still strutting his way through some production of HAIR! somewhere or auditioning for Sir Tim and Sir (Oops! Lord) Andrew for JESUS CHRIST SUPERSTAR! Via Poppa Beuselinck, Steve was introduced to Barry but only after Steve himself had introduced his music and the re-invented Cat Stevens to Chris Blackwell at Island Records.

Steve was consumed with ambition and push and drive and always had been.Where Twinkle didn't want to, Steve desperately did and therein lies the rub and the end of any comparison.

Steve was consumed with his mission to become successful. What he wanted success for, he never questioned. He just went for it. By the time he met Barry, he had been introduced to his producer, ex-Yardbirds bassist Paul Samwell-Smith and MONA BONE JAKON had already taken shape from the fund of some forty or so songs which Steve had accumulated in his catalogue by 1969 and which were to last him through his next seminal three albums before necessity goaded him once again into composition. He must have been terrified. Whereas most artists write as they live and live to write, Steve used his larder of material, like pumping oil from a finite reserve, merely to live. Had he written as he went along, maybe things would have turned out differently.

But, then again, maybe he couldn't ... write any more. Squirrels have been known to run out of nuts.

Chapter Nineteen

THE GOLDEN YEARS

Although we were out and about during working hours, in our free time we were equally assiduous. It was a very pure time in the sense that we were living neither in the past, nor in the future but merely in and only for the present.

Life had improved at Ashley Gardens since I had introduced David Minns to Roger Clifford. Roger was a celebrated theatrical publicist working out of an office in Clifford Street above Michael Fish's famous shirt 'n' kipper-tie shop. Both were great friends of Barry. Roger was especially close to Tony Beckley. Roger, who then lived with hairdresser Stephen August, had already tried to poach me from Barry, unsuccessfully and was still on the lookout for someone like me for his own business. Working for Roger at the time were Penelope Dunkerley and Peter Thompson.

So, enter David Minns who got the 'gopher' job - as it was at the beginning - although this was later assumed by the eccentrically witty and entirely sweet Australian, Ian Kerr who got landed with the nickname of Ivy.

Our jobs put David and I squarely in the same boat and gave us a huge extra shared interest. In the morning, we left for work together, David walking the last few hundred yards between Curzon Street and Clifford Street. In the evening, we would go home together, David arriving at Curzon Street after he had ended his day at Roger's.

By working and socialising in this context which I shall generically call theatrical, I became removed of course from the firing line of intolerance and prejudice which was the lot of many gay men who had to make their own new way dodging the often painful slings and arrows which they faced in the real world. Wolfenden and the resulting Act of Parliament ten years later in 1967 had gone as far as it was deemed politically feasible and practicably possible at the time.

As with all pieces of legislation, the Act was a necessary fudge. The private bit and the lack of specificity might have rankled with gay people and their supporters but it was the underlying sin of making the issue public at all which had left the moral majority of this pure and godly nation with a nasty taste in its mouth.

Private. Yes. Maybe. Except that we queers - soon-to-be-gays - didn't want to be private in the slightest.

I would imagine that kissing your same-sex partner in the middle of the disco floor could still technically be an illegal act given the lack of specificity and the contradictory legislation embodied in the 1956 Sexual Offences Act under whose sickening aegis most of the sexual persecution in this country is prosecuted. I contend that the virulent homophobia in influential, cross-class parts of British society was aggravated even further by the legislation and ensuing events and campaigns of the late nineteen 'sixties and 'seventies. The homosexual was available to be vilified even more. To those who thought they hated us when we existed invisibly, by making us look even dirtier in public, they knew for sure that they hated us and the hatred itself could be made to appear legitimate.

Generally, emancipation was having a nevertheless remarkable effect not only on both gays and women but most males too could ultimately look back on these two decades and realise that the liberation being wrought by their gay brothers would benefit them.

Make no mistake, guys. Gay lib was also male lib. And, it was discovered often to great and perplexing consternation, that real men could also be gay. However, without the collusion of women, straight as well as gay, progress would have been even slower. By 1970 many people on every continent were beginning to see through life's plot and a powerful minority now saw that life - as they'd been told it should be lived - was nothing more than a conspiracy and in it, they wanted no part.

Sexual emancipation was integral in this new found confidence. If there's no need to hide being gay, then there's no need to worry about staying in a job you hate with people whom you find incompatible. Similarly, if, as a woman, you no longer feel that you have to be married by twenty-one and pregnant the next year, there are many opportunities which life will afford you. If people decided they didn't want to be part of the mainstream, they didn't have to be. No surprise that the newly-liberated ultimately flocked to buy the validating music of artists like Cat Stevens.

"Come on over and find yourself ...", he sang, an exhortation to his generation to shuck their shackles and instead of following the piper, to march to the rhythm of a different drummer.

They did. He did.

Gradually attitudes began to change, not least the attitudes of gay people to themselves. Politically, the Campaign for Homosexual Equality and the Gay Liberation Front were organisations which didn't touch me at all, safe, as I thought I was, in my already-out arena. I wish I knew more about their work because it was invaluable in pulling the lavender pot to the front burner in the media forum. I have to say, most gay men ignored their politicking brothers. It would still be many years before the first out member of parliament made gay men start to think that their 'private' codes and attitudes could be constitutionalised. Private still meant another, separate life not just a part of a single whole. Fear was still a powerful vote-rigger.

There was also, almost, a British Stonewall. I was there. Not until 1971 or 1972, I fancy, did the nagging zit which was the stand-off between the police and the newly recognisable face of the out gay phenomenon come to a head. In Earls Court, the Coleherne pub had long been the hub whose spokes embraced the whole spectrum of gay life from leather-clad lads to the limpest of the classic lispers. On a warm summer's night, a couple or hundred of us turned out onto the pavement at closing time and instead of scurrying off to our cars, our motor-bikes our bus-stops and our hole-in-the-wall lives, we stayed on the streets surrounding the pub and chatted. An excessive number of police cars soon converged like angry wasps onto a spilled slew of raspberry jam. Like blood on my terraces, as Freddie Mercury later sang.

It was the ultimate stand-off. It happened on two or three nights in succession. There were no scuffles or arrests on the night I was there, but there was a confrontational atmosphere one could have cut with a knife. It's a very disturbing feeling to touch hate. Also, a deceptively empowering feeling to experience hate which can only have a natural resolution in conflict and thus victory for one of the haters. It must have been the only way two armies could have been impelled to fight each other.

We thought we had good reason to hate. To hate them.

Clubs were still being raided, books and magazines and films were still seized and impounded, theatre productions and movie presentations were still blue-pencilled and censored and the police still milked the shit out of the aforementioned 1956 Sexual Offences Act with agent provocateur tactics of surveillance, entrapment and all the other insidious methods of applying a bad law. It is so bad a piece of legislation that it is still considered too much of a political hot potato for anyone to take up to repeal and rewrite to protect those people it was initially meant to protect instead of being conveniently used to persecute and terrorise a socially and politically expendable minority. Bad law has no place in democratic society where the law is our only freedom.

Learning about the police and the forces ranged against him is the first thing a gay boy should learn when coming out or coming to London to be out. Knowledge is no ultimate protection, however, but bearing the caveats in mind, it alerts him to the risks. He is of course, perfectly free to take those risks and break the law ... To break the law is also one of our freedoms. That there is a price to pay if caught is merely an actuarial calculation.

But sometimes, he who is the best-taught and the most aware forgets ...

Chapter Twenty

BOYS JUST WANNA HAVE
FUN ...

In no particular order, what follows is an anthology of a few of the things we did for fun, out of office hours, in the early 'seventies in London. I have to emphasise that other twenty-three year old gay boys had it very tough both in London, in its suburbs and certainly in provincial towns and cities in the regions of the realm. We didn't and we were very privileged. I didn't know what sexual discrimination was until I had left the musicbiz and returned to civilian life.

And, boy! Did it hurt or what? Ouch.

The very real phenomenon of co-incidence, of people just turning up in one's life seems to be a standard feature of every showbiz, and hence, musicbiz story. Hard to believe, perhaps, but things really did,

"... just 'appen, mum!"

Opportunities simply presented themselves. Even in the 'seventies, anything could happen to a person in London and much of what could happen usually did, to us. Far from being frightening, it made heroes out of the most incurious. I remember meeting Patrick

Walker in Curzon Street one day and being invited back to his lodgings in Chesterfield Street. Going up the stairs, I glanced through an open door and thought I saw Cicely Courtneidge. Had I?

"Yes. Jack must be out," added this wonderfully kind and interesting man about his landlords, Cicely and Jack Hulbert.

Once this precept of accidentalism had been accepted and taken on-board, even though to our parents, fretting at home about our health and moral welfare, our life seemed precarious, the reality was that we lived a life which assumed a, strangely, structured progress. David and I were only too happy to be inseparably associated with the work we did and we were proud to be considered as part of a new breed of professional young people, men and women alike, who had acquired respectable and respected skills not via apprenticeships or training schemes or academic diplomas but in the much-vaunted university of life.

Money was always a consideration for us but never an obstacle. If we didn't have any money, we didn't spend any. Simple. Fact of life. We were the last generation before instant credit, plastic cards and holes-in-the-wall of the totally respectable kind. We were not infected by instant consumer gratification and we were playing by our parents' rules. When we went to pubs, we drank halves and waited to be bought pints. We didn't have drink - spirits, wines or beers - at home in the flat until I was twenty-seven. It was a milestone day for David and I, ranging the spirit bottles and the mixes and my grandmother's sherry decanters and some nice old cut-crystal cocktail glasses on her re-polished deco-ish tea-trolley and wondering who we could invite for drinks! Anyone for sherry? No wonder Hinge and Brackett were so successful. Boys today don't know the significance of a good sherry.

When we went to pubs, it wasn't to the old-fashioned West End bars which even by the early 'seventies had become associated more with rent boys than gay boys. We went to the Coleherne and The Boltons in Earls Court and to the Chelsea ones of which only the Queens Head remains. The Colville - perhaps our favourite - has long disappeared, bought up first to be another flagship of John Stephen's ragtrade empire. Next to the Pharmacy where we bought our amyl nitrite in the glass vials within cardboard tubes (hence poppers because you had to crush the vials to release the gas and the breaking glass duly popped) was The Markham Arms, gay on a Saturday morning where we boys would gather in numbers too great for the interior to hold and so out onto the pavement we spilled.

Grrrreat feeling!

There is strength in numbers. Even writing about it twenty-five years later, I can still sense that wonderful feeling of empowerment, that quickening knowledge that you were part of something greater and not of something lesser as we mingled.

And mingle we did.

On Sunday we would go to the Horse and Groom and the Peg O'Wassail (Pig 'n' Whistle) in Belgravia where the same pavement parade would go on as well as a constant inter-migration between the two pubs. There weren't pubs for this and pubs for that in those days. Britches Queens and leather queens would quite cheerfully mix with nellie queens and dancing queens. Gummi knights and uniform nights had not polarised. Only hearts were worn on sleeves and keys to the right of us, keys to the left was an etiquette of the future. Only a very, very few in that pre-clone era wore the badges of their particular fantasy outside the essential privacy of their own four walls.

And in the evenings, people still had parties. Not just cocktail parties which we groovies had rather eschewed but which the piss-elegant maintained. To our sort of parties, you'd go with a bottle and we'd dance and snog and generally have a lovely time 'cutting the rug' to the sound of Tamla or other American dance records. There was a party grapevine, much I presume like the rave circuit's word-of-mouth. The telephone lines would be red-hot on a Friday evening as the boys mustered for the weekend.

On weekends only, when we had a bit of money, natch, we still patronised the older dancing clubs like Yours or Mine and Henrietta's but there was now not only Napoleon's in Bond Street to increase the choice but also the much raunchier Catacombs in Finborough Road just around the corner from the Coleherne. The Gigolo in the Kings Road assured a hot and sweaty crush at the back of which, many a boy would find his trousers round his ankles in no longer than the time it took to say, "Hello." There was, after all, no escape and if you were jammed in against someone with really foul breath - tough! There wasn't even enough room to drop decently to one's knees.

David and I would assiduously save our money so that once every couple of weeks we could go to April and Desmond's restaurant in Knightsbridge. This place was the seat of the celebrated trans-sexual April Ashley and her business partner Desmond. Housed in a basement, the yards long restaurant was a semi-circular arched chamber of vaulted sand-blasted red brick. To us it was the height of cafe elegance, street-loucheness and our kind of ritzy glamour. There was a grand piano upon which a magnificent flower arrangement always sat. Film stars went there. We often saw Ava Gardner ... This close!

To me, April was the most elegant woman I have ever met. Her gowns were fabulous, her dark, lustrous hair tall and superb and her smile was radiant. She must have known that David and I were fairly challenged as far as social prominence was concerned but she made a point, the same point she made to every table of diners, of making her customers feel incredibly welcome and incredibly special and ... Well, thanks, April. I'm glad that man and not god was responsible for finally shaping you for you helped to make our gilded youth intensely joyful.

For those who remember hot pants, here's a thing. When Paul Hillyer was making leather belts in our kitchen to sell to shops like *Le Bistingo* in the Kings Road, he made me a pair of blue suede hot pants. I once turned up at April's wearing these with knee-length white socks, blue patent Italian moccasin loafers, a white ribbed-cotton vest and a blue suede Levis jacket. I may have looked like a prat to others but to myself I felt I looked like a million dollars.

Neither did I have cause to regret the outfit later when apprehended by one of Chelsea's finest outside the Magpie and Stump off the Kings Road where there was a well-known loo.

"Watch it and behave yourself. If I booked you, you'd look bloody silly in them things in the dock on Monday, wouldn't you?"

"Yes, officer. Sorry, officer."

Nor did I have any regrets when I finally got home and took off the hot pants only to find that the evening's perspiration had conspired with the dye to turn me blue from waist to bollocks which is how I stayed for a week.

There were other restaurants of course but for our first few years in London, we tended to be taken to these by older, wealthier admirers. Christopher Hunter maintained his *La Popote* restaurant in Walton Street and was in the vanguard of many restaurateurs who, both in Pimlico and in the Fulham Road, established their establishments as amusing and congenial places for gay people to eat. Restaurants such as Fergus Provan's and Stuart Grimshaw's PROVANS and, opposite, SEPTEMBER were to become favourites.

I'm sure that Hampstead Heath and Wimbledon Common held out their promise of a fair share of carnal joy but in the early 'seventies we lusted to partake in none of that kind of enjoyment. Ultimately, we were much more romantically impelled. Deepest deep down, conditioned into us, ingrained in our motivation, I think we were like Rock 'n' Doris, in love with the idea of being somehow, someday in love with some nebulous Mister Right and that it would be an in love which would last forever.

On reflection, the way we were going about making this happen was odd. We obviously didn't think we would find Mister Right in anything but a public lavatory. Other than the few pubs, our gay lives really did revolve around the cottaging circuit. As John Lahr so faithfully represented in the ORTON DIARIES, there were hundreds and hundreds of public lavatories which were the venue for both casual and romantic sexual contact. The emphasis was probably on the casual but people did meet whilst ogling each other at the urinals. Sex had to be the prime motivator. Without a sexual contact, there would be no other.

And who was I - or am I - to judge?

As the newly identifiable gay face became more and more recognisable and the debate hotted up, so more and more complaints were purportedly made by the general public as to the activities of men in and around public conveniences. The reaction of police and the authorities was at first gradually, then massively, to target these cottages and try to deter gay men from using them by bringing huge numbers of prosecutions and, when that failed, by closing the facilities down completely.

Co-incidentally, the peak of the closures came with the

exploding gay scene, but that is for a little later. As there was so little mass dancing, a state of fewer drugs was the order of our day. Sure, people smoked pot. A bit. It wasn't until 1974 that I had my first joint. In Amsterdam. Sure, we used amyl nitrite (poppers) but not widely and not generally. I was first introduced to poppers in a Pimlico flat by a doctor, the general practitioner sort, who I suppose really should have known better. I was quite scared as he forced these wicked-smelling cardboard tubes against my nostrils. I could have been asthmatic, I could have been a hysteric ...

But I took to the effect they produced like a duck to water.

There was speed, of course but ... I never wanted it. I was quite high enough on the excitement of my job and my milieu. There were very, very few drugs around. The coke thing didn't start until the mid-seventies, therefore no crack, and heroin, although available, was still a drug whose name was only whispered. Acid was different acid, I guess, to the stuff later produced. Dropping it was accompanied by an almost holy ritual of not being left alone and being in virtual retreat over a whole weekend. I never even wanted to. My mind was quite sufficiently bent already. Any further bending, I fancied, would have resulted in a stress fracture so acute, I would have been left raving, strapped down and gagged on an asylum gurney. All in all, drugs rather passed me by. I am not ungrateful for that.

Those party years now seem remote, removed times. There were far fewer nightbuses. Minicabs hadn't even been dreamed up but London was easier to get around. Parking was definitely easier. Daily bread was definitely cheaper, mortgages were rare, credit existed only as American Express and Diners Club cards, lengthy agreements with hire purchase companies and the rapacious loan-sharks. Foreign travel for Britz was only beginning to be as common as it has become although London was the overseas tourists' mecca every year in succession. Levis were still special, real men were daringly carrying handbags and male fragrances were no longer solely associated with Old Spice and Brut ...

I bought my clothes, other than Levis of course, mainly in Kings Road shops. Take Six had arrived and sold incredibly contemporary clothes which weren't, sorry, an arm and a leg. Peter

Rogers at Cockell and Johnson (now Johnsons and still in Kensington Market) supplied us with innovative shirts, the sleeves and collars and cuffs often being of different, clashing colours and materials. We had particularly extravagant tastes in shoes, however and the bi-annual Bally sale was occasion for a spending spree. I often wandered longingly in front of Piero de Monzi's windows in Fulham Road the contents of which I thought incredibly desirable as was Signor de Monzi himself. In the end, the management proved more available than the merchandise in the shop window and I lost interest in Italian styling.

I did, however, find at least two bitter pips in my bowl of cherries. The first pip was that Dearest Him got married. I wasn't invited to the ceremony, only to the reception which was at some hotel in Roehampton. Her name was Carol and I hope they lived happily everafter. I felt marginalised and uncomfortable and left in embarrassed confusion after having nearly ripped the woman's bridal headress off. Quite unintentionally. I didn't know I was standing on the end of the flowing veil. She walked away. Ouch!

Curtain.

My schooldays were well and truly over.There was no going back. What was it that Gloria Gaynor was later to scream into the disco nights of the world?

"It should've been ..." Who?

The second pip ... God! How could I have been so trusting! It started with a familiar plot. Meet boy in Biograph on Sunday evening. Such a nice person, so sweet, so wonderful. Fall instantly in love in the ensuing hours before Monday morning and swear everlasting bonds of forever.

Now the dumb bit. Leave boy in flat when I go to work.

Spend day in tizzy of excitement. Even buy a bunch of flowers on way home. Return at seven to find ...

To find the whole place has been picked over, ransacked and cleared out. Bastard had used eight empty suitcases and filled them with hi-fi's (sound systems), clothes, ornaments ... And not only mine. The other residents too! I felt so dirty and so, so stupid. I made amends to the others, as best as I could but Ashley Gardens was never the same again and I was left bitterer than angostura and more hardened than a tungsten drill-bit.

196

I think I became an adult that evening. Young and carefree was to be no more. Life was hardening up too. Hardening and widening.

The vast Atlantic was fast being turned into a pond and it was to America that we all looked for the big-time. It was the final invasion, the final revenge for the Boston Tea Party. Although Britain had initially lost her thirteen colonies to Frenchified ideas of Liberty, Equality and Fraternity, for a while in the 'seventies and 'eighties, it seemed the Britz were not only re-capturing the eastern seaboard but all fifty states. Now, the invasion spearheaded by the Beatles was about to recolonise.

The British musicbiz was about to come into its own.

Chapter Twenty-One

THE CAT'S CRADLE

When I started working for Barry, he was perfectly aware of my ambitions to become a writer. Understandably, he was entirely dis-interested. Perhaps, believing that it is frequently better to be cruel to be kind, he told me in no uncertain terms that my future would not be in writing but that some day I might make someone an okay lover ... Whoops!

My perspectives thus adjusted, I didn't really mind. It was so very nice to use his discouragement as an excuse to leave me free to put my own creative drive into the really important things of life which, in no particular order, appeared to be having an extremely good time going to bars and restaurants and staying up very late as often as possible doing unspeakable things with other boys.

So slaked, my creative withdrawal was a doddle. I just let other people, like Steve, fulfill my creative urges. Basking in the reflected glory of the eminently superior and more successful efforts of the creative talent which surrounded me, I felt I didn't have to bother with being creative myself. It was creative enough listening to the trials and tribulations of these great ones and, as far as one could help by being sympathetic and appreciative of their every effort.

It's called arse-licking. Brown-nosing. I am the yes-man, yes. I am the yes-man ... Yes! Endless listening. Bernice Rubens says it's what makes a writer. If so, working with actors and musicians is a serious qualification for the Booker Prize.

After a year or so, even I could tell that life was getting better for all of us when Barry forgave me the ironing and the valet parts of my job spec and, needing an assistant's services fairly constantly, allowed me instead to take his laundry to the dry cleaners a little way down the street. I hung up my iron once and for all and never looked back. We employed the first of a string of office gophers. This one was was ginger and chirpy, from South London. His name was Graham Briley. He could see nothing in Cat Stevens whatsoever but wanted instead nothing more than to be David Bowie who had just stuck his amazing Ziggy face over the parapet of the RCA building on the corner of Curzon Street next to MI5. Our next was Simon Fryer who was tall and lithe and had hair that looked like a spaniel's and whose ambition was to become a roadie.

Most people didn't ask for much out of rock 'n' roll. Just to be there.

For a while, Barry seemed jollier and happier than he had ever been. The realisation that Steve's career had taken off first of all in America came hard on the heels of that first low-key appearance which Steve and Alun Davies made at Doug Weston's Troubadour on Santa Monica Boulevard in West Hollywood, L.A. The implications of such a career launch took longer to be revealed back here at home. Steve's so-called career, until the Troubadour watershed, had been fairly parochial. The highest-flying talks that there might have been were at best infrequent and even then only between Curzon Street and Island Records in St. Peter's Square, Hammersmith.

It was hardly transatlantic and all very much between chums. The people at Island sat at large round tables in open offices where everyone knew a lot about most company matters. It was all very ... comprehensive? And frightfully non-homo. What they made of us is probably unprintable. The dashingly glamorous Chris Blackwell was not a frequent caller at Curzon Street. Island had far bigger fish frying in the early days.

It goes without saying that whatever it was he didn't

know in order to cope with this anticipated but long-time-coming situation vis-à-vis Steve, Barry learned fast and it follows logically that we did too. He had to. We had to.

It was a good thing we were capable of learning for there was no hint of any constructive or structured training at Barry Krost Management. We were there to work and to work for as little money as Barry could get away with paying. To Louis XIV was ascribed the utterance, "*L'etat, c'est moi!*" In exactly the same way did Barry view his company. It was him. Without him, it was nothing and nothing therefore needs no one to run it. No one, ergo, had any significance other than the pragmatic, the functional and, inevitably, the dispensable.

But there were several years to run before my turn came in that inevitable round and in the meantime not only myself but all those who worked at Curzon Street set to with a will.

It became very obvious very quickly that Barry was gut-bored with the theatrical agency side of his business. Very soon after we moved to Curzon Street, Norman Boyack was invited to join as a supplemental agent to Sara Randall. Norman brought some of his old clients with him but basically was there to look after those of Barry's whom Barry couldn't face sacking. Matter of an agent's pride - don't fire them, abuse them sufficiently through neglect so that, disillusioned and broken, they finally leave you. Same with your employees. Make life so miserable, they resign. Richard Eastham succeeded Norman Boyack who quite sensibly went off and became very successful in his own right. And happier. Eastham was a wiry little whipcord of a man, smoked endlessly and was as jumpy as a shrimp looking at a dish of aioli across a steaming vat of boiling water.

His wife, Jane, ran the theatre section of the British Council in Davies Street. That was winding down too. Television was changing our world. Much easier to send a video casette in the post to Malaya and screen LADY WINDERMERE'S FAN to the million Malays with tellies than pack up a ropey old bus 'n' truck of moaning thesps clutching bottles of kaolin and morphine and handfuls of yellowing press cuttings.

This trend was mirrored at Barry Krost's office. The business of management was fast replacing the hassle of agency.

Barry negotiated his way out of his arrangement with Memorial Enterprises. Who was a lucky boy, then? I often wonder if Medwin and Finney regretted their dealings with Barry in the light of the huge income Cat Stevens generated and in which Barry participated to the tune of twenty percent of the gross. Sharp intake of breath. Big swallow. Drink of water, love?

Richard Eastham left us and then so did Sara Randall. I remember sitting with her one afternoon and adding up all her commisson slips for the past two years for the work she had obtained for the artists she looked after in an attempt to calculate whether or not she could make a go of her own business. The figures were good. She made a huge success.

Agency versus Management. The difference? I always described it thus:

Agency seeks, chases and secures work for clients who do it on their own; Management sorts, selects and effects the right work and holds the clients' hands while they're doing it.

And, very importantly, Management involves making sure the world knows what these clients of yours are doing. To this end, publicists and publicity became a large part of our lives. Talking of yellowing newspaper clippings, Durrants Cuttings Service delivered piles to us from every publication it seemed in the known world. Cat Stevens' career alone must have caused the demise of swathes of natural forest. In the end, nothing was done with these clippings except that they were dumped first in green hanging files and when these overflowed the drawers of the filing cabinets, into larger cardboard boxes.

To manage and control the flow of information to the media, the publicists were not staffers but employed. People like the veteran Tony Brainsby, Carolyn Pfeiffer and ultimately the auspices of Rogers, Cowan and Brenner as the company was then called. Steve gave very few interviews which confounded much of the publicists' work. Information about him and his life and schedule was therefore disseminated via press releases. You'd've thought he and Barry were concocting communiqués about the second coming and Brainsby, the prophet, was often kept waiting for days himself.

A long, three flights of stairs led up to the inauspicious glazed door. I remember Jill Bennett and Edna O'Brien staggering up after a champagne-sodden lunch at the White Elephant one day, feigning exhaustion, two mountaineers in mink. Edna looked at me.

"What lovely blue eyes," she murmured. I was instantly in love. "Where are you from?"

"Wales," I lied.

"Ahhh," she murmured longingly. "The Celtic fringe. I just knew it," she managed to say before passing out of my life forever.

Inside the landing door was our attic lair. The first floor of which was a through-room separated by sliding doors, the rear room of which was occupied by Sara Randall and Norman Boyack. The front room, the grander overlooking Curzon Street, was Barry's. After a while, Jill Melford, then married to John Standing, was brought in to choose some furniture for Barry's office and to advise on some oh-so-tasteful blinds and suitable colour schemes. We upstairs, being merely heard and not seen, were left to fend with no interior decorator to soothe our fevered way until Steve took over the building many years later and clouds appeared all over the ceilings. By then, I was a mere memory ...

Upstairs in the rear room, Sally Moore did the agency's accounts and likened working under the coved roof to being captive.

"S'pose you've come to rattle my cage?" she would utter beadily when we went into her office with our queries from all those actors wondering when and how much they were due to be paid because ... Oh! A million reasons, darling.

Chrissie Marshall-Bennett came to take over as our switchboard operator. She was marvellous. Great company and a joy to face a day with. Rhonda Gregory, a tall leggy brunette from Australia also joined up with us for a year or so before going back down under and losing touch.

One of the most important of the new personnel arrived in 1971 in the form of Jill St Amant. She had started off life as plain, old Jill Cooper and had had a chequered and eventful career. She had been a very close friend of Tony Beckley and Barry's and Barry caught up with her again in Rome, where she had fetched up after the moon in her marriage to American painter 'Saint' St. Amant on Mykonos had waned.

Jill was famous on at least two continents. She was an

early example of the species which later came to be known as the party animal. She arrived, much heralded, from Rome and I have a feeling she thought she was coming to be much more than how she ended up. She ended up Barry's secretary, I suppose. But she also did secretarial work for other people. She talked at you a lot and rarely listened. In fact, I doubt if she was interested. Jill was a true star-fucker. My first. That she had fucked stars was undeniable; that she extended that thinking into an area of life where she actively cultivated those who might be socially significant is a talent I sometimes envy but mostly cringe from.

She was tall and thin and came across as blonde although the falls she wore in her hair seemed to dictate her hair colour rather than the other way around. She had a rushin'-about sort of glamour and was forever on the 'phone to a string of people richer and more mobile than she who formed part of that circuit which ran LA-New York-London-Paris-Rome-Greece and back again. She was a socialite without the wherewithal that a wealthy marriage would have provided and she was very important in my life.

So there we have the office.

Because, putting it mildly, Barry wasn't awfully fond of reading, I had a huge amount to read. Scripts were delivered to Barry every day and I would be given them to read and make a brief, few-line synopsis, assessing either the whole nature of the work or merely the part in it for which one of our clients had been suggested. I began to undertake most of Barry's letters too and thus my typing improved dramatically and we all learned to work the new plugless PMBX switchboard, mend photocopiers and Roneomasters and work the new-fangled IBM golfball electric typewriters - the very last word, my dear - as well as the invaluable calculators. Well, most of us did. Barry was a complete technophobe and a lot eluded dear Jill who would do as little as possible that otherwise she could inveigle someone else to do for her. Preferably a man.

So, it was a pretty efficient office too, although I say it myself.

I suppose every paragraph in the rest of this book, really, could begin with the words ... "If Steve hadn't become so successful ..."

And if Barry hadn't become a star too...

I suppose in that latter event, he would have gone on being a theatrical agent and undoubtedly he would have acquired some substantial clients along the way to replace those whom he would have inevitably lost. I would also have learned how to be an agent too, because if I hadn't I wouldn't have otherwise earned my keep and justified my salary and Barry would have made me resign too. Whatever. I know I would have gone on doing Barry's ironing for a helluva lot longer than I did. I would also have watched Steve, unsuccessful, finding himself being pushed further and further down the queue of those waiting for their audience with Barry as Barry tired of the personal side of their relationship. It would have happened.

It did happen.

Steve was very much hands-on in those early days. If there was something to be done, he would do it himself. He didn't have a secretary until auburn-haired Di Hughes arrived some time after we moved into Curzon Street. The offices were gradually being taken over. Organising major music tours not only of England but of Europe, America and the rest of the world is a huge undertaking. Meetings were forever scheduled between whoever the agents and promoters were, Barry Dickens at MAM or Harvey Goldsmith, even Mel Bush later on with Noel d'Abo and Rod McSween. The office really started to buzz when Carl Miller arrived as Steve's head honcho and began to assemble roadcrew and the other touring personnel who accompanied Steve on his conquering sorties. Multiply that activity by three when Barry took on the management of Colin Blunstone and Mike d'Abo too for all three bands could be touring simultaneously.

It was like the Eton Wall Game. Up against it and no rule book.

As TEA FOR THE TILLERMAN and TEASER AND THE FIRECAT successively established Steve's record-selling status the world over, the calls started flooding in from New York and LA as Barry became a very frequent-flyer. Shame there weren't air miles in those days. Nightly calls scorched the 'phone lines to and from CMA (As ICM was called then) where Vincent Romeo handled all the enquiries for Steve's tours and live appearances in North America. New York didn't open for business until two in the afternoon and the lines to LA were hot only after five-thirty. We began to stay later and later at work.

Nat Weiss became a name to conjure with. What did he look like, I thought, this voice that sounded like a face on Mount Rushmore, this ex-partner of the Beatles' manager, the legendary Brian Epstein, this conduit to Peter Asher, now relocated in LA as manager and record producer, and his client James Taylor and all the other assorted high priests of the inner *sancti* of musicbiz power?

When he finally appeared in Curzon Street, Nat didn't look anything like I'd thought. Large and well-covered, he was a funny and centred and proudly professional man. I liked him, especially when I heard that at an airport when Barry went to the first class check-in and Nat to economy, Nat called ...

"Hey, Barry! Why're ya goin' first class?"

"It's safer," retorted the frequent flyer.

"Barry!" Nat exclaimed, shrugging uncomprehendingly, "whoever heard of a plane flying backwards into a mountain?"

But until Sara Randall left and the agency business was finally elbowed, there were still actors ... One of an agency's functions was to attend the end-of-year production at the Drama Schools of which London had its fair share. Six or seven at least. Graduating students would write to prospective agents, enclosing photographs, ceevees and invitations to come to their final year shows. It was an endless and unenviable task. Barry, needless to say, never went and those which Sara couldn't cover, I was allocated. Of all those productions I must have seen over four years, the only actor I can remember seeing was Brian Deacon. What a good thing I never went into casting, where memory is essential.

Di Hughes left Steve's employment at about the same time as Steve's brother-in-law Alex arrived to oversee the accounts and, another red-head, Sarah Harrison took over as Steve's secretary. Sarah had helped build up BROWNS with the Bursteins who took the South Molton Street enterprise over from William Piggott-Brown. The shop really was a flagship of all that was best in European fashion but Sarah wanted to spread her wings.

It was a great time of companionship, hard to sustain and impossible to repeat as we all grew and moved on. I don't know what Barry thought of what was developing into a very tight-knit workforce on the uncarpeted pine floorboards above him. I often wonder if he felt excluded. He was occasionally prone to bouts of really quite nasty verbal attacks. Mostly, however, he would rather send himself up in his one-on-one relationships with female staff. He'd make a joke about pretending to lash some poor woman as a slavedriver might abuse his charge. He often boasted that he'd taught Jill St. Amant how to fellate by showing her how to practice on a coca-cola bottle as an appropriate tool for experiment.

If Barry'd had a good day, we'd know. There'd be a buzz on the intercom around six o'clock - "Can you come down?" - and I'd go downstairs to be asked if I'd go further downstairs, to Stella Richman's White Elephant Club next door and fetch up a bottle of *Moet et Chandon*.

Killer Queen, indeed, my dears. But, as the King of Queen said so famously often, there you have it ...

The White Elephant. Elegant, mysterious with Mark on the desk and George on the door. In and out glid and slid the real movers and shakers. The members-only showbiz dining club was the centre of a web of high-powered contacts in films, theatre and, lately, the burgeoning musicbiz. At White Elephant prices, the bottle of *Moet* was an extravagant gesture. Often, the bottle was for Barry and Steve or Barry and another client but on many occasions Barry would make sure that I and whoever else was working late shared his celebration.

Other generosity was iffy. Barry and I and Steve were standing at the windows looking down over Curzon Street one day and looking at the people coming and going into the National Westminster Bank opposite. Steve turned to Barry and asked, quite matter-of-factly,

"Well? Are we rich yet?"

At that moment, Telly Savalas came out of the bank. I remember him because I always remarked on Telly because he was bald, not because he was KOJAK. He was yet to make KOJAK. Both Telly and Steve must have ended up very rich indeed.

Much has been made of Steve's dilemma based on the 'my-art-versus-my-soul-versus-my-money' dialectic and I have to admit that I had and have a hard time with this theory mainly because I had a pretty hard time financially throughout my employment with

206

Barry. My fault, I know. I should have left and got a better-paid job but it nevertheless pains me to remember that other than a lovely Tom Gilbey sweater Barry gave me one Christmas and numerous cast-off hand-me-down St. Laurent garments, other than small cash bonuses which came our way at Christmas (and then only after a great deal of carrot 'n' stick, shall-I-or-shan't-I from the boss), there were very few crumbs from the rich men's table. But perhaps they thought that St. Laurent crumbs cover a multitude of sins ...

I can only remember Steve's generosity once. What he bought for the women, I've forgotten but for Christmas he bought all of the male office staff a shirt each.

That year he must have sold some five million albums.

My shirt was a blue, denim kind of shirt with a fat, rounded collar and shiny metal buttons. I remember it so well because it never fitted and I sentimentally kept it for many years before sending it to Oxfam. Barry's St. Laurents, however, I wore until the seams rotted. And even then I cried.

Chapter Twenty-Two

ALL CHANGE

David Minns got a new job too. Vincent Romeo had left CMA in New York and was suddenly living in London. At the invitation of John Eastman who was by then looking after Paul Macartney's interests after Alan Klein (Beatles manager *sin egual*) was marginalised, Vincent had arrived to supervise the affairs of Macartney Productions Limited in their office in Soho Square.

Vincent was a very jolly, very expansive New Yorker who had proved invaluable to Barry when Steve's career took off in the USA. The gay mafia proved effective yet again.

David hadn't been happy at Roger Clifford's for some time. Penelope Dunkerley left and was replaced by Sarah Ross-Goobey. Both lent dignity and style to Roger's operation. As Penelope Russell, Penelope Dunkerley still lends dignity and style to all her many enterprises today. Penelope and her sister Theresa lived with their mother in their family house in Burnsall Street just off the Kings Road and we would always call at this warm and loving house whenever we were in the Kings Road neighbourhood and always, always got a warm welcome. Why we called Penelope's mother, Gert I have forgotten but Priscilla (Gert) ... Thankyou.

When Vincent asked me to go and work for him, once again I pleaded loyalty ... What a silly boy. Instead, I suggested David and by the end of that week, David was working for Paul and Linda. Wings were just taking off, pardon the pun and, after RED ROSE SPEEDWAY, their BAND ON THE RUN became huge. David learned an enormous amount and we suddenly had even more in common. Our work was now in exactly the same arena of the industry.

Although Barry was very secretive and would rarely give anything away, even he was forced to work, to an extent, on the favour system which applied in the business. Favours were done and were called in, never as directly, never as bluntly but in our office, if we couldn't help someone who had sent in a tape or a script whom we thought talented, we would call a friend in another management or record company office where we knew the prospective artist would find a more profitable reception. Kinda hippy, I s'pose. Kind of, 'What comes around goes around.'

I understand that business is carried on a little closer to the chest these days. Please, someone, tell me I'm wrong!

David and I also got a new flat.

By the time my dear old grandad had died at the age of eighty-three and I'd inherited a lot of furniture that wasn't wanted by my mother, the Ashley Gardens lease was coming to an end and although we could have stayed as unprotected tenants, leases and tenancies in those days were a minefield.

Albert's death signalled the end of an era for me as well as for him. Not only did I want out of Ashley Gardens, I wanted out of SW One. Even the airless, windowless room behind the kitchen had been pressed into service once again to put up a little gay waif from Manchester called Julian whom Paul Hillyer had found languishing in t'north, imported to London and re-housed in my flat. Big-hearted you may have been, Paul but when we found indelible footprints all over the walls of this tiny closet after stick-thin Julian had been hurled around the tiny bed by some huge overnight trick, I felt that lines should be drawn ... The boy was little more than sixteen and childsplay was getting dangerously ... dangerous? No, dammit. Illegal!

Is this me admitting to all this caution? I'm beginning to

sound old and jaded. Hell. Maybe we were. Anyway, Paul and Melanie moved to Stamford Hill amongst the Jewry and David and I ended up by moving fifteen SW places on the flat-hunting boardgame.

How I found the flat in Montserrat Road in Putney, I don't know but move in to this three-roomed, kitchen and bathroom garden appartment we did on February 11th 1972. There was, I recall, no key-money premium payable and the garden, especially, appealed to both David and I. As far as the drive in to work was concerned, our move coincided with Barry and Tony Beckley moving into 20 Walham Grove just behind Fulham Broadway which meant I could pick Barry up in the mornings on my drive into Mayfair.

The drive to the office through Earls Court, South Kensington and Hyde Park took twenty minutes or so and at each stoplight, I would write down the instructions Barry was tossing out as he thought aloud and extemporarily and thus planned his day.

By the time I'd dropped him and gone to park the car underneath the Hilton hotel in Park Lane, his day's schedule was in place and auxiliary and ancillary courses of action had been decided. It was a fair old way of working and yet work it did. He once publicly credited part of his success to having a good assistant but in the magazine interview concerned, I was never referred to by name.

Natch.

David and I stayed in Montserrat Road for something like a year. I fancy one of the reasons for moving to Putney was that by this time, Micky Hannah had escaped the Twinkle trap yet again and had met Caroline Grey. Part of the Harvey's Bristol Cream Sherry family, Caroline was separated from her husband and, just like Mrs. Brown, had a lovely daughter. She and Mick fell deeply in love and Mick moved into her handsome Edwardian house on the southside of, and overlooking, Putney Green.

Their relationship was short-lived and saddened him enormously when it broke up but he realised and reluctantly accepted that for whatever reason, she would never marry him. He always thought it was that she was ashamed of him and his non-existent roots but I fancy Caroline had greater reason than that. Anyway, as neighbours, it was nice to see more of him than the occasional visit he made to Curzon Street when his successful modelling life brought him to interviews and photographic shoots in Mayfair. He was well-established at Nev's Agency and was fast becoming a very recognisable face in magazines and television commercials.

That bit was at least going to plan ...

Barry's switchboard had been receiving calls for some time from a production office at Paramount in Hollywood. The calls were not concerned with actors appearing in films or directors directing them, they were about Cat Stevens doing some music for a film.

But we were used to handling lots of calls like these.

Would Steve do this? Would Steve do that?

By 1972, we were all pretty much aware what Steve would be likely to do and what he wouldn't. He obviously wasn't a potential opener of supermarkets not a prospective reader-out of nominations at the Academy Awards and he also, as far as we were aware, wasn't in the market for writing any music other than his own albums.

Barry must have taken one of the evening calls from LA one day because a script duly arrived. As I have explained, scripts arrived daily in both posts and that they had been sent at all usually indicated that they would never reach the person for whom they had been intended. For most of Barry's clients by then, a monetary offer or at least ballpark discussions would customarily precede any script.

The Paramount script thus landed in my in-tray.

HAROLD AND MAUDE was already being made. The movie was all but in the can. It wasn't like my reading it and Barry's picking up the telephone was a live-or-die situation for HAROLD AND MAUDE. But the producers were obviously pretty insistent that the script got to Cat Stevens.

I laughed myself off the chair when I read HAROLD AND MAUDE. Scripts rarely moved me to tears or laughter. But, like the movie itself when I eventually got to see it, I didn't want the last page to come. I not only laughed but I cried and cried and laughed and then cried some more. HAROLD AND MAUDE was as moving and funny with just the pictures in my mind as it was when Hal Ashby's production of it ended up on screen.

I suppose it must have been the purity of it, the utterly

sacred nature of the energy that Colin Higgins was writing about. I've seen it and, indeed, experienced it between two men, two women, a man and a woman, between a younger and a very much older person. It had nothing to do with sex or wayward disturbed emotions. It had to do with something so deep-seated and so absurdly powerful that when I wept over the script, I felt that at that moment, had I died I wouldn't have been scared and I wouldn't have regretted anything and I would have been glad to have been who and what I was because I'd experienced that incredibly deep and all-pervasive feeling of having total knowledge.

It's unendurable pleasure, it's holy and yet painfully mortal. It's about incredible strength and undefendable vulnerability. It's about riding every emotional continuum that a man, a woman, girl or boy can experience. I think it's what being human is all about. It's life and death. It's indescribable because it's about pure love.

I not only gave the script of Harold and Maude a rave report, I personally took it into Barry and begged him to read it and begged him to talk to Steve about it. It transpired that the production wasn't after new music. All that was being requested was the use of the songs from TEA FOR THE TILLERMAN and MONA BONE JAKON as they existed.

The production was ultimately to get much more. I stand to be corrected but it was the one of the first times (THE GRADUATE excepted) that a film was to attempt to employ contemporary pop music as a sound track. It has to be said that the production already boasted Ruth Gordon as Maude, Bud Cort as Harold and an assembled cast including Vivian Pickles and Dabney Coleman.

Well, the long and the short of it was that Barry must have spoken to Steve who both talked to Steve's record company, Island and Chris Blackwell and then to Jerry Moss at A and M Records in Los Angeles, Island's licensee and it was all fixed up. Steve talked to Paul Samwell-Smith and the two of them flew to LA to see the film and that, in a nutshell, was how HAROLD AND MAUDE's soundtrack got married to the Cat Stevens 'dub'. Paul and Rosie Samwell-Smith had two Siamese cats for years called Harold and Maude.

So, there we are, except ...

A month or so after all this had gone down, it was New Year's Eve 1972. 1973 loomed. I loathe New Year's Eve and had eschewed parties and the like. I'd taken myself off to Earls Court instead and had been drinking at The Coleherne. I'd come out without scoring a date and walked down Brompton Road feeling chippy, independent and yet strangely pleased that I was alone.

I hung around for a while and walked to the corner of the Earls Court Road and there started chatting to an American. Good-looking guy with deeply smiling eyes, a voice that was partly James Stewart, partly Rod Taylor, full of chuckles and guffaws and I suggested he might like to come with me and drive over to a friend's.

The friend was Micky Hannah and he too was alone. Caroline was with her parents. Everyone seemed to be being alone that night. The American's name was Colin and we ended up having a really great New Year's sitting in Micky's study in Putney in the dark in front of the flames of a roaring log fire and drinking far too much brandy. Colin came back with me and spent the night.

To say we were incompatible in the sack is how best to leave it and we didn't even start to fall in love. We did however, fall deeply into like and the following morning when I drove him back in the West End when David and I went into work, I asked him his surname as we pulled up at one of the lights on Fulham Broadway.

"Higgins," he replied. "Colin Higgins."

The small world theory strikes again with a bullseye.

Q.E.D.

It was indeed the same man who had conceived and written HAROLD AND MAUDE. Whilst a student at UCLA film school.

When it was first released, the movie was not the box office success it later became. It is now legendary and seminal, the stuff of every teenager's emotional bankroll. Oddly, it always was a wild success in continental Europe, especially in France where Cat Stevens was a huge star. HAROLD AND MAUDE played continuously at one Paris cinema, literally, for years.

Thereafter, until he was very rich - which he became in a very short time - Colin would come and stay with us in Putney. When he was writing the English translation of THE IK for Peter Brook later in 1973, I typed up the developing script with him at our empty offices in Curzon Street at weekends. Barry instructed me that I had to secure Colin as a client. I couldn't even bring myself to try. Colin was my friend. And he was someone very special, someone so creative that I always felt pathetically inadequate in his shadow.

Colin was a wonderful man and we shared some wonderful times both in London, Paris, Amsterdam and Los Angeles.

In London one evening, I took him round the corner to meet John Reid, Elton John's manager, at his office in South Audley Street. It was the night that John had clinched the biggest ever deal upto that point in musicbiz history for Elton to record for MCA. I think the advance was some nine million dollars. We all enjoyed a very good dinner.

In Amsterdam, Colin introduced me to my first joint. He rolled it, I smoked it and half-an-hour later I was walking along the canal-side streets thinking every bollard I came across was a thrashing penis, thrusting up through the stones. Bit of acid in there too, perhaps? No. Just wishful thinking.

In Paris, I watched the dress rehearsal of Jean Louis Barrault's production of HAROLD AND MAUDE which Colin had adapted for the stage. (He later adapted it into a Broadway musical but we shall draw a quiet veil over that ...) For the world premiere of Colin's play which has never, incidentally been done in London, J-L Barrault's wife, the divine Madeleine Reynaud of course played Maude.

Somehow, on some wire or some other deus ex machina device, Madeleine seemed to float upwards into the overhead flies when she dies ... In the play.

Little me wasn't even supposed to be in the auditorium. In fact Barrault had banned anyone, on pain of the worst tongue-lashing, from sneaking a look at his *oeuvre* and Colin had given me strict instructions to keep my head down and keep very silent.

So, doubled up with both grief and the effort of not being spotted from the stalls, with tears streaming down my face as the stage lights lowered as Maude goes to heaven and the house lights being brought up, I literally crawled as quickly as I could to what I thought was the exit door I had to take in order to meet Colin, as we had arranged, outside the theatre.

It was the wrong exit.

214

I got hopelessly lost in completely dark and endless corridors. Still weeping helplessly, I groped and fumbled my way forwards, bumping into a chair, some cardboard boxes, a metal bucket ... Finally, almost hysterical, I emerged, sobbing, into the blinding light of the main concourse of the Palais de Chaillot in whose theatre HAROLD AND MAUDE was being presented. In the huge, tall, marble halls illuminated by the vast windows overlooking the cannon-like fountains and, further, the Eiffel Tower, I thought for a moment that maybe it was I who had died and ...

But no. I hadn't died, of course. No one died then, did they? Not in real life. It wasn't heaven at all but the light was a revelation.

All this talk about Colin who died so tragically young in 1988, makes me realise I have to say another word about my grandad. As I've said previously, Albert Frederick had quit this world at the age of eighty-three one Friday night. He died quickly, keeling over in the bathroom having got up to go to the loo. We buried him in the cemetery in Malvern Wells church where he had purchased his plot in anticipation. He now lies next to his father, his wife and two of his sons. The once-empty plot was rapidly filling up. Faster than he'd anticipated. Little had Albert imagined that he'd be put in beside two of his sons. Sons aren't supposed to die first. He always visited the plot every Sunday, after lunch, taking flowers and sitting for a while.

Audrey Cook told me an interesting story. The Wednesday before his death, in the office where he still attended a few hours each day, he suddenly announced early in the afternoon that he was leaving because he felt unwell and that he wouldn't be back. Nor was he, until, of course the following morning when he arrived as per usual at around ten-thirty, having been fed and watered by his housekeeper Suzanane Husson-Saget who had been 'doing' for him since my grandmother's death over ten years earlier.

Later, Audrey found out that Albert had been to visit Mary's grave. Perhaps he knew that he would be unable to go the next Sunday. I like to think that he didn't want her to think he had forgotten. And he died on the same day as his father. Imagine how MY father felt?

Chapter Twenty Three

THE MIDAS YOUTH

A lot of people were attracted by Cat Stevens. It was undoubtedly the Midas Syndrome. Like kissing the Blarney Stone, the perception that rubbing shoulders with gilded people automatically ensures that some of the gilt will rub off is one of the motivating rationales of 'da showbiz'. Not only artists but wannabee managers flocked to Barry's door. Gordon Sutherland was one, Simon Crocker arrived with Juliet Lawson Johnson.

But to get taken on board and to survive there had to be a lot more gang on the plank than merely chance or whim.

The 'right place at the right time' philosophy is, actually, only ever retrospective. It is, willy nilly, accidentalist. Co-incidences can be embraced with no great surprise but they cannot be planned. I have no idea, for example, where I met Peter Burton, my first publisher, for the first time. I know now (and I remember from then) that he worked in Billy Gaff's Management office alongside Mike Gill, marshalling and publicising the careers of Rod Stewart and Billy's other clients like John Mellencamp, aka Johnny Cougar. And I know I did meet Peter in those days but, fifteen years later he publishes my first novel ... ? Right place, right time? Dodgy logic.

Two of Barry's add-on clients arrived in correctly loaded and primed and thoroughly significant forms.

Colin Blunstone and Mike d'Abo.

To accomodate them, Barry also employed Jackie, his brother. All three deserve a great deal saying about them for I found all three very special and one, particularly dear. However, after d'Abo and other thespian acquisitions, I did begin to wonder where Barry's empire-building would stop. His motivation was purely entrepreneurial as theirs was, admittedly, not merely artistic but also commercial. And why not? Music was their job. Some people work in banks. Blunstone and d'Abo worked in the music business. Neither were driven by the same mystical, magical inner demon which drove Steve. Maybe that's why for most of the come-back kids, it's tough ... Steve made it. Neil Sedaka made it. But ...

Please don't write in.

Colin Blunstone became a client of Barry's in 1972. Colin is both blessed and cursed for his voice is one of those in the annals of music history which is so distinctive it is unmistakeably his. Like Dusty Springfield's, like Elton's, like Steve's ... He is one of rock's most gifted interpreters and yet outside the parameters of THE ZOMBIES, he was never to find a relevant long-term career niche. He recorded for CBS and this association brought Barry into contact with a whole other area of the music business which included the celebrated company boss Clive Davis in America, who was first at CBS and later at Arista Records. Useful when re-negotiating a Cat Stevens recording contract. Indeed, Alun Davis, Steve's guitarist and great friend, found a home for his only solo album DAYDO at CBS. Like I said, useful.

I feel Colin Blunstone's voice should have been used as an instrument, as part of a band rather than being hung on the unsuitable peg of a persona which was quiet, shy and incompatible with the high-definition, high-voltage, in-your-face nature required of most stars. I don't think Blunstone was substantial enough to carry a solo career. Sorry, Colin. And by substantial, I mean nasty. This is a compliment, hon. At the time, he had a relationship with Gae Exton who ran a model agency in Bond Street. They split up to go their separate ways, Gae to become the first of the Mrs Christopher Reeves. Superwife.

D'Abo recorded on A and M, a company more like Island in character. Derek Green who managed the satellite organisation whilst d'Abo was there was very laid back. Very cool. D'Abo was a good writer and had a great voice, if not really distinctive and he came across solidly enough. However, outside the MANFRED MANN context and as an individual, he was too nice a guy to cut the cosmic mustard. Married to model Maggie London, he maintained a gentle life style in a comfortable townhouse in Albion Street, Paddington with his daughter Olivia and son Ben. He was multi-talented. He could do too many things too well and probably spread himself too thinly. However, he was loyal and steadfast and true to Twink and I and for the loyalty alone, I salute him.

In those days, artists had to tour. Blood had to be seen to be spilled on the sand. Jackie Krost, Barry's brother, was brought in to hold this side of our management company together. He oversaw the appointment and maintenance of road crews, of hiring and accounting for both van transport and sound equipment as well as the contracting and payment of musicians. Blunstone and d'Abo both maintained bands who were employed individually. They weren't participants in the advance or royalty structure of any record deal. Other than Alun Davis, I knew of no other musician we encountered who became sufficiently indispensable to be included on an individual royalty basis and then only as part of an agreement with the artist directly, not with the record company. But then, I suppose, very few muzos would want to be that tied down to just one other artist other than themselves. Even jobbing muzos dream of stardom and sometimes it happens ... Take Andy Summers again. Who? The Police? Oh, you mean THAT Andy Summers.

Jackie Krost was completely outrageous. As gay as Barry was, Jackie was as straight. All three Krost brothers were totally unalike but no two more than Barry and Jackie. Jackie's mouth was filthy, his appearance zany and over-the-top and his behaviour really did match his braggadocio. He lived to shock and lived up to the after-shock. You've heard all those fabulous stories of roadies and groupies and dressing rooms and dope and sex and rock 'n' roll? They're all true. Just believe them. Jackie was also kind, generous and as golden-hearted as could be in our cage of gilded youth. Jackie soon started to amass a client list of his own. Keith

Christmas, tall, gaunt, long-haired Iggy Pop lookalike and, co-incidentally, ex-Bowie bandsman arrived and Jackie got him a fair deal with Manticore, the management and record company across the road from us in Curzon Street which looked after ELP. Emerson, Lake and Palmer. He also started to reel in the edge-ends of the music business. He worked with a network of local agents and promoters across the kingdom. People like the tremendously kindly and now fabulously successful Maurice Jones from Birmingham. What a very nice man.

And there were other almost-clients for us to think about and ponder. A Barbie doll-like, over made-up girl called Lynsey Rubin came up to see Barry once, introduced by someone. We liked her. She liked us. She became Lynsey de Paul but not at the foot of our stairs. Viola Wills came. None of us could believe she had grown-up children. Gutsy lady. She went on to become one of the decade's disco divas. But she paid the twenty percent to someone else. Not us.

George Lazenby, hot from his badly-handled exit from James Bond-age, was one of the gentlemen callers. We all liked him a lot but he sensibly went to America and did better. David Essex came around a couple of times too. Liked him. He liked us but he stuck with his forever-and-ever manager and became David Essex. Again. I should add his name to the list of successful Come-Back Kids. David Essex had been around for years.

Record producers were beginning to replace film directors in Barry's repertoire of bucks-to-turn. Our last dalliance with a film director after the departure of the unpronounceable Jerzy Skolimowski was Alastair Reid. Barry started a couple of projects with South African Chris Demetriou who produced a duo called DEMICK AND ARMSTRONG but having Paul Samwell-Smith as an independent client apart from his work with Cat Stevens was a far more commissionable prospect. Paul's rise from alcoholism after his departure from THE YARDBIRDS was squarely down to the efforts and commitment and love and care of his wife Rosie. They had a little baby, Nicholas, in 1972 whilst Paul was working on his first big independent job producing a Carly Simon album. Carly, from a comfortable, Gnu Yawk Simon 'n' Schuster publishing background was now singing solo away from her sister and had high industrial

219

hopes riding on her wide shoulders. I never liked Paul Samwell-Smith from the moment he decided life might be better with Carly Simon.

I was one of the ones who helped pick up the pieces in a Hampstead house which echoed with the wailing of a tiny crying baby and which simultaneously throbbed with the hurt shouldered by a loyal wife and friend. I'd seen unhappiness. I'd seen Twinkle sobbing uncontrollably after losing Micky's baby in an Avenue Road clinic. I'd shed a few tears myself over lost loves and comforted others on the loss of their own but up to and including 1972, nothing capped the Samwell-Smith affair.

The depth of hurt that one human being can inflict on another is truly nuclear. Rosie Samwell-Smith was a survivor. There were plenty who weren't. Whilst the tours were out on the road, our office became the hub, the mission control, I suppose where wives and girlfriends would call in for news of their husbands and boyfriends or just ... just to chat, really. Just talk. To a friendly, understanding voice.

Carly herself, an entirely delightful personality in the person-to-person sense, became a sort-of-client for a short while although Barry's management of her was limited to the territory of Europe. I think her name on our list was more valuable than any income which the association might have generated.

The life of an on-the-road muzo has been often documented - no better than by Alvin Gibbs in NEIGHBOURHOOD THREAT, the on-tour story of the IGGY POP Band - but it is rarely mentioned that for those left behind, the limbo is truly strange. It's gotta be. The muzo life-style is fundamentally weird at best and as a *modus vivendi* is incomparable. Well, maybe an explorer ... Mr and Mrs Ranulph Twistleton-Fiennes's perhaps?

Rock 'n' roll widows didn't get the feedback and understanding they required from the women they meet at the school gates or in the doctor's surgery or in the supermarket carpark. They needed to talk to people who knew and who better than us ... The Management. But then we also knew what was going on half-way across the world ... We knew that so-and-so muzo had flown out Miss Yummy Floosie to Arizona where he was bonking the slag dog-rotten in a hotel in Phoenix at the same time as we were oohing and ahhing with Mrs Muzo over her fella's baby's latest new dress or re-assuring and soothing and ... and lying, basically.

It was a rotten business. Probably still is.

And don't think for a minute I'm judging.

Chapter Twenty Four

LEGENDS

There was a nightclub in Burlington Street called LEGENDS. Trevor Clarke used to work there after he'd done his stint at MAUNCKBERRY's. It had posters on the wall, I think, of the great and the good of the century's movie past. Maybe it's still in existence and some tell me it is.

Whatever. Barry Krost Management was about to get its very own legend. A living one. A proper movie star.

Whether Ian McShane arrived before Peter Finch or whether it was the other way around, I've forgotten. Anyway, I'm talking about the legend. Peter Finch.

Finchie, for that was what we called him, was in fact Jill St. Amant's catch. Barry had merely leant on her to call in a past favour. Finchie was by this time married to Eletha Barrett, a pretty Jamaican woman whom he had met during his life on that Caribbean island. She was his, I think, third wife, and was the mother of his, I think, third child. He and Jill St. Amant had met some years previously in Rome when he was going through a bit of a bleak patch.

Having been brought up a great deal in Australia,

Finchie had arrived in England and scored a huge success in the early 'fifties with DAPHNE LAUREOLA at the Royal Court with Edith Evans. He had then made that quantum leap - like Errol Flynn and Stewart Grainger before him - to Hollywood and had managed to crack the combination. 'Though the bottle and the bed had combined to trip him up for a while, Finchie was on the edge of a new phase. He had just made the ground-breaking SUNDAY BLOODY SUNDAY with Glenda Jackson and the aforementioned Murray Head for John Schlesinger and his horizons had lightened up considerably. In fact, his career was pretty damned hot.

Anyway, also hot - for the much argued-over commission which Barry assured her would be hers if she signed Finchie for his agency - was Jill St. Amant. Off Jill duly trotted to Rome where indeed, Finchie was hooked and signed.

It was the start of a lovely time for us. I mean lovely. I'm talking of a man from whose progress spread a bow-wave of bonhomie. Whenever Peter was in London, he would spend a lot of the day between appointments up in the office with we workers. He embraced an entirely unaffected democracy. He seemed to love the atmosphere of organised chaos, the arrival of the stream of roadies with expense sheets, parking wardens with final warnings, people's boyfriends and girlfriends. He was the most unstarry star I've ever met and we all adored him. Equally, Eletha. It was like a favourite uncle and aunt arriving. Of course Eletha was not the most sophisticated soul on the planet but she was true and good and loved her man more than anything and was fiercely and vociferously protective of him and what she saw as his interests. She asked no questions and he had no need to tell her lies. He was not about to leave her and she wasn't about to take him for anything more than her housekeeping. I thought they were very good together and I wish they'd had more time to be good.

Through Finchie's arrival, I also met his very formidable but, I thought, quite wonderful mother, Betty Stavely-Hill who lived in a tiny pink house in Bury Walk almost next to where-once-was-Meridiana and where-now-is-Theo-Fennell in Fulham Road. Here was a fearsomely patrician lady, full of stories, brimming with complaints, at once phlegmatic and passionate. Rather like her son, really. Loathed the idea of his having wives who, as she insisted, bled him dry... Why Finchie never turned out gay is an amazement. Lends total credibility to the genetic theory.

We all took great pride in our movie star. He was inexhaustibly generous with himself. I was invited to his fiftieth birthday party which Barry gave in the White Elephant. Finchie had just made LOST HORIZON which re-united him with John Gielgud. I spent a delightful evening listening to their escapades with John G's hand firmly squeezing my knee all through dinner. At one point, Finchie looked across the table, realised what was going on, winked and mouthed, "Thankyou," nodding and slightly raising an eyebrow in the direction of that verray parfit, gentle knight. I too am now way past fifty. Finchie's dead but Sir John, thank god, soldiered on until he died, almost in harness, at age ninety-six in 2000, having made it to the new millennium.

Though much of the work to which Finchie rented his stature after SUNDAY BLOODY SUNDAY was not of the best - ENGLAND MADE ME, LOST HORIZON - NETWORK was at last sufficient reason to make of him a movie monument. Anyway, it saw him out and won him his Oscar.

He was very special. Looking for the last resting place of Valentino in the Hollywood Memorial Cemetery and having just found Tony Beckley whom I knew rested outside, next to Tyrone Power, I rounded a corner of the adjoining mausoleum, found Valentino, turned round and there was Peter ... Sleep tight, Finchie.

Finchie opened yet more doors for Barry. Our company became instantly legitimised in the domains of the movie moguls as well as the music megabosses. The aforementioned Ian McShane walked through one of these doors. He came equipped with a stand-in who also acted as bodyguard who bore a spooky resemblance to his master. McShane had an unshakeable belief in his future and never questioned the claim he had to stardom. He always makes me think of that Randy Newman song about SHORT PEOPLE. I think Ian was to make only one movie whilst with Barry, the much under-rated THE LAST OF SHEILA. He was another who never made it when he tried his luck in California. His purchase of the LOVEJOY books and his subsequent producing and starring in the television productions finally brought him both wealth and celebrity.

Through yet another door, however, walked Angela

Lansbury.

Angela is of course now hugely famous and hugely wealthy. In those days, she was generally unknown in her native Great Britain and probably entirely anonymous in Southern Island where she had also made a home. She was however, deeply famous on Broadway for theatrical performances in shows like MAME in which she appeared with the then equally theatrical Bea Arthur. Descended from one of the British socialist Lansburys of the politicking nineteen-twenties and 'thirties, Angela and her family went to America for safety like many British families just before the war and stayed there.

She first appeared in Hollywood as the war drew to a close and she appeared in NATIONAL VELVET and in GASLIGHT. Important pictures. But Angela was not a beauty. She was interesting, yes. She had a career of sorts but she was mainly involved in being married to Peter Shaw, a Hollywood talent agent. They had three children, David, Anthony and Deirdre. Deedee. There were five very distinct and distinctive personalities in the Shaw family. Though several of the individuals were dysfunctional, the family functioned just great and this was entirely down to Angela who just hung on in and persevered and was determined. When danger threatened, Angela could make her family do what every family should do for the support of its individual members. She pulled up the gangplank, battened down the hatches, closed ranks and waited for the storm to pass.

The family that strays together, stays together. Despite all her best efforts, they're still straying ...

Any road up, Angela arrived in London to be Mama Rose in GYPSY at the Piccadilly Theatre and the family finally rented one of Richard Page's flats in Earls Court. Lavender country. Covenient. Close to everything. Fritz Holt and Barry Brown were the American producers who came over to present the show which starred Barry Dennen and ... yes, Babette's little Baby Beauty! The very little, very squeaky, very ginger, very ringletted Baby Bonnie. Bonnie Langford.

Terrifying. Art imitating life imitating art. Full circle. Look up own bottom. Stay on carousel. Hang on ... Career.

The show was a huge success. After Angela's run,

Dolores Gray took over and it could have just run and run ... The Lansbury-Shaw connection stood Barry in very good stead as he began to lay the foundations to operate equally from Los Angeles as from London. His uncle's SEALANDAIR travel agency should have been able to float on the stock exchange. Barry's travel account was enormous and his cousin Karen became my best telephone friend. Edgar Lansbury was of course an extremely influential producer in Los Angeles and later, Angela and Peter Shaw's eldest son David went to work for Barry when finally ...

Ah. But that's jumping ahead a little too fast.

Oh. Yes. A third legend arrived up our stairs.

Rose Tobias Shaw was a name not only to conjure with in casting circles. Hers was a name to make grown men quake at the knees. Along with Irene Lamb, Maude Spector ... These women, with the exception of a very few men, constituted that channel which led from the casting call to the casting couch. I jest, of course. The director and the producer, once established as a unit, had to find actors to play the part their writer(s)'s script called for. Other than the starring roles which didn't usually fall within the remit of the casting director's brief, first choices of cast may not be available over the shooting period due to previous commitments. Prices might be too high. The casting director was instructed to check all availabilities, arrange interviews if necessary or at least current photographs and résumés and conclude a financial arrangement with the successful candidate's agent.

Having originally immigrated from Poland in the 'thirties as a teenager, Rose Tobias had come to London from New York, her second home, in the 'fifties after a brief career as an actress and then time in the casting office at CBS. She met and married the actor Maxwell Shaw and never more looked homeward. They made a handsome couple.

Rose knew everyone there was to know in the movies and cast every big American picture which was to shoot - or which had a part schedule - in Europe. Barry lured Rose away from casting with a catalogue of promises. He lured her into a cold, unprotected outpost. Colder than LOST HORIZON which was how and where Barry came to get too close to her.

Pithy, succinct and scrupulously above-board, this

226

elegant blonde New Yorker brought the final stamp of respectability and legitimacy to Barry's management company which, it has to be said, was completely original.

Nowhere in the showbiz firmament at that time was there an outfit with such a diverse client list and with such huge potential. Rose only stayed a brief while but I'm glad she did. Our small worlds were due to collide again.

Chapter Twenty-Five

A MAN OF PROPERTY

David and I moved to Werter Road in Putney. SW 15. One street south of Montserrat Road. Very convenient. A brand-new Sainsburys on the corner of Putney High Street replaced their old-fashioned grocer's glazed-tiled food-hall on the high street proper. Putney was a bit far out but we got used to the journey to and from work. I had bought a two-bedroomed flat on the ground and lower ground floors of a substantial semi-detached Edwardian house at 31 Werter Road, together with sole use of the garden but the property wasn't yet converted. So ... Free of charge, the developer allowed me use of the first-floor flat next door and David and I lived there for six months until the duplex was ready. I was thus able to ask for alterations to the initial plans for my own flat in which the builders readily acquiesced as all my suggestions saved them money. They also saved time.

In this interim period, I'd had a brainstorm. Rather a libido surge. Outside the Coleherne pub one night in November 1973 I had met Alan Zubik, a handsome, hairy twenty-five year old Canadian who, I fancied, had all the worldliness I had yet to acquire. To me, New World accents always make the speaker sound incredibly hip and cool. Mr. Zubik, tall, muscular, turned-on and unphaseable had obviously been around the block a coupla times.

He took me on a sexual rollercoaster ride which taught me a lot but left me, not only breathless but thoughtful. Alan was the first of that generation of North American gays who were not only not queer, but gay and then some. His thoughts revolved entirely about pleasure, immediate gratification and whereas he was also somewhat mystical, I was merely mystified ... I honestly couldn't keep up. I just didn't know how.

I knew from nothing.

He, quite rightly, believed he could sleep with anyone, that he was answerable to no one and that sex didn't compromise his affections. That he fitted copious and frequent amounts of sex into his life, seamlessly and ingenuously, only served to remind me that I was still an uptight, hide-bound little Protestant prig dripping guilt and fierce jealousy all down my gingham humbug.

We spent Christmas in Malvern with my family. Not a success.

I brought the whole affair to an end in January when Barry Krost one night decided to flirt with Alan who had decided it was nice to be flirted with by David's boss. Like,

"Is the dynamite souffle a little too near that romantic candle, dear?"

After taking us both out to dinner, Barry went home with Alan himself.

"You're sure it's alright?" Barry asked, repeating himself at least three times before I dropped them off.

"Alan, wants to," I replied, "he's his own boss. I'm not his keeper."

My face felt kinda egg-splattered that night. Like,

"Eat shit, David ..."

The following morning I called for Barry to go to work as usual. Alan, naked but for the sheet, smiled at me sheepishly from Barry's antique brass double-bed. Barry finally got dressed and announced he was ready to go.

"So," Alan said to me, smiling that devilishly charming, grin, his long, dark chestnut hair falling over his handsome, bearded, otherwise-irresistible face, "I'll be seeing you later, yeah?"

"I don't think so," I replied, quite firmly but with a sort-of smile. "Do you?" I added, cocking an eyebrow, feeling like Joan Crawford delivering a final *coup de grace* with a steely glint in narrowed eyes. I turned on my heel and, for once, Barry followed me out.

And he opened his own car door.

"Is everything okay?" he asked, rather haltingly as we reached the road junction on Brompton Road behind Earls Court Arena. He had to keep his smile up, though. He had to be flip and glib and wise-ass.

"Of course," I murmured. "Why shouldn't it be?"

"Now look, about Alan ...," Barry began.

"Who?" I said and flashed a smile back.

Barry was silent the rest of the way to Curzon Street. I chattered on about this and that and whatever. I felt strangely distant from Barry. It was a distance that was never to narrow. Although he'd never be able to admit it, he'd trespassed and although there was nothing I could do about it, I would never see him as my friend again. He did it to me once again ... year or so later.

It was the killer. The final straw.

When I returned home that Gethsemane night to the flat, Alan Zubik was no longer there. I never saw him again. He'd taken his cue and for that I thank him. He was a true libertine but I couldn't cope with any more sexual cavaliering. As I've already said, a boy can stand just so much competition and although it often takes two, there was only room for one on my learning curve.

Soon after Alan's departure, I learned what it was to forget the rules ...

In Putney there is a famous towpath which runs the length of the river bank between Putney and Hammersmith bridge and late at night, on this towpath, in the dark ... Sparing you the blushes, I fell foul of the law and was arrested by plain clothes police implementing ...the law? Arrested and finger-printed and scheduled for a court appearance, I spent a weekend of sheer misery waiting for the hammer to fall. Newspaper reports, police calling at Barry's office, the press ... "CAT STEVENS ASSISTANT ARRESTED FOR INDECENCY!" All this whirled like razor blades in gravel through my mind. As the incident was to conclude, I was merely fined although this conviction bore heavily on my later life.

And I was one of the lucky ones. Gay men were still, are still, being imprisoned for pursuing their proclivities in private. And whatever the 'rules', I can't understand why the depths of elder bushes half a mile away from the nearest road in the middle of the night doesn't constitute private.

Like a beaten dog, I licked my wounds.

Barry was in London less and less often. New York or Los Angeles were the alternatives. I was left to hold the fort. Jane Asher was pregnant, living with Gerald Scarfe, the intimidating and revolutionary cartoonist who set standards for a new brand of political and social satire. I kept that secret for her full term. It's good to lie.

Did I get a cleverly decorated cake? Hello? I'm waiting.

I acquired a secretary, Alex Foster, younger sister to actress Julia. Alex adored the music business. We worked together for several years. Off and on. Charles Laurence's play MY FAT FRIEND had been a huge success.

"David, d'you know Michael Codron?"

"We met, once. A few years ago in Malvern," I replied and shook the hand that fed a lot of Shaftesbury Avenue in those days. "Malvern Festival ... Public and Confidential?"

Mr. Codron had the grace to pretend to graciously remember. I don't somehow think Ben Levy's play was one of Michael's greater successes. And should he know me from a hole-in-the-ground? Should he fuck.

The international success of Charles Laurence's MY FAT FRIEND opened up a range of opportunities and exciting international outings. Charles's play boasted a deceptively simple story. Fat girl falls for thin man. Thin man goes away. Fat girl diets to please thin man. Thin man returns only to announce that he doesn't like thin girls ... But ex-fat now-thin girl has discovered that life is all about pleasing herself, not thin men.

Very contemporary quasi-feminist philosophy. Women loved it. Good thing. If women don't like the idea of a play, married couples don't go ... Western world runs on married couples. No married couples, big flop!

Plays which have a good London run are traditionally

guaranteed not only repertory and touring income in Britain for some years but also, after translation, productions across the world which can multiply by a tenfold factor the playwright's earnings from the initial show.

The Broadway production of MY FAT FRIEND by Liz McCann and Nell Nugent for the James Nederlander organisation was memorable for Lynn Redgrave and George Rose. It was rather magical visiting Liz and Nell in their offices above the legendary Palace Theatre on Broadway and Times Square.

The Paris production of MY FAT FRIEND was also pretty glamorous and had something to do with a Rothschild and his mistress. All very *fin de siecle*.

Supervising the collection of monies from the several productions of Charles's play on the stages of the world including German and Spanish translations between 1972 and 1975 was an education and introduced me to a world of theatrical production which was interesting, briefly, later.

Charles' second play, SNAP!, was a delicate little piece all about someone catching a dose of the pox. Indeed CLAP! had been the original title and Mr. Codron obviously didn't want to touch such nastiness with a ten-foot pole. Instead, after I had personally delivered the manuscript to Maggie Smith at her half-timbered semi-detached off the Fulham Road, Michael White picked up the option to produce it as Maggie's reaction had been positive. To reading the play, that is.

The subsequent production at The Vaudeville in The Strand was, I thought, awfully funny. Not the greatest success, it ran but a bit and had few if any overseas airings. Working with the Michael White office brought me into contact with the very young but the very easy-to-work-with Robert Fox and his soon-to-be first wife Celestia Sporberg. Very nice people.

In my time with Barry, I think there were two John Osborne openings, both at The Royal Court in Sloane Square. One, WEST OF SUEZ with Jill Bennett was languid and sub-tropically objective about the death of England and Englishness, one of Osborne's pre-occupations. HOTEL IN AMSTERDAM and TIME PRESENT I think also figured. Fifteen years later I read a letter from him published in the London Evening Standard ... "Dear Sir, Etc etc

... and when I go to the theatre now, everything's written by someone called Ron and directed by someone called Les ..." Osborne was a delicious snob.

The second production was A SENSE OF DETACHMENT, random, utterly incomprehensible, full of quotations and hivings-off from the writings of others. All these had to have licences granted for theatrical use and Linda Singer, the Osbornes' secretary at Chelsea Square, was inundated. Barry offered my services to help with the work in order to make the deadline. We must have done okay. No one got sued. Rachel Kempson was one of the company. Actors whilst they're working on a show are unbelievably loyal. At one performance, the audience, as usual, were getting restless to the extent of emitting rumblings of resentment. The redoubtable Miss Kempson, (Lady Redgrave, remember) broke off and strode to the front of the stage. Admonishing one of the louder malcontents, she bellowed,

"If you sit down and shut up you might just learn something!"

Sadly, I don't think there was anything to learn.

Atop the main house at the Royal Court, however, sat the newly opened Theatre Upstairs, a small space but one which had spawned a ground-breaking production which we all trooped in to see and emerged duly converted to a new, even more irreverent form of stage musical. Richard O'Brien's THE ROCKY HORROR SHOW, directed by Jim Sharman pole-axed me. The flagrantly ambivalent sexuality of the show's hero Frank'n'Furter made us howl. I just loved it.

ROCKY HORROR transferred no sooner than it had opened, first to the old Classic Cinema (now demolished) halfway down the Kings Road and later to the old Essoldo, renamed The Kings Road Theatre in the show's honour. The building is now back to being a movie house. Apt.

ROCKY's star, Tim Curry, had given a hugely bravura performance but it was not until a couple of years later that I was to really get to know the depth of his bravura which was, rather disappointingly, the antithesis of the androgyny which he paraded every night on stage and which had become fashionable. David Bowie was braver about things like that then, Peter Straker had fearlessly made it his trademark and someone called Mark Feld wished ... but didn't dare and became Marc Bolan instead. Glam rock as a genre lessened the high-brow profile of the threatening poofter aspect of androgyny and brought the pantomime aspects of men-in-make-up to TOP OF THE POPS every week on Thursday nights. SWEET, MUD, SLADE ... Aaah!

Straight men in layers of Boots No. 7 had never had it so good and not a drop of blood had been shed. The gay boys had already done all the fighting for their straight brothers to come out in a bloodless coup.

Chapter Twenty-Six

OUT OF THE BLUE

Micky Hannah had left Caroline Gray.

Probably sensibly.

He'd taken up with a sweet, bubbly wannabee actress, namely Joanna Lyall, whose parents were wealthy and who lived in a tall townhouse in Brompton Square next to Brompton Oratory. Micky himself had also become a man of property and had bought an elegant, tall-windowed first floor flat in Earls Court and had acquired a fabulous vintage Mercedes sports car.

He had also been seeing a lot of the newly-independent Sara Randall who had been helping him with his acting aspirations and indeed had sent him, successfully, to a series of casting appointments, from one of which he got his first television part in one of the VAN DER VALK series, set in Amsterdam about a Dutch police detective. He was as pleased as Punch and deservedly so. He was still modelling, extremely successfully, and had become well-known for intelligence, punctuality and affability, three qualities photographers often find in short supply.

Micky came around to Werter Road one weekend in the evening to tell me he was off to Spain for a very well-paid job, modelling jeans in an exotic location in the south of Spain, co-incidentally with my old flatmate Mark Ridge. I told him to make sure he gave my love to Mark and to behave. He said he would and he wouldn't. Respectively.

Micky looked fabulous and dashing and so, so glamorous as he waved and accelerated away in his beautiful sports car into the evening light. I felt so proud and so full of love for him that our friendship had endured and was still so strong that he wanted to come and say good-bye just because he was off on a week's modelling assignment. I was surely blessed with a great friend. Not six months earlier, he had driven me down to my parents where a couple of weeks enforced R and R on some anti-depressant drug cured me of a fit of the glooms where I couldn't stop crying ... Mick had more than repaid me for my earning our bed and board way-back-when in Paris in the Hotel Meurice. Then. Way back then.

I thought we'd come out just-about evens.

Having been given the thumbs-down by Emperor Krost, other dear desperate wannabees had even started coming to me. Some of them even started coming to me, just for me. God! It must have been a desperate time.

It was certainly the time when Micky had been insisting that Twinkle get back to work. So inconsolable had she been at ultimately losing him, Twinkle had written for Micky and about Micky a series of songs and I was impressed. Barry was entirely unimpressed, partly, I fancy because for him to have been impressed would have been to endorse my judgment and recommendation and that would have been a toughie. Mainly, however, I think his reasons were that Twinkle came to us cold. No old existing recording or publishing contract to renegotiate with new contacts in the biz.
The truth was that Twinkle was broke and needed a leg-up. Barry didn't work like that. It wasn't to Barry's taste to work gradually with artists he believed in, over a long period of time, nursing them and encouraging them ... He'd done all that with actors and he didn't want to do it any more. Unless Barry could get either a buck or a fuck or preferably both from a business situation, he wasn't interested.

So Mick asked me to do for Twinkle. And Mick and I were honour-bound, weren't we? Forged together for eternity beneath the Indalo's rainbow in the wide, blue yonder. Remember?

Twinkle's writing was immediate and very black-and-white. She wrote story-songs, movies-in-miniature. Some in-house opinions wanting to be clever and, thus, cruel would and could have called her style simplistic and her talent trivial. She most definitely wasn't merely bubblegum. I knew she had something.

That something, it's true, was a million miles away from the Cat Stevens substance which some were going so far as calling poetry. But Twinkle's work wasn't sub-anything.

What Twinkle wrote was English country music. And yet, of course, there wasn't any such thing. No such *genre*. Twinkle wrote aching songs from the heart about loves-lost and loves-gone-wrong and revenge and jealousy and hate and home-making and love-after-death ... Wonderful songs that needed a record company like Island or Chrysalis to get behind her and then a damn good publicist. She was a country writer without a country and no local radio stations to get locally famous on. She was a country artist in a land where country is something green and pleasant and rolling and where there are no tortured hearts nor blood stains on the corn, no hoboes, no dirt roads, no pick-up trucks, no geetars, no guns ... None at least which could be admitted to.

So, when Barry made it clear he wouldn't help us, I started to myself. Geoff Heath at ATV Music liked Twinkle's work and signed her up to a publishing contract which started to involve her once again in the creative world. Weekly writers' meetings started to give her confidence although she rarely spoke a word in the meetings themselves except when spoken to. She started to make demos and started to meet the other artists on Barry's books. All of them she'd known before. They were all her peers. Colin Blunstone she liked. Steve she liked for she had known him the days of the Cromwellian club and the Speakeasy when stars socialised with stars, the Bachelors, Paul and Barry Ryan and Peter Noone, with whom Twink had enjoyed a celebrated earlier liason.

Most of all she liked Mike d'Abo who had produced a single called WHEREVER YOU ARE NOW MICKY for Andrew Loog Oldham's Immediate label in 1969.

Dear old d'Abo. He spread himself even thinner when selflessly - it can't have been for the pootling fee he got - he agreed to produce an album for Twinkle if ATV Music would finance it. I

237

had schlepped Twink's demo tapes all round town. David Croker at Rocket, Clive Banks at Island ... All over the place.

It would have only taken one 'phone call from Barry ...

And dear old ATV. They liked Twink and they gave us a five thousand pounds budget and a non-recoupable fee (against the budget and Twink's advance) to Mike d'Abo.

Before we had finalised the booking of the provisionally reserved studio time, we thought a gig might be in order. How would Twinkle's songs go down with an audience? Jackie Krost came to our help. Colin Blunstone was playing a date at The Palace Theatre in Watford. It had just been realised that Sunday evenings in theatres could be leased out to rock/pop concert promoters and earn a fair old whack and Stephen Hollis, then the director of the Palace Watford was no slouch when it came to opportunity. Jackie had promoted several concerts at this sweet suburban theatre and very kindly gave Twinkle the support slot on his Blunstone concert date.

Quite a family affair, it was. We found pianist Brian Cooke - first husband to teevee's Sue Cooke - and made up a scratch band. The rehearsals seemed to go fine and although she was very nervous, Twink sang her Michael Hannah songs - with Micky himself standing with me at the back of the auditorium - to a very acceptable reception.

So ... all set. We booked studio time at Sarm Studios, Sarm East, in Osborne Street in the East End at Aldgate.

Twinkle had started to see Graham Rogers. Later famous for being the Cadbury's Milk Tray Man, Graham Rogers was not only Nev's Agency's highest earning client but, in 1974 and for some years thereafter, the highest-paid male model in the world. In my efforts to assure the nervous Twinkle that it was perfectly alright, in fact more than alright, to go out with guys other than her beloved Micky, I had invited Twinkle and Graham to come round for dinner with my friend Jeremy Hartley, David Minns and I at Werter Road.

Graham was patently a very handsome man. Physically he had everything but he was far from stimulating. He was very good with his hands - I wish, I wish - and could rebuild a Bentley or put up a conservatory or a fence at whim. Councillor Sid was heard by one and all exclaiming on Graham's handiwork regarding a new fence outside their house:

"Look! What do you think of my son-in-law's fine erection?"

But Graham himself was then very shy and came over as more wooden than his erections which rather accounts for his not being snapped up by Cubby Broccoli when his name appeared on the list of casting suggestions as a replacement for the actor playing James Bond. But he was kind and, then, even-tempered with decent prospects at least and seemed to absolutely adore Twinkle. But maybe Mr. Broccoli had been warned off men who advertise chocolate? George Lazenby had, after all, done a lot for Fry's chocolate cream.

But Graham was okay by us. And he certainly had Micky's relieved stamp of approval. If Graham could stay on the peg, Micky would be off the hook.

After we'd eaten, it was suggested that we have a 'go' with the *ouija* board. Out it came, the glass containing the letters of the alphabet written on scraps of paper and placed round the edge of the polished tabletop. Then I reversed the glass and someone duly lit the candles, turned out the lights ... And so we began.

I knew it was not going to be a fun session. The upturned glass tumbler was sluggish and sullen and slow and screeched like teacher's nails on the blackboard as it slid over the tabletop. I asked it if there was anyone who should not be present at the table and the tumbler medium very quickly went in succinct succession to the letters T-W-I-N-K-L-E. The lady herself was pretty much four sheets to ... In those days she always arrived with her own bottle of scotch and accompanying coca cola in a brown paper bag. Twinkle went and lay down on the sofa and slept.

Which left Graham and David and I and Jeremy.

From thereon in, the spellings were all very comprehensible but the substance was indecipherable. What, pray, were we mere mortals supposed to make of:

"Mother, this is a beautiful place here ..."

or, when asked where the beautiful place was,

"Amalgamamalgamamalgam ..."?

It was getting very late. Twinkle needed sleep. The following weeks would see her back in a proper recording studio for the first time in five years.

I was at home on the Sunday before the start of the recordings. Watching an after-lunch, old, black-and-white movie. As I've indicated, I'd been seeing Jeremy Hartley, the co-owner with Bruce Dundas of the French, Provencal fabric shop in Fulham Road next to Paperchase called Brother Sun Sister Moon. Jeremy had been in Paris, seeing his family and wasn't yet home when the television news in the afternoon broadcast the first reports of a plane crash in Northern France. A Turkish Airlines DC10 had come down in a wood not a few minutes after taking off from Paris. There would be more, it was promised, in the next bulletin.

There was more. Film footage, burning trees, smoke ...

But no wreckage. No people.

Over three hundred people had been on that plane.

Where were they?

Something wasn't right. I had a feeling ... I had a gut feeling ...

My first thoughts were of course for Jeremy and I telephoned only to find that he had indeed just walked in through the door and that he was so whacked out he was staying in that night.

David and I got on with our day. If we went out, I can't think where we went to. I'd just gone to bed when the telephone rang. It was Joanna Lyall. I recognised her voice and I knew what she was going to say.

I knew Mick was dead.

Not only Mick, but Mark too.

All of them. All the models.

I knew most of them.

There had been no survivors.

Over the next few days, it seemed everyone in London knew someone on that aeroplane.

David and I sat up for hours. I don't think I cried. I can't remember. I think I cried later.

When I finally went to bed, I couldn't sleep. I lay in the dark and I swear someone was pounding on my bed. Beating the mattress with invisible fists. I know it was Micky.

How he must have hated letting go.

Amalgam? No. Malaga. A strike had re-routed a direct Malaga-London flight first to Paris and thence, after a change of plane, on a Turkish Airlines flight to London.

It should never have happened.

And yet, we had been warned. Too stupid to heed the warning, too ignorant to know better than to dabble in the dangerous unknown, too arrogant to think past a superficial evening of silly drunken foolishness ...

Amalgam, indeed.

But what would we have done had we known? And who would have believed us?

"Hello? Is that Nev's Agency? Could you tell Michael Hannah to come back to London by train or else he'll be dead? Yes, we think there's gong to be a plane crash."

Hello?

Chapter Twenty-Seven

LEST WE FORGET

For some reason, in Micky's current diary there was a page on which he had written the above again and again and again ... Lest we forget.

In the days afterwards, we did not grieve alone. Our loss was not special like if someone dies of a heart attack or in a car accident. An individual. A one-off. It seemed that the whole of London was numbed by a blanket of grief which settled over our lives like a anaesthetic pall.

I had been truly confused at the prospect of speaking to Twinkle. She was, of course, shattered.

But she went into the studio as scheduled and somehow recorded those songs. There was one called DAYS which was later issued as a single on ATV's Bradleys label.

Don't make me live alone,
Don't make me open
The door of our home
And find nobody there
Just a white leather chair

242

And the smell of the perfume you wore on your skin
How it lingers therein
And the four walls enclose me and grab me within
As I sit and I think in the gloom
Of that once lovely, now lonely room ...

Days
When I adored you
Days
When you longed for me too
I don't want to live
'Cos I still love you still ...

She'd written it ages before.

But then the craziness set in. Contagious craziness. The mediums. The ball-gazers. The entirely fantastical. Even I went to one. Some person in a second floor flat in a south-western suburb. It did me good. For half-an-hour.

Then at the studio one day, Twinkle showed up with Mark Phillips, a young very, very handsome boy who lived with his artist parents just off the Kings Road and whom Twinkle believed quite seriously was Mickey's re-incarnation.

We all became enablers that day; co-conspirators. What did we know about death and bereavement and the attendant reactions? We were grieving ourselves too. If Twinkle wanted to believe Mark was Mick reincarnated, let her ... Who were we? And Mark got a career out of it. He did, in a way, replace Mick in the model-slot. Mark also wanted to make music. He was - is - a good writer.

There was, also, I hate to admit, the covert reaction which ran 'Anything-For-An-Easy-Life'. Sounds awful to say but we also had a record to make. It was a record that Mick had wanted made and I didn't feel bad in the slightest, coaxing and cajoling Twinkle to finish the schedule. D'Abo was very kind and sensitive as were all the musicians and studio personnel. It could have been very, very much worse. And Twinkle, personally, held together admirably.

I also knew with a nagging certainty - like with toothache when you know you're going to lose the tooth - that even though we had to finish the project, nothing would ever come of it. There was now a lugubrious, mawkish, almost sick quality to the idea of a load of songs about a dead guy. TERRY had been TERRY but art imitating life imitating art?

Once again. *Mira! Mira!* Behold, own bottom ...

And then there was Twinkle herself. With the recording over, she understandably succombed. I knew she would never be in a fit state to promote or publicise her work. Normally nervous and vulnerable in public and therefore unpredicatable, now she was obviously dazed, confused and in deep, deep shock.

Chapter Twenty-Eight

LIFE AFTER DEATH

So more of us should have been so lucky ...

Disco finally reached the UK for us gays and it came with a BANG! Having been intimately involved with its opening management, Jerry Collins and Jack Barrie from the Marquee, Peter Burton in PARALLEL LIVES has written succinctly about BANG! I went, we went, everyone went including the straight press who were intrigued. And probably a little intimidated. Because ...

Entirely because of BANG!, a phenomenon mushroomed. It was later to be called The Pink Pound. Money always intrigues even the entrenched establishment. America had already borne witness. Now it was Europe's turn. Not only could we boys dance a lot, in an increasing number of venues but we could read about where to find these venues in an increasingly widely available gay press. In order to enjoy advertising revenue, the pink press had to have things to advertise. Discos came first, then pubs, then restaurants, then boarding houses then the toys'n'boys'n'other lovejoys we now find in back of all the free rags on a Thursday night in every gay bar in the realm.

Out-of-sight became in-your-face almost overnight with

no catholic pogrom nor mass persecution. No real revolution at all. Just those constant, nagging guerilla raids by the boys in blue for personal profit and statistics.

"In pink, in pink, my sister's dressed in pink ..."

Dangerous. Pink can be a very unbecoming shade and doesn't suit everyone. But at the time, it seemed like such a joyous breakthrough. We went, we danced. We thought we were invincible. We thought we really had overcome, even conquered ...

"The people's flag is deepest pink
Instead of blood it's steeped in ink ..."

Our American friend Peter Buckley, now dead, ran AFTER DARK. Dennis Lemon, now dead, ran GAY NEWS. My friend Tim Hughes, still alive thank god, worked on a magazine called ... JEREMY. Frightful name! Of course, there were no videos then, only magazines for boys to wank over and this hardcore porno was mostly imported, accompanied by incomparably awful stories. Erotica had a helluva long way to go despite Mike Arlen's pioneering efforts.

Every pub in London it seemed was suddenly vying to host either gay night at its existing disco or convert one of its upper floors or adjoining function rooms into a dance venue. We had one in Putney High Street. We went. Our friend Malcolm Jones went. Without gay discos, there would have been no gay scene and no gay press. Another endless loop.

Malcolm Jones asked me to accompany him on an evening when he had to entertain his client Neil Sedaka. We went to dinner at Provans, our favourite restaurant where I spent an uncomfortable two hours and then some trying to find as many ways as possible of saying 'no' without being downright offensive. I suppose some people only need 'No' for their answer. Turns them on?

Anyway, I mention the evening only because it raises the whole thing about married men and being just a l'il' bit gay, y'know, all stuff which I've never been able to handle. Especially as I was supposed to say nothing about 'it'. What do I do? Ignore 'it'? What am I supposed to do? The answer to that one, patently, was that I was supposed to forget it ever happened. Well, I can't handle off and on, only when it's convenient, NIFTW - (Like, Not In Front Of The

246

Wife.) Now there's a confession.

I can accept, but I cannot for the life of me understand and I'm damned if I'm gonna condone. I've lied and postured and ducked and dived so often in my life for married or bi-sexual men or gay men lying that I choose now, at my advanced age, to remove myself from their arena completely. I'm not being judgmental, just ... Gimme a break? Has no one ever told people like Sedaka that you can only be married and go with boys with the camouflage of the connivance of others, probably good friends whom you are essentially compromising? Like, just don't be married. Don't lie. It's very easy. Millions of us do it quite successfully.

The 'seventies liberation also ushered in that curse of every progressive, revolutionary movement. Ism and schism. Freedom also entitles you not to belong. And with schism, came gay politics. There were soon gay socialists and gay conservatives. Gay people started to take sides. Against themselves. With organisation came identification and the loss of the luxury of anonymity, privacy and secrecy. It suddenly became incumbent to be out and to belong.

BANG! was not a total surprise to me for I had seen it twice before on the two occasions I had been to America. I'd danced it but I'd had no need to live it. I don't know when Barry relented but relent he had done and instructed me to book myself a ticket and come out to Los Angeles where he had rented a house on Kings Road, just north of Sunset Strip.

1974 was the year Barry left England. It was the start of the beginning of the end of his London company although the end was to take another twelve months in coming. Ends are often so goddam slow.

Since 1971, the more time Barry spent in California the more he liked it and the less he wanted to return to London. Life in Britain was pokey compared to LA. It even felt parochial, slow and backward. Barry wanted to succeed in Los Angeles not merely for business reasons but also because he was at that age and at that point in his life where a gay man needs a lift. A gay man only had to walk down any street in the designated area to realise that lifts there were to be had a-plenty.

Barry had lived with Tony Beckley for many years. They went their own ways sexually but together, as a life unit, they surely

247

were. Or, at least, that's how Tony thought of them. Barry went through a fair few fallings-in-love in Los Angeles before finally meeting Doug Chapin. Then, the idea of moving to Los Angeles permanently took root.

Barry left London. It was as simple and as quick as that. Of course, he left material things behind - shoes, winter coats, furniture, a couple of Hockney prints from Bernard Jacobson's gallery - but the main thing he left behind was his old life and everything and everyone associated with it for we all knew he had left us.

Except Tony Beckley.

It was left to me to drive over to Fulham and explain to Tony that Barry wouldn't be coming back.

"But for how long, Daisy?"

"Never, Tone."

"Never?"

Silence. Incomprehension. Shock.

"Never?"

Tears. Sobs.

"Why didn't he tell me? Oh, Daisy! Why didn't he tell me himself?"

Oh, it was wonderful job, mine. I've played executioner too many times.

I have to explain about Daisy. In the light of later dubbings, my nickname was given me by Carl Miller, Cat Stevens' tour manager. In the early 'seventies, I always wore boots. Cowboy boots. Most of one year, until they wore away completely, I wore a pink pair. With 501's, okay? Cockney rhyming slang turns boots into daisy roots. Hence, Daisy. Okay? This is no faggot thing, right!

America, here I come. I was well-used-to and well-known at the American Embassy in Grosvenor Square. In the past it had been my job to arrange for the artists' working visas to be stamped in the passports by the Immigration staff. This time it was my B1 Visa whose stamp my passport proudly bore.

New York, where my first class flight initially took me was on my itinerary due to MY FAT FRIEND business. It was an amazing experience. Also an amazing experience was my first trip to the Everard Baths. New World bath house culture in pink parlance had been spoken of in awed and whispered tones by those transatlantaeans whose paths crossed ours. The sod 'em 'n' tomorrah licence which liberation had apparently brought with it was mind-warpingly blinding to someone whose idea of being really abandoned was a passing fumble in the loo behind the Magpie and Stump at World's End.

The Everard Baths WAS the world's end as far as my experience of rampant sexual behaviour was concerned. It was an uncappable first in first class experience and I shall remember it forever. My unleashed libido soared on a bungee leash and I felt the power like I'd never felt it and like I'll never feel it again. Like they would be soon be singing in the discos,

"Oh yeah, oh yeah, I got the power ..."

Flying first-class on a jumbo jet to LA on the shores of the other shining sea was also mind-blowing. Champagne all the way. A cabin steward carved roast rib of beef at thirty thousand feet and when he served it, it tasted good!

When I took a cab in to the Hyatt House on Sunset from LAX, I felt as though I was coming home. The skyline of the Hollywood Hills put me in mind of the silhouette of the distant Malvern Hills. The feeling has never been dulled. I always think I'm home. Like sitting on an earthquake faultline has a little in common with living with my family? Seismology must surely also apply to humans.

Barry's new friend Doug didn't exactly arrive with no baggage. Doug had this friend ... who could sing ... and write ... and play. Indeed he could and his name was Lewis Furey, a Canadian Leonard Cohen-cum-Cat Stevens-cum ... Indeed, Lewis was very talented, probably more talented than Steve. And he soon had Barry behind him as he had had Doug. I saw this and winced, for the implications were inevitable. And exactly what must Steve have thought ... ? It was direct competition; Sam Shepherd wrote about the phenomenon magnificently in his play TEETH AND SMILES. The king is dead. Long live the king.

And, of course, into the middle of this champion artistry, I had brought the newly mixed TWINKLE album.

Well, you'd've thought it was a vial of rabies I'd taken out of my briefcase. Plainly, Barry wanted nothing brought over

249

from the old country. The old life. He didn't even hanker for a jar of marmite.

However, Barry did allow me to hire a car for the duration of my trip. I can't believe I was so adventurous in it but in it, I discovered the bath-houses, the clubs, the bars and ... Studio One. On Robertson Boulevard and La Peer just south of Santa Monica Boulevard. It was an almost tripping experience to stand on the balcony of the old cinema and look down on a dance-floor packed with a thousand gay men line-dancing The Madison or whatever the craze was. I soon picked up the step.

In back of the disco there was a cabaret theatre. I saw GOTHAM there and Charles Pierce. Quite breath-taking. And after dancing, one could of course stay up all night and roam the corridors and crannies of the bathhouses where athletic and acrobatic and achievement sex was intoxicating. Sexually, Alan Zubik had been a turning point for me. Not to put too fine a turning-point on it, he'd turned me into a down 'n' dirty sex slut and whatever he could do, I had decided that I could do too; but better.

The continuing fire of abandon kindled in New York was totally joyous, the wantonness was liberating and the sense of self-esteem truly validating. I can honestly say that through sex, I came into my own. The *entree,* however, obliterated immediate thoughts of love and romance. It was an undeniably greedy time. But undeniably very friendly and open. I met some really nice people. I mean, I talked to them. Afterwards.

Selfish? Perhaps. But very, very giving. I wish I could say it was necessary but, as times have since demonstrated, gay promiscuity was a self-determining necessity. I do believe that after so many centuries of hole-in-the-wall existence since the demise of the civilised cultures of classical times, modern gay men had to do what they did sexually, whatever it led to, whatever it perpetrated. Sounds cruel but its the only logic, isn't it? Sort of *per gloryhole, ad gloria?*

I glimpsed America on my first acquaintance from a very privileged perspective and was instantly seduced. Not only did it seem that every radio station was playing either Cat Stevens or Elton John or David Bowie or Carly Simon, but the immediate invitation to be myself was unrefusable. There weren't just little corners where a boy could be gay. There were whole streets, whole neighbourhoods ... In New York, Greenwich Village, in San Francisco, The Castro and in Los Angeles, Boystown as the city of West Hollywood had been dubbed in its aptly zip-coded 9-0-0-sixty-nine location. I thought when I first landed at LAX that I might have arrived in paradise. Via Twa-Twa to La-La land.

But I found the price of paradise too steep. Too steep then and too steep now. I glimpsed another perspective of the LA phenomenon via my friendship with John Reid, Elton's manager, that nine million dollar deal man.

As I've said before, we'd met, I don't know where and had become acquaintances. I'd even spent a night down at his and Elton's Virginia Water house. Hercules, I think it was called. I was led down to Wentworth from London, in convoy, by Michael (John) Howard, John's driver who twenty years later became such a brave public face for the Aids patients of our land.

Anyway, an *ad hoc* intimacy developed which both John and I enjoyed whenever, wherever. No names, no pack drill ... Barry was very jealous and so I never talked about Reid which infuriated Barry further as he was as curious as hell about this entirely more famous manager. Reid was becoming a significant personality in his own right. I think by this time Barry trusted me about as much as Mary Queen of Scots would have trusted a knife-grinder.

Reid wasn't being boyfriends with anyone much at the time and he would take me places where Barry wouldn't naturally gravitate. I was thrilled when he asked me to go to Doug Weston's world famous Troubadour on Santa Monica Boulevard and Doheny. It was where both Steve and Elton had first made their musical marks and thereafter, six thousand miles away, we who remained at home would read, assiduously, every week in Billboard and Cashbox the reviews of the artists and bands currently appearing. My first night at the Troubadour was the occasion of some music industry bash where the great and the good were gathering to view the competition's latest artist in a showcase arena.

It was also the place and the night I was first introduced to cocaine. In a lavatory. Pinned against the flimsy partition by two other captains of the music industry whilst two more, desperate for their honk at the lovin' spoonful, banged on the door and told us to hurry the fuck up! I have to say it didn't do a lot for me. I have had the occasional snifft since but ... No. Not for me.

I could only afford being in California on company expenses; both Barry Krost and Cat Stevens were well able to afford their merest whim on their own accounts. Steve, after all, had conquered the whole of North America and Barry ... Well, he wasn't much interested in Omaha or Nebraska but there were these few square miles of the state of California with which he had become infatuated. Hollywood, Los Angeles, Beverly Hills, Malibu. And Burbank. What Barry hadn't conquered as a child actor, he was now claiming as of right. On the other hand, this was territory in which Cat Stevens was entirely disinterested.

There is something sacred about friendships between men - the David and Jonathan sorts of friendships. The kingmaker friendships. At the same time as they can render the weak strong, simultaneously they can expose the strong to debilitating weakness. Male friendship is truly a double-edged sword for when it goes wrong, it truly goes wrong. When friendships also embrace business relationships, mountains that seem to be immovable and immutable can suddenly appear dangerously frail structures. I'm thinking of John Reid and Elton here as well as, obviously, Barry Krost and Cat Stevens. And Tom Parker and Elvis. And, later, Tom Watkins and Neil Tennant and the Goss Bros. Bowie and Tony de Fries, Don Arden and his people ...

Because America empowers, the feeling that there is so much more to lose is magnified. By giving the illusion of control, America makes you feel that you can do anything, be anything, go anywhere however and whenever you like. America makes the possible likely, makes opportunities out of dreams. It can also make monsters from mere mutations, delusions from pretensions, compulsions out of idle ambitions and addictions out of harmless weekend tokes. America gives you control of everything except yourself. The self-control has to come from you.

It is such excess of opportunity which renders failure so unconscionable.

Of course, I got given the air-ticket so that I could get to know the LA set-up. The new office. The new assistant, Bruce Silke to whom I spoke every night before speaking to Barry. I had been left to run the show in London. We did it by this nightly telephone call for which I prepared a daily agenda. I conjured the questions so that each had a yes/no answer. Alex Foster had left and I had replaced her with John Watson. Bubble hair, bubble butt ... Sort of a very gruff, camper Jane Horrocks.

Without Barry, however, I was beginning to feel horribly redundant. Sure, it all worked but there was no chemistry anymore. To have a successful relationship, any relationship, you have to be able to eyeball the person pretty frequently.

For the others whom Barry had left behind, I can't answer. Personally, I was more than pissed off when he left. I was hurt, I felt let down and betrayed. I can still feel the anger and the pain now and if I felt like that then, I cannot imagine what Tony must have felt or Steve? And, compassionately, how the hell did Barry feel? I'd lied for Barry, cheated for him, censured him, sulked and made up and even allowed him to sleep with my lovers and ... and clients. Why I still loved him, I have absolutely no idea. I even understood why he wanted a new home. It wasn't my idea of home, but ... Someone once opined, I was told it was David Hockney but that's probably apocryphal, on being asked what Los Angeles was like,

"It's like the Holloway Road but with perpetual sunshine ..."

It's not. I live near the Holloway Road and I know that even from its furthest end and even on foot, it would take me no longer than an hour to reach home.

Home, as they sort of say, is where the 'art is and although LA had and has a lot of 'artists', it's a place, commercially, of little heart. Tim Curry had been enjoying huge success at Lou Adler's Roxy Theatre on Sunset Strip in THE ROCKY HORROR SHOW. Tim was the first person I met in LA. I mean person, not merely British person. He was swimming in Barry's pool when I arrived. I introduced myself as a friend of Peter Straker's and we were friends from that moment on until ... Aaah. Until later.

When I met him, Tim hadn't 'signed' with Barry. In this context 'signing' is not a form of communication for the aurally challenged but a rite of passage in which artists and performers seeking fame and fortune are bloodied by giving away twenty percent of their lives to people who say they can make fame and fortune happen. It's the greedy leading the greedy, of course.

But who am I to judge?

For Tim, his future's prospect then was more than merely pink. It was cerisely rosy! He had a great record deal with A and M via Lou Adler, Carol King's producer and he knew he would be opening at some point in New York with ROCKY HORROR.

Tim was living in the Chateau Marmont at the time before he moved to an apartment in the gloriously art deco Sunset Tower on Sunset Strip. Barry made bloody sure that we got on together even more famously than we would have done if left to our own devices. I'm afraid at this point I have to admit that I wasn't being particularly loyal to Barry. I'd mopped up far too many tears to allow loyalty to Barry to ruin a perfectly nice friendship and begged Tim not to 'sign'.

But, hey ho ... A lot of 'art was involved and both Tim and Barry, after all, still call LA home.

I was also, of course, sent out to woo Colin Higgins again but by this time, Colin and I were far too wise. Colin was also getting seriously famous. His script of the remake of SILVER STREAK had just been shot and studio heads were nodding.

Barry asked me to move to LA, to relocate and live and work for him, re-establishing what we had had in London. I declined. I didn't really think too long about refusing and I'm so pleased I did because if I had done, I would be, by now, dead.

I would have been amongst the first to be culled by Aids. Like Bruce Silke. In 1983.

Chapter Twenty-Nine

AN ARTISTIC LICENCE

So, it was all a matter of time, really ...

The second time I went to Los Angeles, Barry didn't have to pay for anything. Chrysalis Records paid because by then, with Barry safely six thousand miles away, my client list had grown somewhat. No longer was I just representing Twinkle.

My second client and still my close friend now thirty years later, was Peter Straker. My third was Brian Protheroe. My fourth was Mike Allison with Pete Sills and my fifth was John Hetherington.

Straker deserves a chapter on his own. No, Straker deserves a whole book. His book. But in the absence of that, here goes ...

His immediate ceevee runs - GANG SHOW at The Palladium as a child, HAIR! in London from 1968, HAIR! in Norway in 1970. Groundbreaking, spuriously autobiographical album PRIVATE PARTS in 1971 for RCA produced and written by Ken Howard and Alan Blaikly. Starred in a movie, BOY STROKE GIRL with Clive Francis and Joan Greenwood, produced by Ned Sherrin in 1971. Coupla outta town jobs in 1972 ...

That Peter was not a major star in 1972 when I first saw him perform at The Kings Road Theatre on one of those Sunday nights, ROCKY HORROR's day-off gigs, was inconceivable. Backed by people like Richard Hartley and Don Fraser in the band onstage, Peter appeared on Frank 'n' Furter's catwalk at the back of the Theatre in a voluminous John Bates couture black silk gown looking like the spawn of Diana Ross, Marlene Dietrich and the long-dead pharaoh Akhnaten. It was like the divine Frank 'n' Furter had ultimately been granted his wish ... TeeVee immortality in stellar heaven.

Peter sang Ken Howard and Alan Blaikley's allegorical COCK ROBIN on his raked way to the stage and brought the house down. Goosebumps still rise all over me as I write this twenty-five years later. All the women in the audience loved him and most of the men wanted to be him. He vamped his way through the rest of the evening backed with superbly apt work by ROCK BOTTOM; the creation of Don Fraser and Annabel Leventon, ROCK BOTTOM also comprised Gaye Brown and Diane Langton and were Howard Schuman's model for the acclaimed 'seventies telly series ROCK FOLLIES which made stars out of Julie Covington, Rula Lenska and Charlotte Cornwell.

And in which Tim Curry played the part Howard modelled on Straker ... Small, small, cruel world.

But beneath the outrageousness and the make-up and the frock there was a career which was deeply compromised both by its conception and its infancy. You see, Peter is Jamaican ... But he's not your standard issue BMW, go-fasta Rasta. Educated, more English than the English, Peter is like semtex. In the wrong hands ...

And, of course, a nightmare to cast. Positive discrimination in casting is seldom successful. And Peter also did everything. He sang, he danced, he wrote ... Hard to pin a label on that. Hard to get that one in a standard agent's closet and make the drawer stay shut. I kind of knew it was an impossible task and, rightly started off by saying, "No." He asked me again. And again I said, "No,". And again and again and then ...

But, he wore me down and so we ended up having a go. I did him no great service professionally although our friendship was forged in alternate links of red wine and tears and our lives have since been rendered indivisible. He had, and still has, a unique voice which no one has used either as orchestral instrument or solo performance. He still waits for the stardom I contend should have been his years ago. He says it's better to still be waiting for it than to have had it and to have lost it.

There are of course, many artists who have been blessed with no greater talents than Straker's but who have been bankrolled to the tune of hundreds of thousands of ...... (fill in appropriate currency) and further funded with that expertise of those who are paid to know what it is that makes a particular career take off at a programmable time.

Of course, we know all about the material having to be sound, the artist-producer relationship being fecund; we know about the need to have the record company solidly in support, we realise the importance of strong management reflecting the essential interest of the artist, we understand the cumulative acceleration of interest that successful reviews of low-key showcases and enthusiastic initial radio airplay can generate ... We know about good publicity, angles just right and spread evenly across the industry not to cause any competitive, resentful backlash amongst the journalists ... We know about good photographs ... We know all about that.

What we still don't know about is stuff like ... The 'X' factor. That factor which defines the indefinable, the moment when thousands upon thousands of individual punters decide to take up the product which the industry has presented them and make that product successful. We know it's about fashion, we know it can be contrived ... But we also know that a great deal of the matter is about one uncontrollable phenomenon.

Luck.

I'm going to quote Rupert Everett again. "You get what you want in the form you deserve ..." I've used this epigrammatic observation so many times. I'm convinced that if it's not gospel then it's a pretty invariable rule of thumb. Everyone who strives and heaves and pushes and forges ahead because they nurse a sore ambition will ultimately get somewhere along the road they wish to travel. Where they haven't got is where they haven't been allowed because ... Their membership dues haven't been paid; or they've forgotten an essential ingredient; or they're not as good as had been thought; unforeseen competition; acts of God contemporaneous with the push ...

Dammit, but I don't believe that any of the above apply to Straker. I'll be there rooting for him 'til they come with the long box.

I got him a singles deal with Pye. Gratis Derek Honey which is how I came by aforementioned male secretary John Watson. Horses for courses, y'know? Pye released a couple of Don Fraser-produced tracks, VALENTINO and TOUCH ME, a Ritz song from the ROCKY HORROR SHOW. But nothing happened. I should have known, I suppose as soon as Peter Prince, the Pye promotions man, suggested quite seriously to Peter that he should, "... try and do something like Barry White ..."

Hello?

If only he'd said, "... try and do something like Donna Summer ..." But vision rarely emanates from record companies. Now, hindsight ... Yes, they're as rich in that as much as they are in catalogue.

However, somehow I persuaded Pye to spring a bit of lucre for a season at the Edinburgh Festival in 1974. We needed a band and I therefore merged the Mike Allison part of Allison and Sills with Straker, Gordon Haskell and George Papanicolou and we took a hall in Newtown. Some churchy place run by a Miss Conway and the same hall where HINGE and BRACKETT had scored such a notable triumph the previous season. What Hilda and Evadne did with a glass of sherry, we thought we'd repeat, essentially, with a box of Black Magic chocolates. I approached Rowntree for a little sponsorship which I thought a logical move. Rowntree/Black Magic didn't want to know ... Maybe if Peter had been white? Or maybe if things had all been a little less ... camp?

Anthony Andrews - later the beloved Sebastian in Derek Grainger's Granada television production of Mr. Waugh's BRIDESHEAD REVISITED - directed our show which was called A LITTLE BLACK MAGIC ... The delightful, if ditzy, and now very dead Charles Brady was our gopher. I often think it was the only job he ever had but he loved it. I paid him out of my own pocket. He blossomed. Before returning to Bradyland.

Our's was a late night production; Peter meanwhile was

playing early evening and matinees in Toby Robertson's Prospect Theatre production of Bunyan's PILGRIM'S PROGRESS. Written by Toby's then-wife, Jane Robertson, the show was called, simply, PILGRIM and co-starred ex-Manfred Mann man Paul Jones as well as Paul Nicholas and John Bowe. Good cast, huh? In PILGRIM, Straker played a variety of devils including an ambi-sexual, a flying monster and something else equally horrid and calculated to deter any sponsor between the Castle of Mey and Brighton Pavilion. The whole thing was, as my friend Richard Hawkes would put it, a frightful carry-on.

Well, the nett proceeding gave me a nervous breakdown and got Peter some splendid reviews. For production money, bearing in mind Barry thought the whole Fringe venture tacky and entirely uninteresting, I'd used a personal insurance payment. This was for a full-length natural wolf coat which I'd lent to Straker and which had been stolen by opportunist burglars from his flat in Hurlingham Road in Fulham. I'd bought the coat, when very, very drunk, the same Saturday when Access cards had plopped onto to the doormats of half the homes across the land. Access was the first of the now excess of credit cards which befell our nation. After spending Saturday boozing and cruising in The Markham on Kings Road, we fell out of the door, onto the pavement at closing time and immediately saw a big SALE sign in a furrier's window opposite, next door to TAKE SIX.

I wonder if that first issue of mass credit cards disabled many more people in Britain other than me? Anyway, hence the floor-length wolf coat and hence A LITTLE BLACK MAGIC. Strange journey - Daisy's fur coat lent to Straker, stolen from Straker's flat which Daisy claims for on his personal insurance to invest in Straker's show which didn't make money and where Daisy lost his investment ... Somewhere, someone still had the coat and the money. But not me. And not, for a long while, Access which was the ultimate unwitting producer of Straker's show, which enjoyed a very reasonable week at The Roundhouse in Chalk Farm.

Odd, that capitalist, angel thing? Did it make me a producer? If it did, I didn't care much for the feeling. Producers have to be made of sterner, steelier stuff than me and they don't need mere dream fairies. They need Mammon.

Brian Protheroe came to me via Nigel Haines at Chrysalis Music. Brian was always an actor. He was an actor first. In fact he was a tall, good-looking actor but he didn't have a great deal of dash or flash about him. I suppose there must have been a sexuality which his girlfriend Anita Dobson, many years away from playing Angie Watts star of EASTENDERS' fabled Queen Vic, must have recognised but which certainly didn't leave me gasping. I wonder if Anita has a thing about the name Brian?

That Brian P also wrote very clever songs, often with Martin Duncan, that he had recorded an album for Chrysalis produced by Del Newman, the celebrated arranger, that he had a charting record with his song PINBALL and all seemed to conspire to make Nigel think of me as a potential manager. Barry's office must have had a widening reputation for mixing theatre with pleasure.

David Minns and I schlepped up the M1 motorway to Leicester where Brian was appearing in one of Ken Lee's musical mysteries entitled LEAVE HIM TO HEAVEN in which Brian played a rock star. Brian and Anita had already appeared in another of Lee's patchwork shows, HAPPY AS A SANDBAG, about the Second World War. Rather good.

Brian was immediately suspicious of me. He was a disciple of an emerging culture of mistrust and cynicism, qualities which, it was beginning to be felt, tarred the entire music industry. They were and still are infuriatingly unattractive qualities and mostly ascribed unfairly. For the first time, I felt I had to work to prove that I was a good guy and one hundred percent on his side. I rather resented that. I'm pretty sure he didn't see the need for a manager and regarded Chrysalis' suggestion that he acquire one as merely a record company ploy to get him to abandon the theatre. The Chrysalis management, record company people to the last man - Chris Wright, Doug d'Arcy, Nigel Haines - were very keen on Brian. They regarded both him and his work highly but, in fairness to them, couldn't understand why a man with such a putatively bright future ahead in the music business wanted to dissipate his energy and time in making the music career, in their view, merely second string. And, in fairness, when they were investing many hundreds and thousands of pounds in their belief in him, money which he was glad to take to record his songs, I can sort of understand Chrysalis' point of view. They must have felt a little used. Therefore ab-used. There are many artists who must also bear responsibility for the tarnishing of the mutual relationship with record companies.

Brian didn't see the situation in the same way. He said he viewed his recording option equally with his career in the theatre. He had a very black versus white perception of the world. I wish it had only been black and white. He was far too suspicious and unfocused for people to want to commit to him. I explained about Cat Stevens and REVOLUSSIA ... That there was another way to handle theatrical interests. That he wasn't the first artist to tread this crunchy path. My words fell like seeds on the same barren gravel.

Even after his tacit acceptance of me, the friendship we managed to develop was never comfortable. I admired his work enormously, I helped him and Martin stage a performance of their musical entertainment LOTTE'S ELEKTRIK OPERA at the good old Palace Theatre, Watford with Anita and all their friends. I arranged for Chrysalis to stump up for a cast recording of LEAVE HIM TO HEAVEN. On Brian's behalf, I acted as agent for the whole company and the director Philip Hedley when Roger Clifford in his latter guise as producer brought the show into the West End to the Cambridge Theatre where there were major confrontational problems.

In February 1975, Chrysalis sent us on a two week promotional tour of American radio stations. We had a wonderful time. Unforgettable. To see a country as huge and disparate as the United States from this privileged viewpoint from San Francisco to Aspen to Buffalo and Albany, New York is a fantastic experience. We also met some very, very nice people as Brian chatted amiably enough to fifty different journalists and deejays about his life and work. I think it rather gobsmacked him how very seriously American punters take their recording artists. Rock 'n' roll was legit culture over there, true art across fifty states whilst in England it was still perceived as flimsy and almost anti-culture. Not a proper job. He wrote a song for me ...

"So come on, Daisy,
Lead me through the crystal air ..."

I did. I tried to stay aloft but he was very heavy. In the end we had to land. Ran out of fuel.

I was not sorry when after some two years, this supremely arrogant young man and I parted company. I was, however, seethingly regretful and somewhat angry at what I felt was wasted effort. Mine. Some five years later, he called me and asked me if I would be interested in managing him again? He obviously hadn't heard, but cynicism and mistrust are indeed contagious.

And finally, to John Hetherington ... Aaah!

Cute, lotta hair, skinny, perfectly formed. Good writer, good singer, greedy - ergo hugely motivated - I rather liked John. We made a deal with Neighbourhood Records, the company founded by the sixties and seventies American folk-rock star Melanie and her husband Peter E ... Phil Symes, now a much more famous publicist than he ever became a record company boss, managed Neighbourhood in London and we formed a decent relationship. Money was always a bit slow in coming but, well ...

This was the client Barry slept with. Coming in from LA for a flying visit, there was John Hetherington in the office one evening and ... Old story. The dinner. The flirting. The Midas thing ...

This time I couldn't forgive either of them and for once didn't see why I should. When I finally left Barry, taking a hugely tentative step to set up on my own account, I explained what my plans were to John and who my other clients would be. I asked him what he thought, what he was going to do.

"Thanks, David," he said as we stood on the pavement outside twenty-seven Curzon Street, "but I think I'll stay where the money is ..."

'Bye, John.

Six months later, Barry didn't have a business in Curzon Street. Or in England.

John Hetherington Who?

Chapter Thirty

QUICKSILVER

1974 and 1975 were densely populated.

I have abandoned chronology. There is too much overlap and spread. My life during these two years resembles a tray of scones in which too much baking powder has been added to the mix. Before being put in the oven, the scones stand separate and perfectly spaced. After twenty minutes, they emerge indistinguishable one from the other, having doubled their size and taken over all available interstices.

But that's how life was then. David and I had developed a huge coterie of acquaintances. People we'd see at dinner tables in restaurants like Christopher Hunter's new place HUNTERS in the Fulham Road where Straker performed most Sundays. There would gather Anthony Andrews, his wife Georgina Simpson of the Piccadilly Simpsons, Esta Charkham, Geoffrey Taylor. Crispin Campbell Lowe and dentist David Healy. Garth Bandell, Eric Roberts and the late and much missed Felix Rice often sang. Peter's own fee was mostly drunk away by his champagne bill but what the heck ...

We also ate a lot at the American clairvoyante

LAURITA's place, a little further down Fulham Road ... Then we'd go on to clubs like Maunckberry's in Jermyn Street and Steven Hayter's Embassy Club in Bond Street where the designer-socialite Michael Fish would be holding court, where Nicky Haslam would prowl and the daring, avant-garde Savile Row tailor Tommy Nutter could be seen before diving into the darker recesses of the night. All these clubs were pretty much multi-sexual. People desperate to be in the limelight don't care a toss about the sexuality of those in whose reflected glory they bask. I was invited home by Nicky Haslam one night. He rather thought I might wear a large, old leather boot on my head for him. I declined.

And on and on ... To the sleazier and far more edifying CATACOMBS where Rae Coates and Steve Jeffers and a lot of the West End chorus lines both loitered and worked the hat check or the Gaggia. Then to ROD'S CLUB above the furniture cave in Kings Road. At both venues, Steve Swindells would hang out when he was a hopeful, a wannabee British Billy Joel and before he too opened and ran club venues; Jordan would come in and dance when she was already a punk but punk was generically unknown. Tom Watkins would be there, looking and learning, with his friend Peter Faulkner. The Bertish Sisters, Suzanne and Jane, the painter Fanny Crichton-Stuart, Sarah Harrison from BROWNS, Cherry Brown who was always Christopher Hunter's right-hand. Hamish McAlpine and his friend Steven Gill. The fabulous Guy Munthe who lived in an eighteenth century riverside house on the south bank in the basement of which he kept a coffin. We took turns getting in. And out.

Guy ended up in a for-real one. Safe journey, Guy.

There was a Rod at Rod's Club. Rodney was indeed a person, a very good-looking, square-jawed Australian boy-person who with his Great Dane (dog) in tow was Christopher Hunter's lover and the apple of many another London boy's eye. Richard Taylor, the owner of the building which also housed the Furniture Cave, was very brave in going for a disco usage of his upper storey premises and it was the first of the larger unisex dance bars. We used it a lot. So did, the Gregg family, Alan Warren the photographer, Mick and Sheila Rock, Derek Jarman who was still a painter and designer and whom I had known most of the 'seventies since when he lived in a warehouse on the South Bank. Derek's was a huge loft space in which his bedroom was a greenhouse full of cushions. He exuded the greatest sexuality of almost anyone I've encountered. This, I envied. Andrew Logan the artist and jeweller was in the same building, his alternative Miss World parties already being famous as were the Porchester Hall annual Drag parties in Bayswater. Fabulously over-the-top occasions. THE COPACABANA opened at about this time in Earls Court Road. Gay life was coming out of the cottages and into the neon. The clubs were beginning to be full of noticeable faces - Nicholas de Jong, Paul Gambaccini, Danny la Rue, Lionel Blair. Dennis Wells was thinking about more clubs as was David Inches. Show business powers like Bryn Lloyd and David White, David Shaw from the Robert Stigwood Organisation were around and about London most nights.

Really late at nights we'd just cruise round the backstreets of Earls Court, Wharfedale Street ... Waiting. Using shadows. We had friends all over the town. Even in these dark nooks of the night. Craig Macdonald, then in charge of publicity at The National Theatre, Murray Salem, the American actor and our friends Graham White and Byron Richardson who often did front of house at Provans restaurant when Stuart Grimshaw was having a bad-hair day.

Byron was sweet and kind. He too went to LA.

He never came back. Thinking of you, Byron.

London was becoming funkily dizzy. It was the era of the T-Shirt, of the plastic carrier bag, of tacky excess and the tabloid newspaper. Punk was creeping in. Mohican hairstyles had been spotted on Kings Road. Rock 'n' roll was also becoming very commercialised. Cat Stevens wasn't much into merchandising on his tours. I believe his tour T-shirts were still being given away free. However, the mugs 'n' posters 'n' scarves brigade of entrepreneurs were well on the way to making their fortunes and turning rock and pop concerts, as these moved into the really big venues, into resembling football matches played in an atmosphere of an agricultural hiring fair.

One night in 1975, a large boat-like Daimler limousine pulled up outside the house in Werter Road. David came in with a riskily exotic flower. Thin and pinched with nervous lips covering a positive horde of unmissable ivory gnashers, long stringy backcombed blue-black hair, eye make-up, one hand painted with black nail varnish, this number arrived wearing a raggedy grey fox-fur jacket which he didn't take off. Tacky beyond belief, the new arrival was heralded as lead singer in a rock band. I'm glad he was. He looked as though he was still wearing his stage clothes. We shook hands, I think and in his there was a hairbrush. I felt like Queen Mary receiving a rather confused and embarrassed Maharani.

I think this person and I also acknowledged each other on the way to and from the bathroom which was on the ground floor of my duplex. David and I never used to bother much with each other's occasional therapy. Because we didn't usually go in for return matches, the trade was mostly the here-today-and-gone-tomorrow sort. But by the following morning, after a night of pretty abandoned bonking may I say, not only was this one not going, he was obviously staying for breakfast.

"What's your band called?" I asked as we padded about in our fragile early-morning sensitivities.

"Queen," he replied.

Oh dear, I thought.

Chapter Thirty-One

CORPORATISING A CAT

Don't believe it. It's really NOT all over after the fat lady sings.

Steve's songs were beginning to reap a harvest of millions of pounds. It was only what he and Barry had been after but having got it, there was left the question of how to keep the lion's share in the face of some pretty toothy tax demands and then of what to do with the balance. Higher rate tax was almost eighty-four percent and after the fifteen percent surcharge for unearned income, the high rollers were supposed to hand over ninety-eight percent of their income to HM Treasury?

Please.

Throughout 1974, plans and schemes became forecasts and yields and growth. It was all done with the aid of some very heavy guns from the city institutions and corporate law firms. Grey suits began to be seen amongst the rush of denim on our stair. Short and neatly kempt hair-do's stuck out like barbers' poles amongst the manes and curls and renegade locks of the roadies and the artists alike who streamed in and out of our door. We'd already taken over the room on the first mezzanine to act as office and overflow reception.

267

Where Barry had met Prince Rupert Loewenstein, I don't know but he was tickled pink to be doing business with ancient European royalty. The fact that Rupert Loewenstein, then at Leopold Joseph, had just assumed responsibility for the management of Mick Jagger's financial interests was obviously a consideration but Barry, now swanning around the town in a chauffeured grey Rolls Royce which Steve had bought him, was equally impressed by the invitations from Prince and Princess Loewenstein to visit them at their country home in Hungerford. As opposed to their London base in Holland Park. Way to go, Barry!

Rupert's suggestions - mainly for deferred income schemes - as to what both Steve and Barry should do with their loot were legal-eagled by the law firm of Theodore Goddard of which the genial and entirely charming Paddy Grafton-Greene was the main champion. David Baker, Barry's lawyer, from the Simkins Partnership also had a hand in these massive arrangements. Neville Shulman our company's accountant and never far from the financial action, was the final party involved.

All this activity was going on against the backdrop of at least two towering horizons, opposite horizons as it turned out. The management contract between Barry and Steve was about to expire as was Steve's recording contract with Island Records. Rupert also became instrumental in the initiation of negotiations between Barry, on Steve's behalf, and Atlantic Records who were more than interested in acquiring Steve's recording future.

And ...

And Steve was displaying not a few worryingly eccentric traits. Eccentric, that is, to us. To him, his behaviour was entirely in keeping with the track his mind was pursuing. Never one to worry about facts, Steve's mindset had always been pretentiously esoteric. He'd already savoured, devoured and spat out Buddhism and numerology and now he was withdrawing into an ascetic, almost hermitic period which preceded his ultimate involvement with Islam. What little sense of humour he'd had, vanished. He displayed symptoms of one clinically depressed. Although he'd got his money, I don't think he was liking what came with it. What he'd ordered from the photograph in life's catalogue didn't show the whole picture.

Whatever dream which ambition decrees should be chased is never what destiny ultimately allows. The rose looks lovely in the florist's window but to hold it, you have to remember it comes with thorns. Steve didn't have many people to whom he could turn. His friends appeared to be few. Alun Davies, his accompanist and Alun's wife, Val and their family and Paul and Rosie Samwell-Smith. He still had his mother and father living in the revamped Moulin Rouge Cafe of his childhood in Shaftesbury Avenue; he had his adoring sister Anita and brother-in-law Alex Zolas who also now worked with us at Curzon Street.

And of course there was David Gordon, Steve's brother, the manager manqué, the thwarted eminence who was forever in our offices with plans and schemes and grand designs which he and Steve and Barry would thrash out for hours only for them to disappear without trace in the course of the ensuing days. David needed appeasing.

Of course, Steve had girlfriends, from the eponymous Patti d'Arbanville, through a flirtation with Barbara Parkin, through Avril Meyer in America and the English model Maggie Gill. But Steve was too cast in the mould in which he'd grown up. He was a loner; even within a group, Steve was always by himself. He was prone to loss of temper and there was a certain violence simmering. He was a poor communicator, certainly no diplomat and there was a feeling of separateness about him. Steve could turn the love tap on and off at will. He could make people feel intimately involved with him and then alienate them into a cold limbo a moment later. He wasn't a happy bunny at all. And yet I couldn't help feeling very deeply for him.

I don't know how he drifted towards god, but he did.

I too would like to think there was a god. Wouldn't we all? That unseen hand, guiding us, even deciding with deft certainty the hour of our death but always through our faith and belief giving us the assurance that there is a purpose, that there is a plan and that we're all going somewhere better. I can't think of a single established religion that doesn't promise something better at the end of the mortal road and that to end up with god is the carrot that tempts each of us onwards to make it through the night of our earthly lives.

I think it must be always easier to cope with life when

you're not at the centre of your universe. Both Steve and Barry to an extent were the centres of their universe. And we all know that any universe can only have one centre ...

God is a very understandable alternative when all that faces you and surrounds you is yourself, your face, your reflection mirrored everywhere you look. Everyone coming to you, everyone firing questions at you, raising problems for you to solve ...

God, apparently, takes all the strain away. God, it is said, removes the pressure. There's a comforting parental quality about the idea of letting God take your hand. Conversion is indeed a re-birth. It makes legitimate children again out of grown people. It allows adults to gratefully grasp the helping hand and to follow instead of always having to lead. A boy can feel taken care of again instead of forever responsible.

The thing about God and the famous is of course not confined to the Cat Stevens story. Soeur Cliff clamourously continues to celebrate being born again as do or did, less volubly, the late John Denver, Donna Summer, Dolly Parton and of course Tammy Wynette and, charmingly, Samantha Fox. And there are Muslim converts too, Richard and Linda Thompson being the most notable and yet least proselytising.

It must be weird to find yourself the one who gets the career which takes off, which hits the jackpot. If it was me, I think that I, too, would need to ascribe the miracle to come greater purpose. Writing as I do, from the other side of famous, it would all appear so pre-ordained, so decreed because mine would have been my only life, a very ordinary, workaday thing. The kind of success that people like Cat Stevens got (and get) is, after all, the incredible made believable. And that is exactly what, to a convert, god is ... the incredible made believable.

One has to be very careful about words these days but I do believe that something religious happened to Steve in the course of the years in which I knew and observed his life. Those first four seminal albums (I'm including CATCH BULL AT FOUR) were his apotheosis. Their creative content and their commercial success enabled him to leave earthly, every-day concerns aside and to consciously and conscientiously look for his god and himself in areas of purer existence, like a monk or a nun or any religieux in quiet, silent corners of the mind.

The very worldliness he had pursued and which he now wanted to eschew could lead in only one direction.

I think I'm glad it wasn't the drug direction. Drugs were just beginning to be a problem. To the authorities as well as to their users. Religions, like drugs, aren't solutions to anything. Both take their toll. From aristocratic opium in the eighteenth and nineteenth centuries to the chic cocaine of Cole Porter, the amphetamine and weed which had crept into popular culture from the early sixties was now beginning to leap rather than creep and its increasing popularity was being augmented by heroin. The cloudy shadow of cocaine loomed only faintly on the horizon at this point.

Unfortunately, the powers-that-be had not worked out ways of how to capitalise on narco-use as they had successfully done with the infinitely more dangerous alcohol and nicotine markets. What cannot be controlled is usually banned and the criminalisation of narco-use had resulted in huge markets being developed which might otherwise have remained untapped. However, there was money to be made.

A lot of people take drugs. A few get very badly fucked up. Caroline Coon had founded RELEASE to help these people. We helped put on a great concert at Peter Morton's newly opened Hard Rock Cafe on Piccadilly at Hyde Park Corner in aid of RELEASE together with Penelope Tree, David Bailey's girlfriend.

I remembered my dead alumnus, Richard Hoyle that night although I still didn't come even close to understanding why ...

271

Chapter Thirty-Two

EVERY TIME WE SAY GOODBYE ...

There was so much Barry had left behind, not least the theatrical production company which he had established with Helen Montagu, who had managed both the Royal Court Theatre and Binkie Beaumont's office and also Robert Kidd, aforementioned Scottish *wunderdirektor*. Both of their talents are now, 2004, sadly no longer available to us. Robert died very young and Helen died late in 2003.

But, back in 1974, there was still a great deal of the theatre in Barry Krost's blood. Indeed it had been germane to his very introduction to Cat Stevens. Along with his recording ambitions, Steve also had theatrical ones. He had come to Barry armed with a musical, entitled REVOLUSSIA, a piece with all the grand-operatic elements of the stage musical. He was as passionately involvede with it as a project as Brian Protheroe was in his theatre composition. Based on the last days of the Romanovs, the Russian Imperial family, it perforce embraced rebellion, sacrifice, murder and death. Luverly. Some of the songs variously appeared on subsequent albums from MONA BONE JAKON onwards. After TEA FOR THE

TILLERMAN, Steve's fervour for the project fizzled out much to the relief of the Island Records committee who, like Chrysalis with Brian Protheroe, always found the REVOLUSSIA project a dangerous sidetrack to what was proving a very lucrative mainline career.

Helen Montagu and Robert Kidd were commissioning plays from everywhere. Tony Warren, the delicious creator of the equally delicious CORONATION STREET wrote an extremely good one; Christopher Hampton, writer of THE PHILANTHROPIST was coming up with one ... Helen and Robert dropped in and out of the offices. But ...

It was all coming to an end.

The circle was narrowing. In Provans one night there was a momentous bit of table-hopping. John Reid was having supper with Freddie Mercury. I was having supper with Peter Straker. Straker is as blind as a bat without spex and couldn't see Freddie, whom I was describing and he was avid to clock the new sometime resident of my flat in Werter Road.

In the end, we all got together. Freddie, I knew, would probably be at my house later anyway, as he would be meeting up with David after his business meeting with Reid. A great friendship was forged that night. Freddie and Straker were closer for sixteen years than two peas in a pod and, of course, under John Reid's stylish tutelage, Freddie turned QUEEN from being a rather tacky glam rock band into a phenomenon of world significance. In those days we all had everything to gain and nothing to lose.

Provans is the site of my favourite waiter story. The vegetables arrived at your table in large, shallow earthenware dishes and were served by a waiter. One night, Fergus being Fergus, one vegetable was mashed turnip - bashed neeps to we sassenachs. Turning to the waiter, a rather clipped but attractive French boy, I exclaimed,

"Oh, turnips! I love them. Tell me, what do you call turnips in France?"

He thought for a moment, poised, bent over the table and then replied,

"We don't call zem anysing. We feed zem to zee pigs."

Collapse of stout party.

Tim Curry opened and closed in THE ROCKY

273

HORROR SHOW at the legendary Belasco Theatre on Broadway. Big blow. Where Barry was, I don't know but although we stamped and hooted and hollered our way through that first night, the reviews were resoundingly pooh-pooh. The show had not come as virgin to New York and I am convinced that the theatre critics and the New York theatrical establishment could not forgive this flouting of convention, this reversal of tradition. The producers had, after all, had the audacity to open ROCKY HORROR on the West Coast! Culture in America moved from East to West, not nice versa. *Quel rocky horreur* indeed!

After the show, we ended up at someone's apartment on the Westside, near the Dakota building and waited. Peter Straker and I and Tim. Little gang of Englishmen abroad contemplating a cruel sea of ink.

At last. The reviews came in.

Tim read them and then went and stood in front of an open window, several storeys up, and looked out over the firefly lights of the New York night. His silence was oceans deep and I felt so, so sorry for him. He had wanted so much to conquer New York. Straker and I both went and put arms around him but there is so little comfort in way of gesture or word that can reach to the bottom of such a bleak void at moments like that.

Sure, no one had died but ... That's what it felt like.

Exit stout party.

However, Tim was to get his wish, sort of ... In a way, not like he wanted but when the ROCKY HORROR PICTURE SHOW came out, it ran - and I believe still runs - for decades at a New York movie theatre. Like the movie of HAROLD AND MAUDE, in Paris.

Later in 1975, we were all back in LA for yet another series of meetings. Barry was now resident of California. Steve and I and Sarah Harrison, now Steve's secretary and Jackie Krost were all visiting. Sarah and I had in fact just flown in. It was Sarah's first visit and the occasion was a joint celebration of Steve and Barry's birthdays. Anyway, Steve was the joint guest of honour at his own party and the party had been organised by Barry at a restaurant. Many of Barry's new LA friends and acquaintances were there. Steve seemed to know few people. He was, don't forget, a huge, huge star as well as just being Steve.

There was an uncomfortable atmosphere from the start. Jackie Krost gave Steve a straight-jacket for his birthday.

Hello?

Jackie didn't have a bad bone in his body and the beautifully hand-painted and decorated device was supposed to be a joke. Oh, dear. Then the cake came on with candles of the sort that don't extinguish when they're huffed and puffed at. Another joke ... Oh dear.

Steve was visibly not thrilled with the jacket and actually hurt himself when he burned himself trying to put out the candles on the cake. The tension and embarrassment in the atmosphere worsened and Steve's obvious distress communicated itself painfully to Sarah, to Jackie and to me.

Steve left. So did we.

Outside the restaurant we all sat in the back of Steve's limo whilst Steve got very cross and then very upset as he ranted that the party wasn't for him at all, but for Barry and where did he stand now in the rankings of Barry's priorities?

That night, Steve hurt.

It didn't take a degree in psychology to realise that Steve was feeling very, very alone and cut off, helpless and rudderless. It also didn't take an MBA from Harvard Business School to know that the time had come when the business and career implications of this state of our principal's mind could no longer be left unacknowledged. I knew from that moment on that there was no future for any of us in terms of our past.

Barry and Steve had lost it. Steve was later to eschew signing his new record deal with Atlantic and left Barry and Prince Rupert with more than egg of their faces. And Barry and I had lost it. Resentment had turned to mistrust which had turned to indifference. Finally, Steve too had lost it. He wasn't writing. He was nervous. He was tired and didn't want what he had. We'd all lost it. It was finally time for each of us to move on.

I've been there, too many times, on those days when you feel like weeping from the moment you wake up, when you don't want to leave the house, when all you want is to be alone and, maybe, remain alone forever. In those circumstances, you don't like yourself

275

at all and any escape route is better than staying both where and who you are.

I realised that what I needed was a new job. I also understood that, like Barry, Steve needed a new life. Although I'd never have thought it possible, as well as changing jobs it is, actually, perfectly possible to change lives.

I don't like postscripts but I guess this one has to be in as does mention of the death of Christopher Hunter in 1996. A brave pioneer who was foolish and generous and infuriatingly forgiveable. And, yes. I did leave the Barry Krost circus. But no gold watch. Nothing ...

Chapter Thirty-Three

I reluctantly decided to start on my own. I talked to David about it. And to Freddie. They were beginning to be inseparable and it was lovely. Way before any Bohemian Rhapsody which was then being composed, cobbled together, created ... whatever ... in that summer of 1975. I talked about my solo move with Straker, with Brian Protheroe, Twinkle. They were fine. John Hetherington, however, was taking no such chances.

Odd feeling, freedom. Heavy feeling. But I had no idea that I'd made so many friends. It seems to be only when you're really ill or if you die that you know what sort of impression you've made on the world.

I had goodwill messages from other managers whom I'd become close to - the Ardens, Mr and Mrs, David and Sharon, Betsy Asher in LA - the agents, Barry Dickens at MAM, Paul Dainty and Ralph Gurnett, theatrical producers and theatre managers, television producers like Robin Nash at TOP OF THE POPS, other record company people James Fisher at RCA, David Most at RAK, Clive Banks at Island, Moira Bellas at WEA, Derek Witt at CBS ...
In a few years, it seemed, I'd immigrated, settled and become accepted in a world of whose existence I'd had no idea when I'd first walked into my orange flat in Ashley Gardens in 1968, still wet behind the ears from university, my extended childhood. And though I didn't know it, there was much more to come. I'd met John Reid, I

liked what I fancied was his way of operating but ... working for him? Please.

And then leaving the business altogether for love, again? And in a foreign land? Too much.

But opening and running my own restaurant? Whoa, boy.

And then, at last, finally finding a degree of peace and contentment and real, real love, that love which exists even after sex? And becoming a proper writer, one who gets paid and who people write to and say they like your work?

Dream on, Daisy.

BOOK II

LAVENDER BLUES

1975 onwards

Lavender blue, dilly, dilly
Lavender green,
I'll be your king, dilly, dilly
And I'll be queen ...

(Traditional. Ish.)

Chapter One

HINDSIGHT

I don't think I was particularly happy during 1975-1976, the period of eighteen months which LAVENDER BLUES covers. Neither, to be perverse, do I think I was particularly unhappy. As an experience on a scale of memorable, however, my twenty-ninth and thirtieth years rate an indelible.

No. Rather a scarring.

No, no, no. Rather, in fairness to everyone concerned, they rate as a touchstone. A straight ten.

Straight?

Okay. A bent ten.

I had unconsciously reached a watershed in the living of my life, from the heights of which I suppose I must have known that I could go neither forward nor back, neither upward nor downward. So I perched there on the ridge, for a while and whilst perching, I appear to have made the third big decision of my life.

The first, dear reader, you may recall, was leaving the soul-destroying greyness of the British Council in 1969. The second was leaving behind the savage mediaeval shadows of my employment in Spain in 1970, bidding farewell to Silvio Narizzano and Win Wells, my purple-pink inquisitors. By the beginning of this, my LAVENDER BLUES, I made my third decision and by doing so reverted irrevocably once again to accidentalism.

Much, much safer.

To remind you, the end of TICKLED PINK saw, me, your hero in this tale, in 1975 at the still-tender age of twenty-seven having worked for the manager/agent Barry Krost for six years as general manager in the theatrical and music agency company which looked after the careers of Cat Stevens, Angela Lansbury, Peter Finch (to name but three of our luminaries). If this wasn't enough excitement, domestic life, shared with my long-term roommate David Minns (who worked for Paul and Linda Macartney) with his new lover, the soon-to-be massive rock star Freddie Mercury from the emerging band lusciously called Queen was enough excitement any boy from provincial Worcestershire should ever have to handle.

In writing TICKLED PINK, I learned that it is indeed possible to improve one's inter-neural facilitation, as Caroline Lee (nee Boucher) calls the phenomenon of trying to remember. It's no more complicated than the games of joining up the dots we used to play on wet afternoons with drawing books bought from Wigley's Post Office, Hemingway's toy shop and Hubert Reynolds' tobacconists, the newsagents closest to the bottom of the road in my childhood Malvern.

Well, maybe there is one difference between those childhood games and the grown-up versions. In childhood, the dots were always numbered. The adult versions provided only the dots. No numbers. We had to find our own way. Still do, dammit.

So, where the hell was the first? Which dot was number one in this bitter-sweet cavalcade of my next eighteen months?

In having to remember, there is so much one does not want to remember as well as so much that does not want to be remembered and it is this latter cocktail which, of the two, is the most elusive. Those inconvenient chokey lumps in the mix are usually the very bits which need to be reserved rather than flushed away. It is not distance which lends enchantment to the view but selective culling of the painful experiences that makes life bearable; watchable. We can only live a strained life, like babies, for whom whole apricots could prove a mortal anathema. Pureed and strained, however, the stuff is nectar ... The very stuff of both life and regular bowels.

So, as I probably said earlier, *per assholes ad astra ...* Onwards and upwards. But how deep is an asshole? Just how high is a star?

1975 until 1977 was a kind of zenith in the annals (sorry) of gay - and my - liberation. Y'see ... It'd all been so damned easy, really. My life had happened, sure and yet, blinking in each morning's light after going too late to bed the night before, it seemed so empty. Life. The life. My life. Life should surely have been so full and yet it had turned out to be so ... So ... Empty? Devoid of meaning. Yes. De void was decidedly unmeaningful.

We had jargon like this by the bucketful. Words. Strings of words which sounded good but were ultimately ... Unmeaningful? Perhaps, after all the hoo-haa and the hype, the later twentieth century had turned out to be a teensy bit disappointing. I mean ... Let's face it. We didn't get further than the moon. Kennedy and Martin Luther King had got shot. The new and successive popes had proved useless. The Cold War still fizzled. The poor were still with us.

On a less philosophical level, as gay men we could buy or steal or con as much stuff - like consumer stuff - as we wanted and yet we still weren't satisfied. To protect this new consumer freedom, we had the beginnings of a little gay press. The start of a primitive debate. We were thrilled. But when an issue of **Jeremy** or **Gay News** was late, instead of being concerned, most of us were irritated. We didn't call up to see what might be wrong. We were merely cross. Like it was The Times. Or the Guardian.

We had never, as Mr Biggest of the Brit-Macs once put it almost twenty years earlier, had it so good. Had we?

Obviously not.

And it was, children, all before Aids in a land that time hardly remembers and yet cannot forget.

Chapter Two

PLANK IS GOD

I suppose most of my professional associates must secretly have thought that my leaving the security and reputation which Barry Krost's office enjoyed in the international music business and starting out on my own was more like walking the plank than a sensible matter of progressive entrepreneurialism.

I suppose they were right.

Even I still don't fully understand my reasons for leaving the comparative financial safety of being permanently employed in the theatrical and music management company which had been my milieu for six years. I am not a very daring person. I hate change and yet I find the phenomenon of change fascinating with regard to other people. To have taken those first faltering steps away from the comfort and cover of my security blanket, I can conclude that I must have been impelled by pretty compelling forces. I must have been more desperate than I have ever been. Writing now, for the life of me, I can't even remember what those forces were.

However, I have a suspicion that my situation was not a little unlike a divorce. I can remember a fleeting feeling of freedom. But I'd travelled that way before and I knew it was a treacherously

283

fickle sensation and certainly no rationale for reasoned behaviour. In conclusion, I think the reason for leaving was that there was nothing to stay for.

I do remember that it was my ongoing relationship with my ex-assistant Alex Foster, sister of actress Julia, which had introduced me to Crispin Cambell-Lowe for whom she now worked. At this time, late summer 1975, Crispin, a dashing young business-man-about-town, was investigating the potential of the video film arena, vis-a-vis both production and application of this up-and-coming genre. He was friendly with James Fisher at RCA, with John Reid too and we rubbed along in pretty much similar milieux. We got on rather well and he was evidently doing rather well with a very sprauncey appartment on the north side of Montagu Square very near Oxford Street and an extremely enviable BMW motorcar.

Crispin offered me an office and a telephone and I took him up on this very generous gesture and moved in. I knew it was generous. There was nothing I could give or lend to Crispin that he hadn't already got. It was one of the very few times in my life when I have been helped merely because of kindness of heart. The favour system was rather beginning to fall into desuetude as the 'seventies wore on and there was more at stake, more to lose, more to gain by either turning away or forgetting to call back.

Thinking I should, I formed a company, David Evans Artists Management Ltd. and had an account at a National Westminster Bank in Sloane Street. Well, there's a how-dee-do! Forming companies at the drop of a hat was indeed just what people seemed to do and I blithely followed where other fools led. The company thing was, in the event, entirely unnecessary and plagued me for years. I should have merely remained a sole partner and not incorporated. It proved an expensive ignorance and I remark that none of the 'professionals' I consulted ever tried to dissuade me.

However, because I had known Neville Shulman for some years, I arranged in the interests of continuity that his office do my accounts and, so, with him and with David Baker from the Simkins Partnership looking after my lawyerly stuff, if I'd taken breath, I would have thought, for just a fleeting moment, that I was fit to burst with pride and ambition. And direction.

But, the god-awful truth was plainly that I still knew

from nothing. Accidentalism may be all very well as a philosophy but it doesn't tell you how. It also - shudder, yearn, shudder - comes with no in-built insurance policy. Screw up once and you screw up period. There are no second chances.

Shoestrings and heartsfaith have nothing to do with managing people's careers. Managing people's careers is to do with money and power when you have no magic and, truth to tell, I patently had neither of those three qualities in any significant combination. There was certainly nothing magical to turn sows' ears into silk purses. When you hold dreams in your hands, without a top hat sprinkled with abracadabra, it's a jolly heavy responsibility. Without the abracadabra, you're the wizard of fuck. Further truth to tell, I didn't know how I was even going to attempt the trick. Let's take stock here.

Instead of doves and strings of coloured silk hankies and a wand, I had Brian Protheroe, an equity minimum actor who could have been a music star but who didn't want to be. I had Peter Straker, a singer who kind of acted but who was so way off the scale that to base any forecast of income from my endeavours on his behalf would be like my pissing into Vesuvius in the hopes of putting it out. Simply Herculean, darlings.

And of course I still had Twinkle. I was such a dumb shit that I never took commission from her. I figured ... I don't know. Maybe I was sorry for her. Maybe I thought it would have been what Mick Hannah, my dead best friend, would have told me to do had he been able to communicate comprehensibly from wherever in the fuck-knows-where ether Turkish Airlines had disembarked his scorched soul on that ghastly Sunday afternoon in 1973 in the forest in northern France. I missed him desperately.

Looking back, I now know that in flying my independent colours, I should have made a business deal with Barry Krost. Continued to look after his clients over here on a freelance basis. But, like I said ... I knew from nothing. Instead, my wings were outspread over a jetstream of prayers. The only real wind beneath them was that produced by a lot of hot air.

But, looking - as we never do - closest to home, I think I had a friend. I think that Brother Mercury was working for me. I can think of no other explanation for what happened over the course of a very few weeks, for I was on my own for an unaccountably short time. I was left, never knowing whether I could have made it or not.

Hell, anyway ... It's what I choose to believe.

Furthest truth? I didn't really want to find out. Honest truth? I've never been any good on my own. Now, writing now, I want to content myself with the thought that I did indeed have a friend who knew this thing about me and who acknowledged it for me and who helped me just a bit with my insignificant little burden.

The title of this chapter, PLANK IS GOD, is a graffiti which I read for years - and am still reading twenty years later - on the brick pier of a demolished railway bridge on the A 40 going to Oxford, now just past the exit to Oxford from the M 40. It's on the way to The Manor Studios. I used to think its meaning unfathomable and would drive for hours deciphering possible alternatives. I concluded that the graffito-ist had omitted the word THE. I fancied that the legend ought to have read THE PLANK IS GOD.

Bismillah! Brother Mercury passed that way many times too, in later years. I knew he would have been amused. He was a great plank-walker too.

The other great piece of road-graffiti still to be seen on a wall in Market Road, North London is:

Beware Mind Control

Think about it.
No. Not for too long.
Hello?

These mid-seventies for me bore just as double-edged a meaninglessness as the Plank is God graffiti. I knew I lived through and past those years because I still see the graffiti on the bridge-pier on the A40. Time and several attempts by the local highways department to chemically delete the legend have not succeeded and, despite several attempts to try and achieve the same with my own memories, I'm still writing about those times like they were somehow the best.

Chapter Three

FOOL FOR LOVE

Like holiday snaps, other people's love affairs are often never particularly interesting to a third party. In fact, sometimes, they're not merely uninteresting, they're downright dysfunctional. Like David Minns's affair. And Freddie Mercury's. The one they were having together. In my flat.

Well, of course I supported them and, on good days, was actively very pleased for both of them. They fought, made up, fell out, made up with the regularity of a laxative. For a long time, I thought that it would end. Then I realised the pattern of the emetic. Freddie needed conflict as much as he needed the stability of being able to conflict in a permanent, non-threatening environment. But that environment was also mine and there was no room for three tantrum-bent, starring-role queens in one coronation. Freddie needed his own.

For the past six years, my domestic, entirely platonic relationship with David Minns and the vagaries of my work had been sufficient palliative for any *chagrin d'amour*. As far as love had been concerned, I was a relative naif. I'd undergone a series of staccato infatuations. I was briefly attracted to a liason with Paul des Salles,

Rosie Samwell-Smith's cousin, only recently 'out'. Rosie'd taken on a crash course in London faggotry which included a stopover for cousin Paul in Barry Krost's office. Paul was undeniably attractive and as Barry was never to be denied; after their particular little omelette had been whipped up, flash-cooked and inevitably overdone, I had my go with the lovely Paul in the big bed in the house in Lansdowne Road.

There was also once a man who was so besotted - oh, what I'd've given on other days - who just couldn't take no for an answer and who simply wouldn't go away; he beseiged the office at 27 Curzon Street every night for days and eventually bought me the Nilson single of CAN'T LIVE IF LIVING IS WITHOUT YOU. After a gesture like that, I had no alternative but to cease any behaviour which might have given him even the slightest hope. I don't remember actually reaching the "Just fuck off and leave me alone!" point but it was close. I can never listen to that song today without feeling horribly guilty that I couldn't even begin to attempt to reciprocate the depth of my swain's emotion. And the awful thing is, I can't even remember his name.

It was almost as though I wanted to do the falling in love. Whenever the falling in love was done to me, it materialised as dangerously like being imprisoned. Doorstepped. Stalked. And I should have been so lucky. After all, it wasn't as though I was drop-dead gorgeous or anything. Plain but perfectly presentable was the nearest I had or would ever come to lovely.

I think in those middle 'seventies I'd gotten to be in that mindset because of a longago Frenchman in the early 'seventies called Jean-Pascal Billhaud whose nickname was Palou. Jill St Amant, Barry's secretary, had introduced us as part of her whirling social scenario. I think she saw me, *in micro*, as the available London totty for the pleasure of her *macro*-mobile globe-trotting rich gay friends. Or maybe she really had my best interests at heart? Who cares?

In late autumn 1970, I fell deeply and essentially in love with this tall, blonde, Frenchman. To me Jean Pascal was ease and grace and insouciance and sophistication whilst I was tense and gauche and naieve and undoubtedly anally retentive to a stress-making degree. I suppose I should never have become so involved with my *Monsieur*, (as my heroine Colette called hers). But I did and maybe I did because it was my first experience of mutuality, of being fallen in love with too. '*Monsieurs*', by the way, are generically entirely different from 'dearest hims' who are positively teenaged by comparison.

It didn't work out and there was, therefore, nothing to last. I hadn't exactly tested myself in the love stakes. I hadn't proven anything yet I hadn't flunked either; nor had I suddenly glimpsed what life could be which might have decided me that one day I wanted to be in a couple, forever and ever.

The fizzling-out process *entre lui et moi* was so vague and ill-defined that it became tediously dispiriting and I was left feeling inconsolably disappointed because at least I now knew that love really did exist.

I must have been writing in those days. Here is a short story in the form of a fairytale - what else? - which I wrote to Palou as a letter. I think it was the 'goodbye' letter. I know I never heard from nor saw him again.

- Once upon a time, in a land so far away that no one had ever been there in the whole history of story telling, there lived a little gypsy boy. His name was Tusitala and he looked like every other gypsy boy whom you might see today or tomorrow in Spain or Mexico or wherever the sun is hot and there are chickens to steal and oranges to pick when the farmer isn't looking. Tusitala was not tall but neither was he short, he wasn't puppy-fat but neither was he too skinny and although he had the darkest of dark brown hair, his eyes were the purplest of blue and piercing, like violets in the dark earth of a wood, parting the ivy and the leaves as the petals unfold in the sunlight.

Tusitala lived in a big encampment with many families and many other children with whom he sometimes played. I say sometimes because Tusitala was a ... a different sort of little boy. He was ... yes, different. He had never known his mother or father and he had no brothers or sisters. He had been brought up by all the other gypsy families in turn although no one family had ever claimed him forever because in the end they always thought him ... strange. Not strange enough to cast out, but just strange enough to keep at

290

arm's length.

Of course, the gypsy men were often away, leaving the women and children behind. Safer, they said. More secure, they added. Best at home, was the common wisdom although Tusitala always wondered. Although he never said as much, he never quite understood this wisdom.

The other children in the camp were wary of Tusitala because although he was quite friendly, he was always remote, distant and he never ever wanted to be a part of their games. He would sit by himself, often for hours, at the side of the open space in the middle of the ring of caravans and tents and merely stare at the others playing their games which were so often the same. He would just stare.

A knot of children would eventually form in front of Tusitala, whispering amongst themselves, wondering what was the matter with him. The gipsy mothers would also whisper and wonder as they in turn watched, even those who had held him in their arms as a child, who had fed him and bathed him as he was growing up. Tusitala was oblivious to their concern and remained impassive, his blue, blue eyes unblinking.

"What are you staring at, Tusitala?" one of the children would finally ask.

"Yes," a mother would say, dropping to a squat and trying to put her brown arms around him, trying to love him, trying to make him love her for they never gave up trying. "What do you see?"

But Tusitala's answer would always be the same as he gently disentangled himself from the embrace.

"You know what I'm looking at, mother. My dreams," he would say, "i'm looking at my dreams."

And, as usual, the women would laugh and then the children would laugh.

"You silly boy! You cannot see your dreams, Tusitala," the children mocked.

"Day-dreaming, more likely," was the verdict of the mothers. "Now be off with you. Go and play properly, with the other children. Don't waste your time with dreams, Tusitala."

Tusitala would neither frown nor scowl. He knew there

was nothing to say and as he got up and wandered away, the women, tutting and shaking their heads, would return to their cooking pots and their gossip and the children would begin their noisy games again and soon they would all forget about Tusitala and his strange, odd behaviour.

When they mocked him, he would wander away into the forest which surrounded the encampment and eventually, tired of wandering the meandering woodland paths, find his favourite and most secret place beneath the branches of the great trees where he would sit and look up at the dappled light filtering through the heavy canopy of leaves above his head. The light would dance, his eyes were almost hypnotised and his head would clear. His thoughts would no longer weigh heavy like grey rainclouds and in the rays of sunlight he would watch the squirrels as they played, chasing each other along the lengths of the boughs. At times like these, Tusitala loved being by himself.

The animals of the forest were unafraid of Tusitala and because of a strong trust which had grown up as Tusitala himself had grown, he had learned that it was safe to love the animals for they would never hurt him as he had been hurt all his life. Unlike the gipsy mothers and children and especially the gipsy men when they were at home, the forest animals never asked him questions and they never talked about him and they never pointed at him when he wanted only to be quiet.

The animals would often come and sit with him. The mice and the rabbits and the rats. The beetles and the spiders and the bees. The foxes and the badgers and the rabbits. But of them all, Tusitala's favourite friends were the forest doves.

Tusitala was always entranced by the elegant landings the doves made on the branches; they came to settle on their perches like fluttering thoughts turning into decisions. Their songs were so soft that he would feel a peace he never experienced in the camp and, at last, he would find himself smiling. When Tusitala held out his arms, the doves would fly down to sit on his outstretched hands. Their feathers were warm and soft when he stroked them and the birds would follow him when he left the forest at dusk, flying overhead in a great circle of grey and white until he reached the safety of the fire in the middle of the camp.

The other children would welcome him with the same question,

"Have you found your dreams, Tusitala? Did you bring any back with you today?"

Tusitala would smile at them but he would take no notice and curl up as close as they would allow him to the fire and go to sleep.

One day, some time later when Tusitala was older, he was in the forest, sitting under the great trees when he heard the crackling sounds of something forcing a path through the thick undergrowth. The animals settled around him all scurried off to hide in the tree roots and in the bushes but Tusitala was not afraid. The doves were still cooing overhead. "They can see who's coming," he reminded himself, "and if they're not afraid, why should I be?"

Through the trees, which grew very close together in that part of the forest, came a big white horse and on it sat a young man. Tusitala did not move but merely stared at the beautiful white horse, so richly caparisoned in finely tanned hides and cloths and adorned with silver saddlery. Tusitala gazed, mesmerised by the handsome young man dressed in suede and velvet, his steel-spurred heels resting in magnificently cast metal stirrups and his legs enclosed by boots of black and buckled leather. The young man carried a long hunting horn slung on a silken cord across his shoulder and at his side hung a beautifully wrought scabbard sheathing a mighty sword.

As the two young men looked at each other, the doves stopped cooing and purring for what seemed the longest moment. Then, the horse whinnied, breaking the magic silence and it scuffed its forefeet impatiently. The doves began their song again and all the animals reappeared from their hiding places.

"Why are you sitting under that tree?" the young man asked Tusitala who chose not reply immediately but merely reached out his hand and fed a nut to a red squirrel on the ground beside him. The young man dismounted and the horse bent its head to feed from the sweet grass of the clearing. The young man crossed to where Tusitala was sitting and sat beside him on the tree root. "I am completely lost," the young man confessed. "So, if you are not lost yourself, can you tell me where I am?"

Tusitala looked up and gazed deep into the eyes of the

newcomer.

"Are you the prince?" Tusitala asked simply. "Are you really Prince Revery?"

The young man coughed and looked at the ground and picked up a twig which he began to turn slowly between his thumb and finger.

"What would you say if I told you I was indeed the prince?"

Tusitala turned away and looked up at the pigeons and stretched out his arms for his friends to to come and sit on his hand and he smiled.

"I would be very happy if you were the prince," he eventually replied. "I'm so pleased you really do exist. I was beginning to wonder." The young man stood up.

"Well, I am. I'm glad that's settled something. Now you know who I am, who are you?"

"My name is Tusitala. Why don't you sit down again?"

"Because I really must find my huntsmen? Will you help me, Tusitala?"

"If you like," Tusitala replied, "but I'd much rather stay here beneath the trees. Wouldn't you, Revery? We have everything we want here. Why do you want to go and find your huntsmen?"

The prince looked at the ground.

"Because I have to," he mumbled. Then he coughed. "I have to, Tusitala. They will worry. They will wonder where I am."

"But you could stay as long as you want. You are the Prince," Tusitala observed. "You can do what you like." The prince threw away his twig and his hand fell to the hilt of his sword which he pulled out just a little once, then twice, from its scabbard.

"But my father is the king," Revery replied flatly, "and he would be angered if I was late for the tournament this evening and his banquet tomorrow at Castle Esperance. I have to be there. It's ... well, expected," he said with a shrug.

Tusitala listened and stroked one of his doves, his favourite and the white bird sang even more softly but even more deeply than ever.

"Do you not like my forest and my friends?" Tusitala asked and tossed the bird high into air. It hovered for a moment,

almost still, as though it were suspended on an invisible cord before it flew to perch with its own friends.

"I love your forest," Revery replied. "I would like to stay for ever and ever."

"It's not like this all the time," Tusitala advised. "Sometimes it's very lonely here without dreams." He looked up at Revery. "But I have my dream now. I know it exists. So it'll never be lonely here again."

Revery stood up once again and walked to his horse which was drinking from a little brook which gurgled through the rocks between the moss and heather on its banks.

"I wish my dreams could come true like yours," Revery said as he took the bridle in his hands. "I would so much like to stay but ..." As he vaulted athletically up and into the saddle, there came the sound of a hunting horn which made the horse toss its head and magnificent mane and rear up on its strong hind legs. Tusitala heard the baying of hounds, the barking of dogs and the shouts of the royal huntsmen as they drew near, following Revery's trail.

The animals once again ran away to hide and the doves flew off in a cloud of panic into the safety of the sky above the forest.

"Will you be my friend?" Revery called to Tusitala as he turned his horse's head in the direction of the hunting party. "I don't have any real friends. No one as close as I would like you to be? Will you be my best friend, Tusitala?"

"Of course!" Tusitala shouted in reply, jumping up with joy. "I will be your best friend if you promise not to hunt any more and not to stay away for more than a week!"

"Good," Revery called back, over his shoulder as the big white horse rode away, crashing into the undergrowth beyond the great trees. "We will meet again, Tusitala. Soon. I promise."

After a few moments standing alone in the clearing, Tusitala heard the sounds of dogs and horns and the shouts of men receding and although all was soon quiet in the forest again and Tusitala was by himself once again, he didn't feel in the tiniest bit lonely.

As usual, with the pigeons wheeling and turning above his head, he walked back to the camp.

"Well," one of the gipsy girls asked him as he lay down

to go to sleep, "did you bring one back today? One of these famous dreams of yours?"

"As a matter of fact," Tusitala replied, smiling mysteriously as he stared into the fire, "I did. I finally did."

The next day, there was a great worry in the camp. The men had returned but they had brought nothing to eat. There had been no deer on the plains around Castle Esperance and no work in the orange groves or the chicken farms for them to earn money to buy food. The gypsy mothers did not know what to do for they had laid in no stores and made no provision against the men returning empty-handed. As the entire camp sat in council, there seemed to be little to look forward to.

Suddenly there was a voice and a figure stood up.

"I will find food," Tusitala announced, shyly. "I have ..." he coughed. "I have a friend who can help us."

The children all laughed. "A friend? What friend?" they derided. "All you have is dreams, Tusitala."

"Don't be silly," chorused the brown-eyed, big-armed mothers. "We can't eat dreams, child. More's the pity."

"Who is this fool?" called one of the men.

"Yes," cried another, "not my son, thank heavens!"

Tusitala was almost in tears as the whole camp laughed and pointed at his lone figure.

"I do," he shouted defiantly. "I DO have a friend," he sobbed, parting the children around him as he ran away towards the forest. He never looked back but stumbled on and on. "You wait and see," he muttered through his tears, "you'll be sorry that you laughed!"

He ran through the forest and didn't once stop, not at his usual clearing, not at the great trees. Tusitala ran and ran. His friends, the doves, flew with him, just above the trees. When he looked up, he seldom saw them but he always knew they were there from the heartbeat sounds of their working wings. It didn't take but an hour or two for Tusitala to cross the forest. His young legs were strong and made him very fast, jumping the streams and the fallen trunks amongst the thick bracken in his path.

It was almost dark when he had crossed the plains outside the Castle Esperance and finally stood in front of the castle's

296

gates which were guarded by two impassive sentries.

"I want to see Prince Revery," Tusitala announced boldly, panting after his long run.

"You can't," one guard said sternly, raising his crossbow and pointing it straight at Tusitala's heart. "Be off with you and don't let me see you at these gates again! We don't hold with gypsies here. Count yourself lucky I don't arrest you for vagrancy. What would Price Revery want with a gyppo, anyway?"

"But ..." Tusitala began,

"Shut it," the second guard said. "You heard the man. Clear off. Gyppo." He spat and both guards laughed heartily at their easy victory.

Tusitala was very, very sad as he slunk away from the castle gates. As night fell, he walked round and round the high, grey, unscaleable walls, trying in vain to find another way in to see his friend when he saw a tall window in which was a face, pressed to the panes. It was Prince Revery.

"Hello!" Tusitala called. "Revery! Hello!"

"Who's there!" Prince Revery called back looking out into the night.

"It's me, Tusitala. Your friend from the forest. I have to see you, Revery but your guards won't let me in. There must be another way in?"

"There isn't," Revery replied despondently. "You can't come in. Everything's locked and barred and so I cannot come out to you either. The king would be furious if he knew I had disobeyed him in favour of a ... a ..."

"A what?" Tusitala. "Do you mean a gypsy?"

"He just wouldn't understand," Revery said, "What can I say?"

"Well that's HIS problem," Tusitala went on, "and anyway, at the moment I'm only concerned for MY people. They have no food. There is none in the forest and no money to be earned so that they can buy any. You and your father have enough in Castle Esperance for everyone." For a moment there was silence. "Revery? Are you still there?" Tusitala called anxiously.

"I do have one key," the prince replied warily, "to a very, very secret door but it only opens from the outside. How can I *get the key to you. It's so dark. If I threw it, you'd never find it."*

At that moment, Tusitala's favourite forest friend, the pure white dove flew out of the sky and perched on his shoulder. He was the only bird who had not returned to roost in the forest. "Yes!" Tusitala said to himself, "thankyou, thankyou!" He was right to be so relieved for the dove could indeed now fly up to Revery's window and fly down with the key held in its beak.

The dove understood without Tusitala having to speak a word and it took off and flew slowly up into the night air, up and up, a whisper of fluttering white shadow against the dark castle walls, hovering for a moment before finding the prince's window.

Revery gave the bird the key but at that very moment, the king appeared behind him and saw the dove flying away, the key glinting in the first shaft of moonlight that night which shone on the bird's beak.

Pulling Revery away from the window, the king leant out and called for the sentries.

"You! You down there. Shoot that gypsy carrion! Shoot it out of the sky!" The moon came fully out as the king shouted out his savage orders which the soldier guards, trained not to question and never to feel sensitive, obeyed instantly. Their crossbows were raised, trained, aimed and with unerring accuracy two bolts pierced the breast of the white bird as it descended to land on Tusitala's outstretched hand.

"No! No!" Tusitala cried out to the night but there was no one to hear for the king had dragged Revery away from the window, slammed it shut and closed the heavy curtains. The dove dropped to the earth like a stone, far from Tusitala's hand.

The guards laughed and returned to their sentry duty and Tusitala, unable to find the wounded bird in the dark, sank down beneath some bushes and cried himself to sleep.

The next morning, he awoke to find the dove lying dead not a few feet away, its feathers no longer warm, but now cold and damp and limp with the early dew, no longer white but stained red with its heart's blood. Tusitala buried his friend as best he could in the hard ground and then started off on the long walk back to camp. There was now no reason to run. There was nothing to run for. Nothing, even, to run from. The useless, mortal key he threw into the

298

undergrowth.

It took him almost all day to cross the plains and then find his path through the forest for he no longer had need to crash headlong through the unknown. There was no more urgency, no longer a quest.

Tusitala collected blackberries and blueberries on the way as well as woodland strawberries and fresh young dandelion leaves, wild chives and sorrel for he was hungry and knew that even such meagre food would be better than nothing when he reached the hungry encampment. And he had, after all, boasted that he would find food, although this ... This poor man's harvest, this wasn't what the gypsy mothers or the gypsy fathers and certainly not the children considered proper food.

When Tusitala finally reached the camp, instead of the heavy silence, he heard sounds of laughter, music and dancing. As he neared the fire, the gypsy mothers called out,

"Tusitala! You're back! Well, well ... Who'd have thought it? You did help us to find food, you know. And you did indeed have a friend. Many friends in fact." The women found this very, very funny and laughed even harder.

"Why?" asked Tusitala. "Why are you all so happy?"

"We should have believed you," said one mother. "Look!" she cried, pointing to the spits over the cooking fires. On them were cooking hundreds of birds, the fat from their plump bodies dropping spit-spat into the flames.

"The men followed you into the forest and found all the food we needed. Wild doves. We didn't know there were so many left! They've shot enough for a week!"

The camp was very, very happy. No one seemed worried any more. None of the children were crying. Even the men looked confident and strong again.

On the other hand, Tusitala, so tired, sat down in front of one of the fires and looked deep into the flames as he pulled from his pockets the handsful of sweet juicy berries and the fresh natural salads he had picked for them.

"Now what?" one of the gypsy mothers called out. "What on earth are you looking at now, Tusitala."

"Nothing," the boy replied, hardly moving his lips.

299

"Absolutely nothing." -

So. Adieu, Palou. There you have it. Another of love's stretcher cases. One seriously wounded Daisy. I think in real life, my prince went on to occupy a high position in the organisation of the Marie Claire magazine. But I could be mis-informed.

Post-Palou, I'd never given any serious thoughts to love, its implications and ramifications and so when I saw that instead of me, it was David who'd been bitten by the love bug, Freddie Mercury's love bug, I found it rather unsettling. What about me, I began to wonder? Not that I was unhappy for either of them. It's just that it wasn't me who billed and cooed over the next twelve months. Being the long-term gooseberry in a fruitcage meant for two is a truly marginalising experience.

With little prospect of the same success at work now that I was self-employed and on my own in Crispin Cambell-Lowe's flat, I began to wonder what else there might be in life other than work? I must add that nothing happened for a year but it took that year to realise that David and Freddie would eventually set up on their own and I would be left in my Putney flat alone.

Did I want another flatmate? Maybe but, equally, maybe not. It seemed almost easier to look for lodgers than for love.

Into the same category in my life in which falls the subject of love in the 'seventies, I find the subject of holidays. I had managed three in six years. The first had been with my dearest Mick Hannah, now two years dead. During the summer of 1972, we had returned to the scene of our meeting in Mojacar and we got there in an orange mini-moke which Mick's erstwhile ex-girlfriend Twinkle had bought for him, part of her constant campaign to buy him back. We drove from London, south through France, experiencing a torrential downpour no sooner than we disembarked in the unprotected little moke in Northern France. It poured with rain relentlessly and, although soaked, we just drove and drove and eventually reached Paris very early in the morning where we slept soundly 'round the clock.

The following morning we set off south for St. Tropez and arrived, once again, very late at night. The weather had turned from rain-sodden to sun-drenched and although we drove merrily along with the moke's canvas roof furled and sun-tan lotion plastered all over our bodies, we ended the day blackened from the exhaust smog and dust and wind-borne dirt we had attracted on the six hundred mile drive. Never had a shower been more welcome.

We stayed in St. Tropez for a couple of days, mainly for me. Mick met no one and was quite content to swim and sunbathe and sweetly ferried me and an Italian prince (I gather that few Italians escape the aristocracy) whom I met one night, out to the *Plage Tahiti* where I and his highness shagged in the sand and in the sea shallows whilst Mickey went on a discretely long walk. Bless him.

Lacking any princely invitation to return to his castle for breakfast, let alone to spend the night, Mickey and I headed off to Spain the following day and arrived in Mojacar to find it much changed in the three years since we had managed our heroic flit. Since our exodus, tourism in that part of Andalucia had grown like the proverbial Topsy. Theresa Sweet had all but moved out of Mojacar and into a second house she had bought in, Bedar, a mountain village some few kilometres further back in the hinterland. We had a pleasant enough time but I didn't feel comfortable in this old stamping-ground. Not at all a good idea, going back.

I returned to London by plane and Mick stayed on for a couple of weeks longer. He drove back to England but as the Moke broke down irretrievably somewhere in the middle of France, he abandoned it and continued the journey by train to Paris and thence by plane to London. Somewhere in a French mechanic's workshop there might still be an orange mini-moke with an unpaid account on it. The interest must be enormous. Please don't write.

The second holiday had taken me with Cat Stevens' record producer Paul Samwell Smith and Paul's wife Rosie to a beautiful villa which they had rented in the South of France just outside Monte Carlo. I remember very little of that holiday except driving down through France with Rosie's mother, Sheila Simon. The Merry Widow had nothing on Sheila. A more redoubtably and pristinely upper middle-class woman in gracious middle-age has surely never lived, but Sheila, divorced from John Simon, her industrialist husband of many years, took to her well-deserved freedom and independence like the first dove off the Ark.

301

We had a wonderful time together, no less in Paris on the return journey when having found an hotel, we agreed to dine separately and meet up the following morning. Sheila had an enchanting time with, I think, a Belgian man who wanted to wine and dine and combine with her and I had a throroughly debauched time in the bushes of the gardens below the jetting fountains of the Palais de Chaillot where I hope I gave as good an account of myself as I was given by that parkful of Parisian peedees, which in French is pronounced pay-days ...

The third holiday was with David Minns in my newly bought orange Austin 1300 Van Den Plas GT (Courtesy of Mary, my very generous mother) to Scotland. This Scottish holiday was of course entirely platonic and memorably successful, unlike the last equally memorable time I had so disappointingly sojourned amongst the lochs, bens and glens with 'dearest him'.

I have just remarked on my propensity for travelling in orange cars and the significance of Scotland in my life. I care little either for the colour orange or the countryside of Scotland so why the great frequency of the significance of both in my life, I wonder?

I was destined not to have another holiday ... I was destined to have a life. Having a life is a kind of total thing. If you have a life you shouldn't be able to tell where the holidays begin or end. It's all one.

Chapter Four

AN HONOURABLE
SURRENDER

Out of all the times I saw him perform, I can just remember Cat Stevens' only concert appearances at The Royal Albert Hall. This, I think, is strange for someone who worked at the very heart of the music business. But on the other hand, Cat Stevens' concerts were never very exciting ... More like reverent religious services. Good practice for him, as it turned out. Me? I'd sat through quite too many holy Sundays for one lifetime.

However, two rock concerts do stick out over the parapet of memory in 1975.

The first was the best concert I've ever been to.

The second concert was the most important.

Elton John and The Eagles and The Beachboys played Wembley Stadium in the summer of 1975. The sun shone, the capacity crowd swayed and ... God, rock 'n' roll can be so uplifting. John Reid had provided some wonderful tickets which gave Straker and I and our party which included Shaun Scott and Yasmin Pettigrew access to the press area immediately in front of the stage and we had the best afternoon. It was one of the bravest concerts too

... Elton played half of an unheard album. No hits. It was received rapturously. It made me realise how very small-time and short-term Cat Stevens was and how very big-time and long-term Elton was and concommitantly, I realised the same about the respective managements. Barry Krost and John Reid. There was no comparison. Or so I thought then.

Back in the Putney flat, those same summer months had seen the final demise of Freddie and Queen's relationship with their managers and backers, the brothers Sheffield. Better the devil you know has never been a maxim in management-client relationships in the music business. So often, what suits at the start becomes ill-fitting and ultimately irrelevant. The Sheffields would never have steered Queen in any other direction than the parochial. Queen would have been big in the *micro* but in the *macro*? Queen needed someone else. They needed a big-time, long-term management strategy which would motivate the recording industry on a worldwide basis.

Don Arden was one of the contenders. Manager of Wizzard and Roy Wood and the ELO amongst many others, Don was, to put it opaquely, rather colourful. Freddie liked Don and his wife and their children David and Sharon very much. And so did we. Tales of Don's behaviour as tough-guy manager, musicbiz godfather are numerous and legendary and although there must, somewhere, be a basis in truth for them, most are apocryphal. The family lived in a delightful Edwardian house with a huge garden bordering Wimbledon Common. Going to parties there and dinners was not only homely, it was positively affirming. Sharon, now married for many years to rock icon Ozzie Osbourne, was my favourite Arden.

Had I not been gay, Sharon Arden would have been the sort of girl I would liked to have partnered up with for keeps. Intelligent, motivated, hard-working with a great eye for style and detail she was also nurturing, caring, patient and honest. I'd bet Sharon never ducked an issue in her life. On one weekend occasion, she gave me a huge diamond ear-stud on the condition that the following week I would have my ear pierced. I said I would and I was as good as my word.

On the way to a meeting at EMI in Manchester Square, Caroline Boucher took me via the earring department in Selfridges which is where boys went in those dim and distant days to get one in.

I am the most squeamish squealer in the world but I didn't squeal. The job was done, the sleeper ring went in and I spent the whole of the meeting at EMI - I think we were asking for money for Kevin Ayers' tour - with my head tilted weirdly to one side as I had a horrible feeling that blood must have been seeping down onto my collar.

Of course, it wasn't. Three weeks later after much obsessive cleansing of the wound with something that smelled like amyl nitrite without the rush, in went the diamond and it stayed there for at least a couple of years until every male in the country below the age of thirty, it seemed, had gotten an ear pierced and the phenomenon was no longer so unusual. I remember there was a great quandary in Selfridges as to which ear I should have done. Right or left.

"Y'see, if you 'ave it done in the wrong one," explained the curly-permed blonde piercer as though she were talking to a severely sexually challenged person, "people might get the wrong idea, know what I mean?"

The left was apparently, in her terms, the iffy sexual ear. These are the same people who in the perfume department perceive there is a gender to fragrance. "But that's for women!" they bleat as my hand alights on Ysatis de Givenchy. However, I was determined to pluck up the courage to stand my ground.

"Honey, I WANT people to get the wrong idea," I muttered vice-like through teeth clenched in terror like any true pioneer and presented my left-hand virgin lobe.

But I hasten too quickly for by that time, Queen - I'm sure heavily influenced by Freddie - had chosen John Reid, not Don Arden, to be their new manager to extricate them from the Sheffield Brothers' thrall, to repackage the remaining years of their deal with EMI and generally re-present them to the music business in a truly global sense.

Freddie must have been mightily relieved for at that time he had an account with a limo company, an account at a restaurant and that was that. Personally, he must have had about ninepence but he had the gainfully employed Mary Austin at home in the ground floor flat at 100 Holland Road and people were very kind to the struggling Mr Mercury in those days. I'm sure that David Minns -

working for Paul and Linda at Macartney Productions - and I even working for myself, earned more than Freddie did in those days in real terms.

But, whereas Freddie had prospects, we merely had jobs.

Before reflecting any deeper on the love thing which embraced Brother Merkles and Brother Minns, I need to take myself on and to do that, I have to remain in the Queen arena for a moment as they, the band, headed for the stable door of John Reid Enterprises Ltd. And, be assured, the second concert I went to that year of 1975 was indeed one on that year's Queen tour of Great Britain.

To most human beings in 1975, the management of the career of Elton John would have seemed a pretty enormously complicated and essentially ongoing prospect, quite sufficient to tax the capacity of even managing directors of most middle-to-large-sized Queen's Award-winning industrial companies. However, for John Reid, it patently wasn't enough. That he should wish to undertake more did not surprise me. I had observed the same trend with Barry Krost who, not satisfied with the success of Cat Stevens, sought to duplicate, even triplicate, it with Mike d'Abo and Colin Blunstone. However, Barry wasn't as hands-on as Reid appeared to be. Barry didn't make stars. They came to him, already established, like,

"... and here's one I made earlier ...".

John Reid, on the other hand, had two unerring instincts, the first of which was in the recognition of that grinding, vaulting, gnawing ambition and rhino-hide-bound determination in raw and undeveloped creative talent which turns a nobody into a star. The second was the ability to choose exceptional staff.

In Freddie, John Reid saw another star. Quite simply. I'm sure he was initially encouraged to take an interest by the enthusiastic record company, just as Barry Krost had been when taking on Mike d'Abo but it can't have taken Reid long to recognise that all the cogs were in place in a machinery that, with his lubricating hubris, was ready to crank out another fortune.

To dwell a moment or two on Reid, he was, famously, Scots, from, I think, Paisley and I don't think his family were other than fiercely proud, hard-bitten working class who knew about struggle and fight and who wanted the finer things in life because I

306

imagine their entire worldly knowledge could have been arranged on a small, tiled mantelpiece.

John is small and pugnacious. He is all that small men are supposed to be. He probably had to defend himself from a very early age. Had he not been gay, I imagine he would have ended up on the floor of many a Glasgow pub with his eyes blacked or his lip fatter than when he'd eaten his fish supper an hour before, the remains of which would have been already barfed upon the bar room floor. Reid spoils for confrontations. He searches out tricky situations. He has radar which homes in on strife and risk and he's always seemed artlessly to run the gamut between punching out an adversary's lights and bawling blue murder because that same person's then tripped him up and he's cut his knee.

He had little formal education. Indeed, to a teacher in his final years at secondary school, John Reid might have appeared to possess few talents. But, as I said, he was not un-endowed. His major, inadmissable talent was that he was gay and pretty with fabulous big, long-lashed blue eyes and somewhere along the line he met television pioneer and supremo David Bell who had encouraged him to move down to London.

Like me and hundreds and thousand of others, the fuel which powered the teenage John Reid was composed of equal parts sex and London although Reid's mixture was spiked with the extra ingredient of quantitative ambition. Having not benefitted from the apologetic middle-class upbringing with which I was saddled, when Reid saw opportunity he merely grabbed at it and held on to it like a terrier shaking a rat until there was no more fight left in the object of his acquisitiveness and surrender was the only way forward. Sweet victory was and is often Reid's.

There was nothing reticent about John Reid. He was like that with people as well as business opportunities for, in a way, business opportunities to a man like John Reid are merely people. People are the necessary steppingstones to cross the puddles of both business and pleasure to the other side, to 'success'. When Reid saw someone he liked the look of, he went after them and never took no for an answer, whether for work or sex. I was always amazed whenever I was made privy to the ever-lengthening list of his conquests and the many additions. Reid's riflebarrel carried

307

innumerable notches. Straight, gay, bi, don't-knows and the conveniently drunk or drugged ... Many whose names are far too numerous to list and many whose names I cannot even remember, nor never knew, fell swains to Reid's charm offensive. He really does bowl you over when he meets you and knocks you flat, like a spare skittle in the alley, when he's had enough.

The initial and lasting impression he makes is one of genuine wide-eyed attentiveness which signals a deep and sincere interest in every word you say. The final and equally lasting impression which many have had of John Reid is a tight and furious little expression, boiling and red like a thwarted baby's as he hurls thunderbolts of vitriol either face to face or down the telephone. He's an A to Z of passion.

Thank the lord I fitted into both categories of attraction, sex and work. For a while.

Whilst working at Montagu Square, I was still without a car. I say still because my beautiful orange Austin 1300GT had been stolen from the Hilton Hotel carpark where I used to garage it during the day. I prayed and prayed that the police wouldn't find it. Found cars were usually delivered back their owners in a terrible state and my insurance policy in those days wouldn't cover the repairs to any damage. Well, of course, the police found the car, abandoned in a department store car park in Twickenham and I had no option but to have it repaired.

When Reid's call came inviting me to the Queen concert in Bristol, I had to initially reply that there was no way I could get there because of my carless state. No problem, he said. He'd pick me up and take me. Fine, I said. I was no stranger to Rolls Royces but Reid's Roller exuded an entirely different aura to Barry Krost's. Barry's was grey and had a funerary interior. Like it had followed a thousand hearses. Reid's was a happier colour, I think, burgundy. Barry's chauffeurs were also weird; one had looked like more like Lurch from the Adams Family than Lurch.

John had really nice people to drive him, the afore-mentioned John Howard had been one, but the current incumbent - and still there at the beginning of the new millennium after twenty seven years - was the lovely Gary Hampshire whose only deviant move was his sabbatical, driving Freddie Mercury in the 'eighties.

So, off we drove down the endless M4 to Bristol. Minns was with us because Freddie had asked him to come and see the show. In those days, although the band all knew the score as far as Freddie's sex lives were concerned, Freddie was still juggling Mary as well as Minns and though the twain met, they never met in circumstances which might have fuelled Mary's suspicions for Freddie had still not 'come out' to her. Mary was with him in Bristol. Ergo, it was okay for David to be there but only with me and under Reid's validating aegis.

I often wonder how much Mary knew ... She was always so sphinx-like, so quiet, so ... attendant. I always thought Freddie's deception was ludicrously transparent and really rather cruel as far as Mary was concerned. It was like seeing movie stars putting on sunglasses - they presumably think they achieve instant anonymity. Instead it's like announcing who they are over a PA system larger than Queen's. Freddie was like that when he announced he was 'going somewhere' - wherever ... the studio, usually - or doing something - whatever ... going to a meeting was most convenient.

Did he really believe that just because he'd spoken, Mary believed him? And the other Queen women, Chrissie May, Dominique and Veronica ... Did the band never talk to their spouses on the pillow? Did the three other Queenies never voice their thoughts amongst themselves and thence to other ears and thence to Mary's? Being men, I suppose they didn't. They were all perfectly reasonably behaved, if a little withdrawn and reticent when I had met them previously and when Minns was around but I never and have never felt that they particularly understood or even accepted Freddie's coming-out and being gay. Homophobia needn't be virulent or violent. It can lurk and fester and irritate like the many other prejudices which we all harbour if we could only but admit. Phobia is, after all, only fear.

Anyway, we saw the Colston Hall concert and it was a revelation. I'd never seen Freddie perform before. Zandra Rhodes' costumes, Brian May in a blouse with sleeves that billowed like spinakers on two America's Cup yachts, fireworks and pyrotechnics, incredibly original and well-designed lighting, great sound. Offstage, the Freddie I had come to know was incredibly shy and retiring in public. He was the last to be first either at home or in private company. Not that he didn't expect to be looked after and waited on hand and foot but I refer to showing-off or being noisy or obvious. He never showed-off, he never drew attention to himself and was never obvious.

I therefore could not believe the phenomenon he achieved when he put himself in front of an audience. He transcended the reality of being someone I passed on the stairs on the way to the loo in the morning and simply became Freddie Mercury, star! I was mesmerised by his incandescence, elated by his energy, poise and showmanship and felt incredibly proud of him, burningly proud just to know him. For better or worse, from that moment, I could never see him as just Freddie. I don't think this inability ever compromised our friendship but I could not escape the ever-present acknowledgement that behind the gentle, funny facade there lay dormant a personality of such stature and power and magnitude which made men and women love him, which cut swathes through crowds and which towered professionally over most of his peers and successors. And all contained in such a stick-like frame. He was as thin as a reed in those days.

King Freddie ... He reacted to an audience like those Chinese, intimately folded-up paper flowers you put in water and which then explode in size and colour. He was the proverbial ugly duckling which turns into a swan. No wonder the swan featured so heavily in his graphic imagery. I also realised that me and my past with David was no match for what Freddie was offering. Not that he was offering anything specific at the time, but the implications were obvious. I saw David's rapt face watching the Queen show and I knew. His mother had recently died and he was alone as far as parents were concerned, his father having died in David's early teenage. I'd kinda felt ... responsible. In loco parentis, I suppose. It's a gross temptation to even attempt to fulfill and one which usually proves unwarranted and unnecessary. Hey ho.

So, grossly tempted, after the concert and the party in the hotel and just before Reid and Gary and Minns were about to leave for London, I pulled Freddie aside and asked him bluntly ... I must have sounded like a putative father-in-law:

"What are your intentions as far as David is concerned? How serious are you because you have to realise that it's my life you're affecting as well."

He replied that his intentions were very serious and we hugged each other and I assured him that I was really pleased for him. I was. But at the same time I felt scared that my domestic security too was about to join my professional gamble in a major craps-shoot.

Somewhere around this time, I had gone out into the back garden of 31, Werter Road where we were proudly cultivating some pot plants and after a little arbitrary snipping and pruning of my infant drug culture, I walked back to the house only to see a dead white chicken lying on the steps which led down to the area outside the kitchen window.

It was quite dead. No blood on its pristine feathers. No visible signs of distress. But it unsettled me. It was like a sacrifice, I thought. An omen. I've hated white things ever since. I think they're all harbingers of deaths and ends.

A couple of years later I remember giving Freddie a collection of I CHING spills collected in a Somerset wood when he saw that I had become intrigued with the ancient Chinese tome. I had been introduced to it by my then neighbour, the director Peter Wood who was also a devotee of the Confucian runes. I too had embraced the mumbo-mysticism wholeheartedly in that woolly new age sort of way that people affect who move to the country professionally and I was consulting it fairly regularly in the hope of making some sense out of my life.

Freddie was fascinated by all the veiled poetic prophesy and the anglicised Sino-imagery which when decoded was supposed to make sense vis a vis the state of one's own existence in the cosmos. I always liked, "Freedom is a mountain lake." Think about it. He did and saw a great deal of meaning in the image as far as he was concerned during a long evening we spent throwing the spills many times to see how they fell for him and which other hexagrams they revealed. I don't think he understood it all for a second but I gave him his own set of these totemic twigs and a copy of the I CHING for his birthday and I wrapped the whole gift in a large scarf of pure Chinese silk. I don't think he ever threw the sticks but it was the white scarf that I became more concerned about. Freddie had little instinct for instinct which didn't relate immediately to him.

311

But the denouement of all that that now implies was not to be played out until very much later. Despite Turkish Airlines, we all still blithely believed in those halcyon days that people were meant to live, not to die.

It was either the day after the Bristol concert or the day after that that John Reid 'phoned up and asked me to go and work for him as General Manager at John Reid Enterprises. I think I must have held out for my independence for at least three seconds. I caved in because, quite simply, I wasn't strong enough to go it alone. I never have been. Someone wanted me and so I said yes. I felt needed. It was as simple as that. It's always been like that for me both in life and in love. And things really did happen that quickly then.

I would like to add a piece of writing by my friend, the television producer, director and writer John Tagholm. I hope he won't mind. It's to do with the 'white' thing ...

In the summer of 1997 I walked a thousand miles across France, following footpaths from Sangatte on the Channel to St.Tropez on the Mediterranean. The personal satisfaction I felt at this achievement, which was undertaken to celebrate my fiftieth birthday, will be forever overshadowed by an event of much greater significance. The nine weeks of my walk were, near as dammit, the last nine weeks in the life of Princess Di. Diana, Princess of Wales.

What does a princess pack for a stay in St.Tropez? Did Diana take trunk after trunk of luggage with her on her fateful last holiday in the fabled resort on the Cote d'Azure? Did she have glittering long frocks for formal evenings, sexy little numbers for the nightclubs and bags of beachwear? I ask not out of idle, ghoulish curiosity, but because now my walk across France seems inextricably linked with every aspect of Diana's final days.

Mind you, on July 4, as I set off from Sangatte, the little village on the Channel just behind the Tunnel terminal, what Diana might or might not pack for her holiday in St.Tropez with Dodi Fayed could not have been further from my mind. I didn't even know she was going there and anyway I was much more concerned with what I was taking with me. For information, it was four T shirts, two pairs of shorts, one pair of 'smart' long trousers, three pairs of knickers, four pairs of socks, a baseball cap, a toilet bag and what seemed like a hundredweight of maps. No dinner jacket, no lounge suit, nothing pretty for the evening. This was a lightweight trip to St.Tropez. Only now do I wonder what Di had with her.

I was celebrating my fiftieth birthday, which would happen in August, by walking a series of footpaths - sentiers de grandes randonees - all across France to St Tropez which I had first visited in 1964. In those days, Brigitte Bardot was the siren which helped establish this little fishing port's exotic reputation. Now I was going again because, I suppose, it represented something from my youth which I wanted to recapture. Anyway, I had walked about two hundred miles and was on the outskirts of Paris before I first read that Diana was already there. It was hard to avoid the news since the pictures of her stretching over Dodi in the back of his yacht were on the front cover of almost every magazine. I was thrilled, of course, because it added a little lustre to my own journey and a certain symmetry. St. Tropez. Brigitte Bardot to Princess Diana. What a place to go if you are at odds with the paparazzi and you want to avoid the limelight.

But for me, as I made my way around Paris on the GR1 to walk along the Seine and the Yonne southwards to Vezelay and the Morvan hills, I didn't give her another thought, except to speculate amusingly when I saw the headline **'Di to extend her holiday in St Trop'** *that she had decided to stay on for me and give me a royal welcome in September. How flippant these thoughts now seem when I read them in my diary.*

Weeks pass and I walk through one of the hottest summers France has had in years. For two weeks temperatures are above thirty degrees celsius but I press on southwards feeling increasingly fit as the pounds sweat off me. I am overjoyed when I eventually step into Provence, crossing the Rhone at Pont St Esprit at five-thirty in the morning to avoid the awful heat in the middle of the day. By now I have covered almost eight hundred miles in seven weeks and I can feel the pull of my final destination. Diana has already left St Tropez and my thoughts.

I am in Vauvenargues, the tiny Provencal village in the shadow of Mont Ste. Victoire. In front of me is the imposing, turretted chateau where Piccasso used to live and where he is buried in the grounds. I am in a 'phone box chatting to David Evans, a writer friend of mine back in England. By now I have got used to being by myself but I find I love to talk on the telephone, full of what has happened on the walk. I am telling David of a curious event that happened earlier in the day.

I was crossing the limestone plateau before beginning my descent into Vauvenargues when the footpath began to narrow and the undergrowth began to close in on me, forming a narrow tunnel only big enough for one person. To make my way along it I had to stoop so I was looking downwards and didn't realise what was coming towards me until the very last moment. A few feet ahead of me, moving slowly and gently, was a white horse.

I stopped but the horse continued forward until we were facing each other. There was no room for us to pass so for a moment I just stood there stroking its soft muzzle. Eventually I took off my pack, fished out a banana which was eagerly received, before squeezing past its warm and sweaty flanks and continuing on my way. There was no sign of an owner, indeed I would have been surprised if there had been, for on nearly every day of my walk I was completely alone. But meeting a white horse in such circumstances is a weird experience.

David was very curious about this strange encounter and I went on to tell him about another odd event earlier in my trip when I was forced to walk a couple of kilometres along the busy Route National 1. I had to pass though a tiny village and in the middle of the road was a woman holding two dead, white doves. A third was lying in the road. The doves in her hand were undamaged, their heads hanging down as she held them by their feet. The woman was bewildered and could not account for their death. She was close to tears as I helped her off the road, speculating that they might have died of broken hearts at the loss of one of their family which had obviously been crushed by a car. Doves, I understand, mate for life.

David was intrigued by the story and asked me if the doves and the horse had been perfectly white, which I confirmed. He seemed oddly concerned that I had told him the two stories but we left it at that. The date was August 30th.

I was staying in a cheapish hotel in Vauvenargues run by a typically efficient and indomitable woman in her late fifties. Since the next day I had to climb Mont Ste. Victoire, about three thousand

314

feet and walk a total of about twenty-two miles, I asked her if it would be possible to have breakfast at seven am. No, she said firmly, breakfast did not begin until seven-thirty. Nevertheless, the following morning I was lurking around the dining room hoping to persuade her otherwise. Alas, she gave me a flea in my ear and I retired to my room. Moments later she appeared at my door, her face completely changed, and asked me to come to her office. She spoke carefully in French. 'You are English,' she said, 'and I have some terrible news for you which I feel you must know. This morning in Paris your Princess Di was killed.' At this point she broke down in tears and between sobs told me what details she knew of the accident.

It is a strange thing to be away from home when a major event like this happens. My immediate instinct was to turn and talk to my family, but it was six-thirty am on a Sunday morning in London. So I set off alone on an acid blue morning and began to climb the steep northern slope of Ste. Victoire. Strangely, the first person I told of the news was the man who had been in charge of building the Channel Tunnel for the French, Pierre Matheron. He was sweating his way up the mountain ahead of me and he stood astonished and appalled by the news, gazing unseen over the magificent views around us. It is a surreal moment to stand with a perfect stranger and discuss the death of a Princess at the summit of one of France's most famous landmarks. It will be hard to look at Cezanne's paintings in the same way again.

It was only when I got to my hotel in Trets that evening and phoned home that the true impact of what had happened came home to me and for the next few days, through Nans les Pins, Signes, Belgentier, Pignans and La Garde Freinet the news makes me feel increasingly isolated. Although I am excited at almost completing my walk and at scraping the figures '1000' into the red footpath just beyond Pignans, the avalanche of flowers outside Kensington Palace, the reports of life totally altered in England, now make my achievements seem most insignificant.

And now, by awful concidence, I will arrive in St. Tropez at the very moment Diana's funeral is taking place. On the morning of Saturday September 6th I leave La Garde Freinet to walk the twelve miles or so to St. Tropez. The walk that will live in my mind for ever is coming to an end just as Diana's body is making the journey that will live in the minds of everyone who saw it by the roadside or on television for as long as they live.

St.Tropez is not a town for mourning and you had to look hard at the international flags fluttering around the beautiful and bustling harbour to see that the sole Union Flag was at half-mast. The fabulous yachts continued to come and go and the throng of people continued to parade in front of them. It was said that the Saturday market at La Place des Lices was 'unnaturally quiet' but it appeared to be going full pelt to me. I was delighted to have finished my voyage, 1056 miles in nine weeks and two days, but as I 'phoned family and friends to tell of my arrival, congratulations were edged with sadness. More than one person, even those who were cynical of Diana, told me there would never be a day like this again.

And for me there wouldn't. I will never walk a thousand miles again, carving ten weeks out of a normal working and family life to fulfill a dream. In the future, September 6th will be the day of Diana's funeral. I will always remember this day as well, but it will come hard on the heels of another memory.

A few days after I returned to England I was chatting to David Evans who told me the reason for his interest in my stories about the horse and the dove. In the Orient and the east, white is the colour of death and mourning and after I had told him on the telephone of the incidents I had encountered, David had been concerned about my safety.

But it was not my destiny that was in question that fateful day in August.

Chapter Five

IN THE KINGDOM OF THE BLIND, THE ONE- EYED MAN IS KING.

The sober, dark blue door of number 40, South Audley Street housed two companies of John's spawning. In the basement were the offices of Rocket Records and the fan clubs of both Elton John and Queen. The backroom and basement personnel we shall nominate in a bit for the organisations over-lapped blurringly.

Upstairs, the first, second and third floors were the realm of John Reid Enterprises Limited. On the first floor, an elegant reception area carpetted wall-to-wall in Wedgewood blue, housed Liz, the switchboard operator who was soon replaced by the beautiful Helen and Jenny Over, John's assistant who had only recently joined after having been David Bell's right hand at London Weekend Television for many years. Finally there was Maureen Hillyer, John's secretary. Through double doors off this reception area where waited roadies, bankers, chauffeurs, drug dealers, wives, insurance sellers, parking wardens and stars was John's office, the inner sanctum with tall, netted windows looking out over South

Audley Street. Same blue carpet, imposing wooden fireplace, big partners desk which had once belonged to Bryan Forbes, high-back leather deskchair, armchairs, even a sofa, I think and a coffee table by Alun Jones, fashioned in the form of skull-capped dominatrix in a green skin-tight leather costume wearing laced high-heeled patent boots kneeling on all-fours.

Yes, it surely had a certain bizarre quality.

Gold discs were on the walls as well as paintings, one - maybe some - by Bryan Organ and there was an eighteenth century-ish cabinet housing both drinks and sound equipment. In this room worked John and, usually, Jenny. He took all his meetings in this room and I came to know it well.

Upstairs on the first floor worked Geoffrey Ellis, big buddy of the late Brian Epstein and lately Dick James' employee whom John had poached. In his later 'forties I would guess, Geoffrey appeared self-effacing, retiring, ineffably and coldly polite and disconcertingly colourless for a rock 'n' roll concern; he was a sort of *eminence grise* and, I suppose, overlooked the whole of John's enterprises. He was a poor communicator and showed little or no interest in the practical aspects of our work. He probably had very little to communicate except in figures which he did to the Michael Olivers of the world and all the other accountants and lawyers who were becoming more part of the business of rock superstardom than any recording desk or roadie ever was. There was a lot at stake, a lot to lose and these guys in suits were on hand to ensure that not a penny more was lost than was legally and efficiently necessary. Geoffrey had a very quiet secretary called Anila, an Anglo-Indian young woman who was the personification of being seen and not heard. I rarely heard her utter a syllable.

Onto the second floor and this was us ... The enablers.

Me, the general manager - me with the, for me princely, salary of £7,500 and a beautiful brown Rover 2000 car which Gary Hampshire found for me. My salary was twice what Barry had been paying me. And of course all the other essential, integral people who ran the nuts and bolts, the everyday, the interface as we would be known today. Interface between artist and industry, industry and public, public and artist ... Me, umpteen roadies, assistants, my secretary, tour managers, gophers, artists way down John's rosta's pecking order, artists at its very top.

On the second floor we planned and co-ordinated and effected the decisions taken by our principals, by John and his artists. Decisions, therefore, made by Elton, by Bernie, by Freddie, by Queen both as a collective and as individuals. By Kevin Ayers, Kiki Dee, James and Gilly Hope, Maldywn Pope ... Oh, yes. There were as many unfamous artists and as much flirting with the whore of ambition as there were celebrities shepherded and worried by the sheepdog known as John Reid. Straker remembers being flirted with as did Annabel Leventon and Gaye Brown and Diane Langton from Rock Bottom.

And who was 'us'? Sorry, were us?

Ultimately, 'us' was Alex Foster whom I persuaded back to work for me, John Brown who came in as gopher who was to gopherther than any gopher had ever gone before, Ian Brown who was drafted in to work for the 1976 Elton tour, Bob Stacey who had long been Elton's tour manager. Later, Gerry Stickells on occasion who was Elton's and then Queen's American tour manager. The relentless waves of roadies, Andy ... Oh, dozens of people who derived their livings from Elton's success.

Another occupant of the top floor at number forty was Jackie Warner, a very cultivated and suave young woman, a publisher who ran Big Pig and, I think, Rocket Music, the publishing arms of the Reid/Elton enterprise. I should at this point add a very important name to make that duo a trio, a triumvirate because I have as yet given no account of Bernie Taupin.

I've just noticed in an old notebook that I jotted these few words about Bernie then ... "Shy poets are more often happy than wordless musicians. Without Bernie (or another lyric writer), Elton could only have hummed tonight on that stage ..." The point being, a point which many people tend to forget, Elton only wrote the music. Bernie only wrote the words. A song has to have both. Words and music. Neither is a consummate artist and neither should argue that he is. Elton is not good at all with words. Separately, they would be bereft. Together, they conquered the world and founded the empire.

Indeed, without Bernie the whole Rocket/JRE thing would have been much more difficult as an imperial project. And in saying that, I have to make mention of Maxine, Bernie's feisty, single-minded and entirely rational American wife. Maxine too was very much part of the political equation which determined the strength of the house that John Reid built. If Elton had become incredibly rich from the income his music made from publishing, Bernie's fortune was equal. And Maxine was part of that. Of course Elton was far richer - concert earnings and record royalties were obviously enormous but Bernie had chosen to throw his lot into their pot. Taupin was a handsome man, again, rather small but where Elton was, sadly, plain, Bernie was very attractive. And, straight. Bernie had no eye for the boys. Also shy, also very unpushy but with equal enthusiasm for what Rocket Records had set out to do - give people a chance. Helping the little people, wasn't it?

But now I must take you from the very top of the building to the very bottom for in the basement were housed the rest of the interface crew who made the magic possible.

Rocket Records was of course the company baby spawned from the potslew of ideas which always proceeds overnight success. A potslew undoubtedly adulterated by the good offices of the wise and tax-efficient, higly paid accountant. Significantly, Rocket Records did not, however, enjoy Elton John as one of its artists at that time. It enjoyed the services of Kiki Dee, the afore-mentioned Maldwyn Pope and was only really to achieve a profile not in Britain but in America when through it, Neil Sedaka was reborn as Golda Disc (Elton's name for him) and Cliff Richard (Sylvia Disc) - a Rocket artist in America only - made it to the Billboard charts but no further. Soeur Cliff may have been lately born again, but resonant in the badlands and heartlands of American musical substance he wasn't.

They also had Lulu. Where and when, we've rather forgotten.

David Croker was in charge of deploying the rocketry and in truth I had little to do with this genial man. I had come to know him well already whilst trying to shop other artists in my personal roster which Reid generously enouraged me to maintain. Croker had had no interest in John Hetherington or Twinkle or Mike Allison and Pete Sills or Peter Straker but he had sufficient heart to make the rejection process as tolerable as possible. There is an art to

320

saying, "No".

However, also working in the basement were David Costa and Caroline Boucher. Costa ran the art department. Quite, quite brilliant. Utter perfectionist. Outwardly calm and measured, quiet, assiduous, often inspired, David was more of an artist than an art director. He was the son of the radio DJ Sam Costa who had figured conspicuously as a voice in my teenage ears and indeed David had played for a while himself in a band called Casablanca which had also been a Rocket signing. David was in charge of the album covers, tour posters, flyers, advertisements - anything graphic which came either out of Rocket or John Reid Enterprises bore his hallmark.

Caroline Boucher who was in the throes of marrying Robert Lee, one of the coming lawyers at Harbottle and Lewis, had been recruited by Reid from her career as one of rock's leading journalists having worked on DISC and RECORD MIRROR alongside and often in cahoots with the now undersung and undervalued Penny Valentine. Caroline was the press officer both for Rocket and for John Reid Enterprises which I shall now reduce to an acronym, JRE. Caroline worked solo until the arrival of both Laura Beggs later in 1975 and that of Laura's schoolfriend Sally Atkins a little later. Caroline was punchy, often brittle but immensely caring and she knew her business backwards whilst acting as sympathetic and encouraging den mother to all her Rocketchiks.

Linda Mullarkey and Marie Thatcher ran the Elton fan club like two corgis guarding the Queen's ankles. Linda was sort of in charge and Marie - who was always called Fuzzypeg because of her fabulous long mane of pre-Raphaelite hair - aided and abetted, keeping visiting fans at bay (Cries of, "Dogs at the Door!" heralded many a first acquaintance of the adoring fan with his or her hero's courtiers,) and generally acting as Rocket's receptionists and switchboard operators. Eamonn, a large, cheerfully dogged, stolid Irish boy had risen from being a fan to the Rocket gopher and apart from all the people I've forgotten or omitted, that was that.

Except ... Except that Pat and Sue Johnson had arrived to run the Queen fan club. I think they had been assimilated but I don't think I would go as far as proclaiming that they had been embraced. Their section of the basement was in microcosm a reflection of how the whole works was feeling.

Like Pat and Sue, I arrived to be piggy-in-the-middle with no history except a very personal one of knowing Freddie. These Rocket/JRE people had all started out with, grown up with and now lived with Elton John and they understandably wore their loyalty like hearts on a sleeve. I think they were as confused as Elton must have been initially about the importation of another principal.

To be fair, I could understand this mood very well. Queen were so comparatively insignificant when compared to Elton. They were only just being talked about because of Bohemian Rhapsody. The single had only just been released, I'm sure with John's encouragement and Sir Joseph Lockwood's influence at EMI ... To say that there was resentment in the camp would be untrue; to say there was suspicion afoot and ruffled feathers only slowly settling would be more precise.

Someone once said that homosexuals should never be used as sticking plaster. I think the implied context was one of other people's marriages and relationships Me? I was obviously supposed to be the Band Aid *extraordinaire*. No one knew how all this mix 'n' match was supposed to pan out. Least of all John and Elton.

It is now about John and Elton that I have to write something for they are obviously pivotal. What was happening around me was the playing out of stage umpetty-pumpetty of the growth of a relationship which still flourishes to this day in varying states of love and hate. Nowadays, 2004, it's hate's turn.

And of course, once again, let's not forget Bernie. Truly, despite his miracle talent with words, the silent partner.

Chapter Six

THE BANDWAGON

It matters not here how or when or through whom they met, but Elton John and John Reid met and for whatever reasons they became friends and then lovers and then partners. Early nineteen-seventies. They were unwittingly at the forefront of the progress of fastest development in gay liberation and swept along by the current they became a couple, like we all were supposed to. Like we could.

But gay men are specifically gay men. They are not, conveniently, one the 'man' and the other 'the woman', one the husband and the other the wife nor are there equal distributions of that gender sexuality in a single person. It's difficult. Then it was more so because there were no handbooks, little literature. One made do, mended and lurched on, one step forwards, two back. Two steps forward, one back. These two rather special examples of the genre were hardly more than boys, in their early twenties. They were far too young for such a commitment especially when each was soon to be beset and confused by celebrity as a mindmate.

I do not know and it's not important when the little family which had been formed and which lived at the Virginia Water bungalow decided to go their separate ways as far as sex was concerned. For a time it hung together but Elton was away a great deal either touring or recording and, let's face it, both were faced with so much temptation in the face and form of the most beautiful boys and men in the world.

And so the first home syndrome, complete with dogs and mothers moved in down the road, was probably destined to break up. John got his own place, ultimately the house at 40 Montpellier Square and Elton got his, the exurbian hotch-potch of a place known specifically and generically as Woodside, the house at Old Windsor. But after all these blue moves away from each other, what persisted between John and Elton was a deep feeling of need and an abiding and positive loyalty which remained, through thick and thin, sick and sin, to the day some twenty-eight years later when Elton finally called it off. For most gay men the first affairs, the early experimental fumblings in domesticity and the sharing/caring life not only never survive but are consigned to the lost and forgotten file for eternity and with enormous relief, together with the halved pets, the pot plants and the unused Habitat catalogues.

For a lot of the time I truly believe John and Elton have hated each other, a little of the time I'm sure they have loved each other and all of the time they have used each other. Also, more than all the time, they have each needed the other, manipulated the conflict, turning it into a torrential dynamic, sweeping everything before it. Their mutuality is visceral, basic and genuine. They were bound not only by a management contract which at the time I joined was drawing to the end of its fifth year, but by spite, revenge, mistrust, one-upmanship, greed, manipulation, political jockeying and a great deal of jealousy. People often got in the way and these were wilfully and carelessly sacrificed, apparently shamelessly in this entente/detente, this stand-up stand-off which has been the story of their lives. Only a very few thwarted the sacrifice and escaped the altar.

They were both children of and parents to each other, always pushing each other to see how far they could go, how far over the parameters of possibility they could push and be pushed. Their power was special and awesome. From little acorns, great oak trees certainly grow and the story of many an imperial legend has started with a kiss.

The atmosphere, therefore, which permeated number forty South Audley Street was incredibly special. It was only describable as magical. An enchanted circle. All the well-crafted, expertly planted stories from this magical kingdom, the legends of both Elton's and John's fabled excesses whether it be in dress or costume or exillion-dollar deals or the huge record sales or punching people in the eye and going to jail conspired to create their charmed existence in whose reflected glory we all basked. Better than any Robert Graves tale about Livia and Claudius and Caligula.

If one of Reid's stocks-in-trade was charm, Elton had the same quality in equal abundance. Came the day when, shortly after my arrival, we were finally introduced. If he had had his forebodings about the arrival of Freddie into his camp, Elton must have thought mine positively Machiavellian. They'd never had a general manager before. Why now?

I forget where in the building we first met. Reid hovered, pretending not to monitor the proceedings. Elton was smaller than I'd imagined - aren't they always? He hadn't shaved. His spectacles were plain, I think red or blue and with tinted lenses. He wore a cap - surprise, surprise. His eyes, even behind the darkened lenses, were the deepest and brownest of any eyes I'd ever seen and he had the most flutteringly long eye-lashes. The eyes were so, so sad. I instantly liked him. I felt like I wanted to hug him and tell him everything would be alright.
And yet at the same time a shiver ran through me as I felt him look deep into my very soul. It was as though one had been frisked by aliens, examined inside and out by a deep-probing fibre-optic neural camera, turned upside down by unseen hands and arms, checked for weapons and proposed for serious security clearance. I know I was passed.

I have to say now that I didn't feel myself in the least bit sexually or amorously drawn to him. Although I loved him on sight, I didn't fancy him one bit and I was very relieved.

My relief, as things turned out, was probably mis-placed. I think it would have been better in the light of later events if I'd fancied the pants off him. I have a feeling it was almost expected. But by whom? By both of them? This was a dangerous *menage* I was entering. A minefield.

It was quite plainly to be realised that in front of me stood and was chatting one bundle of entirely unstable emotional turmoil whose relentless energy was almost dysfunctional. Here was a soul who had known, knew and was to know little peace. Elton was, of course, not the prettiest, not the tallest, not the most physically blessed mortal. Not a satisfactory self for a gay boy to have hauled around for years, comparing, being compared to more handsome, taller and naturally endowed in the family, the form, the sports field, the pub, the club ... To compensate, there was of course the musical talent, the clown's abilities, the show-off's bravado, the bitch-wit of the queens from the far end of the bar in many a provincial gay pub. And, of course, the incontrovertible power gained from the realisation that people found him fascinating because of his fame, irresistible because of his wealth and magnetic because ...

Because of the indefinable magnetism which all this foregoing, babbling paragraph had conspired to produce.

Because, put quite simply, what a voice! What songs!

Larger than life, maybe ... But whose life? Elton John was larger than even Elton John could sensibly manage. He was the most open and yet the most guarded person I've ever met.

Freddie was transparent compared to Elton, much more understandable, much less complex and a much more centred human being.

But they were all of them teetering on the edge of a precipice which could have easily taken all three lives, not just one. Although I didn't know it and had no inkling of it, because I was so utterly green on the matter of drugs, drug-taking and incipient drug-addiction, my arrival on the scene of the Reid-Elton Empire was as a novice into the Convent of St. Cocaine, patron saint of the idol rich ...

"You're so rich you don't have to walk
You're obviously too bored to talk
Your poor old brain can't take the strain,
I know. The answer? More cocaine!"

I've already indicated that my memories of the

dopeheads I'd encountered whilst at university was not good. Everyone had known who they were. I felt uneasy with this knowledge. Intimidated, challenged, compromised and very, very excluded. Since that first occasion in The Troubadour in Los Angeles when I had been with John and been introduced to the golden spoonful, I had had little if anything to do with the sort of drugs one bought from a pusher. The occasional puff of marijuana now made me giggle, we smoked poppers (crushable vials of amyl nitrite contained in cardboard tubes) in the back of Rod's Club above the furniture cave in the Kings Road, Chelsea. But that was all. Coke? Speed? Heroin? Couldn't afford it, my friends didn't do it. There was until now no peer pressure and no psychological need in me. No craving. Interestingly, even Freddie was still vehemently against using these 'recreational' drugs at the time.

All this was to change. The promiscuity which set the seal on the later 'seventies and thereon and which equally embraced the drug culture was taking hold of gay and straight London. Life was hardening. Sex was hardening. Drugs were hardening. The flex and stretch was running out of our lives. It wasn't now merely enough for a gay boy to have a boyfriend. Gay boys now had sex. As much as they could get of it. Achievement sex was as high on the agenda as greedy consumerism. How many, how many times ... All grist to a phenomenon that was to become known in a mere handful of years as Thatcherism which was, contradictorily, not the fault of the blonde lady who lived on Flood Street then in relative obscurity with Denis and their twins, Carol and Mark ...

But then someone always has to take the blame, don't they?

Chapter Seven

Honesty is some conceit, considering the matter
And, possibly, we might agree, it's much the better policy
But, tell the truth and spurn deceit, careers do not get fatter,
So is it any wonder people often slip and tell a lie?

What is the truth? Is it what people want to hear, need to hear or ultimately what they get told? I was soon struggling, juggling with so many sets of other people's truths, I started to forget my own and when I needed my own, I didn't know what it was and wouldn't have recognised it had I stumbled across it or had it jumped up and bit me on the ass. So, I didn't know where to look 'cos I didn't know what I was looking for.

Enough of the conundrum philosophy, already!

To be a manager in the music business is to be able to both instinctively and after consultation make decisions and act on them in your clients' best interests. It is empowering. Probably doubly so because you are acting for two people, the client and yourself. It's really good to kick-ass at the record company because your artist wants to remain Mister Nice Guy and you don't care ... "You couldn't fuckin' sell bananas to a fuckin' starvin' monkey!" I once heard a manager scream down the telephone to a hapless exec at EMI.

However, to work IN management is an entirely dis-empowering experience because you find yourself a servant and, as a servant, one who answers to two masters. Once again, I found that my boss was not necessarily my principal but that I found myself morally bound to render to Caesar that which was Caesar's.

In short, very short, I was employed by John but I found myself contradictorily drawn after the short opening scene to regarding Elton (or Freddie or any of the artists) as my principal for the remainder of the play.

Beware short men bearing promises; that sounds like a stage direction but it was how I was advised once by one much older and wiser. I was responsible and yet I was powerless. Responsibility without power is as dysfunctional as power without responsibility. Useless. The master of two servants is going places. The servant of two masters is severely stuck in shit city.

For the first three months of my employment, it was Queen business which predominated. Elton was away most of those three months recording. Not that there was nothing to do. They were busy organisational days at the end of which there was the daily call to EMI for the detailed sales figures which had to be logged and communicated both to John and to Elton wherever they were in the world. These were kept rigorously as an aid to later checks made on EMI's accounting to ensure accuracy.

And I was getting to know the other artists on JRE's management list. First came Kiki Dee. Elton had always admired her voice, as he had Dusty Springfield's. There was some talk that at one stage he wanted to work with Dusty. Thank heavens he didn't. He ended up with Kiki, a former Motown artist with a voice that would make angels weep and whom John Reid had probably met during his time doing promotion at Motown. Kiki'd already had one Rocket hit, AMOUREUSE and when I arrived, David Croker had just issued another single. Kiki and I were sent out on the road, a short promotion tour of Radio Stations and, whilst we were in whichever town, a press interview - even two - was also usually conducted either at the Radio Station or at a local hotel.

I'm talking of the days when commercial radio was still being introduced, a decision rather enforced on the corsetted broadcasting powers of the day by the activities of the 'sixties pirate stations Caroline, Radio London who operated illegally from storm-tossed rusty buckets masquerading as seaworthy ships from offshore anchorages. It was quite mediaeval really, when I come to think about it but progress has always had to be forced. Change never occurs by magic. It occurs when the rebels show the establishment that there is either money to be made or power to be derived from a brash, brazen new enterprise. Indeed, the Capital Radio Board was composed integrally of men who knew America, who had travelled and who were already powerful in the field of entertainment.

In this media arena, only America had had the benefit of that fabulous system of nationwide WWPCs and WXMPs which made music so exciting and upon which a whole youth culture so retarded in Europe had been built. This system had supported and developed several strands of popular music, country and western, rock, jazz, folk, soul, pop and gave a foundation of category definition which, with generational additions, lasts to this day.

But we were starting to catch up. By 1975 London had Capital Radio as well as smaller less music-oriented stations like the London Broadcasting Company. Manchester had Piccadilly Radio and there were stations in every main regional capital. This blossoming of the radio stations and the general increase in televised music product had of course spawned a whole new generation of smart, street-wise promotions men and women in the music business. I remember Mickey Most's brother, Dave and Annie Challis, Tony Bramwell, then the king of them all and, of course, Clive Banks. These men and women made hit records as much as any producer and certainly more than the artist.

The times also were witnessing the emergence of the DJ and his producer as one of the new powers in the new music biz. The list was endless and usually pretty banal on any cerebral level. Paul Gambaccini was to become a notable exception but in those days he was a mere inkhound. Eversince it had been noticed that this musicbiz thing conferred a glam status as mysterious as transubstantiation, power had become the name of the game. Power to persuade, power to effect records being on a station's playlist or not, power to be invited, power to either take calls or not ... power to be a player.

To an extent this had always been so but now, to thicken

the soup even more, creativity and intellect had entered the communications ballpark and from this magical swirl which spawned the John Peels and the Dave Lee Travises and the Mike Reids emerged the diminutive but towering figure of Kenny Everett.

I first met Kenny via Freddie Mercury. He was at Capital Radio and, as has often been asserted, was probably the only reason why BOHEMIAN RHAPSODY was a hit. It was incomprehensible to most suit'n'tie DJs but to Kenny, who already composed his own jingles, singing the closely harmonised backing onto multi-track home recording facilities, Freddie's huge vision, both the breadth and the height and the depth of it was instantly Kenny's bag. The two became firm friends and Kenny, in the same position as Freddie in many ways - they were both gay men still ostensibly living 'straight' lives with women - derived a great deal of strength to bolster the tottering adult who had emerged after the guilt-onslaughts of a Jesuit catholic upbringing. Kenny was easily led astray, easily persuadable. For a while he had John Pitt, a very centred, feet-on-the-ground Australian to keep him focused but later lovers, such as the fabulous, fatal Nikolai, proved less avuncular.

Kenny and Freddie were certainly equally outrageous in their own public personae and yet both as quiet and shy in private. At core, Kenny was like a tiny child who wanted deep down to be merely swept up by a pair of strong arms and cuddled and held and protected. He wanted, in a way, to be over-powered, to be complemented by the greater strength of another. Hence he found it so easy to be attracted to heavy sexual scenes where being used and abused subsumed the need to be loved for as long as the use and abuse could be made to last. To please his lover meant that he was being loved and this would also please Kenny.

I remember meeting him in Notting Hill one Sunday afternoon. He was driving past in his car and saw me, stopped and asked me if I knew a good doctor. He was very quiet, unusually quiet. I asked why and he told me he'd had an unusually heavy scene with someone the night before and that his rectum had been torn and bruised. It was still bleeding ... I wanted to take him in my arms and hold him and protect him but for some of what I deem the right reasons. All I could do was hug him through the window, give him the name and number of two possible doctors and off he went ... He still felt that for him to have gone to a hospital would have been too dangerous. Press. The Street of Shame might get to hear ... Terrifying.

Kenny was a huge talent, a multi-talent as he later proved in every medium he engaged in. I loved him then, lost track of him in his later excesses as unbridled disco-drug-taking and sado-masochistic proclivities wrecked his life and I miss him like hell now he's gone. He provided for no successor. His talent was too great.

But back to me and Kiki, a long way from London. The promotion tour made for an interesting few days as we schlepped ourselves around on trains and in cabs. Glamorous? Puhleeze. I got to know Pauline Matthews from Bradford quite well. I thought she had the quality of a young French film star in those days. Her short hair was coloured an electric henna by Moulton Brown and it made her look Parisian, together with the artful make-up in which the same salon instructed her. But our Pauline had little enough of the spunk of pure ambition to put fire in the belly of Kiki Dee. She'd started too early and had been doing it all a bit too long to be anything else but a really good singer and Britain, nay the world, has always had a surfeit of really good singers.

Kiki was a nice girl, sensible ... She wasn't wild, wanton or wayward. Hardly rock 'n' roll material. I felt her niche was something in film or on stage and was very pleased when she ended up for so long and did so well in Willy Russell's BLOOD BROTHERS. However, unlike Barry Krost's office, John Reid's was no place for crossovers. As an artist, you were there to join in the musical exploitation but don't for fuck's sake think you'd get acting lessons. Kiki needed them desperately, even if only to teach Pauline Matthews how to 'do' Kiki Dee. But it was a long time before STARS IN YOUR EYES ...

Next in roster seniority - another prefect, if you will, to Elton's head boy (whoops!) - came Kevin Ayers. This was another legendary figure in rock's pantheon. Legendary because there was still enough living memory about to remember the Velvet Underground. Since those beatific days, Eno was doing his stuff, John Cale was still doin' stuff, Nico was probably on Ibiza by now pedalling her ... oh, yes, bike - and Kevin Ayers was living on a houseboat moored in Little Venice with Richard Branson's first wife,

Kristen. Two long-haired, leggy blondes on a narrow boat built for load rather than speed. Where Kevin was probably pretty well-hung, Kristen had an even bigger one and more balls than a bingo caller. Their presence was like that of Zeus and Athena. Philip of Spain's monumental psychedelic Armada to Elizabeth II's dancing disco queens.

John's management of Kevin was always a mystery to me. Kevin was lumpen and stolid and so laid back that to glimpse his drive was like waiting for Halley's comet to come around. The only link between he and Reid as far as I could fathom was EMI Records and so ... hey. Not that I didn't get on with the guy but we had absolutely nothing in common whatsoever. Neither did I with the ex-Mrs. Branson who had obviously gotten very used to the lifestyle she had enjoyed with Richard and was having a tough time coming to terms with her loss of conubial status and her divorcee's pension.

The houseboat drove me mad. I thought it pretentious and pompous. As a couple they were pretentious and pompous, let's face it. They were all statement and no substance. Kevin was making an album when I joined JRE, called, YES, WE HAVE NO BANANAS. Twenty years later, my sister-in-law wrote a television series with almost the same name. Oh dear.

Burning the candle of clients we come swiftly to James and Gilly who were called Hope and hope was about all they had, given the recipe book at South Audley Street. Very nice but just what was I supposed to do with them? They were like ... Like the extra boiled potatoes served up just in case people don't much like roast. Such nice, nice potatoes. People. Parsnips. Penguins. Persons.

Meanwhile, as I left Kiki in the bosom of her family and boarded the train in Bradford to take me back down south, back home, BOHEMIAN RHAPSODY had reached the Number one slot in the charts and remained there for three months, give or take. Most of the time it was there, Queen were touring, playing, it seemed, anywhere and everywhere and consolidating the foundation of their position as a live performance band which would last them the whole of their active careers.

At Christmas they were due to play the Hammersmith Odeon.

We used to watch Bo Rhap on the telly, the three of us,

in the Putney flat. We watched in a kind of disbelief, really. It was more than a kind of magic. The hairs on my arms still stand up when I listen to Freddie's song today. It wasn't until 2003 that I came across that little old black and white plastic Pye television on which we used to watch, Minns, Freddie and I. It was plugless, covered in dust and spatters of what looked like tomato sauce and many inevitable coffee stains. I looked at this museum piece of technology for a full week before I decided I could only dump it in the trash.I really had to. Didn't I? Whatever.

But it was a tough decision and I never plucked up courage to find a plug and reconnect it and so I never discovered whether it still worked.

Odd, though, to reflect that although the hardware had grown old and had became dated and probably defunct, the software is still as vibrant and exciting today as Freddie made it thirty years ago and, ultimately, Mercury's message is even more important that the messenger.

Chapter Eight

LOST IN SPACE AND MEANING

As I write this, it's early April 1997 and I've just driven down through the heart of England to see my parents who still lived in Malvern. Like, they'd even have thought of moving? There were still some constants, thank heavens. Now, in May 2004, they aren't here and it seems there are no constants.

But time itself can never stand still and I was fifty and it was some twenty-two years later ... For the first time since that long-ago, I played Elton John tapes in the car to, I naively thought, wile away the journey. Not songs from the latter part of the career, I confess but the earlier ones when Bernie was his only muse and there was still something for the Empire to fight for.

I used to think that it was the celebrity which must have been the fundamental attraction which lured me into and allowed me to remain in my hallowed showbiz circles. I was always quite prepared to admit my fickle nature which unashamedly borrowed from other people's glory to prettify my own. I'd seen quite enough of famous people jostling to be seen with, sit next to or merely be at the same occasion with those even more famous than themselves that my own paltry jockeying paled into insignificance.

However, as I drove through those Cotswold towns and villages, my journey became one into the past. I suddenly found myself weeping uncontrollably and I realised that it wasn't other people's fame with which I had been in love but that as far as Elton and Bernie were concerned, as far as Cat Stevens was concerned, Twinkle, John Osbore - n-n-n-n - it was the miracle of creativity which moved me. Then and now. That much at least had been constant. The realisation then - as if I needed it - had been that I found myself in the company of people who were saying in words and music what I felt, making me feel a part of something greater, wider, higher, a seminal something which in turn made me feel more, more me ...

So why was I crying? It was as though a voice was calling to me from the other side of a high, high unclimbable wall around which there was no shortcut, whose foundations were so deep no tunnel could burrow beneath them and I was a prisoner behind it.

I understood that I had left something very precious behind. Something?

I'd left my fucking life behind.

It was as though my life was calling to me to come and get it, to bring it home and I was crying because I couldn't. Because the lives on the two sides of the wall are now unjoinable. Like trying to re-unite truth and compromise. The two will never be reconciled. The young know the truth. When we are older, we find the truth palatable only when altered or, more conveniently, ignored altogether. The young can afford to have true feelings. When we are older, true feelings tend only to hurt.

Bernie's lyrics and Elton's music reminded me today how much I have had to leave behind for those songs are still my truth and hearing them reminds me of how much I have compromised since, along the way, merely to survive. There has been so much sadness, so much tragedy and pain since Bernie wrote those words and since Elton nightly chugged and trucked his way relentlessly like the Starlight Express along railroads of driving rhythm, scorching the length of limitless freeways of electrical bop on the edge of the world's most star-striven stages.

Rock 'n' roll was so truly life-enhancing. Why then, oh why, should it have proved also so life-threatening? And why is it that, some days, it's so damn dangerous to remember?

336

Chapter Nine

THIS IS YOUR CAPTAIN
CALLING

I looked up and saw a star ... Noel, noel ... Born is the king of Israel ... Christmas is coming, the goose is getting fat, please put a penny in the old man's hat ...

People had put all their pennies into promoter Harvey Goldsmith's box office hat at Hammersmith and the Queen tour 1976 was coming to a sold-out, not-even-standing-room end. John Reid had flown off to Barbados for the Christmasfest to be with Elton and all seemed well with the world as he had been able to do so safe in the knowledge that Daisy (Me) was the buffer of St. Nick. The fall guy, primed, ready and waiting to take the flak should Brian May, Roger Taylor or John Deacon particularly or severally revolt against John Reid's defection to the enemy camp. Camp, I contend is camp ... There is no enemy, except, then, for the suspect straights. And what the hell I'd've done if they had've revolted was but conjecture.

So there I was, holding the fort in London. Freddie (Mercury)? He cared not a whit. If anything he would have preferred to have been on Barbados with Elton and John rather than schlepping the stages of the venues of the rocktour circuit but there was final work to be done - the Hammersmith Christmas show was due to be recorded and broadcast by the BBC - and all that was, after all, Freddie's job, wasn't it? As my job was mine.

So why on earth, a week before Christmas, did Jenny Over, John Reid's assistant, come up to my office to say she had had a 'phone call from Barbados which instructed me to go to Cartier the following morning and collect the Christmas presents which Elton had ordered to distribute amongst his houseparty on Christmas morning and fly them to the Caribbean? My going would, of course, leave no one technically 'in charge' of the London office, precisely the situation which I thought John had employed me to avoid. I wonder now if there was not a few power politics going on. I think someone was exercising a little muscle. I think someone had to ensure that they were still number one, still top dog, still Captain Fantastic ... Someone must have had one of someone's celebrated, seldom-recorded 'little moments ...'

Of course, I had no choice. I told Freddie who was at least mollifiable and I was helped by David Minns (my flatmate, his then-lover) who was, on my behalf, thrilled at my chance of my having such a wonderful adventure. But Freddie also had the burden of the band's irritation to contend with and so yet another of those situations arose where he was pleased for me but selfishly - and quite understandably - didn't care to deflect bandflak by making excuses either for my absence or for Reid's to the other three Queenies. And they had a point. They had, after all, signed up at a massive percentage of their income for personal management. The management is hardly personal if the management's not there. Queen were a doomy, gloomy lot *en masse* but their Queendom was never anything but fiercely democratic. Tantrums were not merely the prerogative of an individual. Collective tantrum beset the band throughout its existence.

Reidrule in the realm of the Two Queens was not starting well.

But hey ... I was off to Cartier, Minns waiting in the car outside in Bond Street with John's driver Gary Hampshire to collect the swag which was presented to me very graciously by Mr Castle, famous for his associations with the famous *arriviste* clientele, who paid his salary and perpetuated what was once a classic reputation –

from my perspective, Cartier's current existence was as lonely little onion in a petunia patch, to misquote another common ditty. Mr Castle was always on the guest list for any Elton/Reid bash. I suppose if I'd've got famous, I'd've insisted that my favourite checkout person at Sainsbury's at The Angel be invited to all my book launches. But there, we have it ... I never knew Mr. Castle's first name. He was always down on the guest list as merely Mr. Castle. Had Elton had anything to do with it, he would have surely have been nick-named Barbara. How did Mr.Castle escape?

But there I was with all those little red boxes ... I felt like a cabinet minister I had so many, disguised on the way home to Putney in a Sainsbury's plastic carrier bag. Minns had already helped me to choose a travel bag for my trip. Because we'd never had holidays and since the Ashley Gardens burglar had made off with all my good luggage, I had nothing to carry the swag in and so we bought a scuba diver's holdall from a shop in Fulham Palace Road.

The night before the flight I hardly slept. I hadn't dared open even one of the boxes. Diamonds? Certainly. Watches? Probably. Incalculable value. Between worrying about burglars and fighting off Minns and Freddie who begged in vain to be allowed sight of the booty, I was a worried bunny. My fears were hardly allayed when I got to the airport the following morning. Needless to say, the red boxes never left my side and came with me on the 'plane. I'm pretty sure I was travelling first class, at least club if there was such a category in those days and the westward flight to Barbados was uneventful although what the cabin crew and my fellow passengers made of this slight, untravelled English lad clutching a Sainsbury's carrier bag to his chest for four and a half thousand miles, I never knew. A chic new crumbcatcher for the *canapés*, perhaps? It would have been understandable; punk had just surfaced as an identifiable trend.

Down we came at the right airport - always a miracle to my unscientific mind - and off I got. Caribbean island airports still have passengers disembarking - even off Concorde - onto the tarmac in front of the terminal. We had already had one stopover on Antigua where machine-gun toting military men had patrolled us, herded us as we disembarked for a breath of air and a bottle of fizzy from one of the corrugated iron airport buildings. I clutched my bag even closer to me. Stranger and stranger they must have thought.

And so from one banana republic to another, even from a hundred yards away I could recognise Reid on the first floor of the Barbados terminal. He had, thankfully, come to meet me. He'd said he would but ... Well, you never know. He was wearing white - shirt, shorts - but even from that distance he looked rather too contrasting. As I walked closer, the contrast manifested itself as a vicious sunburn, scaldingly pink which made him look like a prawn, sandwiched as he was between two very dark Bajan ladies waving from the balcony at my fellow-arrivals. Reid gestured, pointing downwards, by which he meant he would see me in the arrivals hall after clearing customs.

Customs.

Never even crossed my mind, your Honour ... And it was true. I'd never given any real thought to mere officialdom. Where must my brain have been? Was I so comfy in the illusion that as I was the emissary of the court of King Song I was therefore immune to the banal chorus of ordinary diplomatic and contraband regulations affecting mere mortals? I suppose that must have been the case. Blithe was nowhere in it.

Dumb, on the other hand, is a good word.

Thus, to the question, "Do you have anything to declare?", I probably murmured rather grandly, looking the other way, "No, only Elton John's Christmas presents to his houseguests!"

"Elton who?" came back the irritated and entirely unimpressed response. Elton John obviously meant as much in Bridgetown as Baa-Baa Blacksheep. At that point I could see John Reid, even more conspicuously sun-grilled, behind a glass wall in the heat and fug of this tropical evening for it was now past dusk. He looked even more like a boiled prawn in a glass casserole full of enormous, flailing tadpoles. I must have flashed a smug grin in his direction. I must have for I remember noticing how his expression was turning from the beaming to the bewildered, from the dimpled smile of pleasure to the furrowed frown of concern. Reid, more *au fait* with these circumstances than I, had surely twigged. I hadn't and soldiered on with the foolish arrogance of the ignorant.

"So what in d'ere?" barked one of the officers.

I felt an appalling attack of stammering overtake me.

"C-c-c ..." I just couldn't get 'Christmas presents' out. Being a seasoned stammerer, I knew the verbal escape routes and so I therefore tried for 'Gifts'. I opened my mouth and the word strangled itself on then intitial 'G' somewhere between my larynx and my epiglottis. 'P' was usually pretty safe and so I took a deep breath and, hey presto, out came, "Presents!" I nearly blew the customs officers away in a cloud of spit and spray.

"What sorta presents?"

Oh, lord! I launched into the intimate, *sotto voce* repetition of, "Surely you know who it is I'm staying with ..." routine delivered in the sort of sublime whisper I fondly imagined must have been used by equerries explaining to Queen Victoria who Oscar Wilde was.

Absolutely nil reaction. The dear Queen, after all, would have known exactly who Oscar Wilde was whereas my current wild man had neither knowledge of nor interest in queens of any description or lineage. My smug little grin slid off my face like a greasy fried egg from a fatted frying pan.

I don't know exactly why or when the scenario concerning me and the customs men started to turn really sour but it did. I glanced at the prawn through the glass. He was chewing his fingers with the look of a terrified child watching the ritual disembowelling of a live sacrifice. I looked at him beseechingly as the customs men pointed to the Sainsbury's carrier.

Their fingers wagged insistently.

Once again, I looked beseechingly at Reid. As I tipped the bag open and the myriad jewelcases clattered out onto the counter, Reid pulled his fingers out of his mouth, slapped his hand disbelievingly over his mouth and turned away ... He actually turned right about face and stood with his back to me, those pinkly grilled calves pressed so hard against the glass that I thought the anointed sun-burned skin would have stuck to the pane.

I was bundled away from being interviewed on the public concourse and into the privacy and secrecy of a blind interrogation room. Thank heavens I'd actually declared the Cartier loot. If I hadn't, matters would have been much more serious.

As it was, things were not going well. The law in all its forms has always terrified me - I make pathetic attempts when

341

passing customs or stopping at a light next to a police car to turn my face into a brazen mask. However, this West Indian manifestation of the law, black men with badges and berets and huge pistols holstered on their khaki hips, forced my heart into my mouth. Eight hours worth of champagne and mid-air picnic churned in my guts and dropped dangerously into my lower bowel.

"But look," I protested as a vain explanation, "Mr. John (Mister John!! Makes him sound like a chain of shops selling toilet bowls) is not importing these objects at all. They have been bought as gifts for his houseguests on Christmas Day and these guests will be leaving Barbados soon afterwards, taking their Christmas gifts with them."

I was starting to get really worried. Could this be interpreted as smuggling? It was scary. The spectre of confiscation had also just reared up on my mindscreen and the prospect of actually being the cause of one of 'Elton's little moments' instead of a mere sidelines observer was not exactly sweet. In the humility of reflection and in the light of what I was later to see was the standard of living then enjoyed by the majority of black Bajans, I have to immediately concede the obscenity which the sight of the contents of my bag of little red boxes must have created in the perceptions of the customs officers who, although obstreperous and high-handed, were, after all, only doing their jobs. Not since the days of Henry Morgan and Long John Silver had this paradise island's shores seen such a hoard of treasure. There were brooches, necklaces and rings. Gold bound address books, pens and watches ...

As slowly as the boxes had been opened, they were just as quickly snapped shut, twenty-five or more pairs of leather jaws snapping closed like so many piranhas in a pond.

It was then thought that the import tax could be paid and perhaps refunded. "But no, officers," I almost wailed, "I don't have the receipt!" Without a receipt, what value could be placed on the goods? And without a value, no percentage duty could be calculated. I felt my case melting away like an ice sculpture set too close to the fire. It dripped away like the perspiration on my brow.

Impasse. Elton's presents were as likely to see a Christmas tree in 1975 as a fairy with a hangover.

Heads were shaken. Tutting tongues tic-tacked out

negativity, no, non, nein, never, nohow, no way ... The end of the matter was that the consignment be temporarily impounded but then restored to me upon my departure. That departure, I now calculated, would obviously be the next plane when Elton found out that he wasn't getting his Christmas presents. In the meantime, I was free to go. What had been an hour's grilling on top of a very long flight was over. But what was to come?

Very dejectedly, I made my way through to the public exit and there was Reid. I could hardly bear to look at him when I explained what had happened. After a few very brief moments of, "I'll kill the bastards!" and "Just who the fuck do they think they're fucking playing with?", as there was nothing left to do, we made our way to where he had parked his car.

How odd, I thought. For just those few moments, where was all the power and the glory? Where was all that all-conquering, irresistible *force majeure* which usually surrounded Reid like an inviolable cloak? There, on the tarmac of that tiny little island, miles from anywhere, he might have been ordinary. So, I thought for the first time about my hero, so it's not true. He can't do everything. He's just as fallible as I am.

The drive to Landmark, the house Elton had rented in the parish of St. James close to Barbados' swankiest hotel The Sandy Lane, took a while. Bridgetown looked positively tumble-down and although it was dark, I could see that while on one side of the coast road, the beachfront properties of the rich were obviously quite sumptuous, on the landward side, the Chattel houses of the workers as these traditional dwellings are called and which then existed in profusion, were little larger than my grandparents' summer house in their garden where the deckchairs, tennis racquets and croquet mallets were kept in sleepy middle-England.

It was my first experience of a developing country and of our much vaunted imperial past and I was later to be much sobered by it. Nudged by the day's experiences, a little much-needed perspective was starting to simplify the images in my hitherto riotously infatuated kaleidescope of feelings about the new company I was keeping.

The house known as Landmark can still be rented to this day and I'm writing in 1997. It's a beautiful, planters plantation style house with many open walls and set in delightful grounds at the sea's edge. I cannot begin to describe my first experience of the tropical lushness of the vegetation. I felt well-and-truly foreign and undoubtedly abroad for the first time in my life.

The company was already assembled and instead of being bawled out, ridiculed and made to feel responsible, Elton was adorably sympathetic as were Elton's Personal Assistant Mike Hewittson (whom they called Brenda for some godawful hair reason), Tony King, David Nutter, Bernie and Maxine Taupin who had taken the house next door and Graham Carpenter, John's cook who had made a delicious dinner. In those days, Bajan food was indescribably awful, mainly flown in for we honky tourists from Miami and Graham's presence to make the Noelfest a success was essential.

"Oh, Christ!" Elton exclaimed half-way through dinner, "if Daisy had such a problem with the bijoux, what's going to happen to my Harrods turkeys?"

Chapter Ten

EX-PATRIOT LEGENDS

There was a sort of holiday camp atmosphere to the place the next morning when we awoke. I was sharing a room with the always gorgeous, ever-young Graham Carpenter but any dreams of being ravished in the night remained merely dreams ...

Elton was bouncing around from an early hour. He had brought with him from England some garish pop record whose title I wish I could remember but it had everything to do with pink and bubbles and froth and made for an insistent *reveille*. I fancy it could have been 'Baby Face'.

On that first morning, I think Elton went off to play tennis at the Sandy Lane and we others spent the day lounging about, reading, lying on the beach in the company of a very large black man called Dalton who taught things like water-skiing and whatever else people do on coral strands. I seem to remember a constant trail of people trying to sell everything from ganja spliffs to gunky aloe vera gel.

Why can I live without these things?

It emerged that I was to be staying three nights before flying home as more people were arriving.

John and I had taken a long walk up the beach to Heron Bay, the superb house owned and built by Penelope Tree's father Ronald which stands shaded by huge Manchineel trees on the beach at Coral Reef, just south of Glitter Bay. Even the names on the island were enough to send me into paroxysms of romantic spasm. We found out that Penelope wasn't at home. Reid couldn't bear just to stand outside and look at this fabulous re-creation of the famous Italian villa at Vicenze. Reid has no fear. Me? I have to have written permission just to look over someone's garden wall.

On the second night, after dinner, we all de-camped to Alexandra's, the only discotheque on the island and bopped about a bit but because boys don't bop with boys on Barbados, we came home rather early. One of the callers during the day had been Verna Hull, one of the island's residents. Verna, the heir to the Sears Roebuck American shopping catalogue fortune lived in a lovely house further along the beach, way past Holetown and all but next door to the elderly actress Claudette Colbert with whom she maintained an ongoing feud. I think I should have described Claudette more respectfully as 'eternally youthful screen siren'! Take your pick.

On a subsequent day, not that I was loitering mind, I glimpsed, Miss Colbert, a true Hollywood legend, emerging from the sea, only to wrap herself mysteriously in large fluffy lengths of terry-towelling robe, don huge dark glasses and hurry like a very small sheik through the white banked sands to the sanctuary of her beachside hideaway.

Verna, a large lady in her sixties, was very much like a bullhorn in a muu-muu. I think it was she who organised the Alexandra's expedition and she was certainly into organising the Reid-Elton entourage as a social force to be visited. Visitors were henceforth, forth-coming.

My second full day proved even more languorous than the first and was an ideal accompaniment to the languorous night. The two visitors - either to drinks or dinner or both - whom I remember were a young dress designer called Simon whom I greedily shagged in the sand in a purple haze of dopesmoke in the early hours of the morning and, secondly, more significantly in a way, Oliver Messel.

Staying with one legend, sighting another and meeting yet another. Three in three days, this, the third, being an oft-quoted, eponymously illustrated designer of theatre and film sets, costumes, designer of interiors, fabrics, houses ... He was fabled. The contemporary of Cecil Beaton, Syrie Maugham, Noel Coward, Terence Rattigan, uncle to Lord Snowdon via his sister the Countess of Rosse ... Oi vay. If my friends could see me now!

Messel was a delight. Very quiet, obviously rather shy and patently completely bemused by the outrageous modern, cross-class out-ness of the predominantly gay company at the rented Landmark. He was small, small-boned like a featherless sparrow and his eyes twinkled as bright and dark as those of a small bird in a head which seemed almost too large for his body. He was sun-tanned and rivettingly alluring. I couldn't take my eyes off him. So alive ... vital. The juxtaposition of he and Elton was in a way shocking. But he loved the over-the-top quality which Elton brought to the company. No wonder Messel's colour was green, green for life and living for there was the green to which he gave his name. Messel Green. It's my favourite colour for interiors and exteriors. Cool and practical and welcoming and clean ... Whereas Elton is not and would not be content to be merely part of the rainbow; his greedy gaudiness ensures that he is the very spectrum.

Messel lived, along by Verna Hull, in a house called Maddox (sp?). Sussex-by-the-Sea? Later in my life, in another lifetime, I not only looked over many of the houses he had designed on the island but I got to look over his own garden wall. Did I have a chit? Sort of. By that time Penelope Tree was never at home again. She had moved to New York, had had rainbow babies and her father, Ronald Tree was dead, having founded the Barbados National Trust. Courtesy of that august body, we were looking over a house called Crystal Springs on its 'open day'; it was next door to Messel's Maddox.

Fucking on beaches, which I'm sure Mr Messel knew all about, also comes with sand as the occupational hazard but it was a hazard I was only too pleased to entertain when the formal part of my last evening on Barbados came to an end. But surely, a man should fuck on a beach at least once in his life and I fancy that I detected that the body beneath mine that night had had a mite more practice. We kissed goodnight, the dress designer and I and I crept back to my prim little single bed alongside Mr Carpenter's.

The following morning, I packed my scuba bag and vacated my billet as there arrived more company. Linda and Seymour Stein, he who later sired Sire records and thereby brought us first the Ramones and then Madonna. This schmoozingly oozing New York couple arrived with another American gen'leman whom I fancy owned a fleet of radio stations. I mean! Elton didn't invite just ANYBODY on holiday!

I bade my goodbyes and either John or Graham Carpenter drove me back to the airport. The thought of what had happened to the bag of *bijouterie* in the hands of a customs force who'd probably only ever seen a hoard like that in the movies had been haunting me all the time I'd been on the island but the prospect of now having to find out had churned my guts to water. John seemed to think that there would be no problem - indeed, it wasn't his problem - and bade me farewell.

With my little piece of paper in hand I went through an hour- and-a-half of frustration and anxiety the like of which I had never experienced and hope never to experience again. The time ticked on, no one came back with the jewels and it seemed a dead cert that I would miss the plane. The time for the departure came and went and I heard noises of jet engines being started outside - the airport in those days was like a provincial rugby stadium - and I started to lose my rag. I started to shout, I was almost in tears. I'm not the most fearless flyer, never have been and in the years following Mickey's death, my trepidation was unrestrained.

At last, the bag was brought. No time to check the contents. What am I saying? I'd never even thought to count the number of boxes and even if I'd done so, I had no idea of the contents. It would have been one of those crazy games people play at parties, trying to remember the contents of a tray in thirty seconds ... Unceremoniously, an impassive customs official pointed the way to a door which led out onto the tarmac. There stood the plane, engines blasting and, under heavy escort to the very door of the plane, I hurried like I had the wings of Mercury himself on my heels and clambered up the steep, metal moveable staircase. Not until I was inside the plane did the customs men take their eyes off me.

348

I knew I was travelling back economy. We had been told that there had been no other space available. The only seat was the one I was shown to in economy and it was one of a pair, the fellow seat being occupied, nay, overpopulated by a lady of such gigantesque proportions - bless her - that the only way she could fit into her seat was by having the armrest up and her ample hips and buttocks half-occupying the seat I had been allocated. Her seat belt looked like an elastic band tethered to the Hindenberg.

I simply refused to sit down. I made such a fuss that the plane, already late, was even further delayed. It was most unlike me. It was a 'me' I had never seen. Although I have been often told that in private I can compete with the best of 'Elton's little moments', publicly I am usually the soul of discrete, bitten-lipped politeness.

The temperature inside the cabin was either unbearable or I was in such a lathered two'n'eight ... It wasn't as though the cabin crew didn't understand my plight but it was only after the purser had authorised that I was upgraded to a seat in first class.

So! There WAS a seat there after all! I sank into it as though easing into a velvet-lined bath. The cacophony of the packed economy section faded away to a muted hum no more invasive than the monotone drone of the jet engines slung beneath the wings outside in the tropical night. I felt immediately stroked.

I spent the easterly nightflight across the Atlantic swathed in a haze of champagne bubbles. Being a big-mouth, I'd told the cabin crew about the incident and apart from laughing gratifyingly at the funny bits, they were extremely sympathetic too when they heard the full tale.

We landed at Heathrow in the morning and I went straight to the office where Jenny Over thankfully took charge of the jewellery and put it into the office safe where it stayed, undistributed for months at least. Baubles? Trinkets? When they were finally distributed, their recipients were probably completely different from those for whom the gifts were originally intended. After those few weeks, the court could easily have changed its courtiers. Those in favour at Christmas might easily have been leprous outcasts by Easter.

Oh, I don't know. It's very very difficult in life not to be judgmental. One tries not to judge because one would not wish

349

particularly to be judged and found wanting oneself. But being that close to so much wealth, to so much expense and to see it being treated with no more reverence than would be shown to an armful of fairings from the travelling circus does something to one's sense of values.

But then it was the start of the age of the 'take me, show me, buy me' generation. The beginning of astronomical deals, mind-boggling grosses, telephone number prices. I wonder what Elton did manage to give his guests on Christmas morning? I.O.U's?

Chapter Eleven

INFLUENTIAL FRIENDS

1976 brought many partings of the ways. If I'd been prescient, I'd have seen it as the strands of the rope splitting, breaking and the skein of the rope's core unravelling.

The first and most significant 'nice-knowing-you' was between Peter Straker and myself, closely followed by Twinkle and Brian Protheroe. I found I couldn't do justice to either of the latter and with the former, Freddie's influence superseded any strength that mine might once have had. Minns had by now left the employ of Paul and Linda Macartney and Freddie was busy finding him something to do.

One of things they found for him to do was Peter Straker, though Minns' involvement was not something that thrilled Straker whose relationship with Freddie - and vice versa - had turned in one way into a thing of enviable beauty, so close and interdependent was it. There was room for little else of an institutionalised nature, like a permanent lover.

In another way, however, Freddie and Peter's relationship was beginning to destroy the very credibility that Peter had been building up since 1973 when he had been at the point of quitting show business altogether. Freddie Mercury, long a fan of the operatic tenors, adored, was needled by and therefore envied Straker's voice which is one of the most unusual the British musical stage has ever heard. But the key word is 'stage'. Peter is a theatrical performer. His many forays into records and recording had brought no residual or cumulative dividends.

Freddie however was convinced that it was he who was going to turn Straker into a rock 'n' roll star? Or was it? Did he really want Straker to be as successful as he was or did he in reality only want to 'own' the voice. Freddie, let it not be forgotten, was a great collector and let it also not be forgotten that although it's very nice to be in a great collection, one runs the risk of becoming forgotten, perhaps drowned in the spate of further acquisitions.

I wasn't going to compete or vie for Peter's trust nor was I about to compromise my relationship with Freddie. Freddie was nothing if not single-minded about anything he either did or wanted and he behaved accordingly. I might have been forgiven for feeling that perhaps he was rather taking over my world. Like he'd got Minns, now he had Straker? At least he never had me, except as a friend on mutual terms, I'm pleased to say.

So, Straker went his own way, his career tended still for theatrical engagements by Clodagh Wallace of Brunskill Management. Clodagh would also come to 'look after' Tim Curry who was equally desperate at the time to become a rock'n'roll star just like Freddie.

I still had a ways to run with Tim although because he was playing in THE ROCKY HORROR SHOW in America for the time I was with Reid, I saw little of him. Despite his interest in the person, Reid never expressed an interest to me in wanting to manage the career of a drag queen. It would have been an easy enough move to make. However, Tim, sporting himself as Frank 'n' Furter, despite the attentions of Lou Adler and the very butch Jerry Moss at A and M Records, was a whoops-perhaps-not phenomenon on the cough, spit 'n' curse American music biz scene. After all, Elton was still merely a madcap young fella. Come out? Way-to-go, not! Not profitable at all. I think in those days, even Liberace's psycho-psyche was left unassailed, safe on the outer limits of the off-limits closet.

Show business, whilst founded on careers of rock solid negotiability, has to have its gold rushes, the perceived motherlodes whose claims people grab for, fight over and then abandon. As far as Tim being another Iggy Pop or Billy Idol, the future was entirely Meatloaf's.

And so Tim's and my real time as friends was yet to come for he was there and I was ... Hey ho. Straker's and my time had come to an end and the professional parting was amicable enough ... I was pleased that it appeared that he was going to be at least financially sound with Freddie talking handsome sums both for Straker's recording schedule and his daily maintenance. Well, so it appeared ... What was important was that I was both too busy to do more for Straker or to want to and he was too busy to have cared less. Freddie was so busy that he didn't notice that he should have been noticing other things.

And as I've said, Brian Protheroe and I were coming to an end too. Influences such as his co-writer and friend Martin Duncan and the director Philip Hedley - lately longtime artistic director of the Theatre Royal, Stratford East - seemed to negate any positive influence I had on my constant attempts at describing the territory of rock 'n' roll as not necessarily the land of tyrants, exploitation and victims. What they all were afraid of, I don't know. The theatre was obviously as holy and as undefilable a shrine as ever was and there were too many white chickens roosting in the dead tree.

Brian Protheroe was onto his second, or perhaps third album with Del Newman, the fabled string arranger who was producing him but he was at the same time, as I have mentioned earlier, preparing to go into a West End Show, Ken Lee's LEAVE HIM TO HEAVEN, which was all about a rock 'n' roll hero. Or is that a contradiction in terms? An oxymoron? I think it might have been to Brian. Both Brian's record company, Chrysalis, and I were running out of patience. His arrogance was demeaning both to them and to me. I found I could live without it. We parted amicably but our association drifted quickly away on the winds of time, sealed in a bubble, never to be burst.

Twinkle too. 'Bye 'bye. She was still blaming me for Micky's death. She didn't have to say. I knew. Still know, even twenty-eight years later. She hated to admit any complicity, see ...

Other people are always to blame in some worlds.

And so that was that. I think I earned a little from residual overseas sales from Brian Protheroe's work but David Evans Artists Management Ltd. only stayed open as a bank account to receive my stipend from JRE. Too much time and too much self-revealed truth thus set the seal on any notion I might have had of being an entrepreneurialist like Barry Krost or John Reid.

But for all the good-byes, there were many hellos. Getting to know the people at EMI brought me into contact with Eric Hall, now a sportspersons' agent, who was in charge of 'promotion'. He was forever "Monsta-monsta'-ing" at any and every industry bash and generally obliterating any trace of sophistication or decorum which might better have been the order of the day. Other than Kim Osborne (later Mrs. Pete Brown), I can't remember the others at EMI ... Isn't that awful?

The Decca record company boss Ken East and his wife Dolly, major friends of Reid's, were very kind to me and often invited me to their flat in Warwick Square where I met the likes of Cliff, later Soeur Cliff, Richard who droned on endlessly about religion in a social setting where most people had found their own gods to validate them long ago. These gods had been reasonably easily found inside the seekers rather than them having to turn to an outside god to lend substance to a life and personality long devoid of common reality.

I remember Twinkle telling me on a later occasion, with two children to bring up, that she had become so broke that she'd written a begging letter to Soeur Cliff, a man she had known once as a friend and as an equal. Not a jot of any help was forthcoming. Nevertheless, when he could see that it suited him, Cliff could appear incredibly generous. I remember once at Top of the Pops, one of Kiki Dee's backing singers hadn't shown or hadn't been able to make it through traffic and Cliff, also on the show and also on Rocket Records in the USA, obliged by warbling the necessary harmony behind a screen. I guess he wished it could have been on screen, but what the heck. Was anyone gonna out-sing Cliffie? On your bikes.

Charitably, I have later thought that Twinkle's begging letter never actually reached Soeur Cliff. Although the opener of the letter must have known who she was? I have lately (2003) calculated

354

that there have been less than a thousand occupants of the number one position in the British charts in the past fifty years. When Twinkle wrote to Cliff there would have been half that number. In other exclusive clubs there are safety nets to catch the fallen members. Even the acting profession has one such club. Says a deal about the music industry, doesn't it?

And there, as Freddie would say, you have it, dear ...

I have to say that a few admissions wouldn't have gone amiss with Cliffy ... He was about as invulnerable as a rubber soufflé. I realise that he was a star practically before I was born and one whom, rumour had it, was one over which my nightly wet wank as I perused the sticky fan mags wouldn't be wasted. But in the flesh, the ageless one was, to me, a complete dinosaur, a sort of *passé* puppet on a dangerously fundamentalist string. Despite the sunny-side-up personality, I always suspected a morass of seething complexes and in-turned motivations beneath the surface. But, sadly, I was never privy to them, had they existed at all and thus I always found him obdurately nice, unfailingly boyish and about as substantial as an undercooked meringue.

And of course Clive Banks and Moira Bellas. Then, Clive was in charge of the promotion at Island Records and Moira was, as she always has been, at Warners - Warner/Elektra/Atlantic (WEA). Clive had worked for Elton and John when Rocket Records first started and had started off, amongst other positions I believe, as the company gopher. Or the go-far, in Clive's case. My principals, John and Elton, had found him sweet and adorable as a late teenager and, indeed, so did I now he was a little older and in a different prime. I still feel incredibly fondly towards him. His ingenuous, no-side affability masks a very canny and a very lucky soul. He had tenacity and perseverance and, when Chris Blackwell sold Island Records, our Clive, then managing director, got his well-deserved share of the pot too.

This whole business of being a rock/pop star and being gay and, ergo in 1976 as opposed to 1956, wondering whether to come out or not had surfaced in a very real way sometime just after I joined Reid when Freddie and Queen were on tour and promoting Night at the Opera. Caroline Boucher had set up an interview with a journalist called James Johnson. He was a very, very nice man entirely sincere and quite without malice. However, it was fairly well-known up and down the Street of Shame that Freddie was gay but also still living with his 'girlfriend', Mary Austin. Caroline therefore also knew that James was going to ask Freddie directly about his sexual proclivities.

Well, we - Minns, Freddie, myself and whomsoever - turned this old chestnut over for many an evening, wondering what was best to be said as the interview was scheduled for the London Evening Standard.

Freddie was on a high of 'in-loveness' at the time with David Minns and initially was all for throwing caution to the winds. Straker was of a very different opinion. In some ways, caution was his wind. However, after several comparable careers were examined and Freddie'd listened to what all his friends had to say, he reached a compromise which he found acceptable and one which embraced not only any and all proclivities known to Western man but one which was considered digestible by Western media and ultimately, most significantly, palatable to Western woman. If Freddie's 'admission' was palatable to Western woman, then it would be palatable to most Western men who usually think and do what their women tell them.

And so, the unspeakable was spoken about ... The love that dare not speak it's name was given a bit of an airing. Something about Freddie sleeping not only with both men and women but also animals and if he had a choice of animal it would of course be a cat. Even cats. Plural. Not just one cat at a time.

Shocking?

Course not. And nothing came of it. There wasn't a lot that could be said. Not a lot can be made of the truth. Rumour, denial, hearsay ... That's what the Street of Shame thrives on and Freddie rather successfully pulled the rug from beneath further speculation and went on to live a very happy, open gay life for many years until ...

Until they got their pound of flesh. In the end, they always do. But that's yet another story.

The people at BBC's Top of the Pops programme also became our new best friends. The programme was incredibly influential in those days, the most important avenue for national proclamations of music product. I'm talking of a time so longago, so wreathed in the mists of time that in 1975, about the only video that had ever been made that at least had been powerful and sales-effective, was the Queen/Bruce Gowers' Bohemian Rhapsody. It was simply unheard of for bands or artists to make videos and, thus, either live performance or mime to a backing track was the only means of appearing on the show.

Allow me just look at both these two options for a moment.

First, live performance. For a singer guitarist with a simple folk ditty this was no problem technically although often, the simplest performance was the most complex and another factor, a horrid, malign 'X' factor would come into play, one like ...

"God, she's cross-eyed"

or

"Sad. Not a camera natural, huh!"

Second, live performance for a band playing their own instruments but often unable to use their own PA could result in such an appalling sound quality that the appearance would produce a performance which was so bad when compared to the original record that many a band did themselves a gross dis-service and never broke the surface of public recognition again.

In the same category, live performance for a solo singer who could utilise the BBC (Musicians Union staffed and organised) Orchestra often made hits out of crap songs and crap records which should never have seen the light of day.

Finally, appearances on Top of the Pops by artists or bands miming to a backing track was a category fraught with horror. The backing track had to be approved by the Musicians Union. This body, as we will see in a later anecdote, was absurdly powerful. Should it be suspected and then proved that a band had in fact not recorded its own backing track for an appearance on Top of the Pops, the appearance would be cancelled and the band, and probably the record company, blacklisted during her majesty's pleasure, the majesty in question being that of Robin Nash, the programme's editor/producer. Individual band membership of the Musicians Union was thoroughly vetted and confirmed and woe betide those people who hadn't paid their dues.

The whole thing was far more to do with fascist than ever it was to do with fun. It was like the music police patrolling the prescribed boundaries of by-the-book correctness.

So, you finally made it onto Top of the Pops. It was about as glamorous as a knees-up in a Bailey's Nightclub or a third rate gig in a university dance hall. The sets and stages were messy, dusty and rarely dressed, dressing rooms were little more than utilities; there was no reception room other than the BBC bar which was always full of style-less bluestockings - and their commensurate bluesocks - who looked down their elitist noses at their sanctuary being infiltrated by the common horde of us hoi poloi from market-place, buck'n'cent country.

Ugh!

And for this we kissed ass for miles. Brown-nosed like moles.

One person who made it bearable was the delightful Gordon Elsbury, one of the BBC staff directors and later part-time producer/director of Top of the Pops. Gordon had something to do with a skating rink up at Camden Town in the Electric Ballroom and we went there on several occasions to find out what falling flat on your ass was really about! Even Freddie came, once. He loved roller-rinks. In New York he went every week. But rarely to skate. Gordon's dead now. In America somewhere in the mid-eighties.

Both Minns and I had gotten to know Robin Nash, the initial producer of both TOTP and also the Basil Brush (ugh!) show, from late-night encounters on Shepherds Bush Green. He was like an old colonel, or an archetypal squire. Ebullient, joky, more than faintly patronising but tough as old boots and with a determination and will of iron. On every level but the venal, I never knew what he was thinking and could never predict a decision ... Like,

"Hi, Robin ... Queen can't be in the studio this week, can you use the video again as they're still number one?"

You'd never know until the day. Fame was such a lottery.

Our own circle of friends was expanding too. We used to see a lot of Ronnie Fisher who worked at Harvey Goldsmith's office. Ronnie was sweet. He's died.

Hamish MacAlpine was one of the boys then and lived

for a time first with the late Stephen Gill, then with Rupert Everett before moving into the house next to Billy Gaff's over a shop in the Fulham Road with Ian Brown, of whom more later. Rupert was petulent and unformed in those days. I could have cheerfully smacked him and I was therefore so relieved to see him acting so wonderfully in ANOTHER COUNTRY several, character-forming years later and more so as the delightful Christopher Marlow in the 1998 Oscar-winning movie SHAKESPEARE IN LOVE. I often wondered whether Rhys Waveral, the hero of Rupert's first novel, HELLO, DARLING. ARE YOU WORKING? bore more relation to fact than he did to fiction.

We also saw a lot of Bias Boshell, a wonderful song-writer signed to Rocket Music and who played keyboards for Kiki occasionally. Sweet hippy-haired Bias.

And there was also my family, still safe in the fastness of The Land That Time Forgot, locked away in the safety of the Worcestershire countryside, who must have been terrified to receive even a telephone call from me, let alone a letter. My life must have been incomprehensible to them and we never talked about it. They had no references, I knew they had no references ...

Jesus! What am I saying? I had no references any more.

Chapter Twelve

1976 AND ALL THAT ...

The New Year dawned. It was a time for taking stock. A breather. We needed it. For a time it seemed that there was little immediately for such a huge organisation to do. The ensuing hiatus was probably the reason why no one really took very much notice of Reid's rarely being in the office. But then taking stock isn't the same as stock-taking. Not the same as counting, is it?

In fact neither my principal nor his clients, Elton and Freddie, were ever very much in evidence in the office for those first new months of what was to prove the longest, hottest summer for years. Of drought proportions, even.

Having both been liberated from their mutual co-habitant and ostensibly monogamous state, both Elton and John were, I presume, exploring the possibilities. Reviewing their situations, as the late Lionel Bart's version of Dickens' Fagin memorably said. I fancy that their brave new worlds were rather empty, devoid of any kind of stability for both of them started to rattle and bang about and kick up enough white dust to obliterate any signposts showing the proof-positive way to tomorrow. 'Tis ever thus. Breaking up is really, really hard to do.

However, the tempting horizon of this apparent new wealth of opportunity for both of them was made even rosier when seen through hazy veils of chemically induced euphoria; as both *rex* and *imperator*, each, their habits were only obvious to everyone else but me. Having never 'done' drugs in any depth, I was oblivious to the effects that drugs had on people's everyday ability to function when the drugs in question were thrashed to such excess. What Elton did, I know not for his freedom to be gay and out and about was severely curtailed by his celebrity. His drug use, however, was by his own later admission never in question. What's more, it now seems that most of his intimates also imbibed. In a way, they would have had no alternative but to fall in behind their leader for how else to eliminate censure? Lions do not, contrary to idealistic hopes, ever lie down with lambs longer than to ask for mint sauce on the side.

What Elton did for kicks, he had to do in the privacy of his own clique, to the sound of his own claque. Still does. He was never to be seen in the London clubs Freddie was regularly to be found in and therefore pursued his proclivities more often in America than in England, in Los Angeles rather than London, where it was much more possible for pulchritudinous young men of ambition to be introduced to stars like him who, in return for their 'being nice', would be 'helped' in the furtherance of their own careers. America was also where cannabis, cocaine and all the other music business drugs of a pharmaceutical persuasion had long been known. Drugs, their effects, their supply and demand had been exploited all the way through the jazz age, in and out of the succeeding swing era and now fundamentally underpinned the solid, three-chord rhythms of rock 'n' roll. On the LA scene, the young men who came with these drugs, each equally available to Elton, may have often been hookers but they were also lookers, far superior to the London menu and there were respectable-enough figures around who were pleased to have their own celebrity-ranking endorsed by being a part of the Elton entourage, even if their function was as pimp and pusher.

Elton's lifestyle, when compared to Freddie's and Queen's, was not quantitavely better or worse. The comparative lifestyles, however, showed up qualitatively in the music. Elton was beginning to marginalise himself in terms of inspiration and motivation. What Elton merely heard once removed on the radio,

Freddie felt as a live pulse in the clubs. Sharon, Princess of Pinner, slept on a mattress where the pea was never silently ignored. Freddie was always immediately touchy-feely and spent many a splendored night on a bumpy mattress. Having been only lately come-out, he had a lot of lost time to make up for.

But unlike Elton, Reid was not similarly compromised. I don't know if either was consciously searching for any permanent replacement for the other in their lives but the casting couch for whatever position was being advertised was audibly creaking and groaning in both, separated households. And because Reid hunted at night, after business buddies had been seen off, it was usually in the early hours that his quarry would be finally brought to ground. And it was probably dawn by the time the last toot had been snorted, the final surrender signalled and vanquished's halfpenny claimed by Mr. Reid. What am I saying? Probably?

Definitely.

How did I know? I'd been there on several sunrises.

Reid, painful though it is now to admit, was only human; he had to sleep, dammit and quite simply in the light of the previous paragraph, was therefore rarely seen anywhere near South Audley Street until after at least a very late lunch.

True, he was often in the office all evening, only leaving to dine with a client or other business contact and thence to boogie on down with same at one of the West End's disco-wonderland nightspots.

But the plain fact was that he wasn't at the office when most of us were there. When we and when his clients needed him to be there. Reid wasn't, as was the Elvis camp, taking care of business in office hours and certainly never in any kind of a flash. What Reid did in and around the LA office, run for him by Connie Papas, was no-one-in-London's business but I guess the format was about the same.

The man I had known occasionally for several years as a friend, fuck-buddy - whatever - was not the same man I was now working for. Separated from Elton - for they were both mere halves of, and therefore smaller and weaker than, their joint whole - Reid had to work twice as hard to establish himself socially. And, make no mistake, John Reid had huge, huge social ambitions as could only be conceived by a boy who felt he needed to make good, who still felt conscious of his trailing roots and who needed more than anything to be loved. Promiscuity, whether social, sexual or drug-related always achieves in the short term a lessening of that malignant feeling of being alone and unloved. I know what I'm talking about, believe me. But that was how both John and Elton worked. How they functioned. They had to make you love them and then and only then could you be trusted and only when you were trusted could you work for them.

However, although I didn't know it then, I for one had begun to fall out of love with this infuriating but intensely lovable little Scottish person. I'd known others who had fallen out of love with him but I hadn't believed them, ignored them and their vituperative blandishments about 'the real John Reid' and banished them from my company.

But all reactions were indeed possible. As easily as it was to fall under his spell, fall in love with, become infatuated with Reid, it was a hundred, a million times more difficult a) to admit to falling out of love and b) to be able to do anything about it. By then, it was often too late. There was too much at stake. Too much glamour, too much reflected glory. A lot of people found out how costly it was to hang their personalities, their careers and their futures on Reid's peg.

And for what I've just said about Reid, read double for Elton.

I suppose it must seem odd that anyone should want to write in depth about these two frail characters and explore their relative strengths and vulnerabilities so passionately but the truth of the matter is that the moods these two woke up to every morning affected a whole habitat, an entire ecosystem as indeed do our own waking states affect the lives of our own nearest and, well ... dearest. And each, of course, was indispensible to the other. It's impossible to read one without having first read the other.

Reid's house - in those days he just had the one - in Montpellier Square, number 40, had been bought from the merchant banker Julian Gibbs and for a while John lived in it without 'doing' anything to it, content to wait and see. Along with the house came another circle of acquaintance; Julian Gibbs's 'set' included James Fisher, an executive at RCA Records as well as the member-of-parliament Norman St. John Stevas (before his elevation) and the pre-MP Martin Stevens, (before his elevation).

John's ambitions were always more political than Elton's. Elton liked to control his position in the industry from a position outside and made the industry his whole life. Reid was more disseminated, wanted to be part not only of his industry but also the wider establishment. There will be more about these ambitions later but suffice for the while to remark that Reid loved being involved with these aforementioned powerful, suave, sophisticated people from such a different background, doyens of such a different class whom he must have regarded as people of substantial power, real movers and shakers.

They in their turn were also, let it not be forgotten, not unsympathetic, shall-I-say, to queerdom and the benefits of knowing John Reid. Excitement was always to be had around Reid. Young and new people always clustered around Reid. The socialites learned quick. It was all very much the operation of the much vaunted, infrequently identified 'gay mafia' of which membership was not exclusively restricted to homosexuals. But if there was respectability for Reid to be had through the merchant wankers, it was only by the back-door. There may have been a pro-tem welcome for a queer, but not automatic social acceptance. Eligibility for that still depended on the good old class and pedigree rules. Other, lesser men with money – the *parvenus*, the *arrivistes* - were and are allowed to visit but they will for ever strangers in a strange land. Perhaps their children ... if they'd been to the right schools ... Maybe if a title was in the offing ...

And I, of course, little me fallen into this shallow deepend, was as nosey as all get-out. This aspirant milieu was one into which I had been introduced very early on after my own arrival in London in 1968. Reid and I were in many ways not unalike. So, it was therefore not unwillingly that I took up any and every invitation (some called them commands) from Reid to attend upon him at 40 Montpellier Square when so-and-so was expected to dine. Jenny Over, John's assistant, was similarly press-ganged. Was it that we made reasonable conversation? Was it that we were aware of the appropriateness of the correct placement of the knives and forks?

Who knows. But not who cares for it was through one of

these invitations that I met two people who were to become hugely important in my life and who had already been hugely important in the lives of both Reid and Elton.

Bryan Forbes and Nanette Newman were, as far as I was concerned, movie royalty and I was as pleased as punch to find myself one night seated at Reid's table in their company. What a relief not to have to talk about the music business. Neither Bryan nor Nanette, despite having been the creators of THE SLIPPER AND THE ROSE were in any measure afficionados of pop music but they were, showed themselves to be and continued in being, great supporters and champions of Elton's work. They had long lived on the Wentworth Estate at Virginia Water in their splendid between-the-wars house which Elton had dubbed 'The Gaumont' and it was to a road three distant from their own gracious gates that Elton and John as a couple had moved into the big bungalow which Elton had in turn dubbed Hercules, his own newly-assumed second name. Elton Hercules John. Captain Fantastic.

Nanette Newman is the nicest woman in the world. The most trusting and the most generous. Her capabilities are enormous not only as an actress but also as a writer, an entertainer and as a cook. Nanette doesn't just write about cooking, she cooks, self-taught and self-developed. If you need her assistance in any way, she helps you with her whole heart and soul and both she and Bryan adopted the two boys from across the road with all the substance they have always displayed to people they like. Nanette has one other true talent. She is a very real family person. Having enjoyed a pretty peripatetic childhood herself, she knew the value of a solid domestic life in as far as that could be achieved in the itinerant vortex which Bryan wrote about as 'that despicable race', the gypsy life of 'da show biz'. They were a truly mutually reliant couple, classically interdependent and together produced two daughters, Sarah and Emma, of whom more later.

Not only did the Forbeses learn from the Reid-Johns but the latter, both sponges eager for all forms of knowledge, lapped up all the sophistication and social savoir-faire which these two kind neighbours were well-endowed. Royal introductions were effected so much so that it was not long before Elton was playing piano and entertaining the Queen Mother and Princess Margaret at White

Lodge in nearby Windsor Great Park.

Bryan, at the peak of his career as screenwriter-producer-director, had been instrumental in making and securing the broadcast of a masterful television documentary about Elton made over the period that Elton was recording at the Chateau d'Herouville in France. All golden grist to the fabrication of both the respectability, acceptability and durability of the growing legend of Elton John in the eyes of at least the accessible parts of the British establishment.

The Forbes family, such emiment villagers in the small settlement of Virginia Water - where Elton's mother and then husband Fred Farebrother lived and ran their decorating shop - played a very large part in the lives of my principal and his erstwhile client. And let us once again not forget Bernie and Maxine Taupin for the Scribbler and the Tiny Dancer were also residents of a couple of Wentworth's finest acres.

Returning to the unfolding year of 1976, I think the schedules of the stablemates panned out fairly well for the first couple of months. Queen went off to tour in America and Canada and Elton too was recording in America. The televising and broadcast through Europe of the prestigious date of Christmas Eve of Queen's Hammersmith Odeon concert had been very successful. My mother sent me a clipping from the regular Peterborough column in the Daily Telegraph taken on 8th January 1976. It reads:

"I am sorry I missed a late-night BBC2 programme on Christmas Eve, advertised by the Belgian Broadcasting journal *Tele Moustique ... 23:00 Old Grey Whistle Test - Show de Noel avec la participation de Sa Majeste La Reine.*"

Yes. But at least my mum and dad were beginning to acknowledge that rock 'n' roll - even when called graciously "artists' management" - was at least a life of some consequence. However, I intuited that it still fell rather short of accountancy or being a diplomat for the British Council and was certainly not a conceivable career. But whatever they thought, they'd never said when I was at home for Christmas that year.

I remember from that time a fabulous pair of *mukluks* coming back for me as a present from Freddie via one or other of the itinerant Queen entourage. *Mukluks* are not naughty eskimos with dirty minds but merely the rabbit fur-lined boots worn by naughty eskimos with dirty minds. I loved my beaded boots to distraction - Freddie was a great present chooser - and I wore them for fifteen years. I finally had to admit defeat when even the cat wouldn't lie down in the same room. They were consigned to the trash just a few months before Freddie died and of course I now deeply regret such profligacy with the precious past and I miss them desperately. Now he's not here anymore ...

Chapter Thirteen

HAPPY NEW YEAR

If 1975 had been a Queen year, then 1976 surely belonged to Elton and I'm talking world domination here, not just merely the empire of South Audley Street. Queen were recording again by Spring, Elton had just come out of the studio and, as part of that canon of work, under his arm he bore a very poppy little tune he and Bernie had come up with called DON'T GO BREAKING MY HEART ... There was also a tour planned. It was also a long, very hot and very dry summer which, by its end, saw everyone more than a little crazy.

Caroline Boucher worked very hard for Elton. As a journalist herself, her connections with journalism, fellow journalists in particular and the Street of Shame in general made for some eyebrow-raising front pages, especially in the London Evening papers. One such stunt pictured Elton escorting the late Princess Margaret to 'the pictures'. Not so much of a date either for Elton or for the then still attractive Princess but more of a means to an end. Wherever the Princess's life and loves had led her at that time, Elton's had led him to the need for establishing a platform for the *Blitzwerke* which would be 1976. Whether it was on that 'date' that

368

she opined to Elton that "… your music is louder than Concorde!" I have no idea but Elton latched onto the 'louder than Concorde' bit and the royal pronouncement was commuted into the title for the upcoming early summer tour. David Costa in the all-but airless art department in the basement of South Audley Street was trawling for ideas, there having been none submitted or even suggested by our fickle principal with his pet concept.

I have to mention, if not to re-iterate here, that it was rare for John Reid to appear in his offices before the afternoon and Elton showed up even less frequently, not that there was any reason for him to be around any longer than a meeting with John or a conference with David Croker in the Rocket Records department might take. Their absences gave rise to frequent conference meetings between ourselves, trying to decide on a series of options which we would submit to our masters in order that they might cherry-pick and make a decision as to how we should proceed. Louder Than Concorde, which ended up as a thirty plus date nationwide tour, had to have a face, a logo and be somehow branded into a ticketing reality which could be successfully advertised by the promoters in the press.

The sharp end of the music industry was also growing up fast and was just about entering the marketing and merchandise era and the tour's 'branding' was therefore essential. We were all-too-readily sent photographs of Concorde by British Airways – but how to make rock'n'roll out of an airplane? How best to combine two great icons of the nineteen-seventies and make sense of a visual union? A photograph of Elton wearing a glittering Bob Mackie jumpsuit and brandishing a baseball bat at his recent Dodgers Stadium concert supplied the Elton part of the equation and a full-face, head-on photograph of Concorde on the runway did the rest of the algebra. Elton beating back Concorde – the ultimate in decibel competition. And so, we found the face of the tour and the gods saw that it was good and it was so …

Bohemian Rhapsody had spent nine or ten weeks at number one and I forget how long Don't Go Breaking My Heart remained in the same position. Not that we were competitive of course but the figures sorted the office out into Elton sheep and Queen goats. One thing no one could fight over was the reason for this compounding success for the John Reid Enterprises juggernaut.

The reason was 'the video'. I remember seeing jukeboxes in the sixties which also played a short section of film with the record selected but the video age consigned this memory to yet another of civilisations' *oubliettes*.

Not only was the pop video the new kid on the block in terms of promotional tools - it sure beat the hell out of payola, 'entertaining' and chart-rigging – it brought its own dimension and dynamic to the song which was being plugged. It also put the power back in the hands of the punters – for a while. Unarguably, no longer would a song be an audio creation but it would be visual as well. The resulting integrity could either be a tremendously forceful two-edged whammy of substance or a doubly silly, extra-super-fluffy piece of contrived pap. As extremes of the invading genre, both were equally effective and, boy, did we know! We had our own in-house example, If Bo Rhap had an artistic flair and genuine experimental solidity, DGBMH had neither. Where DGBMH had vitality, exuberance and exuded a sense of summer fun and carefree hedonism, Bo Rhap could only acknowledge *nul points*.

For DGBMH, maybe the situation could have been different although had it been so, hindsight must rule that alternative unwise. The reason for the almost throwaway quality of the DGBMH video was just that – the very opportunity of making it was indeed almost thrown away. Bruce Gowers– any sane manager's first choice for a director – who had so successfully constructed the Bo Rhap video was unavailable and this it fell, after a brief consultation with Eric Hall, then head of EMI promotion, that Mike Mansfield be given the responsibility. Mike was a television producer/director and had become pre-eminent in his field as the power behind the casting for appearances on pop television shows. Mike had no office/studio facilities of his own and indeed demanded no pre-production meetings or script sessions or concept discussions. Such strategies were unheard of then. We were merely given a time, two to four, at some London Weekend Television Studios on the South Bank where we had to show up on a Saturday afternoon! Dammit – no peace for the wicked, another weekend's plans shot and certainly no compensatory overtime for us! And there was a rub – of course. Our studio slot and Mr Mansfield's talents had to be shared with Rod Stewart who, with Billy gaff his manager, also had cottoned on to the necessity for an accompanying video.

"What! Share with fucking Phyllis!"

I believe that was approximately Elton's reaction when I told him of the plan for the afternoon. We had arranged to meet at South Audley Street at one o'clock. Oh, I have forgotten to mention that it was then or never as far as the video was concerned. Elton was booked on a late afternoon plane to America – I think he was making final mixing adjustments to his forthcoming album. Oh. Another slight complication … Come one-fifteen, Reid still hadn't turned up.

I thought Elton was going to go ballistic. He was furious, and rightly so. It was one of those celebrated 'tantrum' moments. For Reid not have been on time was humiliating and insulting not only to Elton but to Kiki who was understandably embarrassed, managed as she was by John Reid Enterprises but wholly obligated to Elton as the fount of all charity. Sorry, employment. As I found out that afternoon and subsequently, the incident was one of the nails in the coffin of the 'will I sign or won't I' drama of Elton's re-commissioning Reid as his manager. But then, on the other hand, I'd shown up that afternoon. I was on duty, wasn't I? Me. the punch bag, the alibi, the peacemaker. What I had figured was the strategy intended to work for Queen tantrums was now working for the 'other' client. I had never reckoned on Reid not showing up for Elton. Ever. Whatever the current state of game-playing inter-personal politics.

"Well, I'm going!"

That was Elton talking. The ultimate threat. I knew he could mean it. This time I knew he did. I am at this juncture, stumped. I have no talent and no experience for handling this situation. But I know I have to. It was why, for God's sake, I was employed in the first place. In management, one manages. In management, one is managed. All very fine theory except I am but me and he is Elton John! And yet we're the same age, of reasonably equivalent intelligence – why am I going through this nightmare? Why does he not want to make his video? Why should I care? Perhaps because I was being paid to listen and then to talk. In Reid's place. But this time, there could be no listening. DGBMH, the very first of what has become a tradition of duets in the music industry, was not necessarily a sure-fire hit. My personal hindsight judges that

371

the video made it so.

So I start to cajole 'the artist' ... And to explain ... and to mollify ... Kiki helps. And finally, reluctantly, off we go to the South Bank and into the dressing room and there is Mike Mansfield and all is fine and dandy and campy and witty and brittle and 'dear' and ... surprise, surprise! Everything's suddenly all right. Clothes are changed. The atmosphere is joky, almost theatrical. But, still no direction or policy format for the shoot. Off we go down the echoing stairwell to the studio and ... what on earth to do? Elton doesn't know. Kiki sure as hell hasn't got the foggiest idea and ... still no Reid. So. They, 'the artistes', stand in front of the two microphones someone has set up. Tape rolls. Cameras turn. I can't remember how many takes or parts of takes but it wasn't a lot. Three or four. Someone must have said, "Be yourselves!". They made a pretty good stab at being whoever they thought themselves were.

Then Reid shows up, all smiles as if he's bang on time. Elton is sulky after an initial side-swipe which anaesthetises the vitality in the studio for the necessary while. Tantrums at this point in the career aren't usually thrown in front of directors and strangers. And then, thank heavens, our time is up. What is done is done, in the can. It's a wrap. We go back up the, bare concrete echoing staircase to the dressing room and on the way pass Phyllis and the Gaff/Riva posse on their way down. Laughs, jibes, goads, wit, jollity, good-natured banter and wicked camp humour. A storm in a teacup. Whatever. Elton goes off to the airport, probably with Mike Hewittson. Reid hangs around and I escape as quickly as possible.

Whatever Mike Mansfield did or didn't do to the tape, it was perfect. Reid loved it, EMI loved it and Elton's opinion was only heard by Reid. The record was already out. Even great stars, when faced with no options can only sensibly acquiesce and put on a brave face. In this case there was no need for a brave face. The broadcast tape said all the song itself said and yet amplified the scant substance by showing two great friends having a great time and not giving a shit. It was liberating, actually, a faux intimate insight into the happy times enjoyed by great pop stars and their protégés. It worked like a charm. " ... Don't go breaking my heart",
"I couldn't if I tried ..."

Too right, dears. Many would say you haven't got one to break. Not even one between you.

Chapter Fourteen

GOOD COMPANIONS

At some point in late Spring, I was appointed to accompany Elton to the Midem song festival in Cannes. I enjoyed it all hugely and travelled with Elton, first class of course, along with many other industry luminaries. Quite why Elton went, I'm not sure except, perhaps, at the behest/invitation of EMI who threw him a fabulous dinner in one of those very chic restaurants high up above the *corniches* in Eze or Saint Paul de Vence. Forced to remember, I think it was the Le Colombe d'Or. God, it was glamorous. It was my first experience of a truly great cuisine and I loved it. Elton was presented at some point with some sort of certificate for ISLAND GIRL and, as he returned from the podium having accepted the accolade, he thrust the certificate into my hands for safe-keeping. I kept it so safely that a couple of years ago, when searching for some other piece of paper, I found it, rather crumpled with a very expensive wine stain on it. Of course, I returned it, via John Reid's office. But it was the time when Elton and Reid were having that law suit … Knowing Elton, he would have missed it in his collection years ago and would have demanded a copy. I hope.

I have forgotten where it took place, that first whispered

intimation, that clandestine suggestion and so I am, for convenience, using this jolly to Cannes as the context for setting my realisation that Elton was not happy with Reid's management. Or, so he, for whatever reason, gave me to understand. This conversational intimacy terrified me much more than the now almost-forgotten thought that he might have wanted to have explored my private parts.

In hindsight, I can remember thinking that I had dreamed the conversational exchange for with it had come the implied re-assurance that I was doing such a good job ... That he thought I was very capable. And with all this was presented, obliquely delivered and in only just-opaque, wrappings, the implication that ... Me? Be Elton's if-not manager then part of some sort of post-Reid management organisation? I must have burbled some nonsense in reply, at least in acknowledgement, to what was undoubtedly a compliment, but what I know I did do was to immediately try to forget that the incident had ever happened. I certainly wanted no part in such high-powered shennanigans and consciously remember reminding myself that my loyalty was to John Reid and not his principals.

But, before the summer was out, it happened again. After this second occasion, I knew that some all-consuming power-play was going on around me and it scared me to death. I began to feel more and more vulnerable, abused and fragile and I stupidly spoke to no-one about it. To Reid? Impossible. To whom would he be loyal other than himself? To Elton, of course. Others would have thought me crazy, over-stressed, hallucinating, even ... The pressure of my quandary corroded that long, hot summer.

LOUDER THAN CONCORDE was the first major tour I had ever undertaken as it was indeed to prove the last. At Barry Krost's office, the overall view was maintained by Carl Miller, the tour manager and there was always so many other artists' needs to fulfil, let alone my employer's. At John Reid Enterprises it was entirely more focused. For the purposes of the project there was only one client. Elton's tour manager Bob Stacey was 'it' as he had been for several years. Gerry Stickells had not yet appeared on the Elton scene and indeed had yet to undergo his apprenticeship with QUEEN in the USA before adding Elton to his 'to do' list. John invited his brother Bobby Reid to join the team and also his and Elton's old friend Ian Brown appeared at work one day and introduced himself. If Reid thought that someone's appointment was a good idea, they started work regardless of the exact functions they were to fulfil and with no introductions or discussions with other employees whose jobs could have been seriously compromised. Ian Brown was a wonderful character, sharing an apartment with my old acquaintance Hamish McAlpine next door to Billy Gaff's rooftop eyrie above a row of shops in the Fulham Road.

And so, we had a team and a poster and a promoter in the shape of Mel Bush and his Birmingham-based operation and, after a week or so, we had a tour, some thirty plus dates covering the kingdom. The augmented band were to come from America, both Americans and British musicians alike. Elton wanted a choir on a couple of dates. This whim was made flesh when after a little research and a long night-trip into the middle of the Suffolk countryside, Ian Brown and I persuaded a somewhat suspicious assembly of gospel singing service personnel from an American airforce base to sign up to LOUDER THAN CONCORDE. I imagine permission would have had to be sought from the Pentagon and the CIA itself.

But that negotiation paled into insignificance and was never as difficult as the knife-edge, to-and-fro, will-they-won't-they bargaining and pleading with the Musicians Union in London when it was discovered, by the Union, that no agreement had been reached for Elton's American musicians to enter the country to work. I imagine that Davey Johnstone, Roger Pope and certainly Ray Cooper's situation (as bona fide Brits) was *hors de question* but no application had been made for James Newton-Howard, Kenny Passarelli and the others to work. I and everyone else pleaded ignorance. I had no experience of Cat Stevens or his musicians crossing the Atlantic to work in a westerly direction and I since assume that such matters were taken care of by the American tour promoter.

There's nothing like a baptism by fire to ensure a lesson is learned and this is what I learned. In order to work, the Musicians Unions on both sides of the Atlantic had a *per diem* exchange arrangement which basically meant that if four American musicians want to work in the United Kingdom for five days then five British musicians can perform in the United States for four days. Oh, what a troublesome calculation this was for the implacable officials in Victoria to contend with and what a great and terrible joy they derived in putting me through their hoops of miserable bureaucratic fire. Just as in Barbados with the Cartier cargo, the whining 'But it's for Elton John' argument initially cut as much ice as an empty blow torch on the day hell froze over.

But all was well although I think I aged visibly in the course of my afternoon's grilling. Reid was waiting for me to re-emerge, much as he had done at the airport in Barbados, to see what, if any bacon, I was bringing home. And, as with all great triumphs, the moment lasts but a moment. The tour indeed thundered ahead and was also a distinct triumph and was memorable to me for three reasons, all of them people, and one major event. One of the people was David Nutter, appointed by Elton as the tour's photographer with a view to producing a later book of the event. David, brother of celebrity Savile Row tailor Tommy, was sweet and funny and great company, the man who never contacted me in later months to warn me that every photograph of me was to be ultimately cut out of the book. I wonder who had ordered that spiteful little coup?

The second person was Ray Cooper with whom I had the pleasure of travelling on at least a couple of inter-city legs. The third and final person was the writer and broadcaster Nina Myskow. In those far-off days, Nina was JACKIE magazine, the incredibly influential teen organ and one of the successes of the D.C Thomson publishing empire based in Dundee. At the gig in Dundee, not knowing who she was, I refused to allow her in to the backstage area. I learned. There were no hard feelings, we later became firm friends and remain so to this day.

The event I remember was when the tour arrived at the Earls Court Arena. There were, I think, two or three dates at this major London venue, all of which were sold out. On the afternoon of the first gig, I went down to the Arena to see how progress was going – it was a prestigious London showing and expectations were high. I went into the darkened gallery above the arena and it was as though spots appeared before my eyes. Hundreds of white spots.

However, not spots at all, dear reader, but flyers, little half-A4 pieces of paper advertising the upcoming concert tour by

David Essex which Mel Bush was promoting. He was taking every opportunity to ensure that David would be playing to full houses. I on the other hand failed to see why the supremely Elton John nature of this particular occasion should be alloyed by the presence of thoughts of the fair and dimply David and ordered the flyers to be removed. It was another of those Damascene moments when, twenty minutes later I noticed that the flyers had all been replaced. Mel could hardly contain his joy when he announced that the restoration had indeed been authorised by John Reid himself. It was the first intimation I had that my days were numbered … A pea had inserted itself under the mattress of my authority.

Chapter Fifteen

BORDER CROSSING

1976 was indeed granted a hot, long, dry summer. Britain reacted accordingly in the way that only the Brits do. I believe every red-blooded Brit has a pair of shorts hanging on a peg behind the front door. Evidence of even a single full day of sunshine turns everyone into an Aussie. London behaved as though Bondi beach was only a coupla bucks worth of bus ride away.

One project which had come to fruition and which needed the attention of 'management' was the book of lyrics which was the spawn of the partnership between Bernie Taupin and Alan Aldridge. It was surely Bernie's moment to shine in a solo limelight. THE BUTTERFLY BALL had been Alan Aldridge's calling card and the Bernie Taupin book of lyrics was given a great send-off at SEPTEMBER, a pale green and cool restaurant in Fulham Road, opposite Provan's and the sensationally evocative Fulham cemetery. Bernie was enjoying the benefit of Lynsey de Paul's charms at the time and although he seemed to enjoy his own spotlight for a while, he didn't emerge from beneath its glare with a literary aspect which could ever do without the panoply of the rock 'n' roll fanfare. The fanfare had, it seemed, become part of him. He was a joy to work with, highly intelligent, sensitive and great conversational company.

I had hopes, for a while, that Reid might have started an associated publishing company which could have dealt with Bernie's – and others' – literary work. It's not as though we didn't have product. David Nutter's book, for example? Bernie, although a delightful man, struggled beneath the weight of a personality which was compromised by his writing partner's flash 'n' dash. I felt that Bernie's career, whatever it would emerge to be, would always be compromised. Independence from the Elton-Reid regency was in those days an impracticable perspective. I liked and admired Bernie hugely and, although I bought his subsequent novels, I did so from loyalty rather than conviction.

But notwithstanding, we still had to go to work and mine continued to involve Brian Protheroe whose chart success had at least given him appropriate status in his theatrical world. Ken Lee's LEAVE HIM TO HEAVEN, produced by my friend Roger Clifford if I remember rightly, directed by Philip Hedley who was soon to assume command of the Theatre Royal in Stratford East for the next thirty years. The Ken Lee Show lumbered down the counties and into the Cambridge Theatre. A rock 'n' roll catalogue compilation show, it featured all the favourite period rock 'n' roll songs which the cast performed magnificently, the plot woven as thickly as possible for a pastiche effort around the central thread of death-and-glory career moves in the annals of music legend. Brian was superb, very heroic and the rest of the cast including Brian's then girlfriend Anita Dobson, matched him elegantly. It was sort of GREASE before GREASE, really.

Interesting, as Brian's manager I was called – unpaid of course – into the arena a couple of times to sort out problems with either Roger Clifford's management or the relations between the cast and Chrysalis who, more out of duty than enthusiasm, had agreed to record a cast album of the show. Acting for the whole cast in these situations was rather a kick – I can sort of understand now how trades unionists or United Nations diplomats might feel when taking on the might of real tyrants. And the joy was that Roger and I never fell out over my representations on behalf of his stroppy cast.

LEAVE HIM TO HEAVEN also came in very useful later in the year. In Scotland. I had only ever been to Scotland three times before, once, secondly, with David Minns on a rare, snatched holiday from Curzon Street two summers before, the first occasion being the ill-fated neo-honeymoon with 'dearest him'. The third occasion saw me in Scotland with Peter Straker in his show directed by Anthony Andrews. This time, my fourth, I went to Scotland because of John Reid's naked ambition and his friend David Bell's bright idea. Scotland had been about as successful for me as it had been for the English army soundly drubbed at Bannockburn. But all disastrous campaigns start with someone's bright idea so, first, the bright idea ...

David Bell, suave, educated and elegant, had been controller of light entertainment at Scottish Television but had lately moved to London to take up a post at London Weekend Television which enabled him to produce and direct his friend Stanley Baxter's famous Christmas Television Show. There might be few now who remember these superb pieces of entertainment. Baxter was a huge influence on and hugely influenced by the panoply of the contemporary comedic scene and David's support was paramount to the lengthy process involved in the creation of the legendary television programmes. He is sorely missed.

David Bell, older than Reid by a few years, had been mentor to John Reid's equally eager ephebe and Reid benefited from having several of the roughest of rough Paisley edges knocked off his battering character and the two maintained close ties. David had heard that there was, in Edinburgh, a family called Maxwell – no relation – who were keen to divest themselves of an asset they held which took form and frame of a disused cinema which stood at the top of Leith Walk just behind the towering magnificence of the rear of John Lewis's. Would John be interested in acquiring this property which afforded the lucrative potential of a three thousand plus seater auditorium? Answer: yes, because John would also be very eager to do anything in Scotland which would raise his profile in his homeland. John would be pleased for this because he was now harbouring an ambition to become an MP. No, not a military policeman but a Member of Parliament, an elected representative of the Scottish people, serving their interests in the nation's Parliament in Westminster. I suppose the received thinking was that representing Elton John and Queen was qualification enough for representing the interests of upwards of sixty thousand constituents in the national political tableau.

And why not? I suppose the merchant wankers and their political acolytes and liggers had raised his social stakes even higher. Or, perhaps the delusional effects of imbibing too many recreational narcotic substances were taking their effect? So, what did all this politicking mean for me? Elton's tour was over, Queen were touring (I think) in the USA, Kevin Ayers had toured and his album NO BANANAS was doing what it was doing, Kiki was on the inside-out of DGBMH and so there wasn't much else to do. John and I and David Bell flew up to Turnhouse airport for a meeting in Edinburgh with the Maxwell family and a butchers at the theatre.

The Playhouse was indeed a magical place. Walking into it was like exploring your granny's old handbag, full of hidden pockets, occasional nuggets of delight and a lot of dust in the creases and corners. Masses and masses of potential. It had been built as a variety theatre at the beginning of the twenties, just at the time when Variety and Music Hall were capitulating in the face of the onslaught of the cinema and had only ever been used to show films. The warren of dressing rooms behind the stage, state of the art for the time of its construction, had hardly ever been used. Now, the cinema function of the building had succumbed to the ravages of the television age and even though the City of Edinburgh was pleading the need for a new opera house, the future of the Playhouse in this mode was obviously *hors de question*. Second hand was something even the usually thrifty burgers of the Edinburgh artistic hierarchy could not – would not – consider.

John and David were enthralled. Initially, I was appalled at the anchor that this white elephant could represent to the fortunes of both John Enterprises and John Reid Productions, a company of which I was a director and which would be responsible for taking on of the Playhouse. I counselled caution in the face of all the thoughts of buying and/or renting the building and wondered, off the cuff, whether a trial season of concerts might not be the thing before any irrevocable decision be made. A season of concerts to co-incide with the Edinburgh Festival itself, at the end of August, beginning of September that year?

As I write this down, I can see why some might have

easily questioned my own sanity. There was no more than a two-and-a-half month window to achieve such a feat of presentation. To convert a building with insufficient power supply, insufficient loading space for the massive trucks which would be bringing sound and stage equipment to the theatre ... The prospect was quite a madness. But it was a fine madness and one embraced immediately by John and David. By the end of the morning, there was a done deal, set against an outlined secondary deal which would kick-in if John liked what he saw after the initial exercise; we agreed terms for the rental of the building until the end of September 1976.

In the cooler light of London, it was decided to run a three week pop and rock festival to coincide with the wider cultural context of the official Edinburgh Festival. Other than the opportunity of this challenge, the long drives to and from Edinburgh gave me plenty of scope to allow the corrosion of Elton's early implications to focus my addled brain on what the future was going to hold when September had come and gone.

Almost the first night I arrived in Edinburgh on my own to begin the on-site organisation, I met a man. I was booked into a big room in the charmingly old-fashioned Caledonian Hotel at the Jenners end of Princes Street. I felt very far-away from London and my home that first night back in Edinburgh. I had left behind an organisation seething with politics, I had all but ignored the importunings of arguably one of the biggest rock stars in the world and I had left two happy people making love in my flat where I was beginning to feel more and more marginalised.

So, dinner done and bib and tucker exchanged for some raunchy jeans and the ubiquitous Daisy Roots (boots, remember?), I was out for a stroll after my first few hours sussing the city for the fourth time. Sex reared its urgent head yet again. From previous visits, I had known about the delights of Calton Hill on a summer night. I had been made aware of a few 'cottages' which were said to be fertile hunting grounds for the cruising gay man both from out of and inside the town. And as I had a very good memory, I knew exactly where I was going.

From what I have written earlier about David and Freddie, I might suppose that I was actively looking for someone more permanent than a ten minute gasp. (Golly, I've just remembered that I used to smoke in those dim and distant days. Cigarettes not friction, you understand …) Since I might suppose it, I shall suppose it and when I found Ed Murray, I could not help but admit that if I was looking for a – at least sexually perfect – partner, he was it.

The locals had called the place where I found him GHQ. The local gays, I mean. My destiny that night was played out in my destination, a vast subterranean gentleman's public convenience at the Waverley Station end of Princes Street, frequented by both visitors and townsmen alike. The traffic was sterling, the cruise quotient meteoric. The seasoned hunters from the town parked their cars in the dark cobbled lane at the back and the visitors, who stood out like priapic pastries at a Polish wedding, came blatantly to be hunted. GHQ of course stands for General Head Quarters and the head in question was nothing to do with seniority. Bingo. Dais scores first time out, first time on the carousel as the phantom hurdy-gurdy played show tunes from BRIGADOON … Harry Lauder was calling me from the wings, the purple heather was being gone around tempestuously at least twice a day and I was as thrilled as a haggis in boiling water. My libido could not believe its eyes.

Ed Murray was, and is, to say the least a complicated character. He was a highly successful antiques dealer, his speciality being centred on Continenal European furniture although his eye for any object of quality from clocks, to jewellery to porcelain was not only excellent but should he have practised his trade some twenty years later, his mien and character would have meant that David Dickinson might never have been on celebrity Come Dancing. His mother, Jessie Swanson lived with him, a true Scot from Anstruther on the opposite Fife coast, and his father was a Polish military man who had arrived in Scotland as had many other Poles at the beginning of the Second World War but had been dead for some many years.

The child was brought up comfortably but with little love when his mother married into the Murray family of Dundee. The young Ed was indeed brought up by Jessie and her husband and, by default, but also, mercifully, by two indefatigable aunts, Aggie and Belle, who when they died left Ed the money to finance his passion for antiques in a recognised business-like way. He emerged from the shadows of the lesser-known Midlothian sale rooms and ultimately hung up his shingle outside a premises in Dundas Street in Edinburgh and moved into a magnificent apartment made of two top floors of a house in the elegant oval of Moray Place, just behind Charlotte Square, overlooking the Waters of Leith, a usually gentle 'burn' which ran through gardens which embraced two sides of a steep ravine.

It was wonderfully respectable. Downstairs in the Moray Place house lived an advocate, no less. In London, we called one of those a QC, one of those characters who was always played by Dirk Bogarde. Advocate versus QC. It was my final lesson in the reality that Scotland and England are not only two separate nations but entirely different cultures. Upstairs, in the flat, it was curiously barren. Beautiful, highly desirable and valuable furniture but not a single finger-print of personality. Anyone's.

But to ice my personal cake, Ed Murray had no earthly clue as to who Freddie Mercury was and had hardly even heard of Elton John. It was enough to allow me an inkling that there might be a life after rock 'n' roll. So, that first night, after I'd bolted the door of the room in the grim, old Caledonian and refused to let him leave, instead of staying for the duration of the Scottish Project at The Caledonian, I eschewed the delicacies of haste versus speed and moved in with him. And his mother. And his soon-to-be, in-the-process-of-splitting, almost-ex lover George Elas. Another Pole. Talk about polarisation. What a silly boy I was.

Obviously, as I began to establish an office in the Playhouse building and started to develop a schedule and concert timetable, all the John Reid acts were booked and dates offered to other promoters. Regrettably, I cannot remember specifics although the arrival of Ritchie Blackmore's Rainbow caused several palpitations in the hearts of even the most seasoned roadies. How the actual Rainbow was ever made to fit through the scenery dock doors, I shall never know. And there was a special development on the staffing front which was to affect my life forever. John's friends Bryan and Nanette Forbes had a daughter. In fact they had two but the daughter in this scenario was Sarah, their eldest who had been left behind in America after Bryan had finished filming STEPFORD WIVES to attend another year of high school in Connecticut. Sarah had just returned to England and needed – sorry, wanted - a job. So, John facilitated and Dais, me, executed. Sarah was sixteen, had never eaten fish 'n' chips out of paper and was about as useful as a band aid in an amputation. But I loved her from the start and still do to this day. She arrived in Edinburgh, initially, with her school friend Felicity Dean who went on to become an actress of great repute and, when the booking office was up and running in the foyer of the Playhouse, I sent the pair of them out in the advertising car with the loudspeaker shouting the odds for our programme of concerts.

Another arrival was that of David McCowan Hill, a contact of Anthony Andrews who had been invaluable to us with the Peter Straker show. He came on board as local co-ordinator and was an invaluable member of the team as was Duggie Wragg, a sensitive, calm but very practical Scottish hands-on technical adviser. The final 'signing' was the re-employment of Mick Walker who had been Elton's personal security guard on the LOUDER THAN CONCORDE tour and whose presence was indispensable on the 'disco' evenings. In my wildest of expansive entrepreneurial moments in the planning of this Scottish event, I had thought that one of the first floor foyer spaces would be ideal as a revenue-earning disco.

Disco was beginning to be all the rage, everywhere and weekly 'nights' had emerged as a draw in many pubs the length and breadth of the land. So, why not Edinburgh? The reason why not was simple. I had no idea of the power of alcohol in Scottish society. Thus fuelled, the Scottish fighting spirit in male and female alike is irrepressible. The disco nights became a hell and I came to dread them as I'm sure Mick Walker did too. However wonderful our security and 'bouncing' strategies and personnel might have been, there was no way we could stop the anti-social violence. I wanted to curtail the disco programme. Reid wanted to continue it. He had rented himself a bijou little cottage in a very quiet neighbourhood bordering the Waters of Leith for the occasional nights he spent in Edinburgh. He was rarely - if ever- at the disco but saw the event as something which would also raise his profile in the city. The populist profile.

However, on this occasion, I won. My flat refusal to have anything to do with more discos was, in hindsight, more a measure of the confidence that my growing desire not to be part of this operation was giving me. Rationally, what did I care if drunken yobs of either sex beat themselves to a pulp every evening? I should have been more loyal to the profit motive of the company which employed me and the political motives of the man who employed me. However, irrationally, I was not proud of the debacle. If Reid wanted to be associated with it, let him. I didn't. Wouldn't. Couldn't. My instinctive distaste towards the situation I now found myself in was beginning to turn into principled aversion.

And there was another matter of worrying eminence on my *grise* horizon. Sarah Forbes came to me one day in my oak-panelled office above the theatre's foyer to announce that she and John Reid had fallen in love and were actively consummating their passion.

Oh, no. Oh, god!

My first reaction was irritation, then a fury with Reid and then an impending sense of disaster when I imagined what Bryan and Nanette would have to say about the matter. I needn't have worried. I don't think they twigged for ages, until they were asked to announce an engagement. But all that is *ex parte, hors de combat,* outside the time frame of these scribblings. I merely throw into the pot, my later observation that had Sarah been a sixteen-year-old boy, my reactions would have been entirely different. Sexist, or what? I too had been a sixteen-year-old boy.

It all started well. The civic Festival Parade which wound its way through the Edinburgh streets was held on a fabulously sunny Sunday. Lacking finesse or tradition, I had plumped for sound and fury as the thematic keynote for the parade float which represented and, of course, advertised the Playhouse and our parvenu enterprise. I persuaded Chrysalis Records – dear Doug d'Arcy – to fly up the cast of LEAVE HIM TO HEAVEN and have them perform the songs from the just-completed cast album on the float. Those magical roadies of ours had somehow rigged up for it to be possible to have huge speakers on the flat-bed lowloader truck trailer and that, other than the gaily caparisoned and period-costumed cast, was all we needed to blast the parade's spectators out of their politeness and irrevocably announce the Playhouse's position in the upcoming *Kulturfest*. Unforgettable. Anita Dobson gyrating and jiving along with the other twenty or so … It was as I've said, like GREASE before GREASE had even been thought of.

The highlights of our season of concerts – I'm obviously biased - were the Queen and the Elton Shows. I think even Peter Straker who was performing as part of the official festival fringe at the George Hotel, managed a respectable audience in the Playhouse which was, when not full, like an aircraft hanger. In the main, the concerts panned out … some were sold out, like the Queen shows and some, the operatic concert given by diva Rita Hunter for example, not so sold out. Only one show significantly stood out and stands out in my memory still. Elton's.

It was unforgettable. I hope the memory of it is mutual.

He had no available band, was very keen to perform at the festival and yet didn't know how. Where have I heard this story before? After the CONCORDE tour, the musicians had gone their separate ways. Other commitments. Session work for many, stardom and fame for one – James Newton Howard, whose name seems to be on the credits of every Hollywood movie I see.

Elton made the extraordinarily brave decision to play the venue alone. Just him and a grand piano. We were all breathless with a sort of concern mixed with admiration sprinkled, after a moment's necessary reflection, with unrepentant admiration. David Bell suggested filming the event. There was a new medium afoot in the halls of entertainment hardware – the picture disk. It is now, of course, defunct, redundant and largely forgotten. The ultimate spawn of current technology, the picture disk was trampled in the rush to next base. I believe that the plan was that after initial television broadcast, the whole performance was going to be put onto a picture disk and the total package would, of course, be owned by John Reid Presentations which was, I think, the name of the off-shoot company of the main John Reid Enterprises, of which I was a director.

We had to dress a stage the size of two tennis courts … with what? Answer, most of the contents of my new friend Ed Murray's antique shop. Everything from tall French armoires, to tall Welsh dressers to delicate French Empire boudoir furniture … A black and gilt, Japan lacquered grandfather clock. All very tastefully arranged on a sea of grey Wilton carpet and beautifully lit by, who else, our in-house 'sparks' and genial love-hunk James Dann in association with the telly people from David Bell's arena.

The show was brilliant. I had always thought that Elton and Bernie's songs had sounded best live with that incredibly dynamic, solidly chugging band underpinning them and with Elton, the showman as the great rock 'n' roll ring master but that night, in Edinburgh, as well as the Saturday Night Elton and the B-B-B-B-Bennie Elton, he appeared as the troubadour, the master of an art which wrung tears from the hardest heart as Daniel flew away on his plane, as the Rocket Man went into orbit forever and as The Sun threatened to go down for the last time on us all …

Billy Connelly had a gig booked at our Playhouse and it co-incided with Elton being there. And Elton's birthday. Sarah Forbes and I were despatched to search for a venue for a birthday party concomitant to the significance of our principal's main event and we found a restaurant at the last moment which agreed to accommodate the 'gig'. The date co-incided with Billy Connelly's show and afterwards, the assembled and joint *entourages* traipsed across Edinburgh for the celebration. It was almost at the end of our three-week schedule and it didn't seem a day too far away that we would all be able to go home. Go anywhere. Sarah and I had spent a long time and a lot of love in choosing the menus for Elton's day. For example, we knew he liked Spotted Dick and we knew for certain he liked runny custard. So, we had menus printed up including this and other of his favourite delights.

How mortified were we, after lengthy and dedicated meetings with the restaurant to produce the best possible feast, that Billy – for the Big Yin read Big Head – trashed the party and began a pudding-slinging match which embarrassed the whole company, let alone Sarah and I who were left with the onerous task of reaching a reparations deal with the restaurant the following day. Thanks, Billy. It urgently reminds me how much the majority often suffer for the behaviour of the few and that those 'behind-the-scenes-headlines' which bolster the reputations of the few have repercussions which are never reported. It's only rock 'n' roll, I know, I know … But when trashing other people's livelihoods and reputations involves potential loss of said livelihood and reputation, how rock 'n' roll is that? Sure, John Reid Enterprises initially paid for the damage and the clean-up. I only hope that the amount was re-charged to Elton.

Probably not. Connelly and his then girlfriend Pamela Stephenson both ultimately become clients of John Reid's.

It was a sordid ending to what had been an initial success for John Reid Enterprises at The Playhouse. But for me, the sun was indeed going down for the last time as I had already decided to leave not only John's employ but also the music business. It had been a hard decision and it was made even harder when, at the end of his triumphant show, Elton thanked me from the stage for all my hard work, made reference to Sarah and her help and glowed in the genuine admiration of his enraptured, enthralled and entirely entertained audience. I don't know if Elton knew but I had handed in my notice to John already. There was only time left before we all parted company. I left the theatre that night in a torrent of tears. Why? How had this point been reached? Was there no going back? What had I done?

When not in the throes of panic, I was comforted by the self-knowledge that I had always proclaimed that one should quit whilst ahead. I always thought that rock 'n' roll was a young man's game and I was, after all, almost thirty. Freddie M always said that he couldn't even imagine performing on stage as an older man and found the antics of many in that age-bracket embarrassing. He was far from being ageist, just being himself and I sort of knew what he meant … I had told him about my plans. My non-plans. I don't think he was very pleased but he had lots of good and new friends around him by then and there were rumblings already that the other Queenies weren't entirely happy with Mister Reid's management of their career, although the split was not to come for another year.

And thus, where else would I have gone in any considered career move? It would have been impossible to move upwards. Reid's was the biggest and best management company in the world. I could only possibly have moved sideways. America? I wasn't keen. Never had been. All very well for a cultural mind-fuck as well as general physical seeing-to on the venal level, but live there? And who to work for? Had I managed to be employed by Peter Asher, for example, it would have only been to work for an equivalent Colonel Parker? He only had one act. I knew it was only a matter of time before Reid would fire me. OK, I might have been able to work for Elton but, practically and morally, even that distant possibility would have been impossible. And what might have happened if record companies had decided that another manager of the status of Reid should be later instated? Yours truly would be unceremoniously out in the coldest of the very cold.

I knew that I had somehow arrived at a state of damnation whatever I did and the best move, to me, at the time was to be somehow kidnapped by friendly aliens. And conveniently, as you know, my alien had already appeared. But would permanent residency in Edinburgh work? And was the alien friendly? Academic, my dears, because at that time, the future wasn't even being offered as a possibility.

Chapter Sixteen

WHEN AU REVOIR REALLY
MEANS GOODBYE

Earlier that summer, I had had vague thoughts of going to Arizona to have a week's holiday on a tennis ranch much favoured by those in my line of work. The vague thoughts were immediately dispelled as I faced the prospect of not earning. My much vaunted £7,500 salary would be gone and I'd have to turn my thoughts to another livlihood.

I wasn't able to go to Queen's triumphant concert in Hyde Park which happened on the final weekend of the Festival in Edinburgh. Instead, I stayed north of the border and cleared up the Edinburgh aftermath before returning to London to check in the car and bid farewell to my colleagues at South Audley Street. It didn't take long. As you might imagine, I had at last broached the laying of plans to remain in Scotland with my alien although these had never been finalised. The alien's ex-boyfriend, George, had plans to fill the gap that my departure would have left on the London gayboy circuit and indeed emerged from his association with Ed Murray with sufficient funds and enough antique stocks to hang up his own shingle in a shop in Moulton arcade. Maybe my presence precipitated his exit … If it did, I apologise for, in true ignorance, I believed what I was told, that he wanted to leave. I sort of, accidentally, found that I was going to stay with Ed. There was never any plan, no agreement … In the event of going, I just stayed around.

John Reid gave me a generous settlement, considering I had only worked for him for a year and in those days, half a year's salary would go a long way. When I returned to Scotland, the autumn was well on its unremitting way. The fall falls early north of the English border. The grey skies and the rain and the sheer granite dourness, the dreich slate hues of the land, sea and sky do something to a man's soul, especially to the soul of an unseasoned Sassenach. I had horrible withdrawal symptoms. I suffered the torments of hell when I realised that there was no going back. The loss of status, the absence of power, the unglamorous horizons didn't make for a good beginning for my future out of the sun.

But I was bequeathed something entirely new, utterly unexpected and very strange … I finally realised that I had been delivered of a unique opportunity, a chance to develop a passion which had only ever surfaced occasionally, badly misunderstood and as frightening as that choice of ten years before when I seriously wonderered about going to drama school and becoming an actor.

It seemed that I had been invited to write. And so, I started to write.

I had had a serious flash of inspiration, the physical shock of a kick start from somewhere outside me. Literally, a flash of light inside my brain accompanied by a jolt, as though I had been harmlessly struck by a massive surge of elemental energy. It happened in Ed's flat, in the soul-less front drawing room, overlooking the bleak oval garden square. I fancied the culprit might have been Mick Hannah because from that day forth, I started to write his story in the form of a three-part novel, A SHADOW ON THE GREEN, telling, putatively, his life from a conception in Ireland to that terrible day in France in March 1973. Whoever muse it was, whatever muse it was, I can only humbly offer my thanks.

I saw Freddie thereafter. Many times and in great depth and our relationship was one of ultimate substance. I maintained all my valuable old friendships, Straker, Tim Curry for a while, Minns, The Forbes family and all these, other that Tim's, I cherish to this day. Some friendships have retreated into a bubble of time but I still know where to find them. I hope they know that I too can still be counted on. I even saw John Reid on several occasions, once especially when he offered me my old job back but reneged at the last moment. But then, he and Elton had 're-signed' with each other and I was, as I always thought I would be, *hors de combat*. A whore of combat. But I didn't see Elton again for several years and although I deeply regretted the passing of our association, when I did see him again, I was so relieved that he had all but forgotten who I was. I should have known that going back to where one has been unhappy is not an option for a Gaderene superstar. Elton is well-known for expunging from his reality anyone who has 'crossed' him. I'm sorry that he should have seen my behaviour as directed against him but then, if you are a world superstar, I suppose you see what you want to see. Bit like God, really, whoever he, she or it might be but I fancy that even Gods have their good days.

I started to keep a journal from the moment I lived with Ed Murray in that flat full of antiques and valuables and so I have no need to write any more. It's already written and it's of immediate interest only to me, although I'm pleased to say that my return to 'ordinary life' turned out to be far from dull. But all that's for another time.

Chapter Seventeen

A BIT OF A DO ...

Almost twenty years later ...

On Friday 17th May 1996, there was a gathering at 102 Hamilton Terrace, the home of John Reid and his partner Doctor James Thompson. James wasn't there, probably precisely because the gathering was a reunion convocation of those employees of John's whom he chose from an initial list of forty-three available living specimens to sit around the twenty-seater dining table and partake of reminiscence.

James must be very wise.

We'd all been in a frightful two'n'eight, especially Penny Valentine and Caroline and me. We three convened at my home in Ripplevale Grove in Islington to have a first fortifying drink before schlepping across North London to St. John's Wood at the appointed hour of seven-thirty. No one wanted to arrive alone.

Sarah (Forbes/Standing) was not invited and she had been in a lather of curiosity for the weeks running up to the 'do' as she was decorating one of the mews houses Reid has bought at the end of the garden of this rather lumpen cream stucco house which looks like a very expensive private tooth peeking through a rather plain national health prosthetic. The place is a pile.

Well ... Perhaps that's harsh. Whatever the house is, it's not pretty.

Poor Sarah. She had after all been a bona fide employee of John Reid Enterprises, e'en though for only a few months, and as such had a perfect right to attend. John'd told her, when she'd asked if she could come, that no more could be seated round the table and that, anyway, she was "... in a different category ..." from the rest of the guests. I presume that means that she is a friend.

Charming.

Penny Valentine was adamant that the whole thing was a mere 'cleaners' dinner' and was determined that the tenor of the evening would be so. She was proved incontrovertibly, one hundred percent right. This was definitely not the A list. Though it might not have been exactly an alphabetically challenged list, it was certainly a mite alphabetically confused.

But what did Reid want with us after all this time? Why, we asked ourselves? We had been invited spouseless except those two, David Croker and Laura Beggs who had met whilst employees but who had later married. Sarah had deduced the guest list. It was no surprise to learn that there were to be no surprises. The surprises weren't there. They hadn't been invited. Alex Foster, Clive Banks ... There are a lot still left alive.

The final guest list ran thus:-

Me, Jim Doyle (I'm trying to go round the table), Jenny Over, Maureen Hillyer, Garry Farrow, John Reid, Helen Dann, Gary Hampshire, Caroline Lee, David Costa, Robert Key, Penny Valentine, Graham Carpenter, Sally Atkins, David Croker, Laura Beggs, David Larkin, Chrissie Craybourne (his wife I think), John Hall, Eric Hall ... So, no one really who might disgrace the occasion and stand-up screaming at Reid, "Get thee back to hell, Satan!" in the middle of pudding.

Well, we got there at seven-forty-five. Lots of people there already. They must have been door-stepping since seven-fifteen. Whatever. A butler opens the front door. Not Reid. Sets the tone for evening through which will be woven the two other waiters. I've brought a copy of my BLONDES book for John which I am too embarrassed to bring into the drawing room to give to him personally in front of a crowd of grinning ex-sometime cronies. So I dump it, bound in its red ribbon of blood and time, on a side table in the hall. Yes, Peeve, I think there was a marble floor but let's never mind.

Then, into the drawing room. It is like walking into the unopened tomb of a long-dead Borgia. The paintings on the wall are mightily classical, post-renaissance and I'm sure terribly valuable. But they're gloomy and depressing and heavy. Like palls on the walls. There is marble and ormolu and gilt everywhere. The windows and the sofas and anything that can be is swagged and draped and jhusshed like baroque altar cloths. The whole place reeks of blind nuns with bleeding fingers and washed-in-the-blood-of-the-lamb perfection. Not a single dragged thread in the carpet - specially woven, green garland with red ribbon on taupy-beigey-sand ground - and nary a snagged cord on a cushion. It is entirely unreal. It's the home of someone who never does but who pays others to do. It's like a turn-of-the-century bordello/saloon in Chicago. Or San Francisco. It's ... It's not like any of our homes, I suppose is what I mean. It's an hotel, a very private and very expensive Helmsley hotel.

There is champagne. I don't catch the label but it's lovely, served in heavy cut and gilded flutes. Or there is wine, white or red but not a crisp in sight. Later I am told there was a discrete bowl lurking beneath a Caravaggio. Missed both.

Lots of waiter attention but not a canapé to be had. Sarah had told me that there was to be caviar. Not a sturgeon's ovum in sight of any colour, my dear. Beluga, beluga be-buggered!

I talk to Laura Beggs whom I had last seen last year at the Hampton Court Flower Show and who has had two books published, one on asthma from which she suffers and the latest on anaphalaxia, the body's allergic reaction. I chat to Sally Atkins - Laura's schoolfriend, I had forgotten: from Weymouth - who works for Stock, Aitken and Waterman and who is writing a novel. Good for her. I chat with Jenny Over and we are joined by Eric Hall, a late arrival. Ghastly man. Wouldn't have him wash my windscreen at a traffic-light! Monster, monster, boom-boom-boom indeed ...

Reid glides round being the mingling host. He's in good shape, I must admit but still careers around like a two-seater sofa on jerky casters and now with a No. 4 haircut of the style the right-stuffed sport. I look at him like I'd watch a chocolate box full of semtex. Wary isn't in it. I just don't ... believe. I am no longer a believer. I left the sect.

I feel strangely apart and yet oddly still wounded. My partner, Nigel, had asked me earlier in the day when I was at my most neurotic what exactly it was that I found so disconcerting about Reid. I listed three occasions of our acquaintance, three instances ... He was convinced. There was no need to go on. And time has allowed discomfort to rather mellow into disinterest. Not a pretty commute on either side of the change.

However, had I stayed with Reid or in 'the business', I remind myself that I would have been dead too. Like Neil Carter. And Julie, John's secretary whom I never met who is heavily featured in a spotlit photoframe in the drawing room. It is a grisly rosta which includes that poor boy Guy about whom at least Elton'd later written a song. In this company, I have to keep reminding myself that it was Reid turning me down in 1979 when I was very much adrift after I had left Ed Murray that saved my life. Had I stayed, I would have been dead by now for sure.

Then there is Helen Dann, very sweet. Still blonde and petite and with two children by the eternally-shaggable James who still does lights for shows and discos and stuff. He could do my lights any day. Helen is so complimentary and so nice, I now wonder who I was in those days, that person about whom she is so generously effusive and upon whom she had looked from behind her seat on the switchboard in the reception area at South Audley Street. *Incroyable* am I.

I later discover she was mind-bendingly widdled that night. We variously chat and natter and bludger on for over an hour before we are called into dinner. This whole shtick is more like a reception. We are being received. Not entertained.

Into the dining room.

Oh! The dining room! Into the valley of d-d-dining room rode the ...

Of an elongated rectangular shape, the dining room has apparently been built onto the back of the original house. Planning permission? It contains a highly polished banqueting table - and that I think I recall, is all - which runs the whole length of the room and round which are twenty fully upholstered armed chairs. The over-pledged wooden surface is littered with silver candelabra, salts, cruets ... Like the fallout shrapnel from a downtown explosion at Asprey.

A huge classical painting which I was far too rat-arsed to remember dominates the room; there are yet more marble columns, tiers of pilasters, a fair yardage of friezes, a crazed and confused cornucopia of architectural orders. Swagged windows give out onto a terrace and thence to a garden which looks bleak and forlorn, not unlike a municipal park in between plantings. There is a painted ceiling.

"I had two dykes on their backs for a month doing that!" exclaims the de-toxed and now thoroughly clean-living penitent from Paisley as he worries at our heels like a border collie, chasing us to our pens. Sorry, seats. Visions swirl in my mind of the *il glorious papa* and the divine but overworked Michael Angelo ... Oh, stop it, Dais!

There are place cards, each held in silver place-card holders. Individual calligraphics. Like Reid's done them? Puhleeze! Yes. It is just like an embassy reception. The location of the bordello-in-the-mind moves effortlessly from Chicago to Monte Carlo. Now I know why the Monagasques needed Grace Kelly!

And those *placements!* They are indeed truly from hell. It has taken true talent to magimix this lot. A great delia talent.

And why? Still the nagging question, why are we here? What has he dragged us here to do except to exhume the corpses of memories we were only too happy to bury? PV and Caroline are shepherded to the far end of the table to scintillate in the company of Robert Key and David Croker. Take my word, that was a doddle compared to my end ...

I catch their eyes.

They are *desolees!* I am *'elpless.*

I find my *placement.* I am at 'the head' as Reid puts it, next to Jim Doyle to my left and John Hall to my right. Whoopee! I say I'm always very good at head and Reid says he remembers. Ha, ha! Such publicly-blown intimacy is truly worrying. John Hall runs something called Portman Productions and they make movies. Do I push myself to get some work? Do I, fuck. He is however polite enough to ask what I do and I burble something banal ... I'm such a pathetically retiring and Janus-headed little C-U-Next-Thursday.

398

Jim Doyle was something at ATV Music and remembers me as having had to do with the damnable Twinkle but really he likes to ski more than have to do with music. He tells me ...*Quelle surprise* ... that he is now going back to work for Reid after a two year sabbatical. That's about where we get to because both my dinner-mates are hanging on other words. Absent friends are mentioned and I toast them, to the 'head' group, and then Jenny Over talks about David Bell and how wonderful the Westminster Hospital is.

Maureen seems to be sweetly giggly and quite pie-eyed and sort of oblivious but then hatchet people have to be, don't they? She's been wielding Reid's hatchet for more years than I care to remember.

"I was only obeying orders," I believe was the plea at war crimes trials.

Dinner starts. Leek and potato soup with cream and croutons. Nice. But I do better. It's a facile comparison. Then chicken breast - very large and heavy chicken breast - with a sauce I can't quite handle ... I mean name. I try to recall the ingredients the following morning and Nigel says,

"Call it *Sa Sauce Mystere*, dear."

Nice mangetouts and carrots and potatoes with onions ... Pommes lyonnaise, I think they're called. Good Chateau Talbot. Full and round. Also in gilt and cut thick claret glasses. Matching.

Cheese ... store-bought. Unripened Pont L'Eveque, a Herb and Garlic Roule still with the plastic bit on the bottom and some other supermarket purchases ... PV is vindicated. The cleaners' dinner. Nice cheese shops around? I should coco. We who also cook are judged and judge ourselves by our cheese course!

Enfin le Pudding.

Dark and white chocolate mousse with a strawberry in a stemmed glass. Nice. With a cookie. Nice-ish.

Reid stands up. Speech. Nice to see us. How grateful he is. Blah blah blah. Gary Farrow now head of Sony ... It's like Jim Davidson being in charge of Rio Tinto Zinc. Can't honestly remember what else Reid says. Coupla jokes. We all laugh. He sits down.

So that's why we're here! He feels good. He feels great. He's forgotten every single thing that, through working for him, plagues us, has plagued us and will continue to plague us until the day we die. He has absolutely no idea what it was like to work for him because he has absolutely no idea who or what he was. Or did. Or is. Or still does!! Jesus, but it's sad and I'm one of the assembled enablers. One of the really guilty. There should be courses in John Reid. At universities, yet.

Into the drawing room for coffee. Nice. Then a tour of the house. Gary Hampshire materialises. Looks like a ghost. Dark circles under his eyes like the Avebury Rings on chalky cheeks. PV tells me later he told her he's had a heart attack, at the wheel of a car? Shit. So sweet. He's worked for Reid for twenty five years. Must be a fucking saint.

The rest of the house is perfection too, like the ground floor. Master bedroom with four poster with a purple coffer at the foot which at the press of a button rises and opens up to reveal the tellie. Lovely. Master bathroom all mahogany with rousched and pleated blue stuff on the closet panels. Marble tiles, huge bath ... Upstairs again, James' room and study complete with stethoscope. To show he's a real doctor? Not just a thinker? Up here it's plainer than the 'master-floor' below but just as perfect.

"Imagine the National Health patients up here!" Reid exclaims.

I try. It's hard.

Then, another floor. Sort of study place. The carpet here has a single J woven in the middle of the garland. I like it. J for John and J for James. But it doesn't spread throughout the house. Only safe, wholesome perfection is permitted to spread throughout John's house.

Helen Dann and I are ensconced way-up here on the fortieth floor, she asking me if I am mystical. I hate these kind of moments because I know I am and never know what to say because if people have to ask then they're not ... I want to escape but she pinions me and talks on. Reid comes up. We chatter on and it's so unreal that all I want to do is go. Finally stagger downstairs to find my girls. Caroline is snuffled up with the rottenest cold and feels like soaked cork and Costa says he'll take her home. I see Graham Carpenter and have to embrace.

"Stay in touch," he says.

"Yeah," I say.

Hello?

I take PV and we leave. Phew!

We drive home squawking as we remember gems of the previous few hours. Peeve is desolate yet vociferous. I am totally drunk but can't tell her in case she gets out and leaves me to drive home alone! Just now I could not bear to be alone. Tonight I feel as sensitive as though I'm an autumn lawn, naked and worm-cast that's just been cleared of its leaves by a squadron of metal-tined rakes. So we chatter and rant on in turns and we come to Highbury when she does get out 'cos that's where she lives and that's it ... All done. Over. Onwards and upwards, darlings. Per assholes, ad astra. And god speed, Peeve. It shouldn't have been you to go so soon.

Except that David Croker was also - and next - to die. In 1998. Of a heart attack. I don't think he was yet fifty. He too was back working for Reid at the time of his death. Worried that Reid was going to close down the management company, stressed and fearful of what he would do next to pay his mortgage and educate his two young daughters. Just after Croker died, Reid did indeed close down.

Elton had finally left him, more than twenty years later than the end of this story. Where Elton would have gone twenty years earlier had he left Reid in 1976, I have no idea. I'm sure he had even less.

Sad isn't even in it ...

THE END

" ... posthumous fame seems, then, to be the lot of the unclassifiable ones, that is, those whose work neither fits the existing order nor introduces a new genre that lends itself to future classification."

HANNAH ARENDT

By the same author ...

Fiction:

SUMMER SET
A CAT IN THE TULIPS
A HOLLYWOOD CONSCIENCE (by pseudonymous Ned
Cresswell)

All three titles published by Millivres Books, now
GMP/PROWLER, all out of print and available only through the
author.

A LETHAL DOSE OF MURDER will be published in 2004 by
Tusitala Press.
PORNSTARS Inc, a sequel to A HOLLYWOOD CONSCIENCE, is
to be published in 2004 by TUSITALA PRESS. 0207 609 7005.

Biography:

THIS IS THE REAL LIFE ... Freddie Mercury with David Minns
THE BOY WHO LOOKED AT THE MOON ... Cat Stevens
SCISSORS AND PASTE ... Dusty Springfield
FROM MAE TO MADONNA ... The Glamour Blondes. Thirteen
studies spanning the twentieth century.

All published by Britannia Press Publishing, now defunct but all
now available from Tusitala Press 0207 609 7005

MISTER MERCURY (with Peter Freestone) was published in 1998
by The Tusitala Press. Second hardback edition by Omnibus Press
in March 2000, entitled FREDDIE MERCURY An Intimate
Memoir.

THIS IS THE REAL LIFE was republished in November 1997 by
Antaeus Books.
FREDDIE MERCURY – The Afterlife by Peter Freestone and

David Evans is published by Tusitala Press, available from Tusitala Press. 0207 609 7005.

ROCKY HORROR - From Concept to Cult - written with Scott Michaels was published by Sanctuary in 2002 and is still available.

Short Stories Published by Robinson in anthologies MAMMOTH BOOKS OF GAY EROTICA and GAY SHORT STORIES as well as Prowler's anthologies YOUNG AND HUNG and HARD AT WORK, scheduled for December 1999.
THE BAD BOYS BOOK OF BEDTIME STORIES, a collection of short stories under the pseudonym Dan Tusitala, was published by ZIPPER/MPG in September 2001 and is still available.